My Haunted Vow

Praise for *My Haunted Vow*

"*My Haunted Vow* is a captivating romantic suspense novel that weaves together a gripping plotline, emotionally rich characters, and poignant themes. Louise Davis delivers a compelling narrative and a must-read for fans looking for a story that balances heart-pounding suspense with heartfelt romance."
-**Ashley Mansour**, International Best-selling Author, Founder of LA Writing Coach and Brands Through Books

"The stakes have been raised and the suspense continues with Louise Davis's sequel to *Haunted by You*. *My Haunted Vow* will immediately draw readers in as the characters navigate their new normal in New York. But, as fans of Davis know, not all ghosts are dead and danger seems to lurk around every corner. In *My Haunted Vow*, Davis weaves a story of love, loss and the importance of family that will keep readers invested long after the last page."
—**Jessica Reino**, Author, Author Coach and Senior Literary Agent

"This is the perfect recipe—a dash of suspense, a love story folded in. The characters pulled me in and never left me in this stunning sequel. A perfect, haunting tale for this fall season."
—**Susan Shepard**, Author of *Curse of the Winter Lord* and *The Gardiens Series*

"*My Haunted Vow* is a testament to the strength of the human spirit and the enduring power of love. Davis's deft storytelling draws readers into a web of intrigue and suspense, where every twist and turn leaves you breathless for more. A must-read for fans of gripping thrillers and heartfelt romance alike, this is a book that will stay with you long after you turn the final page. Prepare to be enchanted, enthralled, and utterly spellbound by this unforgettable tale."
—**JoAnna McSpadden**, Author of *Obsidian Tide*

"Louise has mastered the art of keeping readers on the edge of their seat. My Haunted Vow delivers exactly what a sequel should - taking the reader by surprise, building the stakes, and diving in deeper to the characters who you wanted to know more about after Haunted by You. The combination of romance and suspense is perfectly balanced to keep you turning pages and wanting more!"
—**Jen Woodrum**, Author of *The Severed Fates Series*

A NOVEL

MY HAUNTED VOW

LOUISE DAVIS

NEW YORK

LONDON • NASHVILLE • MELBOURNE • VANCOUVER

MY HAUNTED VOW

Published in New York, New York, by Morgan James Publishing. Morgan James is a trademark of Morgan James, LLC. www.MorganJamesPublishing.com

Publisher's Note: This novel is a work of fiction. Names, characters, places, and incidents are either products of the author's imagination or used fictitiously. All characters are fictional, and any similarity to people living or dead is purely coincidental.

Proudly distributed by Publishers Group West®

Morgan James
BOGO™

A **FREE** ebook edition is available for you
or a friend with the purchase of this print book.

CLEARLY SIGN YOUR NAME ABOVE

Instructions to claim your free ebook edition:
1. Visit MorganJamesBOGO.com
2. Sign your name CLEARLY in the space above
3. Complete the form and submit a photo
   of this entire page
4. You or your friend can download the ebook
   to your preferred device

ISBN 9781636984315 paperback
ISBN 9781636984322 ebook
Library of Congress Control Number:
2024932102

Cover Design by:
Rylan Bird
www.voodooartsstudio.com

Interior Design by:
Chris Treccani
www.3dogcreative.net

Morgan James is a proud partner of Habitat for Humanity Peninsula
and Greater Williamsburg. Partners in building since 2006.

Get involved today! Visit: www.morgan-james-publishing.com/giving-back

For my dad,
I miss you every day.

Prologue

The blood red index cards on the counter leer up at me.

"I see you." Written in bold, black ink.

All four of us got the sinister red cards with the same message on them at school today.

Again.

The tiny fingers of fear claw their way through my body and I shudder, rubbing at the raised flesh on my arms.

This time, the notes were found when all of us were in different classes at our various locations—the high school, The City College of New York, and Juilliard. Different classes, different buildings even, than where they slipped the previous disturbing red cards into our bags. Like whoever is leaving them for us is trying to prove they know where we are at all times.

They are watching us wherever we go.

No place is safe, no *one* is safe.

We have nowhere to hide.

Message received loud and clear. *But why?*

Why are they watching us? Why do they care what a bunch of emotionally beaten and broken teens are doing and where they are going? And what exactly is their end game here? Are they just trying to scare us? Or is this a warning of more to come?

My eyes are fixed on the cards, maybe if I stare long enough they will reveal all of their secrets.

But of course they don't.

How can we hide from someone who vanishes like they never existed every time law enforcement thinks they have found another lead?

Ghosts from my past mingle with the ghosts of my present, making my grip on reality feel like it is slipping away. Just out of reach—my fingertips barely brushing the answer before it disappears all together.

Dread settles heavily in my stomach. The urge to look over my shoulder is now constant, as my paranoia that someone is watching us is once again proven a legitimate concern.

Why can't we just be left to live in peace? Haven't we been through enough already?

And why do I feel like this sick game is just getting started?

October

Two months earlier

Chapter 1

Violet

Adulting is hard.

Why I was in such a rush to grow up is beyond me. How I wish I could go back to the days when my biggest concerns were what to wear that day, getting my homework done, and if the boy I currently liked thought I was cute.

It has been eight months since my parents died.

Eight long months of figuring out how to change from fun, carefree Juilliard student to responsible adult and guardian of my youngest sister, Konnie. My sisters, Genevieve and Konnie, both moved to New York with me, as well as Genevieve's boyfriend, Steve. Technically, Genevieve is eighteen and I'm not her guardian, but I feel like I need to be.

We aren't supposed to have to figure out life on our own. Our parents are supposed to be here to guide us, love us, and help us when we make mistakes.

How am I supposed to fill that role for my sisters?

I'm only nineteen, and it wasn't very long ago that Genevieve was keeping me on track. Genevieve would've been a better guardian to Konnie than me. But she hasn't been the same since Mark and the elusive Sebastian took our parents from us. Neither has Konnie. Genevieve is more anxious than she has ever been, and Konnie is angry. Angry at everyone and everything.

Just last week, all four of us went on a drive in Steve's Jeep. We all needed to get out of the apartment and decided a hike would be the perfect way to spend our Saturday. Well, Steve, Genevieve, and I decided it was a good way to spend the day. Konnie grudgingly packed a lunch and got in the car with us. As we were driving along the High Peaks Scenic Byway, all the trees were displaying their vibrant fall colors—reds, oranges, and yellows mixed with the occasional

1

evergreen were breathtaking. Even Konnie's ever-present scowl had softened as she looked out the window.

As we wound through the Adirondacks, one of Mom's favorite songs started playing from Genevieve's playlist. Genevieve and I both gave each other sad smiles before Genevieve turned up the volume and we started singing at the top of our lungs and dancing in our seats. Steve would glance at us occasionally with a smirk on his face, but the winding road kept him from joining in. We were having fun until I noticed Konnie wasn't participating. She sat with a stiff posture, tense against the door, a look of fury on her face.

The anger in her eyes made me stop singing.

There were no tears, no sadness, just pure anger radiating from her, until she exploded in a fiery ball of emotions, screaming at Genevieve to turn it off and startling Steve enough that he jerked the wheel hard, almost running us off the road. Genevieve, also not sure what was going on, quickly turned off the song and asked Konnie what was wrong. Instead of responding, Konnie pulled her ever present headphones over her ears and turned up the volume, turning her back to all of us and looking out the window.

My sweet, happy baby sister is gone. Replaced by a resentful teenager who looks at me with disdain every time we're in the same room.

"Violet! Get your head out of the clouds." Ms. Yvette snaps.

I stumble out of the arabesque I had been holding for a count too long and she gives me a glare that could wither the healthiest of plants. Glancing around the brightly lit dance studio with its mirrors in front of me and the large windows behind me, I shake my head, trying to clear it of the constant worry for my little sisters.

"Sorry, Ms. Yvette," I respond, getting myself back into position as she starts counting again.

Back home in Moncks Corner, South Carolina, I was always one of the top dancers in my class, but here at Juilliard, I'm struggling to keep up. Falling behind during all the chaos of my parents' deaths and moving my sisters to New York didn't help me either. My technique is turning sloppy—I'm falling out of pirouettes that I once was able to do in my sleep, my arms drooping when they should be held high, and even my once perfect posture now has an ever-present slouch brought on by my physical and mental exhaustion. But my new failings don't end there. I can't seem to remember new choreography and I'm always a count behind on every move no matter how hard I concentrate, something I've never had trouble with before.

It's not only dance that I'm falling behind in. I just can't seem to keep up with anything. My grades are slipping. I've never been the best student. Genevieve has always helped me with things I didn't understand, but I've never gotten D's or—heaven forbid—flunked out of a class before. I haven't failed a class yet, but I came close last semester. And my once vibrant social life is now collecting cobwebs.

I love every kind of dance, but ballet has always been my first love. Ever since that first ballet class Mom took me to, I've dreamed of being a professional ballerina. Regular school work and the redundant activities of daily life have never been easy for me to keep up with. But not ballet. Ballet has always come easily to me. The movements were just a natural extension of myself.

Dance was my safe place, my escape.

Until now.

Forgetting what comes after the pas de bourrée, I stumble again. I try to catch back up with the rest of the class before anyone notices.

No such luck.

"Violet Clark!" Ms. Yvette's shrill voice echoes through the dance studio. "Are we wasting your time here? Or are you going to actually pay attention at some point today?"

Taking a deep breath, I force down the sassy comment that comes to mind and say, "I'm sorry, Ms. Yvette, I'll try harder."

Her threatening gaze meets mine. "I don't want you to *try*, Violet. I want you to *do*."

Dropping my eyes from her gaze I nod and get back into position. Learning the choreography for the New Dances performance has been more difficult for me this year. New Dances at Juilliard is one of the main recitals we do. Every fall, each class is taught a new routine by a prominent choreographer for the December performance. Rehearsals for the New Dances kept me from going home for Thanksgiving last year, but this year I'm even more behind. So much has happened and I have so many new responsibilities. Instead of the college life I expected—classes, friends, parties—I'm now making sure my little sister gets to school on time, has lunch money, and gets her homework done.

And the bills. Don't even get me started on the bills.

No wonder Mom was always so grumpy on the days she had to sit down and pay them all. You might as well light your money on fire; at least that is how it feels. The life insurance payout left us with a reasonable nest egg, but it is stressful watching the funds disappear bit by bit each month. *Why are groceries so expensive?* And I now know why Dad was always yelling at us to turn off the lights. It really does matter. Now that I'm trying to keep up with so many additional tasks, I realize how much my parents did for me, how much I took for granted, and the rigorous dance schedule that I've always loved and thrived off of has become daunting.

Trying hard to pull my head from my never-ending thoughts, I focus on the choreography. I would rather not get called out for a third time in one rehearsal. If I can let myself get caught up in the movement and beauty of the dance, I can pretend for just a moment that my life hasn't turned into such a dumpster fire.

As we move through the pirouettes and grand jetés of the dance, my world is right again, until rehearsal ends and I'm pulled back into reality.

"You're doing great, Vi," Jocelyn, my best friend here at Juilliard says, her dark skin glistening with sweat. She gives me one of her cheerful smiles that can brighten anyone's day. "Don't stress too much, you've been through a lot since school started. You'll get there."

"Thanks, but I didn't hear Ms. Yvette yelling at anyone else. Just me. Which seems to be happening pretty regularly now. I can't seem to get my head in the right place."

She grimaces in solidarity. "What you didn't see up there in the first row was every time she would stop and turn that death glare on one of us who wasn't adhering to her expectations." Reaching over, Jocelyn squeezes my hand before zipping up her bag and throwing it over her shoulder. "With everything that has been going on, I'm not surprised you're having trouble concentrating. Have you looked into seeing if you could take a leave of absence for a little while or something?"

Glancing over at Jocelyn, I sigh, "I don't want to get that far behind. And I really want to keep dancing with you guys, I would hate to dance in the year below us. Our group has become like a second family to me. Seeing you all dance without me would hurt."

"Well, I'm here. Extra rehearsals, babysitting, late night cry sessions with ice cream. You name it. I got you."

"You're the best Jocelyn. Hopefully, I won't be needing any babysitting. Konnie is sixteen."

"Have you seen the anger rolling off that girl? I'm pretty sure she might need more than a babysitter. Have you thought about a full-time bouncer? Not to protect her, but to protect anyone she comes into contact with."

Laughter bubbles up and escapes my lips. It feels good to laugh. I can't remember the last time I felt happy. There's been a whole lot of devastation, guilt, and anxiety these last few months.

"A bouncer might be a good idea. Maybe while I'm at it, I can hire someone to remind me how to dance."

"Girl, you're literally paying a school to teach you how to dance. You just have to pay attention."

My smile falls. "I really am trying."

"I know. I didn't mean it that way. You just need to relax a little bit, get some of your spark back."

"How?"

"I don't know Vi, that's something you're going to have to figure out on your own. Maybe try taking time for yourself—relax, take a bath, buy a new outfit, binge your favorite TV shows. Or come out with us occasionally like you used to, we miss you. But whatever you decide, I've got your back while you're finding yourself in this new normal."

New normal.

That's a good way of putting it. I've been searching for my old normal, but it isn't there anymore. I've got to figure out how to navigate this new role I've been forced into. Last year when Jocelyn and I were roommates, life was so different. Dinner out with Jocelyn after rehearsals has been replaced with going home to make dinner for my sisters and Steve. Late nights on weekends with my friends, laughing and dancing until the early morning hours are now filled with me trying to recreate our old typical Saturdays together as a family. Homework study sessions at Juilliard have turned into me trying to study at our kitchen table while also helping Konnie with her schoolwork.

Following Jocelyn out of the studio, we walk the short distance to Hearst Plaza and sit down in the shade. Jocelyn unwinds her knotless braids out of the bun they were in for rehearsal. I envy how easily she can switch from looking like someone who was just rehearsing to someone ready to go out on the town. Even in her leotard and joggers, she could probably fit in anywhere she went.

"You want to go grab something to eat?" Jocelyn asks, her brown eyes focusing on me.

"I have to get home and make dinner for everyone. Plus, unlike you, I actually have to do quite a bit to not look like a drowned rat after rehearsal."

Jocelyn laughs. "A drowned rat?"

"Yes! Look at me, hair all sticking out everywhere, skin flushed." I point to my dark brown hair sticking out in every direction, showing no semblance of the tight, neat bun it was in at the beginning of the day. My olive-toned skin—a feature I got from my dad—is reddened and wet with sweat.

I gesture toward Jocelyn, her dark skin with maybe a slight sheen of sweat showing. "You just took your hair out of your bun and look ready to go out for the evening."

"Well, thank you, but I think you're exaggerating a bit."

A text from Genevieve interrupts us.

> What's the plan for dinner?

> Want me to make something?

Standing up I grab my bag. "Well, duty calls. I better run."

I send a quick text back to Genevieve before Jocelyn responds, "Don't burn yourself out. It is okay for you to relax a little and still be responsible. Your sisters need you, but they don't need you to run yourself into the ground."

"I'm trying. I'm just not sure how to relax right now." I sigh and try to give Jocelyn what I hope is a convincing smile.

She looks at me, not quite able to mask the concern in her eyes. "I know, Vi. I'll see you tomorrow."

With a wave, I walk toward the subway, trying to keep the forced smile in place. But it is hard to smile when all I feel is overwhelming pressure from all sides.

At what point am I going to break?

Chapter 2

Matiu

It's nice when all the pieces fall into place easily. Glancing up at my partner, Detective Armstrong, I close the folder in front of me, sliding it to the corner of my tidy desk to wait until it gets filed away. His desk is directly in front of mine, the fronts of our desks pushed together. The busy office is full of cubicles with desks in various states of disarray, as each detective sorts through the information they are given.

Our desks are complete opposites. Mine is clean with a place for everything, and his looks like someone just dropped a whole pile of junk onto it. Piles of files and papers litter the surface, with pens and paper clips jumbled in the mess. I shake my head; I have no idea how he finds anything in that clutter, but his weird messy system doesn't seem to slow him down. I am glad this most recent case was tidy, like my desk, and not a jumble of misplaced information like Detective Armstrong's work space. It doesn't normally happen with cases, but thankfully this case was an easy one to close.

Unlike the Clark case.

I clench my fists in frustration and take in a deep breath and try to relax. The Clark case, now labeled the Lykaios case, will haunt me until it is fully closed. The poor Clark girls got caught in the middle of a blackmailing gone bad. That disastrous night ended with six people dead. There were three suspects: Mark Lykaios and two low-level lackeys. Mark and one of the suspects died that night. We know the deceased thug is the one who shot and killed Tony and Charlotte Clark—we just don't know why the Clarks were a target to begin with.

It was satisfying throwing the only living suspect we got against the car, hard, before I put him in cuffs. Unfortunately, he didn't know much, only that Mark Lykaios was getting instructions from his uncle to retrieve weapon blueprints from Tony. Other than that, he seemed to be low on the totem pole and didn't have any useful information. He claimed to only get instruction right before a job, and always only the details he needed to know to complete his task. He didn't care what he was told to do as long as he got a paycheck. A paycheck he will never get again because he will be spending life behind bars. He may not be the one who killed the Clark parents, but he did murder two innocent victims on the ghost tour that night. Victims that were just in the wrong place at the wrong time.

Through our conversations with Mark's roommate, Steve Adler, we learned that Mark lived with his uncle Sebastian in New York City before becoming a student at Charleston Academy. Sebastian used Mark to get close to the middle sister, Genevieve, to try and get blueprints that their dad had access to. *But how did Sebastian know to target Tony Clark in the first place?*

Seven months later, my first big case is unsolved and Sebastian Lykaios is still unaccounted for. When we learned he had a residence in New York we asked the NYPD to look into it. There was no record of a Sebastian Lykaios owning any property in New York City, but a large house owned by Mark's mother Irina was discovered. When the NYPD searched the luxurious property, Sebastian was nowhere to be found. He had apparently left in a hurry, leaving documents behind that linked him to multiple drug and weapons deals, both in South Carolina and New York.

We are told not to let cases get personal. Don't get too attached emotionally.

Leave it to me to break all the rules right from the start.

As that night played out and I met each one of the sisters on the worst day of their lives, it instantly brought back the day we lost my little brother, bringing my first big case barreling into personal territory.

I was immediately attached to the girls as I watched them go through each emotion, emotions that revived my own feelings from the investigation of Nikau's disappearance.

Mark had opened fire on the officers that night resulting in his own death. I watched officers help Genevieve up after the shootout. Her eyes wide with terror, then confusion and sorrow as she saw Mark's body on the ground, a pool of blood slowly forming around him. Her fear mingled with the same terror and confusion in my beautiful mum's eyes when I told her Nikau never came home after our bike ride.

But it didn't end there. Only a few short hours later I walked that same young, once vibrant, senior in high school down the long brightly lit hallways to the morgue and watched her face crumble in heartbreaking grief as she identified both of her deceased parents, bringing back images of my parents faces crumpling when we realized Nikau was gone. He wasn't coming back.

It wasn't just Genevieve though; the youngest sister, Konnie, who looked broken mentally and physically like my own sister did and the oldest sister, Violet, who, in one horrific night, went from college student to guardian. Violet was forced to grow up in an instant, just like my sister and I were forced into the world of adult fears, when we realized that our safe haven wasn't actually safe at all. That it only took a small moment to change our lives forever. Our happy carefree childhoods became a thing of the past in the blink of an eye.

I am haunted by the pain etched into Violet's face when I had to recount the events of the night, the same pain that was mirrored in my parent's eyes as I recounted my last moments with Nikau.

And then Konnie. Officers found her unconscious, with a broken leg in the woods behind her house. Thank goodness she didn't see her parents get killed, but she heard the gunshots. She saw the men grab her father before her mother told her to run as fast as she could into the dense vegetation. When I talked to her at the hospital after the horrific events, I had the horrible thought that at least we found her, unlike my baby brother. *Were his last moments filled with fear as he tried to flee from his kidnapper?*

I still haven't been able to close either case.

These images plague me. They keep me up at night, tossing and turning, staring at those glaringly bright red numbers on the alarm clock as night turns to morning before I finally find sleep. And when I fall into a fitful slumber, I watch the replay of that night mingling with the worst day of my own life, until I can't distinguish one from the other. The two cases have become one in my nightmares and I don't know how to separate them. I close my eyes every night and get a constant reminder that I have no answers. I have failed these girls and my own family.

Just like I failed Nikau.

I need to find Sebastian, give the Clark girls answers to why their family was ripped apart. I don't want another family to go through the years never knowing, always wondering, like my family has these last fifteen years.

I reach into my pocket and rub my fingers against the toy dinosaur that I always have with me. Dad helped me drill a small hole through its back and attach small metal links to turn it into a keychain when I was a teen. It has been my constant companion ever since. The paint is faded and the rough skin of the small dinosaur is rubbed almost smooth by years of running my thumb across its side.

But I can't think about Nikau right now. I need to do my job.

Listening to the sound of the busy office around me, I try to focus my thoughts back into the present. The clicking of fingers on keyboards, the scratch of pens on paper, papers rustling against themselves as other detectives flip through all the information they have. Trying to make connections where others can't, trying to find the missing piece of the puzzle to solve the crimes that come across their desks.

Where did Sebastian disappear to? And what was he planning with a weapon that big?

Because of the risk this weapon could present to the American public, authorities are viewing this as domestic terrorism. With the worry that Sebastian may have secured other weapons, and the lack of resources needed to handle a case this big, the FBI is taking over. But everything has been put on hold for the last seven weeks while we all wait for NCIS to conclude their own internal investigation of the incident.

Waiting to move forward on anything has been frustrating to say the least. In the meantime, the file we have built on him contains everything from weapon deals to the documents found during the search of his New York mansion. Documents that link him to drug runs in Charleston and this whole blackmail fiasco with the Clarks.

So far, he has either been too smart or too lucky to get caught.

I'm assuming he's too smart. Since his involvement with the Clark case, there have been no sightings of him. The FBI has constant surveillance at all the locations we have gotten leads on—his mansion in New York closed up with no sign of him returning there, no contact with his sister living in upstate New

York, and no withdrawals on any of the accounts that his sister told us he has access to. He must have accounts we don't know about.

It is almost like he knows what we are going to search for next. When we think of another avenue to pursue, he has already wiped it clean. There is nothing scarier than an intelligent criminal, especially one we can't put a face to. We still don't even know what Sebastian looks like, even during the searches of both the mansion and his sister's house there wasn't a single picture of Sebastian found.

How are we supposed to catch a ghost?

My phone vibrates on my desk, pulling my thoughts from the Sebastian nightmare. Picking it up, I answer quickly. Any distraction from the unsolvable case is welcome.

"Detective McAllister."

"Is that how you answer the phone when your own mother calls you now?"

My agitation lessens at the sound of my mum's warm voice. I can almost picture her walking around the kitchen as she talks, pulling along the cord from the wall phone she refuses to upgrade. It brings a smile to my face.

"Sorry Mum, I didn't even look at who was calling before I answered."

"Why do you sound so serious?"

"I'm at work. I'm supposed to be serious."

Her sigh filters through the phone. "Well, lighten up a bit, aye?"

A smile tugs at my lips. "I'll try. What's up?"

"You're coming to whānau dinner on Sunday, right?" she asks using the Māori word for family. "You've missed the last three! I almost can't remember what my own son looks like."

This pulls a chuckle out of me. Both my parents, Tane and Katarine McAllister, are high energy and loving parents. They expect family to come first at all times, so missing the weekly whānau dinner is a bigger crime than the ones I solve.

McAllister whānau dinners are full of lots of good food, teasing, and the warm feelings of acceptance and love. I look forward to our weekly dinners with eagerness. So not only do I feel guilty for missing the last few, but I feel like I need the recharge of my emotional batteries that my parents and sister provide every time I am around them.

"I'm sorry, work has been busy."

"Nothing makes you too busy for whānau. Do you hear me, son?" The colonial twang of her Kiwi accent becomes thicker with her frustration. I have always wished that I had lived in New Zealand long enough to acquire the accent both my parents have. The mix between a British and Australian accent with a bit of Irish thrown in is probably one of my favorite things to listen to.

And maybe if they had stayed in New Zealand, Nikau would still be here.

Guilt and grief bundle together, creating a pit in my stomach. I can't let my thoughts go down that road.

"I hear you, Māmā. I'll be there." My use of the Māori word for mum seems to settle her, letting her know that I am taking everything she is telling me seriously.

"You better be. Your sister is going out of town for a college tour soon, and you need to see her before she leaves."

"I promise I'll be there on Sunday, but I have to go. I'm at work."

"Whānau comes first, Matiu. Remember that. Everything can change in an instant."

Flashes of the last time I saw Nikau's smiling face race across my mind. His missing front teeth and that cheerful grin plastered on his face every time I had a new idea for an adventure. I know everything can change in an instant, not just because of the darkness I see at work every day, but because of my sweet little brother Nikau, and how one horrible day changed my family forever.

"Trust me, Mum, I know that better than anyone else."

"Then why do I have to keep reminding you, aye?"

The crackle of the phone changing hands and sounds of my protesting mother come through the line as my dad gets on the phone.

"Hey son. You doing okay?"

"Yep, hangin' in there, Dad."

"Just making sure, haven't seen you in a while."

"It's only been three weeks."

"You sure? I'm not sure I remember what you look like."

Rolling my eyes, I laugh. He only needs to look in the mirror to remember what I look like. Dark hair, cut short in a high and tight hairstyle, clean shaven and our dark copper-toned skin that all four of us share from our Māori ancestry. "You and Mum both need new jokes. I promise I'll see you on Sunday."

"You better be here. Your mother is driving me crazy. She thinks you might be having a scandalous relationship and getting ready to elope. Nothing else could keep you from whānau dinner for three weeks."

"No relationship, scandalous or otherwise. Just been busy at work."

"Well, work isn't everything, my son. Remember that."

"I will. See you Sunday."

As I disconnect the call, I can't help but feel that insistent internal push to give closure to the families of each case I am working on. There is a need buried deep within me to solve every case that comes across my desk, because I know how it feels for the worst day of your life to linger over you like a dark heavy cloud that just won't let any trace of sunlight through. How it feels to go years not getting any answers, living up close and personal with an unsolved case.

And now I have another unsolved case. Another dark cloud rolling in, hanging over me, reminding me of my failures.

I slide the file of a different case in front of me and get back to work. Work may not be everything for me, but my work is everything for the families waiting for answers that may never come.

Chapter 3

Violet

"Earth to Violet! Am I not going to get a lunch today?"

Konnie's condescending tone brings me back to the present. The butter knife in my hand paused, hovering in the air above the sandwich I'm making, the glob of mayo waiting to be spread across the bread. This has been happening a lot more lately. I zone out all the time now. Maybe it is my brain trying to reboot back to its former self when it actually worked properly.

"Right, sorry." I say as I put down the knife and walk into the front entry to fish some money out of my bag. "Put all of that on your lunch account, okay?"

"What else would I do with it?" Konnie says with a dramatic roll of her brown eyes as she pushes her sliding glasses back up on her nose.

"At this point, I'm not sure. Maybe you'd use it to keep your bad attitude fueled."

Konnie doesn't even respond, pulling her headphones back over her long brown hair pulled into a tight ponytail. Her once ever-present braids are gone. She walks out the door, slamming it hard behind her. The vibration rattles the front entry, making my red umbrella slide from its spot propped up against the wall and clatter to the floor. Sighing, I walk over to pick up the umbrella, leaning it back up against the wall before going back to making my sandwich in the kitchen.

Konnie's surly mood first thing in the morning could put the happiest of people in a bad mood. She may look like Dad with her dark hair, glasses, and olive-toned skin, but her demeanor is nothing like our happy-go-lucky dad. Turning back to my task, I catch a glimpse of Genevieve leaving Steve's room and heading toward our bathroom where all her stuff is.

Yep. I'm definitely failing this whole big sister turned guardian thing. Once again, I question my decision to let Steve be our roommate. Was that really the best idea? But then I remind myself that he doesn't have any family left; he doesn't even have any siblings to rely on like we do. Not to mention that after everything we all went through none of us are comfortable with a roommate we don't know. And we need a roommate, rent is too expensive otherwise. Steve insists on paying half the rent each month instead of just the fourth he should be responsible for. I gave him the master bedroom on the opposite side of the apartment, with his own bathroom and everything, telling him that I insisted he have the larger room if he was paying half the rent. But I was also trying to put a little bit of space between him and the bedrooms and bathroom my sisters and I share. Konnie and Genevieve share the larger of the two rooms in our hallway and my room is about the same size as my closet back home in South Carolina.

Sure, Genevieve is eighteen and technically I'm not her guardian, but I know my parents wouldn't be okay with Genevieve sleeping in her boyfriend's room every night. And at what point did follow-the-rules Genevieve turn into this version? She hadn't even gone on dates with any boys before Steve, and now she is sleeping in the same room with one night after night.

Genevieve comes out of the bathroom with her long auburn hair in a ponytail and dressed for school. Tears threaten the backs of my eyes. She looks so much like our mother; it hurts a little bit every time I look at her. It's weird how both of my sisters look so similar to one of our parents and I'm a good mix between the two. I share Mom and Genevieve's facial features, but I have Dad and Konnie's olive skin and dark brown hair and eyes. Genevieve grabs a bowl out of the cabinet and the box of Cinnamon Toast Crunch out of the pantry. I watch as Genevieve fills her bowl to almost overflowing before adding milk. If I ate that much sugar first thing in the morning, I'd be sick halfway through the day.

Taking a bite out of my whole wheat toast topped with avocado slices and an egg, I reach around Genevieve to grab Mom's favorite teacup out of the cabinet and heat some water for tea. The teacup was one of the keepsakes I made sure to bring with us when we moved; it makes me feel closer to Mom having it here.

"Has Livi finally rubbed off on you?" I ask.

Genevieve looks confused. "What's that supposed to mean?"

"Gen, there is no way that Mom and Dad would be okay with you sleeping in Steve's room every night."

Okay, that came out a little harsher than I meant it to. Apparently Konnie's attitude this morning was contagious. The hurt look on Genevieve's face from the mention of our parents sends a wave of guilt through me.

A blush creeps onto Genevieve's freckled cheeks. "Nothing is happening Vi, the nightmares are relentless and sleeping next to Steve is the only way to keep them away."

Worry washes over me. "You're still having nightmares?" How haven't I noticed? Even I have nightmares about our parents' deaths and I was in a different state when everything happened. I can't imagine what the nightmares are like for Konnie and Genevieve.

Genevieve looks at everything but my face. "Yeah. Every night I sleep alone."

"You share a room with Konnie, you aren't alone."

"Yes, because Konnie is such a ray of sunshine right now. She definitely puts me in a state of relaxation." I can't help it. I snort a laugh, and Genevieve gives me a genuine smile before continuing. "We'll get through this Vi, it's just going to take some time and a lot of grace. None of us knows how to navigate this. We *all* have to be patient with ourselves and each other."

She gives me a small side hug, relieving some of my stress, before eating her cereal. I watch as Steve comes out of his room and plants a kiss on top of Genevieve's head before grabbing a protein bar out of the pantry. I can't help but feel a little jealous of their relationship. As much as I hate to admit it, I envy Genevieve. Steve is always there to comfort her with a hug or a kiss on the forehead. When she is having a bad day, she has his arms and support to come home to. Yes, I have Genevieve's support, but the support of a sister is different than the feeling of someone choosing to love you for you, instead of loving you because you were born into the same family.

"You ready to go?" he asks Genevieve and they both wave goodbye and shuffle out the door to school, leaving me sitting alone at the kitchen table with my guilt and the breakfast mess I have to clean up.

The sounds of honking horns and the busy New York traffic float through the quiet apartment. I don't do well in silence anymore and even with the noise from outside, the empty apartment makes me feel uneasy. Rinsing the dirty cereal bowls and placing them in the dishwasher, I rush to finish my tasks—tasks that Mom used to do—like finishing making my sandwich for lunch, tidying up the apartment, shutting off all the lights, and locking the door after everyone leaves for the day.

I'm definitely not equipped for these new roles, and I'm far from being mother material.

At least for now.

I was supposed to have time to grow up first. I was supposed to make mistakes that I would learn from before I was in charge of another human being. Yes, I'm their sister, not their mother, but I can't help but feeling like that is the role that I need to take on. I need to do more, be more for them.

I should have been more for them months ago.

I should have taken Genevieve seriously when she was asking for help with what to do when she found out Dad was being blackmailed.

I should have called my parents more and told them I loved them every day.

I can't change the past, but I can do my best to make sure my two beautiful sisters have the best possible future.

Pulling out my phone, I text Livi, Genevieve's best friend and one of my closest friends back in South Carolina.

> Hey! Has Gen said anything to you? Do you think she is doing okay?

> Do you mean how is she doing after a psychopath she thought was her friend killed her parents and then almost killed her?

I roll my eyes. Leave it to Livi to not sugarcoat anything.

> Yes Livi. That is exactly what I mean.

> She seems to be keeping it together in true Genevieve fashion.

But to be totally honest, she seems to be putting on a happy face every time we talk. I'm not sure how well she's doing, but I think she's doing as well as can be expected after what we all went through.

You were on that tour with her. Are you having nightmares?

Sometimes. The tour was terrifying.

But I didn't have the same experience that Genevieve did. And I still have my mom to help me through everything.

That stings, and I can feel the pinpricks of tears forming behind my eyes. It's not fair.

Why does one horrible night get to take everything from us? Who's going to be there when I inevitably mess all of this up?

How are you doing Vi?

I'm fine.

No you're not. But I'll be here whenever you need to talk.

Noticing that I only have twenty minutes to get to school, I rush to grab my lunch and my bag heavy with books, dance clothes, and ballet shoes. Flinging it over my shoulder, I check the weather on my phone. No rain today. October is usually a pretty dry month in New York City. Leaving my red umbrella propped in the corner, I walk out the door and lock it behind me before turning toward the elevator.

The outdated hall is heavy with dark beige paint, full of chips and scrapes. Big floral paintings line the wall, their colors faded with age. I squeeze my way through the narrow elevator door and push the button for the lobby level. The white noise of the elevator hums in the background as it descends the three stories to the ground level, lulling me back into my ever-present thoughts of what I should or shouldn't be doing to take care of my sisters. The ding of the

Louise Davis

elevator arriving at the lobby level startles me back into reality. Checking my bag to make sure I grabbed my phone before leaving the apartment, I bump into a kind looking middle-aged man with a smile on his face on my way out of the elevator, making him drop the book he was holding.

"I'm so sorry," I say, reaching down and picking up the book and handing it back to him.

He looks vaguely familiar, blonde hair sprinkled with gray, tan skin, a scar under his right eye. His skin mottled with the criss-cross of scarred skin that healed after a burn. I must have seen him in the lobby before, but I can't remember when exactly.

He gives me a wide smile. "No problem at all. You have a good day."

Why can't everyone be that pleasant? Pretty sure if I bumped into Konnie and made her drop something right now, I might not live through it.

Giving him a smile, I rush out the door. I can't be late for school again.

Chapter 4

Matiu

The warm, welcoming light escaping the windows of my parent's house beckons me as I pull into the driveway and park my car. Unable to pull myself out of my stressful mood from work I stay sitting in the car looking at the house. When we moved to Charleston, my parents initially lived in a rundown apartment, and we stayed in that same apartment for longer than we should have, but Mum didn't want to leave in case Nikau found his way home. When my parents were forced to move due to our apartment building being sold, Dad bought Mum her dream house. She never wanted anything grand or over-the-top, but she loves the southern plantation style houses with the big, towering pillars in the front, and the wraparound porch with a set of rocking chairs to watch the sunsets with plenty of room for whānau dinners.

Nikau should be here for whānau dinners. We should have happy memories with him here in this house, not just in the rundown apartment where my parents no longer live. I don't always want to dwell on my sorrow of Nikau, but I can't seem to stop lately. Reaching into my pocket, I absentmindedly brush my fingers across the dinosaur. Nikau loved this stupid dinosaur so much. We had toys that were so much more interesting and fun to play with, but he never went anywhere without this miniature Brontosaurus, which he called a Long Neck. Pulling it out of my pocket, I look at it. The texture and paint are worn off on both sides. I will never forget the day I gave it to him.

I wanted to use my own money to buy Nikau a birthday present for his sixth birthday. I was only eight, but I spent weeks helping Mum and Dad do extra chores to earn some money—helping Mum with dishes, washing the windows with Dad. Finally, Dad took me to the toy store to pick out a gift. The toy store was brightly lit with wonders all around. Every toy caught my eye, begging me to take it off the shelf and play with it. Nikau loved dinosaurs and when we went down an aisle full of more dinosaurs than I could count, I found the perfect one for him: a massive T-Rex that I could barely pick up myself. It moved and made sounds; it was perfect. He was going to love it!

"I'm sorry Matiu, that one is just too expensive. How about some of these over here?" Dad said, gesturing toward a bin full of small dinosaurs that could fit in the palm of my hand. Glaring at the inadequate bin, I dug around until I found a bright blue Brontosaurus—Nikau's favorite color. With a furrowed brow, I walked up to the counter with Dad and paid for the toy.

Later that day, I was embarrassed to give him such a stupid toy. Dad put his hand on my back and gently pushed me forward, urging me to follow through. When my brother opened the small, wrapped box, his face lit up. He took it with him everywhere after that. His blue Long Neck; a constant companion always nestled in his pocket.

Until it wasn't.

My parents weren't always overly protective, but after my brother was kidnapped and never found, something irreparable broke inside of them.

Something broke inside of all of us that day.

I was nine when it happened. It was a sweltering hot summer day in July with no breeze. One of the large South Carolina thunderstorms had rolled through the night before leaving large puddles and heavy humidity behind in its wake. It was one of those days where the humid air makes everything stick to you. Sweaty, clothes clinging to our overheated bodies, and grumpy from the heat, seven-year-old Nikau and I decided to ride our bikes to one of the corner stores. Back in those days, it was still common to see parentless children riding around close to home on their own. We needed some ice cream to cool off and Nikau loved the sandwiches that have chocolate chip cookies with ice cream in the middle; if Mum let him, he would have eaten a box a day.

Mum gave us some money, and we hopped on our bikes and raced to the closest corner store. It was one of our favorites. The owner had so many different ice cream bars in the freezer section. Walking into the store, the sweet smell of candy wafted over us. Nikau's eyes filled with excitement, wide with delight as we rushed over to the freezer holding the ice cream. Opening the door, we both lingered too long in the cool air drifting out of the freezer and cascading over us.

Nikau grinned at me with a wide smile, missing his two front teeth, and picked one of the chocolate chip cookie sandwiches, as usual, and I grabbed one of the frozen Snickers bars. We bought our ice cream and sat on the sidewalk in the shade of a large Magnolia tree, trying to eat the dripping ice cream faster than it was melting. The fragrant Magnolia blossoms, their sweet floral smell with hints of citrus, overpowered the scents of the city. Even though I was eating so fast I gave myself an ice cream headache, the melting ice cream was rolling down my arms, creating a sticky mess and dripping off my elbows onto the sidewalk. When I finished my treat, I looked over at Nikau, who wasn't even halfway done eating his. Melted ice cream covered his hands and face, dripping onto his red shirt.

"Mum isn't going to be happy about your shirt," I teased.

"It's just ice cream. It'll wash out. It's fine," Nikau responded between bites of melted cookie sandwich. Growing more uncomfortable in the hot, sticky humidity, and with my hands and arms covered in melted ice cream, I grew restless. Nikau was taking way too long to finish his frozen sandwich, so I jumped up, hopped on my bike, and yelled over my shoulder, "Last one home is a rotten egg!"

Racing away, I laughed as Nikau yelled after me, "Wait! No fair. You got a head start."

Ignoring his pleas, I continued to race home, not wanting to risk losing the race.

But Nikau never came home.

And I never forgave myself for leaving him alone.

I never got to see that grin again. Never got to play in front of our apartment together or ride our bikes to the store for ice cream.

Never got to say sorry.

My chest still constricts, a horrible, aching pinch that flares when I think about how I laughed as I rode my bike away from my innocent little brother. I should have waited. I should have been with him the entire way home.

At first, Mum thought maybe he had stopped at a friend's house on the way home. But after calling everyone she could think of without anyone seeing him, she got worried. She told me to show her the exact path we had taken to the store and back. We walked it, over and over, searching and calling for Nikau without finding him or his bike.

It was like he had just vanished.

On the walk back home, a glimmer of bright blue caught my attention near the edge of one of the puddles left between the sidewalk and the street after last night's storm. Tugging on my frantic Mum's hand, we stopped. Dread filled me when I saw the Brontosaurus lying in the muddy water. Its long neck the only thing visible, sticking haphazardly out of the small inky pool.

No matter how mad Nikau was with me, he would have never thrown this away.

Reaching down into the puddle of warm murky water, I picked up the dinosaur, rubbing my fingers over it to get all the mud off.

Mum's gaze fixed on the dinosaur. She covered her mouth with her hands, choked back a sob, and grabbed my hand. We rushed home to call Dad and the police. We hoped and prayed for so long that Nikau would be found.

He never was.

July 21, 2009 changed our lives forever.

Detective Darryl Armstrong, a middle-aged man with salt and pepper hair and a warm demeanor, was assigned to Nikau's case, and he searched tirelessly for my little brother. Every clue he found that seemed promising always ended up being another dead end. Dead end after dead end until our broken family was forced to try to heal, missing one member.

Detective Armstrong checked up on us regularly and Mum and Dad insisted he come to all our major get-togethers—birthdays, BBQs, you name it, Detective Armstrong was there.

After watching him search and search for a little boy he had no connection to for such a long time, I gained respect and admiration for detective work. Watching him solve other cases throughout the years—coupled with my need to solve my brother's unsolved kidnapping case—made me want to become a detective.

Once I decided investigative work was what I was going to do, nothing could stop me. I graduated from high school early with an associate's degree, then went on to college getting my bachelor's degree in criminology. Mum wanted me to go to medical school or a similar field, something that wouldn't put me in the line of danger, but I was set on becoming a detective. I wanted to make sure that my work could help prevent another family from going through the heartbreaking ordeal that mine did.

At twenty-one, I started training with the Charleston Police Department, and nine months later I was on patrol. I felt like I was helping as a patrol officer, but I still hadn't reached my goal. I gave up any semblance of a social life, worked hard and studied even harder to pass my exams with flying colors, and maintained a near perfect record at work.

Detective Armstrong, now a seasoned detective, his salt and pepper hair looking more like just salt these days, vouched for me in the Homicide Unit nine months ago. I became his partner and the youngest detective in the department at the age of twenty-four. I had only been a detective for a few short weeks before we were assigned to the Clark Case.

Sure, I get some snide comments from fellow officers about how nice it must be to have someone pulling strings for me, but I got here with hard work and determination. I am where I want to be. I love learning from Detective Armstrong and I have the added convenience of our unit handling cold case files, where Nikau's case has sat for years.

I will solve my brother's kidnapping case so my family can finally find peace. I won't let the Clark girls share my family's same fate. I *will* find answers, for *all* of us, even if it is the last thing I do.

I will never stop searching.

Shaking off the melancholy thoughts, I open the car door and walk up the front path to my parent's house. The path is lined with beautiful bright flowers running along each side. Mum sits on one of the rocking chairs on the porch, slowly rocking back and forth, watching the sun slowly sink down below the horizon. The evening glow framing the large, fragrant Magnolia tree in the front yard, the sweet smell bringing back memories of my last moments with Nikau.

"I was wondering if you were ever going to get out of your car, son," she says as she pats the empty rocking chair next to her.

I sit down and lean back. "I was just thinking for a bit."

"What's bothering you?"

"Nothing specific, just regular work stuff."

"I know you're sick of me asking, but are you sure this is what you want to do with your life? I know you've worked so hard to be where you're at, but do you really want to be surrounded by such sadness every day?"

Mum and Dad are overprotective, but it has never felt stifling. They radiate love and have always been supportive of anything my sister or I want to do, but they aren't shy about helping us question our choices when they think we are unhappy.

"It isn't really that I want to do it, Mum. I feel like I *need* to do it."

"If this is about Nikau, you don't need to let his disappearance make you feel like you have to do a job you don't want to do."

I sigh and run my hand across my face. "It *is* about Nikau, but it's also about all the other families I can help. We didn't get any answers, but I try hard every day to make sure I do everything in my power to find answers for those that I *can* help."

Mum reaches over and grabs my hand, holding on tight. My gaze fixes on her tā moko, a small tattoo on her hand that links back to her Māori ancestry before looking up into her warm brown eyes framed by her wavy black hair. "You have such a big heart, Matiu. No one knows what the future holds, but I know you'll do great things."

We watch the last wisps of the orange-red hues of the sun disappear, and sit without speaking, listening to the sounds of the cicadas' nightly symphony. Mum's relaxed demeanor calms my nerves. She stands up and pulls me up with her, wrapping me in a tight hug. I may be much taller than her now, but her hugs always make me feel safe, wanted, loved. A calm peace settles over me. It is nice to be home.

Life may not have been easy for the McAllister family, but Mum and Dad have always had such a positive outlook on life. As we walk into the color-fully decorated kitchen, a mixture of delicious smells assaults us and Dad turns around, rolling his eyes.

"I thought you two were never going to come in here and give me a hand with all this food," he grumbles playfully.

I take in the assortment of food littering the counter. Some southern dishes, like homemade mac and cheese and a big pan full of pulled pork, mingle with some favorites Dad misses from New Zealand, like minced meat pies and Māori fry bread.

"Were you planning on feeding an entire rugby team, Dad?" I ask.

Mum laughs. "Your father couldn't decide what he wanted for dinner tonight, so he just made everything that sounded good. We'll be sending some kai home with you, and even then, we still won't be cooking another meal this week."

Mum's use of the word kai, the Māori word for food brings a smile to my face. I love that even though they have been in America for over twenty years they still make sure my little sister, Miriama, and I have our Māori heritage sprinkled into our everyday life.

"Can I help you carry some of this to the table?" I ask and he puts me to work.

I was born in New Zealand, but Mum and Dad moved to the USA before my first birthday. There was a position with a large pay increase that opened up in the company Dad worked for. He is a biomedical field service engineer, so he fixes, installs, and maintains all the important equipment that hospitals use every day—like X-ray, MRI, and CT machines. Nikau was the first to be born in the USA, followed by Miriama two years later.

I love listening to my parents talk in their melodic accents and even though I have loved my life here, I can't help but wonder if my parents had never moved to the USA how different our lives would be. Would Nikau still be alive sitting at whānau dinner, laughing and joking along with the rest of us? Would we be a complete family without the scars left by the loss of a brother?

"I'm here!" Miriama announces as she walks through the door, her ebony hair piled high on top of her head in a messy bun. She brings her happy, playful energy into the room with her. "I hope dinner is ready because I'm starving," she says dramatically.

"I see how you are, showing up last minute so you don't have to help with anything before eating as much as you want," I tease.

"Maybe you should learn some of my tricks," she says with a wink and then squeals as Mum swats her with a dish towel.

"Come help carry some of this food to the table, Miri," Mum says as she piles dishes into Miriama's arms.

"Apparently, I should have waited just a few more minutes," Miriama jokes, earning her another swat of the dish towel from Mum.

As usual, the food is great and the company of my family is comforting.

"How long are you going to be gone on your trip, Miri?" I ask.

"A couple of weeks. I'm going with a group to tour several college campuses. Thinking I want to change things up for my bachelor's. It's been fun staying close to home for my associate's, but I think it's time for an adventure."

Mum groans. "Not too far away, aye?"

"Don't worry Mum, I'll call you every day, and I won't stay away for long." Miriama reaches over and gives Mum's hand a squeeze.

My phone dings from an incoming text and I pull it out of my pocket.

Hello Detective McAllister. This is Violet Clark. Just wanting to check in and see if there are any updates on the case?

I had given the eldest Clark sister my personal number back in February, yet another breach of personal space. We had communicated quite a bit about the case in those first few months after the incident, but it has been five or six months since I last heard from her, and I haven't had any new information to send her way.

And just like that, the peaceful calm that I was finally feeling shatters and the real-world creeps back in. The overwhelming weight of responsibility to those I have let down settles back onto my shoulders.

And Tony and Charlotte Clark's unresolved murders continue to haunt me.

Chapter 5

Violet

"Your fouettés are sloppy, Violet. Get it together." Ms. Yvette's sharp voice grates through the room.

Jocelyn bumps my shoulder with hers. "You've got this. I've seen you do beautiful fouettés. Stop overthinking everything."

Easier said than done.

I prep for the turn, and after just one rotation, I lose my balance.

Again.

What is wrong with me? I can't even do something that I should be able to do in my sleep. How can I be falling behind in something that used to feel like second nature to me?

I'm falling behind in everything—school, family… life. I just got two assignments back that I got Ds on. It probably doesn't help that I don't sleep well; I'm worried about my sisters constantly. No wonder Mom was always so high strung. Being in charge is exhausting. I don't know how she did it.

Last night, I got into another fight with Konnie. This time it was about a rude comment she made when I burned dinner. Steve and Genevieve were good sports, trying to gag the disgusting burned casserole down, but Konnie wouldn't even try it.

To be honest, I don't blame her, but she still doesn't have to be such a brat about everything.

How do you know what to worry about and what isn't important? When Genevieve told me she overheard Dad talking about someone blackmailing him, I didn't think anything of it. Dad was such a rule follower; he did everything by the book. I didn't think there was anything that someone could possibly use against him.

I was wrong.

What if something small that I do today affects one of my sisters' futures?

Maybe I'm not giving Konnie all the vitamins she needs. What if her diet is not healthy enough? Could I give her health problems in the future?

What if I'm not enough? What if I mess her up so badly trying to be her parent that she turns out to be an inadequate adult and I start a whole generational cycle that won't break for hundreds of years?

We need our parents. I'm not cut out for this.

Brushing off Genevieve's worries about Dad will forever haunt me. If I had called the police right away, our lives might be dramatically different. Dad may have ended up in prison depending on how dark his secret was. But even if he was in prison, at least he would've been alive. Both of them would still be alive. I have a feeling that Genevieve might know what happened during Desert Storm, but she hasn't told any of us.

I stumble again. The thud of my foot hitting the dance floor at the wrong time echoes through the studio.

"Miss Clark, go ahead and excuse yourself until you can take rehearsal seriously." The shrill nasally tone of Ms. Yvette's voice is about as pleasant as nails on a chalkboard. "Quickly. The rest of us have work to do."

I glance at Jocelyn on my way out of the studio, and she gives me an apologetic grimace. Grabbing my bag, I make it into the hall before stopping to lean against the wall. Hands shaking and tears starting to form, I slowly slide down the cold, hard surface until my butt hits the floor, resting my forehead on my knees.

How can I get past this? Everything feels like it is piling on top of me.

Pulling my phone from my bag, I reread the text from Detective McAllister.

> So sorry, nothing new yet. The case is in the process of getting turned over to the FBI.

> I haven't given up. I'll keep checking in on the progress of the case, even when it is out of my hands.

> Are you doing okay?

The text came through shortly after I sent him a text asking for updates last night, but I haven't responded yet. I don't know how.

Nothing is okay, but I can't really text the detective working on my parents' case about my swiftly dwindling mental status. I'm supposed to be Konnie's guardian—except she seems to do whatever the heck she wants, regardless of what I say.

I'm not even sure what I'm expecting from Detective McAllister. We know who killed my parents, but we don't know why. Maybe we never will, but I need some sort of closure as to why my family was targeted? And even though we've been told that we aren't in any danger with Sebastian on the loose—my sisters and I don't have access to classified weapons plans like Dad, and we don't have anything that Sebastian would want—I still can't shake the feeling that he isn't done with my family yet. I don't think I'll feel safe until Sebastian is found and in custody.

I reread the text one more time as class lets out, my stomach clenching with the knowledge that Detective McAllister will no longer be over our case soon. I don't know him well, but I trust him and I'm nervous about someone new coming into our lives.

The hallway fills with bodies heading to their next classes and Jocelyn stops and holds out a hand to help me up.

"You okay?" she asks.

Why does everyone keep asking me that? Do they really expect me to tell them no? That I need help? That I feel like I'm drowning in responsibilities and uncertainty every minute of every day?

Almost like she can read my mind, Jocelyn's deep brown eyes look into mine and she says, "You know it's okay to *not* be okay, right?"

And dang it all, tears start to roll down my cheeks, without my permission I might add. Jocelyn drops her bag, wraps me in a warm hug and lets me cry. I'm thankful that she doesn't expect me to talk; she just lets me cry until my tears dry up and only short unladylike hiccups remain.

"Don't you need to get to class?" I ask.

"Some things are more important than class. I'll catch up later."

"That's what I keep telling myself. It doesn't seem to be happening."

"Have you thought about talking to a professional? I think the school has some counselors that you can talk to."

Louise Davis

"It probably wouldn't be a bad idea."

"If you need help Vi, all you have to do is ask. There are so many people who would love to help you. We just don't know what you need or want help with."

"That's the problem. I don't even know myself."

Jocelyn gives me another squeeze. "You don't have to carry this burden alone."

We pick up our bags and head to our next class. At least I won't have to see Ms. Yvette again until rehearsal this afternoon.

Looking at the text from Detective McAllister one last time, I send a reply before walking into class.

I will be okay.

Chapter 6

Matiu

Where is that slippery snake Sebastian hiding? And why can I not find any leads? At this point, I would take the tiniest of breadcrumbs as long as it sent me in any direction other than standing still. Sebastian has to make a mistake at some point, right? Nobody is perfect.

Back in February, right after the NYPD found the documents linking Sebastian to weapons deals and drug runs in Charleston, we pulled any and all information the CPD had on the connected cases. Going through the files, we started noticing an unidentified man, always wearing some sort of facial covering, in a good majority of the surveillance photos as well as rumors of a man named Sebastian pulling the strings behind the scenes in the written reports.

I grab a stack of the best printed pictures of the masked man that we have. Flipping through them I notice that not only is he always wearing either a bandanna or, after the COVID years, a fabric medical style face mask, but he is always wearing gloves and a jacket with a tall collar or a turtleneck. By the style of dress and his face always being covered, I am confident that this is the same man in each of the photos. Frustrated, I run my fingers through my short hair. I wish surveillance photos were better quality.

Switching to the computer, I scroll through the most recent photos taken within the last five years by an undercover officer. I search for the man with the mask. Finding a clear, decent image, I stop and stare.

Cold, unremorseful, soulless eyes glare back at me from the computer screen, eyes that look vaguely familiar. Longer blonde hair is pulled back into a low ponytail leaving those eerie eyes uncovered and piercing. His mask covers from his nose down, a turtleneck covers his neck, and the ever-present gloves hide his hands.

What is he trying to cover up? Identifying tattoos? Birthmarks?

Zooming in on the current picture, I notice a small portion of skin is showing in the small strip that is uncovered between his mask and turtleneck. It is leathery, mingled with shiny areas which stand out compared to the unblemished skin of his forehead. It might have been severely burned at one point, maybe even some skin grafting by the looks of it.

Is he hiding skin that has been burned significantly?

Moving back to his eyes I zoom in and inhale sharply. Pulling up a picture of Mark, the masked man has similar longer blonde hair and dark brown eyes. I zoom in on Mark's eyes as well. The eyes are eerily the same, except for the wrinkles that come with age and the large scar under his right eye peeking out from below the mask. How had I not noticed this before?

Picking up the department phone on my desk I dial the Forensic Services Division. I don't have to wait long before someone picks up on the other end.

"Hey, this is McAllister from Homicide. Would you be able to tell if two people were related using facial recognition?"

"In theory, yes, there are algorithms that can compare facial profiles to verify genetic relationships."

"What if one of the suspects is wearing a mask covering the bottom half of his face?"

"That would definitely make it more difficult, but it is possible to get enough facial markers from the top half of the face to make a connection."

"Okay I am sending over two photos, can you analyze them and let me know if the two could be related?"

"Sure thing, but just a reminder, most facial recognition data isn't recognized as valid evidence in court."

"I know, thanks. I just need to make a connection between the two before I go further."

"Alright, send it over and I'll let you know what I find."

Hanging up the phone I sigh and lean back in my chair wishing we had a decent picture of Sebastian's entire face. That way, I could at least know exactly what the monster I am searching for looks like. Staring at the picture in front of me, I will him to make a mistake. The Sebastian in the written reports never had a last name, but Sebastian Lykaios has most likely been causing problems in our city for years. My gut tells me the masked man in the surveillance photos is Mark's uncle.

Maybe I can track him down by looking for burn victims. But who knows when or how he got the burns, and if that is actually what he is covering up.

It frustrates me that the Lykaios case is turning into such a cold dead end, and it doesn't help that I haven't been able to do much work on it since NCIS took over the case seven months ago and claimed jurisdiction until they finish their internal investigation.

And soon I will have no jurisdiction over it at all.

I am haunted by the Clark girls' faces every time I close my eyes. The same emotions I have seen in the mirror the last fifteen years are reflected in their expressions.

Broken. Alone. Guilt-ridden.

Violet's last text, "I will be okay," has been pestering me. I haven't responded. Maybe I am reading too much into her word choice, but she didn't say that she *is* okay; she said that she *will* be okay. That would insinuate that she *isn't* okay right now, right?

"Did you get a hit on the fingerprints we got this morning?" Detective Armstrong asks, breaking through my wallowing thoughts, bringing our new burglary-gone-wrong case back to the front of my mind where it should be.

"Not yet. Apparently, they're pretty backed up down there. It might be a while."

Detective Armstrong walks around my desk and looks at my computer screen. "Don't get too caught up in a case that is getting turned over to the feds. It's their job now. We have other cases that need solving."

"I know, I'm sorry."

He gives me a sad smile. "There are always some cases that just stick with you." He stops to give me a meaningful look. "Quite literally sometimes."

I smirk. "Noted, Detective Armstrong."

"Oh, for Pete's sake, stop calling me that. We've been partners for months, and I've been at every birthday party since you turned ten. Call me Darryl, for crying out loud. Or at the very least Armstrong, like the other detectives."

"I'll work on that."

"See that you do," Detective Armstrong huffs.

Turning back to my computer, I look for the results of the fingerprints we are running, but they still aren't back. Refreshing the page again, I sigh in frustration. Stuck once again. Another case going stagnant, with me searching and searching for information that just never seems to manifest itself.

"Armstrong, McAllister. A call just came in. You're needed at a scene." The rough voice of a fellow detective calls across the room. "Dead body over on King Street."

I lock my computer screen and grab my keys as I stand up, my fingers brushing over the smooth surface of Nikau's dinosaur as I shove them into my pocket.

"All right, let's go. Who's driving today?" Detective Armstrong asks.

"Me, definitely me. It would be nice if we get to the scene sometime during this century."

"Ha ha, you're so funny," he says with a roll of his eyes and tosses me the keys to our department-issued vehicle.

With a laugh, I catch them and follow Detective Armstrong out the door, leaving Sebastian for another day.

But the text Violet responded with yesterday still nags at me.

"I will be okay."

Is she okay? Or is she just trying to put on a brave face for everyone around her?

Chapter 7

Violet

Today is going to be a good day.

The soft glow of morning sunlight filters in through the blinds on my window, the sounds of the city that never sleeps filtering up from below. I stretch, trying to banish the constant exhaustion from my body. Despite getting an unusual full night's sleep and my excitement for the day, I still feel tired. It's Saturday, and rehearsals have been canceled today, due to cleaning crews doing a deep clean of the studios over the weekend—giving me a rare and much needed break from disappointing Ms. Yvette at school. I probably should practice, but I'm not going to think about that right now. Steve is going to be working on a group project for one of his classes today, so it will just be Genevieve, Konnie, and me. Between school and our various school-related activities, mixed with having Steve living in the same apartment as us, I feel like I never get any one-on-one time with Genevieve or Konnie anymore. Steve is great and I love the guy to death, but we haven't had much sister time since we all moved to New York.

What else makes a Sister Saturday awesome? Pancakes.

Climbing out of bed, I stumble to the kitchen, still a little groggy and bleary-eyed with sleep, but determined to have a full day of quality time with my sisters. I dig through the recipe book I brought from home and find the recipe for Mom's sour cream pancakes—they're delicious and we all love them. Pulling out some flour, sour cream, milk, eggs, and butter, I start mixing the batter and get the homemade buttermilk syrup simmering before pulling the flat top out and cooking the pancakes. The delicious, sweet smell of the syrup and the mouthwatering aroma of slightly sweet bread and browned butter waft through the kitchen as the first pancakes sizzle on the hot surface, bringing a smile to my face and making my stomach grumble. The familiar scents finally banishing the last lingering tendrils of sleep.

Memories of lazy Sunday mornings at home flood my memory—Mom cooking these same pancakes, pulling them straight off the griddle and placing them onto our plates one after the other.

"You girls sure have an appetite this morning," Dad would say, looking up from the paper he was reading at the table as we drenched the pancakes in syrup and practically inhaled them before asking for more.

Mom's melodic laughter would fill the kitchen and she would always say, "They're growing girls Tony, I'll make as many as they'll eat," before turning back to the griddle and placing more on our plates.

I miss them so much.

The creak of a door opening shatters the memory and an exhausted-looking Genevieve comes out of the room she shares with Konnie—her messy hair sticking up at odd angles and lines on her face from her pillow. She doesn't look like she slept well but at least she is coming out of her own room this morning. Konnie follows closely behind with the countenance of a storm cloud.

"Why are you up this early on a Saturday?" Konnie grumbles and I choose to ignore her negativity.

"Yum! Are those Mom's sour cream pancakes?" Genevieve asks.

At least someone appreciates me trying. "Yep. Thought it would be a good start to Sister Saturday."

"You're naming our Saturdays now?" Konnie grumbles. "I plan on spending my Saturday in my room. You and Genevieve can have your Sister Saturday without me."

Genevieve looks at me and raises her eyebrows. Being Irish twins and with birthdays only ten months apart we've pretty much been attached at the hip all our lives. I struggled for my first few weeks away from home, missing Genevieve and Livi and their constant company the most. For as long as I can remember, when I wasn't dancing, I was with Genevieve and Livi. Finding such a great friend in Jocelyn and my love of dancing at Juilliard took some of the homesickness away, but I still miss my old relationship with Genevieve. I need my best friend back. I need both of my happy sisters back. Today is supposed to be a fun day and Konnie is already dampening it.

Grabbing plates for the three of us, I set the table and put the towering stack of pancakes in the middle. Sitting down in my chair, my sisters join me at the table. Genevieve grabs the syrup and we all devour our pancakes like we haven't eaten in weeks. At least Konnie still has her appetite.

"Did you know our apartment is haunted?" Konnie says around a mouth full of pancake.

Genevieve rolls her eyes. "It is not."

"No, it really is! Jenna, the girl I go to school with who lives in apartment 42C, told me that not only is this apartment haunted, but it's cursed too."

Great, all I need is to have Konnie making Genevieve terrified of our apartment on top of everything else. "Konnie, our apartment isn't haunted or cursed. Knock it off," I say.

But Genevieve is already getting sucked in. "Why do they say it's haunted?" she asks Konnie.

"Well, the apartment has been empty for a while, but the last person to live here before us was an old woman who had like a gazillion cats. She died one night and her cats ate her after they ran out of food. Nobody found her for like a month."

Konnie's eyes are bright with excitement and a mischievous smile stretches across her face. This is the most animated I have seen her since our parents died. I'm torn between letting her continue her story and possibly scaring the crap out of Genevieve, or shutting it down before Genevieve decides we need to move. But I can't remember the last time she actually had a full conversation with us, so I don't say anything.

"Gross." Genevieve scrunches up her face. "That doesn't mean it's haunted, though."

"They said that the whole month before someone found her, the neighbors could hear her calling her cats to dinner. That's why no one thought to check on her." Konnie gets a mischievous look on her face. "And then, after her apartment had been cleared out, they could still hear her calling for her cats every night."

I sigh. "We've lived here for months and never heard an old woman calling her cats."

Konnie continues. "Then the family who lived here before the old lady had a son that died under mysterious circumstances. They moved out when the ghost of their son wouldn't stop slamming the doors at all hours of the night."

"Also, never had a door slam in the middle of the night," I point out. Konnie glares at me.

"But the worst one is the person who lived in the apartment before the family. He was a serial killer. He would take women into the apartment every weekend and no one would ever see them leave."

This one makes Genevieve's face go pale. "He was killing them in our apartment?" she whispers.

"Yep! Then when he got arrested and sentenced, while they were transporting him to prison, they got in a car accident and he died. Jenna says that every once in a while, someone sees him walk down the hall and disappear into the apartment."

The butter knife I'm using to butter another pancake slips out of my hand and hits my plate with a loud clink before clattering to the floor. Startled, Genevieve flinches hard enough that orange juice sloshes out of the glass she is holding and it hits the floor with a wet splat.

"Okay, that's enough," I say. "Our apartment isn't haunted. Change the subject."

"Haunted and cursed," Konnie pipes in.

Genevieve is so focused on what Konnie is saying, she leaves the spilled orange juice untouched on the floor. I sigh and reach down to wipe up the juice; Genevieve has always hated getting scared. I still don't know how Livi and Steve convinced her to go on so many ghost tours. I tried for years to get her to come to the Halloween-themed fun at Cypress Gardens, but her aversion to anything scary always kept her safe at home, far away from anything that could frighten her.

"Why is it cursed?" Genevieve asks timidly, like she has to know the answer, but she isn't sure if she wants to.

"Because someone in the apartment always dies. No one living here makes it more than a year without a death," Konnie says, making her tone of voice spooky.

"Konnie, stop!" I snap. Genevieve's face has gone pale, her eyes wide with fear. "Nobody is going to die and our apartment isn't cursed or haunted. Like I said, we've been living here for months and nothing weird has happened unless you count Konnie's transformation from Wednesday's happy, bubbly roommate to Wednesday Addams herself."

This earns me a death glare from Konnie as she pushes herself back from the table and stomps into her room, slamming the door behind her with enough force to knock one of the throw pillows off the edge of the couch it was balancing on. I sigh and squeeze my eyes shut, rubbing my temples as a headache starts to form. Konnie's constant anger is really getting old.

I open my eyes and look at Genevieve. "See, we don't need ghosts to slam the doors. We have Konnie for that."

Genevieve giggles. "Be nice, Vi."

"I'm trying. She just makes it really hard."

"Trust me, I know."

The doorbell interrupts Genevieve. I get up and look through the peephole, bright red flowers filling my view. Curious, I pull open the door and see the kind man I bumped into coming out of the elevator the other day peeking out from behind the blossoms.

Weird, I'm not sure why one of our neighbors would bring us flowers.

"Hi, nice to see you again," I say, putting a neighborly smile on my face

That same wide smile he had the last time I saw him spreads across his face, but I notice it doesn't quite reach his dark brown eyes. "Why thank you. These flowers got delivered to my apartment by mistake. I thought I'd bring them to the correct apartment. They're pretty, though. I thought about just keeping them for myself." The man laughs heartily at his own joke, and I notice a small hint of an accent laced with his words, but it is so faint it doesn't have any distinguishing qualities.

I reach for the flowers and take them from him. "Well, thank you so much."

"Anytime, that's what neighbors are for. You girls have a great day," he says. His eyes seem cold, which doesn't match his facial expressions or the kind tone in his voice. Turning around, he walks back down the hall.

"Who was at the door?" Genevieve asks as I close the door behind me.

"One of the neighbors. These got delivered to his apartment by mistake."

The flowers are a beautiful mixture of Roses, Dahlias, Tulips, Carnations and Amaryllis—all different shades of red. A small red card is tucked into the flowers with Genevieve's name on the front.

"They're for you," I say and hand them to Genevieve, annoyed at myself with the bit of jealousy that flashes through me. I'm happy for Genevieve, but that nagging want of someone to love me unconditionally keeps pestering me.

"Oh my gosh, they're beautiful!" Genevieve takes the flowers and places them on the kitchen table before pulling the card out of the fragrant flowers.

Her face lights up as she reads the card. "They're from Steve. It just says 'I see you' on the back of the card. How sweet. Remember me telling you about when he took me to Magnolia Plantation? It has kinda been a thing we say to each other ever since."

"Aww, that's so cute," I say, genuinely happy for my sister.

I lean in to sniff the flowers as Genevieve pulls out her cell phone to call Steve and say thank you. Inhaling the sweet floral scent brings back memories of Mom's fragrant blossoms she would cut from the yard and place in vases around the house. Loneliness pushes away my happy feelings. My chest constricts from the weight of missing my parents and the sister that I didn't used to have to share with Steve.

"Thank you so much for the flowers!" Genevieve says in a giddy voice when Steve answers.

Our eyes meet as her smile turns to confusion and then worry.

"I thought they were for sure from you. The card has my name on it and then all it says on the back is 'I see you.'"

Genevieve listens to Steve for a while, her face draining of color before she hangs up.

"Vi, the flowers weren't from Steve. Who would've sent them? Especially with that message?"

"I don't know. Livi maybe?"

"You're the only other person I told that story to besides …" a sharp intake of breath stops her sentence.

"Besides who, Gen?"

"Mark." The name escapes her lips in a whisper.

Small tendrils of fear begin to creep in as I peer at the card. "That message just went from cute to creepy real quick."

"Right? What do we do?" Genevieve asks with a tremble in her voice.

"I'm not sure."

We can't call the police and tell them that someone delivered us flowers. That isn't a crime, even if the only other person who knows the story is dead. They can't arrest a ghost.

I pick the card up and look at it again. This time the red card and the red flowers don't seem so beautiful.

They feel like a threat.

Fuming, I pull the flowers from Genevieve's hands and drop them into the garbage—glass vase, card, and all. Angrily I cinch the plastic bag tightly, pulling it out of the trash can. On a mission, I stalk through the door and down the hall and dump the bag down the smelly trash chute.

Just as quickly, my anger turns to fear. Hands shaking, I walk back to our apartment. I close and lock the deadbolt behind me. The click on the lock sliding into place calms my nerves some.

But not enough.

We don't know how close Mark was with his uncle. Would he have told Sebastian a seemingly random story Genevieve told him in confidence? Would Sebastian even remember it if he had?

Detective McAllister said they thought we were safe, that Dad's blackmailing had nothing to do with us, so it should be over.

What if he was wrong?

Chapter 8

Matiu

They never show how much paperwork you have to do as a detective in any of the movies. It gets monotonous. Glancing at the stacks of folders that I still need to go through and get ready for filing, I close my eyes and rub my temples. I am going to need some caffeine. It feels like I have been doing paperwork for hours. In reality, it has probably only been thirty minutes, but I am ready to be done. Taking a peek at the clock again, I am relieved to see it is 4:45 p.m. The workday is almost over. Stretching, I clean up my desk, place my pens back in my drawer, and tidy the piles of papers and files that will be waiting for me tomorrow morning.

Our captain walks up and stops at my desk. Rapping his knuckles on top of it, he says, "Armstrong, McAllister, the FBI and the NCIS want one of you to join in on a meeting about the Lykaios case. They want you to go over all the information you've collected so far. Armstrong, gather what you need and be ready to meet with them tomorrow morning."

My stomach drops. I know Detective Armstrong is the senior partner and is who should go, but I really want to be in on that meeting. I'm not sure if NCIS will give any new information, but I want to be there nonetheless.

Detective Armstrong looks over at me. I lock eyes with him and silently plead my case to let me go instead, and it must work. "I think we should let McAllister go to the meeting, Captain. He knows everything about the case and has worked night and day on this one."

Captain looks between the two of us. The seconds seem like hours as we wait for him to make his decision. "Done. McAllister, don't be late."

I sigh in relief as I watch our captain walk back toward his office. "Thank you."

"Don't thank me yet. Relinquishing full control of the Lykaios case might be more torture than you realize."

Oh. Yeah. I didn't quite think about that. I won't have access to updates or be able to step in and help. I won't be able to help find Sebastian and close the case. Clenching my jaw in frustration I try to think about the benefits of passing the case to the feds. They will be able to throw more resources into finding Sebastian and they can cross state lines during their investigation. Any progress in the case will be better than this standstill we have been at for months.

"I don't care who solves the case as long as it gets solved," I say, trying to convince myself.

Detective Armstrong chuckles. "You keep telling yourself that, kid."

As long as Sebastian is found and the Clark girls can get some closure, that is really all I care about, right? Maybe if they find Sebastian and the case closes it won't haunt me anymore.

Images of that night flash through my mind as if my desire for the case to close conjured them—the red and blue flashing lights reflecting off the old city jail, an officer pulling Genevieve from the ground, leading her way from Mark's lifeless body and helping her into a patrol car, the numb shock on Violet's face as she tried to process all of the horrible information—those big brown eyes filling with tears and searing themselves into my memory.

With the disturbing images fresh in my mind like they happened yesterday, I watch the clock as the final minutes of my workday pass at a painstakingly slow pace. At five sharp I clock out and rush to my car, but instead of going straight home I make a slight detour to drive past the Old City Jail. A few minutes later, I park and watch a tour group disappear into the ominous building.

The Old City Jail has always creeped me out. Even when we were younger, Nikau and I would ride our bikes as fast as we could past the jail, not wanting to stay near it for long. The jail just feels wrong. The old sinister building and the ancient trees surrounding it cast menacing shadows over the street. Shadows that seem to come to life, moving and twisting with the branches, a chill always in the air even on sweltering hot, humid days. The serene beauty of Charleston cannot be felt here, where history is mixed with terror and the rumors of lingering ghosts—restless spirits of the people who did unspeakable things.

Kids in high school would always dare each other to do dumb stuff by the jail, like sneak past the locked gate and see if you could see Lavinia Fisher's ghost in the courtyard or try to break in and stay the night. As far as I know, no one ever successfully got into the jail. Maybe it was because the tour companies have it locked up tight or maybe it was because nobody really tried that hard, because no one in their right mind would want to spend the night in that building alone.

It has always given me an uneasy feeling, but after the horrific tour in February, it is even more disturbing. I'm sure the recent tragedy brought more business from the morbidly curious to the tour company. I wonder if having one of their own employees responsible for the bloodshed has hurt business, or if it has increased sales. From a business standpoint I understand why shutting down the tours that go through the jail wouldn't be a smart move, but I can't help being uneasy with how quickly they opened it back up.

Getting out of my car, I walk to where I can see the courtyard where the shootout with Mark took place. More flashes of the tragedy bombard my thoughts, the images dancing across my mind like a movie.

Sticky blood coating the floor inside the building.

College students and tourists whose lives were cut short by Sebastian's plan.

Mark's last words.

Words that are permanently engraved in my memory.

'If you have a message you want to send to hell, give it to me—I'll carry it.'

A chill runs up my spine and I shiver. Why Mark would want to quote such disturbing last words from Lavinia Fisher is beyond me. I had even researched as much as I could about Lavinia to see if there was any hidden meaning behind Mark's final statement, but I couldn't find any connections. Only disturbing stories about the first female serial killer in America and more questions about how people can be so evil.

After reading so much about Lavinia Fisher, if I believed in ghosts, I wouldn't be surprised if she was forever wandering the halls of the jail.

But I don't have time for ghost stories.

I have enough real-life things that are haunting me.

Not all ghosts are dead.

Chapter 9

Violet

The vibrating phone in my pocket is a nuisance as I try to get ready for rehearsal. I'm running late, as usual. Pulling it out of my pocket, I see Konnie's school's number calling. *Great, what did she do now?* I answer the phone and try to sound pleasant.

Instead of an actual person, I hear an automated voice on the other end. "To ensure the safety of all our students, this is a call to inform you that your student, Konnie Clark, has been marked absent. Please call and verify this absence at your earliest convenience."

The call disconnects. *Why isn't Konnie at school?* I look at my phone and realize that this wasn't the first call from the school. They had called first thing in the morning too. She hasn't been at school all day?

I try to get a hold of Konnie. She doesn't answer.

I call Genevieve and wait impatiently for her to pick up. "Gen, have you seen or heard from Konnie?" I ask in a panicked voice.

"Isn't she at school?"

"No, I just got a call from the school saying she isn't there."

"Did you look to see where she is on Find my Friends?"

Oh. No! How could I forget about that? Putting Genevieve on speakerphone, I quickly pull up Find my Friends and click on Konnie. It loads for what seems like forever before saying 'location unavailable.' Fear settles in my stomach, thoughts of accidents and murders and everything that could happen to a teenager in a big city flash through my thoughts.

"It says her location is unavailable," I tell Genevieve in a shaky voice.

"Don't panic, Vi, go to rehearsal. She probably just ditched school and went home. Steve and I will go home and see if she's there. We're done with class for the day anyway. We can study at the apartment."

"Why is she not showing up on Find my Friends?"

"She probably turned her location off. You know as well as I do that she does everything we ask her not to do and doesn't do anything we ask her to do these days. It's getting really irritating."

Taking a deep breath, I tell myself that Konnie is fine, she's just being a rebellious teenager. "I definitely won't disagree with you there. Let me know as soon as you find her."

"I will. Go to rehearsal and Steve and I will head home."

"Thanks Gen," I say before hanging up.

Konnie is probably safe at home, just being a brat, I tell myself. But my heart races and I panic as my traitorous mind runs through all the worst-case scenarios. *What if she got into an accident on her way to school?* Why do I not take the subway all the way to her school with her every morning?

What if it has something to do with the flowers?

Telling myself to stop, I take a long deep breath, trying to calm my nerves and walk into rehearsal.

"Places everyone!" Ms. Yvette snaps and we all scamper to our various spots.

She counts "five, six, seven, eight" and we start marking the routine with counts like we do at the start of every rehearsal. Ms. Yvette starts the music and the group falls into the routine we've practiced countless hours. Despite all my practice it doesn't take long before I forget a step and Ms. Yvette's shrill voice is reprimanding me.

And it happens again.

And again.

And again.

"Miss Clark. Trade places with Miss Smith," Ms. Yvette says without feeling. I look behind me and notice she's putting me in the very back. The worst spot in the entire dance. "Perhaps back there your constant mistakes will be less detrimental to the group, but if you don't get your head where it needs to be, your spot will be given to someone else entirely. Maybe we need a pretty tree in the back for the performance. You might be able to handle that."

I can hear snickers around the studio.

"I'm sorry, Ms. Yvette. My sister didn't go to school today and I'm having trouble focusing because I don't know where she is."

"I don't care if your sister flew to the moon instead of going to school. When you enter this studio, you will give me your full, undivided attention or you *will* be cut. Do you understand?"

"Yes, ma'am," I grumble and hear more snickering around the room. I find Jocelyn, and she gives me a reassuring smile before the drill sergeant resumes rehearsal.

As soon as rehearsal is over, I rush out the door with Jocelyn right on my heels.

"You don't know where your sister is?" she asks.

"No, she left the apartment but apparently never went to school today."

Pulling my phone out of my bag, I call Genevieve. The worried tone of her voice when she answers tells me they haven't found Konnie yet—I don't even have to ask.

"Steve and I have been looking everywhere we think she might have gone. We're headed to another spot now," Genevieve says breathlessly.

My stomach feels like it's full of rocks. I disconnect and send a text to Detective McAllister.

> We can't find Konnie.

My phone is vibrating almost instantly with Detective McAllister's name popping up on the screen.

"What do you mean you can't find Konnie?" he asks instead of a greeting.

"She left the apartment this morning like every other day, but she never made it to school. I don't know where she is."

"She's probably just being a teenager. Can you think of anywhere she may have gone?"

I try to think of all the possible places Konnie would go in New York if she was skipping school. "Konnie hasn't really made any friends, so I can't think of anyone she'd be with or where she'd go. She's usually at school or at home."

"Have you called the police?"

"Yeah, I texted you."

"No, I mean, have you called the police in New York?"

Duh, why didn't I call the police? I didn't even hesitate before texting Detective McAllister. Why? What good could a detective down in South Carolina do? When did he become the first person I call when I need help? Probably shortly after all the other adults in my life got taken away.

"Uh, no. I haven't."

Pulling off my ballet flats, I shove them into my bag and lace my tennis shoes up over my sore feet, practically running out of the building with Jocelyn following close behind.

"You should definitely call them if she hasn't been seen all day," Detective McAllister says.

Rushing out the door and across the street Jocelyn and I sprint past the Elinor Bunin Munroe Film Center and skid to a stop, sighing with relief. Konnie is sitting at a table in Hearst Plaza.

My relief quickly turns to anger. "I found her."

Detective McAllister breathes an audible sigh of relief. "Good. Call me again if anything else comes up."

I appreciate his offer, but I need to deal with this. I disconnect the call and send Genevieve a text letting her know I found our sister. Stalking toward Konnie, anger boils up inside of me, I'm ready to yell and scream. *How dare she scare Genevieve and me like that after everything we've been through?* But when Konnie looks up at me with tear-stained cheeks, my anger dissipates.

Jocelyn tells me she'll see me tomorrow, and I walk over to Konnie. She doesn't say anything, and I don't know what exactly is going on, but I wrap my little sister in a tight hug and let her sob until the tears stop. Konnie stands up and wipes her eyes without saying anything and I wrap my arm around her waist as we walk toward the subway.

"Do you want to talk about it?" I ask.

"No."

"You want to tell me why you weren't at school today?"

Konnie pulls away, and her irritated look that I've come to know so well slides back into place before she stalks toward the subway with me chasing after her.

"Konnie, wait. You can't just skip school and expect nothing to happen. What's going on? Why are you so upset?"

She spins around and the anger in her eyes is a little bit scary. "Why am I upset Violet? Probably because both of my parents are dead."

I'm speechless, trying to come up with the right words to say to my obviously hurting little sister. Grasping at straws, my mind latches onto the first coherent thought it has. "But what happened today to make you ditch school and come here? How come you didn't text me? I could've come out here earlier."

"Nothing happened today. I just wanted to be alone. Is that too much to ask, Violet?" she shouts angrily.

"You're always alone lately Konnie, that's all you do is shut yourself up in your room away from us."

She stops yelling, but her voice drips with venom as she says, "Yeah because my parents are dead and my stupid big sister is trying to replace my mom. You're not Mom, Violet! Stop trying to be. Just leave me alone."

Her words sting. I don't think I would've been any more surprised if she had turned around and slapped me. I'm not trying to be Mom. I don't want to be Konnie's mom. I'm just trying to keep what is left of our family together and help Konnie make it to adulthood in one piece. I'm doing it all without knowing what in the heck I'm doing pretty much 99.9% of the time. And I still don't know what I'm supposed to do next.

I follow Konnie onto the subway and we sit next to each other in tense silence until we jerk to a stop at our station. We don't speak for the rest of the walk home and Konnie stomps past Genevieve and Steve when we enter our apartment, slamming her room door behind her.

"What was that all about? Where was she?" Genevieve asks.

I don't think I can keep the waver out of my voice to answer so I shrug and make my way to my own room, shutting the door behind me with a click. The tears come quickly, falling down my cheeks faster than I can swipe them away. I half expect Genevieve to come see if I'm okay, but she must think I want space because her soft knock at my door never comes.

Without thinking or giving my thoughts time to talk myself out of the phone call, I sit down on the floor, lean against my bed and click on Detective McAllister's name. The phone only rings once before he answers.

"Is everything okay, Violet?" he asks with a concerned voice.

"Um, yeah." I pause, my brain finally catching up to my actions. *Why did I call him?* Frantically trying to come up with a reason for the call I start panicking. "I just wanted to call and say thank you for your help earlier."

A nervous chuckle comes through the line. "You're welcome. I didn't really do anything."

Ugh. Could this conversation get any more awkward?

"Well, I just wanted to let you know that I appreciate everything you've done for us these past few months."

"I haven't done enough," he says quietly.

I'm not sure how to respond, so I don't and after a short silence he starts talking again.

"I'm sorry that I haven't been able to give you and your sisters more answers, Violet. I'm sorry I can't find Sebastian or help you get the closure you need."

The pain in his voice breaks my heart a little bit more; I'm not sure how much more breaking my heart can take.

"It's not your fault," I whisper.

"Isn't it? Isn't it my job to find you answers?"

"Yes, but I think that some answers just can't be found."

Detective McAllister lets out a long sigh before continuing. "Well, Violet Clark, I vow to find you your answers. No matter how long it takes me to uncover them."

I can't help the smile that creeps onto my face and the giggle that escapes my lips. He sounds ridiculous even if it might be the most meaningful thing anyone has ever said to me.

"My very own personal knight in shining armor. How did I get so lucky?"

Heat floods my cheeks and I'm glad he can't see me. *Did I really just say that out loud? Am I flirting with our detective?* I hold my breath waiting for his reply.

"You know, my mum always loved to paraphrase a quote from Tremendous Trifles written by G.K Chesterton in 1909. The actual quote is much longer, but it essentially says that children don't need fairy tales to tell them dragons exist. They need them to tell them that the dragons can be killed."

He pauses for a moment before continuing. I think this is the longest I have ever heard him talk and although I have no idea where he is going with his rambling thoughts, I find myself just wanting to listen to his soothing voice.

"I guess the point I'm trying to make is, I think that sometimes when we can't kill our own dragons, people are put into our life who can kill them for us."

"Are you volunteering to kill my dragons, Detective McAllister?"

He chuckles. "Yes Violet, I'm volunteering to kill your dragons, they just happen to be evading me at the moment."

"Even the biggest of dragons can't hide forever, right?"

"That's my hope."

Didn't he say that the case is getting turned over to the FBI? He might not be our detective much longer. Nervous energy courses through me for a whole new reason. I don't want someone else to be searching for Sebastian.

I want Detective McAllister.

"What happens when the FBI takes over our case?" I ask.

"I'm not one hundred percent sure. But I'll do everything in my power to keep my promise, even if I personally don't solve the case, I'll continue searching to the best of my ability until Sebastian is found. And I'll be there celebrating with you when it's all over."

I can hear the distant sounds of traffic in the brief silence before he speaks again. "How are you really doing, Violet?"

"I don't know how to answer that question."

"How about honestly."

I sigh. "Honestly, I feel like I'm drowning. I can't keep up with school, Konnie hates me, and I'm just so extremely tired."

"Why do you think Konnie hates you?"

"She's just mad at the world right now, and I'm who seems to be getting the brunt of her anger."

Tears start to fall again and I angrily swipe at my cheeks.

"She doesn't hate you; she has good reason to be mad at the world right now and you're her safe space. The only person in her grieving world that she can lash out at in her anger and still be safe. Let her feel her anger Violet, give her the help she needs when she needs it and be there for her when she's ready to let her anger go."

The tears are unstoppable now, I can't see through them and I don't even bother trying to dry my eyes.

"But who is going to be there when I need someone to run to?"

"Me."

My breath catches in my throat. Warmth floods me and feelings start to surface for Detective McAllister that are anything but professional, bringing along confusion and anxiety with them.

"Thank you, Detective. I really needed to hear that tonight. I'm sorry that I bothered you earlier when we couldn't find Konnie. I was panicking and I didn't know who else to call."

"I meant what I said when I told you to call me anytime, Violet. If you need me, call, and I'll be here."

Butterflies replace the confusion and anxiety that had settled in my stomach as I disconnect the call. I'm not sure what is happening between us, but one thing I know for certain is that during our conversation, Detective McAllister has given me a small amount of peace. And with the turmoil of my life constantly surrounding me, that little sliver of peace is the most beautiful thing I've felt since I got the call telling me that my parents had been killed.

If Detective McAllister is offering to slay my dragons and bring peace back into my life, I'm going to let him. Even if the peace that he brings into my life is just knowing that he'll be there if and when I need him.

He's only a phone call away.

Chapter 10

Matiu

Captain told me not to be late to the meeting with NCIS and the FBI, but I got through traffic quicker than anticipated and I am thirty minutes early. I go through security, check in at the front desk, and a no-nonsense woman in a suit leads me to a conference room. I thank her and smile as she leaves, but she doesn't return the smile and I am left waiting alone in the empty space.

The conversation with Violet last night replays through my mind, again. It has been on repeat in my head since we hung up last night. I sounded like such an idiot. Who says they vow to do anything these days? And why did I make so many promises to her that I'm not sure I can keep? I have no idea how this meeting will go today, but it's likely I won't have any access to the case when I leave this room.

But one thing I know for certain is no matter how dumb I feel, if I had a chance to re-do last night's conversation I wouldn't change a single thing. I had never heard Violet laugh before and that contagious giggle of hers is something that I will never get tired of hearing.

Even if I have to make a fool of myself to hear it.

Two people in suits stroll in—a tall, blonde man and a petite, caramel-skinned woman. These must be the FBI agents. I stand up and shake their hands, hovering for a minute, but when they continue to discuss something in hushed voices, I sit back down. I can't hear what they are saying, so I observe their body language trying to get a feel for them and hoping that these agents are competent enough to take over this case that has become so important to me. We don't wait long before a brooding giant of a man in military garb enters. He is obviously the officer from NCIS.

Imposter syndrome kicks in and I start to feel way too young and under qualified to be in this meeting; I am starting to wish Armstrong had come instead when the blonde FBI agent stands up, towering over all of us, and clears his throat.

"Thank you all for coming. I'm Agent Alec Sullivan and this is my partner, Agent Delgado." He waves a hand toward the petite woman. "Now that NCIS has finished their necessary investigations, we can move forward on a federal level to pursue Sebastian Lykaios. We appreciate your cooperation and expertise regarding his case. Let's start from the beginning, walk us through what you know."

All eyes turn and focus on me. Apparently, *I* am the beginning. "I'm happy to give you all the information we have collected. I just want Sebastian found, no matter how it needs to be done."

Agent Sullivan smiles, crinkling the corners of his blue eyes. "It's great when everyone can play nice together."

I nod and proceed. "Moncks Corner Police Department got a 911 call. A neighbor reported hearing gunshots at the residence of Tony and Charlotte Clark. When officers entered the home, they located the two deceased adults. The perp used a standard 9mm. Close range. No signs of forced entry. Analysis of the scene suggested someone exited through the back door into the woods behind the Clark's home, so officers searched the area."

A cough escapes my lips, my throat parched. Agent Sullivan hands me a bottle of water, and I thankfully take a drink and continue. "The neighbors mentioned the couple had three daughters, one who was away at college in New York, and two high school-aged daughters who lived with them. The Clark girls weren't at the house, so we put a flag on their cell numbers. An hour after we discovered Tony and Charlotte Clark, Charleston PD received a 911 call from the Old City Jail. It was Genevieve Clark's cell phone, the eighteen-year-old daughter. Her boyfriend, Steve Adler, made the call."

Sullivan holds a finger up to halt my story. "How does the jail connect to what happened at the Clark residence?"

"After sending units to the Old City Jail, we discovered three suspects at the scene. Mark Lykaios, an eighteen-year-old from New York, opened fire on officers and was killed by return fire. The suspect who shot Tony and Charlotte Clark was also killed after firing on officers inside the building." Stopping to take another drink of water, I continue, "We took the remaining suspect, Clyde

Fletcher, into custody. Unfortunately, they took several hostages and there were two more homicides inside the jail. Fletcher is still in custody awaiting trial on charges for those homicides."

Agent Delgado stops me with the raise of her hand. "So just to clarify we now have a body count of six people. Where exactly does Sebastian fit into these murders?"

Okay point taken, not so many details. When Agent Sullivan asked me to walk him through everything, he didn't actually mean everything.

I clear my throat and take a calming breath. "Fletcher claimed that orders were coming from Mark's uncle, the previously unknown Sebastian Lykaios, and that they were only given information as needed. Steve Adler and Mark Lykaios were roommates at Charleston Academy. Mr. Adler told us that Mark had mentioned living in New York with his uncle. We contacted NYPD to assist with a residence search, but no property was found under Sebastian's name. They did find a house owned by Mark's mother Irina Lykaios. By the time NYPD arrived at the residence, he had fled, but they did find documents linking him to weapon and drug deals both in New York and South Carolina. After going through the information of the connected deals in Charleston I noticed rumors of a Sebastian in the written reports and a masked man in multiple pictures."

I stop and pull a picture of Mark and one of the pictures of the masked man out of the folder I brought with me. Both Agent Sullivan and Agent Delgado lean forward to look at them.

"When I was looking through the photos, I realized there was a resemblance between the masked man and Mark Lykaios. I had the Forensic Services Division run both pictures through several algorithms. It was confirmed that Mark and the man wearing the mask are related. I think this is Sebastian Lykaios," I say pointing to the picture of the masked man.

Agent Delgado raises one of her perfectly shaped eyebrows. "You think this is Sebastian? Do you have any proof? You know as well as I do that facial recognition software will hold no weight in court."

My cheeks grow hot. "Yes, I'm aware, but this is all the information on identifying Sebastian I've been able to uncover so far."

"It's not a lot," Agent Delgado scoffs. "We can't even see his face. We have nothing to go on."

Narrowing my gaze at Agent Delgado I try to wrangle my irritation. I have been trying to connect dots that aren't there for months. Good luck to her if she thinks she can do better.

"Thank you, Detective. Will you go over the blackmail evidence you found?" Agent Sullivan interrupts.

"Yes. We found several text messages and letters threatening Tony Clark and his family if he didn't give Sebastian blueprints to a weapon. They were threatening to expose something that happened during Desert Storm, something that Tony must have been privy to. There were pictures of the family taken at various places and an old photo of Tony with some men he served with in Desert Storm." I pull copies of each picture out of my folder and place them on the table.

"Do we know who all of the men are in the military photo?" Agent Sullivan asks the intimidating NCIS Officer.

"Yes, all the men in the photo are now deceased except for Miguel Baros and the possibility of Andrei Lykaios, who was labeled MIA in the Gulf War and presumed dead."

My head snaps up at the mention of another Lykaios. I search the Desert Storm photo for anyone who might be related to Mark and my eyes find him. Andrei Lykaios. He has Mark's eyes, with the same cold anger that both Mark and the presumed Sebastian share. *Are they all related? How did I not catch this before?*

Agent Sullivan looks back to me. "Anything else we need to know about the blackmail?"

"Genevieve Clark later found the blueprints for the weapon hidden in their tree house and contacted me. I let NCIS know, and they retrieved the documents."

Agent Sullivan turns his attention back to the NCIS officer, who has a sour expression on his face. "Do you have a copy of the blueprints?"

"The blueprints are classified. We are confident we recovered all confidential materials and don't think we need to pursue the case further. If and when Sebastian Lykaios is found we will press charges for blackmailing an officer, but we don't think Sebastian actually got any classified information from Warrant Officer Clark. It is apparent that Sebastian knew some past confidential information and he was blackmailing Warrant Officer Clark with it."

"What was the information he was using for blackmail?" Agent Sullivan asks.

"That is classified information that I am not at liberty to disclose," The NCIS officer says with a completely emotionless face.

Agent Sullivan exhales slowly. "Well do you know how Sebastian got a hold of this classified information? Is he ex-military?"

"We have no record of a Sebastian Lykaios serving during the Gulf War."

"And would someone need to be serving during the Gulf War to have access to this information?"

"Again, that's classified."

"Well, this isn't going anywhere," Agent Delgado snaps.

Agent Sullivan nods and I realize that the NCIS officer didn't even bother to introduce himself. "If that is all, I will take my leave."

Agent Sullivan motions for him to leave with a wide sweep of his arm. "Well, apparently I spoke too soon about us all playing nicely together."

I chuckle. I like this guy. If someone new is taking over the Lykaios case, I think I am glad it is him.

"Even though Sebastian didn't get his hands on the weapon from the Navy, we know he was trying to," Agent Sullivan says. "Based on the connections you made to Sebastian's dealings between New York and South Carolina, we're happy to step in. We might have a domestic terrorist situation on our hands or we might have something totally different going on. We need to figure out what his plan is, and we needed it figured out yesterday—which is difficult since we currently have no idea how or where to find him."

My gut twists. *What is Sebastian's end goal? Is his plan already in motion and he is just staying out of the way to watch it unfurl? Are the Clark girls safe?*

Is Violet safe?

"Agent Sullivan, with the possibility of Sebastian being in New York City, which happens to be where all three Clark girls are currently living, I think it might be a good idea to keep an eye on the girls. I'm not completely convinced that they're safe."

"What would the Clark girls have that Sebastian would want?" he asks.

"I don't know. I just have a feeling."

Agent Delgado scoffs. "Do you have any evidence? It's like we're getting a case handled by a bunch of kindergartners."

A rush of shame fills me, heating my cheeks once again. Agent Sullivan silences her with a pointed look. "I agree with McAllister. It's a little too convenient that Sebastian could be in the same city as the Clark girls. We need to keep track of all the puzzle pieces, at least until we know which puzzle we're putting together."

She rolls her eyes and starts packing up her things.

Realizing the meeting is ending and I might lose complete access to the case I blurt out, "If you have any other questions feel free to give me a call, I would love to help out if I can."

"Not likely," Delgado says as she walks past me and out the door.

Standing up to shake my hand, Agent Sullivan gives me a small smile. "Her bark is worse than her bite. Thank you again Detective for all your insights. I'll be in touch."

A small sliver of hope that I might be able to keep my promise to Violet creeps in. I really hope Agent Sullivan does call. Just like Detective Armstrong warned, I am not quite ready to give the case up completely.

I was relieved when Violet found Konnie unharmed last night. I had a powerful reaction to Violet's fear, and that worries me; her terror had my stomach in knots, my heart racing. Maybe Armstrong is right and I am letting this case get too close, but I don't think it is the case that I am getting attached to—I think it is Violet. Yes, I want the case solved and to give all three girls closure, but during our conversation last night, when I made a complete fool out of myself, I realized I genuinely meant every single word I said to Violet.

I am drawn to her.

And I can tell myself as many times as I want that it is because of the Lykaios case, not her.

But I would be lying.

I have an intense need to protect her, make sure she isn't only safe, but happy too, and I don't really know how to process that.

Despite my worries, I pull out my phone and send a text to Violet.

There is still something off about all of this and I have a horrible feeling something is coming.

And it is coming soon.

Chapter 11

Violet

Ever since my phone conversation with Detective McAllister after Konnie ditched school, we've been texting every day. Our texts have started to blur between personal and professional, usually just checking in, but he did give me an update on the case after his meeting with the FBI. From what Detective McAllister heard at the meeting, I'm relieved that it sounds like the FBI will be watching for Sebastian closely in New York, making sure my sisters and I are safe. Knowing that the FBI will be watching us is reassuring, yet a little unnerving at the same time. Detective McAllister told me that they just want to make sure we're no longer a target, because Sebastian could likely be in the same city as us. He didn't say anything directly, but I get the feeling that he is worried Sebastian isn't gone, and he's still a threat we need to be worried about. I really hope that's just my own anxieties coming through as I decipher his texts.

I reread the text from Detective McAllister for the millionth time as I walk out of the subway station and continue toward our apartment.

> How are you holding up?

> I'm here if you need anything.

I'm not sure what exactly has changed in our relationship, but I can't deny that I look forward to his texts. They remind me I'm not alone. I've stopped viewing Detective McAllister as an authority figure and now consider him a friend. I'm not sure he feels the same way, but if I sent out Christmas cards every year, he would definitely make the list now.

Maybe I should start sending out Christmas cards now that Mom isn't here to do it.

The crisp fall air feels refreshing. Hot and sweaty from rehearsal, the shower in my apartment calls to me. I can't get there fast enough. Bright orange and red leaves crunch beneath my feet as I walk up the path to the front doors of our apartment building. More brittle leaves drift down to the ground from the large maple trees on each side of the path. Our apartment building is older and in need of some updates, but it's nice and well kept. The patches of grass and the ancient maple trees out front are the main things that drew me to this building in the first place. A little slice of nature surrounded by the big city.

Taking in a deep breath, I'm reminded that I'm not surrounded by nature. The aromas of various foods assault me, mixed with exhaust and a slight hint of chimney smoke.

My thoughts drift back to Detective McAllister. Even though he's in Charleston, hours away, his consistency and concern for my sisters and me makes me feel safer.

Is that totally insane? I'm not sure what he could do all the way from Charleston. My cheeks flush as I remember him asking me if I called the police when I couldn't find Konnie and I told him yes, I had called him. *What exactly did I expect him to do?*

Reaching to slide my key into the door, it moves out of my reach when I bump the knob, the creak echoing down the hall.

Why is the door cracked open? I was the first to leave the apartment this morning. *Did one of my sisters forget to close the door completely on their way out?* I should be the first person home today. Steve and Genevieve are supposed to be meeting friends after school and Konnie is staying late to work on a school project. Pushing the door slowly open with my sore, tennis shoe clad foot, I wince at how loud the creaking hinges are in the silence.

Anxiety fills me, my nerves screaming that something isn't right.

"Genevieve? Steve?" I call out, peeking around the door.

No answer.

My heartbeat picks up its pace. With slow silent steps, I move into the apartment and stop short. The dining room table and chairs are tipped over and scattered, the couch pulled from its spot against the wall, its cushions on the floor several feet away.

The picture of our parents on one of the end tables is lying face down, small glass shards littering the surface next to it. All the board games have been knocked off their shelves and even our mail is strewn across the living room.

Peeking into the kitchen, even our cabinets have been relieved of their contents. Cereal is scattered and the milk I bought just yesterday is spilled all over the floor, the creamy liquid slowly creeping across the linoleum.

This is definitely not the work of my sisters; even with how angry Konnie is at the world, she would never do this amount of damage to our apartment.

I immediately call Detective McAllister.

By the time he answers, I'm almost too panicked to get any words out. "Someone broke into our apartment and completely trashed the place."

My breath seems to catch in my throat, not fully making it into my lungs. Hyperventilating, I try to pull in quick gasps of air.

"What do you mean someone trashed your apartment?" his calm voice responds with a concerned edge.

"I just got home from school and the door was cracked open. I thought one of my sisters might have come home early or something, but when I came inside, I saw that everything has been turned over and dumped out. The whole apartment looks like a tornado went through it."

"Violet, listen to me. Don't touch anything. Get out of there."

"I really don't think whoever did this is still here."

"Does it look like they took anything? I still think you should get out of the apartment and call 911."

"Okay, I'll go down to the lobby and call. Nothing seems to be missing. Our TV is still here, granted it's tipped over, but still here. And Steve's Xbox is unplugged and on the floor."

Walking around the wall that divides the kitchen and living room, I gasp. There's something sitting perfectly on the counter amid the chaos. Something that I couldn't see when I glimpsed into the kitchen from the other end of the wall near the front door.

My gut tells me I don't want to see what it is, but I can't help myself and slowly creep closer.

The color drains from my face and goose bumps prickle my skin.

The book Mark gave Genevieve for Christmas is sitting right in the middle of the counter. It has a small hole through the middle of it.

Is that a bullet hole?

A wet, thick, scarlet substance covers the book, dripping off the edges onto the counter. It leaves behind streaks of red across the white pages as each drop plops onto the counter in a steady rhythm.

Fear grabs a hold of me, stopping my heart for a moment in its vice grip. My lungs freeze. The goose bumps move from my arms all the way up the back of my neck and my hands begin to shake.

Whatever was going on between Dad and Sebastian is definitely not over.

We are not safe.

The breath that was caught in my lungs finally releases as a scream rips up my throat and out of my lips.

Chapter 12

Matiu

Violet's chilling scream shocks me, shooting me to my feet, my desk chair rolling back from the force. Dread fills me. The same sense of helplessness I had the day Nikau went missing comes flooding back. Hands clammy with fear, I try to take a deep calming breath to steady my nerves.

This isn't the same scenario as Nikau. Violet isn't missing. I can still hear her panicked breaths on the other end of the line.

"Violet, what's wrong?"

No answer. Her screaming has stopped.

Konnie or Genevieve could be severely injured. The boyfriend, Steve, could be knocked out, unable to protect them. The intruder could still be there *with* Violet, hurting her or ... worse.

"VIOLET!" The desperation in my voice surprises me and has several of my fellow detectives looking up from their desks. Armstrong stands up and rushes to my desk, giving me a questioning look. "Violet, talk to me. Are you still there?"

"Yes." Her voice is so soft it is almost inaudible.

Even though she is obviously terrified, the fact she is still conscious has my heartbeat slowing down slightly. I wipe my clammy hands on my pants one at a time, switching the phone from one ear to the other.

"Are you okay? What's going on?"

"I think you're right. Sebastian isn't gone."

My heart stutters to a stop and I inhale sharply. "What? Why?" I have never been so impatient for someone to spit out information.

Violet finally tells me what she is seeing. Relief floods me as I realize no one is hurt, but my insides twist. It is too much of a coincidence—the bloody book Mark gave Genevieve with a bullet hole through the middle. Mark was shot right in front of Genevieve and now the book he gave her has a hole through it and is covered in blood.

This is clearly a message. But what is Sebastian trying to say?

Is Sebastian after the girls now? What happened to his bigger plan that he needed such a large weapon for?

I cover the mic on my phone with a hand and look at Armstrong. "Get Agent Sullivan on the phone, we have a lead on Sebastian."

"Call NYPD and have them send units to this address." I say pointing at an officer as I pull up Violet's address and scribble it on a piece of paper, handing it to him.

"First the flowers and now this." Violet's worried voice snaps me back to the phone call.

"Wait, what flowers?"

"A few days ago, Genevieve got a really pretty delivery of flowers with a note in them that said, 'I see you.' At first, she thought they were from Steve, but when we realized they weren't, it kinda freaked us out."

"Did you call the police? You didn't say anything to me about them."

"I figured if I called the police and told them that someone sent my sister flowers, they wouldn't be too concerned."

Why do I feel like Violet just delivered a punch to my gut? Turning away from Armstrong and the other detectives in the room, I lower my voice to respond.

"Okay, valid point, how come you didn't tell me?" The slight whine in my tone, the hurt leaking into my words, is embarrassing.

Color floods my cheeks and I try to cover up my reaction by standing up and walking into one of the empty conference rooms, but Armstrong follows me in.

"I wasn't sure it was something to be worried about," Violet says with hesitation.

Trying to rein my emotions in and sound more professional, I switch to work mode and try putting the puzzle pieces together. "Where are these flowers now?"

"I threw them away right after we figured out they weren't from Steve."

"Did you at least keep the card?" I ask, trying to keep the frustration out of my voice.

"Um, no, I threw it away, too." Violet's quiet response tells me I didn't do a very good job.

"Who delivered the flowers? What company?"

"I don't know. One of our neighbors brought them to our house. They got delivered to his house by accident."

I doubt it was by accident. It was probably to make it harder to trace back to whoever sent them. Grabbing a pen and paper from the conference room table, I pause to write. "What's the neighbor's name that brought them to you?"

"I don't know. I've run into him a few times. He's older. He seems really nice, but I don't know him very well. I don't even know which apartment he lives in."

Okay. What am I missing? I jump when Detective Armstrong nudges me.

"Everything okay, kid?" he asks.

Nodding, I hold up a finger, letting him know I will have to fill him in when I am off the phone.

"Does this have to do with the Lykaios case?" Armstrong asks, insisting on answers even though I am still on the phone.

I nod and watch as Armstrong's eyes go cold and narrow at me. "McAllister, you have no business with that case, leave it to the feds, it is out of our hands now," he orders.

I ignore him when Violet starts talking again. "I'm worried that this is Sebastian," she says in that same quiet defeated voice.

My gut says that it is Sebastian, too. We were stupid to think the girls were safe in the same city we know Sebastian lives in. Why didn't we push harder to look in New York? It is clear Sebastian has intensified his sick game, he wouldn't get sloppy and get caught just for revenge, would he? Leaving ominous gifts related to his nephew's death is a sure way to slip up, eventually. On one hand, this might be a good thing. If he continues, it gives us more clues, more opportunities to track him down. It also doesn't bode well for the Clark girls, but Violet is already freaked out and I don't want to panic her any more without concrete evidence.

"I have officers headed your way. I need you to hang up and go down to the lobby and wait for them, I am going to touch base with Agent Sullivan. Don't touch anything and you should probably tell your sisters to steer clear of the apartment for a bit. I'll do what I can from here." I lower my voice. "And please be careful, Violet."

I disconnect the call and turn toward Armstrong. "Did you get a hold of Sullivan?"

"No. I didn't even try," he responds, anger lacing his voice.

"What? Why not? We need to let him know we have a lead on Sebastian."

Why didn't Armstrong call Sullivan when I asked? Irritation and anger mix with my confusion, but Armstrong is my superior and I try to calm myself down. He probably just wanted some clarification before he called.

"Was that the Clark girl?" he asks.

"Yes, someone broke into their apartment."

"Why are you still in communication with her? Didn't you tell her we turned their case over to the feds?"

"Yeah, I guess she just feels comfortable with me because we were her original detectives." I try to squeeze past him out of the conference room. I need to get back to my desk and call Agent Sullivan since Armstrong didn't.

His eyes narrow and he blocks the door with his arm, jerking me to a stop. "Matiu. Step back from this case, stop answering her calls. Give her the contact information for the agents taking over and focus on the cases that you're actually supposed to be solving."

I am not sure how I am going to get out of explaining this to him. How much information do I want to divulge to him? Do I really want to let him know Violet is constantly on my mind? Especially since he told me not to let this case get too personal. He has made it clear that he doesn't want me working on the Lykaios case now that it is in the FBI's hands. I am not sure how he would react if he knew I started communicating with Violet more regularly.

I don't want to find out.

"I'm not going to ignore her, Armstrong. She's scared."

"It sounded like you were pretty scared yourself there for a minute," he says.

I was. I was terrified. I know this isn't my case anymore and what Detective Armstrong is telling me is valid, but I can't just drop it.

Ducking under his arm, I get to my desk and look for the card with Agent Sullivan's number on it. I should really just add his info into my phone. I pick up the phone on my desk and start to dial, but Armstrong disconnects the call.

I glare up at him. "What are you doing?"

"I told you to drop it McAllister," he says, raising his voice and drawing the eyes of the other detectives and officers in the room who stop and watch our growing exchange.

"I heard you the first time," I snap back, my own voice growing in volume. Pushing Armstrong's hand off the phone on my desk I start to dial Agent Sullivan again.

"This conversation isn't over McAllister," Armstrong says, venom dripping from his words as he sits down forcefully in his desk across from me. His dark eyes narrow and his silent disapproval emanates off him as Sullivan answers and I fill him in on what Violet told me.

Logically I know I should listen to Armstrong, he is my superior, but for the first time since I started working with him, I feel like he is going in the wrong direction. I should follow his orders and stop following leads on the Lykaios case, leave it to Agent Sullivan and Agent Delgado. I also know that I should leave Violet alone, stop texting her every day and answering every time she calls.

But I can't stop.

I *won't* stop.

And I realize with a bit of uneasiness that I will always answer when Violet calls. Even after the case is solved and put to rest.

Not because I feel like I have to, but because I want to. I *need* to.

Violet isn't just a person from one of my cases anymore.

She has somehow become more.

Chapter 13

Violet

My fingers tremble as I push the elevator button. Konnie's phone goes straight to voicemail, so I send her a text to wait at the school until either Genevieve or I come to pick her up. The elevator doors open and I escape into the lobby.

Rushing to the front of the building I stare out the windows at the front courtyard, the last of the colorful fall leaves clinging to the trees. One leaf makes a slow descending journey from its branch to the ground. It looks so peaceful. Yet peace has been evading me for months and I know that just past the courtyard is a busy, bustling city. The tranquil setting in front of our building gives a false sense of peace to those who walk through it.

"Is everything okay?"

I startle at the concerned voice coming from right behind me. My phone flies out of my hand and I whirl around to see the neighbor who delivered the flowers. "Oh, you startled me," I say, clenching my hands to my chest.

His grin wrinkles the skin around his dark eyes, but once again, the smile doesn't quite reach them. "Are you okay? You look like you've seen a ghost," he asks as he bends down to retrieve my phone and hands it back to me.

I try not to stare at the mottled skin, scarred from what looks like a severe burn peeking out from above his turtleneck. "Someone broke into our apartment. I'm waiting for the police now."

"Oh no, I'm so sorry. Is there anything I can do to help?" he asks.

"I don't think so. Thank you for offering, though."

My conversation with Detective McAllister and my paranoia of anyone I don't know comes rushing back. I still don't even know this man's name or which apartment he lives in. He seems like a kind older man, but I don't feel like I can trust anyone new right now.

"I'm sorry. I'm just realizing I never asked for your name. I'm Violet," I say reaching out to shake his hand.

"It's nice to meet you, Violet," he says taking my hand into his gloved one. I can hear the distant sound of sirens approaching. "It sounds like the calvary is approaching; I hope they can figure this mess out for you and your sisters." He lets go of my hand and heads toward the elevators.

As the elevator doors close and hide him from view, I realize he never told me his name and I never told him I had sisters. He could've seen us together, he probably even saw Genevieve when he dropped off the flowers, but an uneasiness settles in my stomach. Shaking my head, trying to clear it, I turn my attention back to my phone and call Genevieve.

She answers on the second ring. "Hey Vi, what's up?"

Willing my voice to sound calm and normal, I try to act like nothing's wrong. I really don't want my sisters to see the apartment like this, and I don't want to ruin Genevieve and Steve's afternoon with their friends. "I was just hoping you and Steve could swing by and pick up Konnie on your way home. She's working on a project at school."

"Sure, but you sound stressed. You good?"

"Oh yeah, everything's fine." Even I can hear the tension in my voice.

Genevieve sounds skeptical. "Where are you? Are you rehearsing again?"

Ugh. Why does Genevieve have to be so observant all the time? "Nope, I'm home already."

A police car pulls up and parks on the street, their red and blue lights flashing. Two officers exit the vehicle and walk toward the building. I need to end this phone call now or she'll for sure know something is wrong. "I'll see you later tonight, Genevieve. Gotta go."

"Wait, Vi. Why are you acting so weird? Did I hear sirens?"

"We live in New York City, Genevieve, hearing sirens is kinda part of the package deal."

One of the police officers walks up to me. "Are you Miss Clark?" I nod. "We got a call about a break in? I'm Officer Martin and this is Officer Rodriguez." He nods toward his partner.

"Who is that, Violet? Did he just say something about a break in?" Gene-vieve's nervous voice says through the phone.

"Gen, everything's fine. I need you to stay where you are and pick Konnie up from the school, please."

I disconnect the call and glance at the two officers.

"Can you show us to your apartment?" Officer Martin asks.

"Of course," I say and lead them to the elevator.

Once inside the elevator he asks, "Was anyone home during the time of the break in?"

"No, we were all at school."

He nods. "Who was the last person to leave and when? And were all the doors and windows locked?"

"I'm not sure. I left before everyone this morning. We usually make sure to keep everything locked up."

The elevator makes it to our floor and they follow me out of the elevator and down the hall. I stop when we reach our apartment door.

"Ma'am, please wait here," he instructs me as both officers pull their guns from their holsters and approach the door.

Officer Rodriguez knocks, before opening the door and announcing, "NYPD! Is anyone inside?"

They disappear through the door and time seems to move in slow motion as I wait for them to come back out into the hallway. By the time they tell me it is safe to come in, my body is thrumming with nervous energy.

"Did you notice anything missing?" Officer Martin asks when he comes back out into the hallway.

"Not that I've noticed yet," I say as I follow him into the apartment and take in all the destruction again. Clothes from our rooms are tossed into the hallway, the lamp on one of the end tables is tipped over and the bulb's pieces litter the carpet below. Both officers are pulling gloves onto their hands and one of them says something into their radio that I can't quite make out.

"How long was the apartment empty today?" Officer Martin asks.

"All day. We left for school this morning; my sisters usually leave the house around eight. I was the first one home."

"We've been made aware that there is an active case involving you and your sisters. The FBI agents in charge have asked us not to move anything until they can process the scene." I nod, but don't fully comprehend what he's saying to me. I watch as both officers inspect the bloody book on the counter.

I reach to close one of the cabinet doors and Officer Martin stops me with a gentle hand on my arm. "I'm sorry, Miss Clark, we really need you to not touch anything for now."

Hurried footsteps and a gasp from the front door tell me that Genevieve ignored my request to stay away and rushed home with Steve, anyway.

Genevieve's shocked face takes in the mess as she reaches for me and wraps me in a warm hug. "What happened?"

"I don't know," I whisper. Now wrapped in Genevieve's arms, I'm realizing just how much my sisters are keeping me from falling apart after everything we've been through. Why can't we just catch a break for a little bit?

I can feel when Genevieve sees the book Mark gave her. Her breath catches and her body trembles as she lets go of me and walks toward the kitchen counter where the officers are still standing.

Her face crumples. I can't tell if it is with fear or grief or maybe a little bit of both. A small sob escapes her lips and Steve is immediately at her side, taking in the scene as well. The only indication of his feelings are his clenched fists by his sides, but when he notices the pain on Genevieve's face, he unclenches his fists and pulls her into a hug.

Genevieve has struggled with coming to terms with Mark's betrayal and death. He was her only friend for months and through all our conversations, since our parents and Mark were killed, I know deep down Genevieve has held out hope that maybe all of it wasn't a lie.

Steve has his arms around Genevieve, but I walk up and wrap mine around her, too. "Are you okay, sis?" I ask.

Tears are flowing freely down her cheeks. She glances at Steve before answering. "That was the only thing I had left that Mark gave me."

Steve tenses up and anger flashes in his eyes, but he still doesn't let go of Genevieve. This has got to be super weird for him too. His roommate, who let Genevieve think Steve abandoned her, is still causing problems from the grave.

"Are you upset that the book is ruined or are you upset that it's bringing back up all the feelings from Mark's death?" I ask.

"Both. Neither. I don't know." Genevieve sends a cautious glance toward Steve again. "All of this is so confusing."

I reach for Genevieve's hand and give it a squeeze. Her eyes, brimming with tears, meet mine. "When Steve was gone, Mark was my person. He was there when Livi was mad at me; he brought pizza and movies over to watch with Konnie and me when I needed cheering up. He listened to me months before Christmas when I said I wanted to read that book and then gave it to me as a gift," she says quietly.

I didn't know Mark well, and I honestly don't understand how Genevieve can harbor any good feelings for him after his role in our parents' deaths. I try to put myself in her shoes and think of how I would feel if one of my best friends was a part of something so terrible. Betrayed. Angry. But knowing my sister and her kind heart I can imagine how hard it is for her to fully believe that everything that Mark did and said was a lie, especially because she did feel so close to him.

Steve removes his arm from Genevieve's shoulder and glances back at the book. Genevieve takes a shaky breath. "I guess I was just hoping that not all of it was a performance." She swipes at the tears that have escaped her eyes and have started rolling down her freckled cheeks. "I wanted a small piece of my friend who is gone, even though sometimes I feel like a bad person for even mourning his loss at all. Especially when it's because of me and my friendship with Mark that my parents are gone."

Apparently, that was too much for Steve. He steps back, his eyes full of anger. "Genevieve, you can't blame yourself for any of this. Mark made his own decisions, and I understand why you hope that there was some genuine friendship in all that you went through, but Mark was playing a game. He wasn't your friend. He wasn't my friend. He and his deranged uncle got your parents and several other people killed."

He pauses and runs his hand through his hair angrily. "I didn't realize that Mark gave you the book that has been sitting on your nightstand all this time. What were you doing? Torturing yourself by looking at it every day. No wonder you have nightmares sleeping in your own bed."

Genevieve's tears are coming faster now, and her eyes fill with... remorse? Guilt? I'm not sure, but she's in a battle with her emotions now, and it doesn't look like she's winning. Her eyes dart from Steve to the book and back to Steve again. "I wasn't torturing myself. I'm just trying to move on and process everything, just like everyone else."

"By keeping a gift Mark gave you? Did you have feelings for him?" Steve's voice is quiet but hard. The muscles in his jaw clench.

"He was my only friend, Steve."

"No, he wasn't," Steve almost shouts. "I tried over and over to get a hold of you, and Mark knew where I was. He never told you Genevieve. He wanted you to feel alone. He wanted you to feel like he was your only friend. *He* put you in that situation."

"You just don't understand," Genevieve says quietly.

"You're right. I don't understand. What makes you think that Mark had any genuine feelings for any of us?"

"He pushed me down," she says quietly.

"What?" Steve asks as his hurt eyes search Genevieve's face.

"Before he started shooting at the police officers that night, he pushed me down onto the ground. Why would he do that if he didn't want to save me?" Genevieve looks up at both of us, her cheeks stained with tears.

"If he truly cared for you, why would he put you in that situation to begin with?" Steve asks angrily.

"He was scared of his uncle; I could tell by the way he talked about him. He didn't even want to live with him, he was forced to. I think his fear of Sebastian was stronger than any other feelings he had."

"Ghosts may be the least scary thing in this world," Steve says quietly.

"What's that supposed to mean?" I ask.

"It's just something Mark said to me once." Steve looks lost, his eyes focusing on something no one else can see. "Regardless of his fear or his feelings, Mark did horrible things. Forgive him if you need to in order to let yourself move on. We honestly probably all need to so that we can find peace again. But I can't. Not yet. And if you need to grieve him then do it, Genevieve. But you *need* to move on. *I* need you to move on. Stop lingering in the nightmare of his shadow."

He waits a moment, but when it's apparent Genevieve isn't going to say anything, Steve grabs his keys and storms out of the apartment.

More tears stream down Genevieve's face as she starts to quietly sob. I can see both sides, but I kind of have to agree with Steve on this one. Genevieve holding onto hope that Mark's friendship was genuine seems like a lost cause. Especially since the only person who can answer that question is dead. I need to make sure Genevieve is getting that grief and trauma therapy she said she was going to sign up for at school, but now isn't the time to bring it up.

Officer Martin comes over with a tall, blonde man in a suit and a petite woman with long dark hair. "This is Agent Sullivan and Agent Delgado, with the FBI."

"Hello Violet, Detective McAllister told me you called him after the break in. I understand Detective McAllister is who you're used to communicating with, but from now on I need you to make sure you let me know about anything else that happens," Agent Sullivan says as he hands me a business card with his number on it.

I nod, but don't say anything. My stomach feels uneasy. I've gotten so used to calling and texting Detective McAllister, I don't want to stop.

No, that's not right. It's not that I call him because I'm used to it. I call him because I want to talk to *him*.

He calms me.

No matter what I'm feeling, his soothing voice and calm demeanor seems to make everything else in my life seem less stressful, less damaged. Just seeing his name on my phone when a text or a call comes in brings a smile to my face.

Is there some sort of syndrome for someone who clings to authority figures who help them? Maybe I need to go to therapy too. I mean, we probably all should have started therapy immediately after our parents died. We all know Konnie isn't handling it well, and maybe Genevieve has a Stockholm connection with Mark. That actually makes a lot more sense when I think of it that way.

Yet another thing I'm failing at, I should've gotten us all into therapy as soon as we got to New York.

Noticing Genevieve's pale face and once again realizing that it is now on my shoulders to take care of my sisters, I try to shake off my uneasy feeling.

"Detective McAllister told me that you got a strange flower delivery. Can you tell me about that? What do you know about the neighbor that delivered them?

I take a deep breath and swallow, trying to focus. "Yeah, it was a couple of weeks ago. I'm sorry we threw them away. I realize now we should have told someone. I actually saw the neighbor in the lobby while I was waiting for the police. I asked his name, but he still didn't tell me. I'm sorry I don't know his name or which apartment he lives in."

"That's okay. Can you describe him for me? I'll have officers ask around your apartment building. It would be good to find out if anyone saw anything this afternoon as well."

I give the agents a brief description before Agent Delgado starts taking a look around the apartment.

"We're going to be collecting evidence for a while. It might be best if you all go get some dinner." He looks from me to Genevieve and then back, compassion filling his eyes. "Officer Martin, do you mind escorting the girls to dinner? We also need to make sure their sister is accounted for."

"Of course," Officer Martin responds.

"I'll call you when we're done, Miss Clark. And if you think of anything else, don't hesitate to call. Go to dinner with your sisters, Officer Martin will make sure you all stay safe."

Wrapping my arm around Genevieve, I lead her toward the door. Looking back over my shoulder I see Agent Sullivan walk into the kitchen where Agent Delgado is putting the bloody book into an evidence bag. A shiver runs through me as Genevieve, Officer Martin, and I walk out into the hallway. Her tears have stopped, but she seems out of it.

The three of us file into the elevator. I don't think I've ever seen Steve and Genevieve get into a fight; I don't know where to start.

"You doing okay, Gen?" I ask.

She nods. "I don't know why Steve got so mad."

I half laugh, half snort. "Are you serious? Would you be upset if you thought Steve had feelings for someone who purposefully kept you guys apart for months, held you at gunpoint, and had a hand in killing his parents?"

"I didn't have romantic feelings for Mark, but I felt like he was one of my best friends. How am I not supposed to have any feelings?"

"I don't know Genevieve, but regardless of how you felt for Mark and how confusing all of this has been for all of us, Steve watched Mark try to steal you from him and then hurt you in unimaginable ways. I don't blame him for being upset that you kept Mark's gift or because you're still struggling over the loss of his friendship. I agree with Steve. Mark was never a genuine friend."

"You weren't there, Violet. How would you know?"

Her words feel like a slap to my face. I know I wasn't there. It haunts me every single day, but I don't want to fight about it and I don't want Steve and Genevieve to be upset with each other, either. Their relationship is something I hope to have in the future. To have someone look at me the way Steve looks at Genevieve.

"Just try to see it from where Steve is coming from, too," I say quietly as we exit the elevator into the lobby.

I send Steve a text asking if he can pick up Konnie and meet us some place for dinner. In true Steve fashion, he lets me know he would be happy to.

When we finally decide on pizza, we plan to meet Steve and Konnie at Joe's Pizza on Broadway. Genevieve, Officer Martin, and I beat Steve and Konnie to the restaurant, and we get in line to order. Officer Martin does his best to lighten the mood and get our minds off everything by asking us questions about school and what we like best about the city. It doesn't really work, but I appreciate the effort.

Steve and Konnie join us in line when they get here, and I'm relieved when Steve and Genevieve both apologize and wrap their arms around each other. Steve rubs small circles on Genevieve's back while we wait in line and another uncomfortable twinge of jealousy washes through me.

I want what they have.

I want someone who is always there for me, even when I'm at my worst. I'm trying to support my sisters and keep up with school, but who is going to be there to help me pick up my own pieces? Assuming there are any pieces left to pick up when we make it through this never-ending nightmare. Is Detective McAllister's offer of him being who I can turn to genuine? And why is it that the only person I feel like I can count on to help hold me together lives in a different state?

When we get the go ahead to come home from Agent Sullivan, he meets us at the door. "There will be a unit outside all night. If you see anything suspicious, even if you think it might not be something worth mentioning, let us know."

After thanking both Agent Sullivan and Officer Martin, we walk in and close the door behind us. A long night lies ahead. Fixing the destruction that was left behind is not going to be an easy task.

Konnie begins angrily shoving things that are broken beyond repair into a garbage bag and Steve and Genevieve start righting the furniture in the living room. Walking toward the broken picture of our parents still lying face down on one of the end tables, I pick it up. More glass shards join the other pieces of glittering glass littering the tabletop and I stare into my parents' smiling faces.

We haven't even been able to pick up all the broken parts of our lives after our parents were murdered, and now we have to pick up the literal pieces of our apartment. How far can we bend before we're irreparably broken?

Maybe we already are.

Konnie stomps through the living room with her garbage bag and disappears into the hallway. Steve and Genevieve move around each other like orbiting planets. If one goes off course, the other one will follow. Konnie has her anger. Steve and Genevieve have each other, and I just feel broken. Alone and unsure of where I'm supposed to turn next.

My parents' faces look at me from the picture frame. For a moment, rage surges through me. *Why is it my job to pick up everyone's shattered pieces?* Maybe I can let my anger control me just like Konnie, but the anger doesn't stay as I watch my parents' faces blur behind my tears. Mom and Dad wouldn't want us to be angry. They would want us to live life to the fullest. Lives filled with laughter and love, just like they always made sure our house was filled with love and happiness

My phone vibrates with a text from Detective McAllister.

How is everyone doing? Any updates?

I don't even know how to respond. I type something and then delete it multiple times. I'm pretty much the farthest away from okay I've ever been. Still not sure how to respond, I jump when my phone vibrates again, this time with an incoming call.

From Detective McAllister.

"Hello?" I answer, my uneasiness creeping into my voice.

"Sorry, I probably shouldn't have called." He sounds nervous. "I just saw the typing start and stop multiple times on the text and thought maybe it would be easier for you to talk. How are you holding up?"

The tears I had barely managed to hold back start to fall. "I've been better."

"Oh Violet, I'm so sorry you're going through this. What can I do to help?"

My breath catches. He said, 'I'm so sorry you're going through this.' Not you all. Not you guys. *You're.* As in me. I'm probably reading too much into that sentence, but for a minute I don't feel quite so alone.

My voice is wobbly with emotion. "I honestly don't know what to do. So, I don't even know what others could do to help."

"Did Agent Sullivan give you any information about what they're thinking?"

"No, he just said they'd be in touch and now we're trying to clean up the apartment. I just feel overwhelmed and for some reason I feel alone, even though I have my sisters and Steve here with me."

He sighs on the other end of the phone. "It makes sense to me, Violet, you're taking on so many new roles, roles that your sisters aren't having to take on themselves. It *is* overwhelming."

"Thanks," I sniff, my nose now running with my tears. "I feel a little bit less crazy now."

He laughs. "You're definitely not crazy, I'm actually a bit in awe of you. I've seen so many others shut down and stall in life after traumatizing events. You haven't looked back once; you just keep moving forward."

"I think it might be because if I stop, I won't be able to start back up again."

"Don't worry, you're not alone. If for some reason, you do stop for a while, you have so many people who will make sure you get back up again. Including me."

My heart picks up its pace. I've felt like Detective McAllister was becoming more like a friend than our detective. Is it possible that he's starting to feel the same way about me, too? Or am I just so desperate for connection that I'm seeing things that aren't actually there?

He clears his throat and continues, and I realize I didn't respond. I can be such an idiot sometimes. "I'm always here if you need to talk."

"Thank you," I manage to say before he says goodbye and disconnects the call.

Steve and Genevieve have moved on to re-shelving the board games and picking up the mail strewn across the living room. I can hear Konnie and her anger slamming drawers shut in the bathroom. Grabbing the dustpan and broom, I gently sweep the broken glass from the picture frame off the end table into the dustpan and carry it to the kitchen garbage.

As the tiny bits of glass tinkle across the dustpan and into the garbage, I sneak a peek at the counter. The police took the book and someone has cleaned up the blood, but there is a stain from where the pool of blood dripped off of the counter onto the floor.

I grab some cleaner and a scrub brush and frantically start scrubbing. It doesn't take long for the stain to disappear, but even with the stain gone, I can't stop scrubbing. The break in, the mess, the disturbing display left on the counter, all of it leaves me feeling violated.

Anger bubbles back up inside of me. My sisters and I had nothing to do with Sebastian's devious plan, whatever it may be. He's already ruined our lives. *Why can't he just leave us alone?*

I continue to scrub the no longer existing stain. Angry tears race down my cheeks as I scrub until my hands are as sore as my overworked feet.

And I keep scrubbing.

The blood stain on the floor may be gone, but I feel like I'm stained. We're all tainted by the horrible things that have happened in the last year. *Will we ever be able to heal?*

Sometimes the worst scars left behind are the ones that no one can see.

November

Chapter 14

Matiu

It has been two weeks since someone broke into Violet's apartment and the air is still tense between Detective Armstrong and me. Sitting in this desk right across from him every day is becoming daunting. Detective Armstrong gives me an uneasy glance as we get ready to head home from the office. I stack my papers and put my pen back in my drawer. He has been cleaning up his desk to go home for a few minutes himself, but his cluttered desk doesn't look any different to me. This tension between us is foreign. I usually take everything he says to me seriously and try to implement it, but this is not something I am willing to budge on.

"You've got to let it go, McAllister," he says as we are walking to the doors exiting our building.

"Why don't you want to know what's going on in the Lykaios case? Don't you want to see it solved?" I snap.

"Of course I want it solved, but it isn't our problem anymore and you need to step back and see that you've let your personal feelings get in the way."

Our captain stops us on the way out. "Glad I caught you, McAllister. The NCIS has given the FBI all the info they are going to share, but Agent Sullivan has requested that you come to their New York office to give more insight and consult on the case."

They want me to come to New York? Excitement and relief fill me. It will be a breath of fresh air to get away from Armstrong and his judgment for a while. I silently try to work out my emotions. My initial excitement worries me. Without thinking, I reach into my pocket and run my fingers over Nikau's dinosaur. I should be excited to go see New York City and work on the case I so desperately want to solve, but the first thing that flashes through my mind when I hear the news is that I would be able to see Violet in person.

Detective Armstrong fidgets with a pen in his hand, looking uncomfortable. "I think maybe I should go for this one, Captain. I'm the senior detective and I have more experience."

"They requested McAllister specifically. He's who will be going." He turns to look at me. "You travel tomorrow and you're expected at the FBI office first thing in the morning the day after."

"Yes, sir, I'll go home and get packed tonight. Any idea how long I'll be there?"

"They didn't say. I would plan for at least a couple of weeks."

I nod and continue walking toward the exit. Detective Armstrong catches up and stops me with a hand on my arm. "Look, I just don't want to see you get too emotionally attached to a case that you'll most likely not be a part of when it's solved. I know a thing or two about getting too emotionally attached."

I know he is talking about Nikau's case and taking me under his wing. "I already told you I don't care who solves it as long as it gets solved."

He gives me a tense smile. "Just be careful. You might end up with a kid that becomes your responsibility, like I did."

He squeezes my arm before dropping his hand. Armstrong has helped me countless times on my road to becoming a detective, and I am truly grateful for where I am right now. Even if he is being hard-headed at the moment, I know I am only here, already a detective this young, because of him.

This brings a tentative smile to my face. "Am I really that bad?"

"I wouldn't want to be working with anybody else. Just keep it professional, okay?"

"Okay," I say, but I already know it is too late.

The complete terror I felt when I wasn't sure if Violet was okay or not was *way* beyond professional. I have never wanted to be someplace else more in my entire life. The fact that I can now go to New York and be closer to Violet—no the Clark girls, not just Violet—has me wishing I could already be there.

Rushing home, I pack as quickly as I can. While I am throwing clothes and toiletries into a suitcase, I dial Mum and she answers on the second ring with her usual warm greeting.

"I just wanted to call and let you know that I have to go to New York for work, so I'm going to be gone for a bit."

"New York? Why are they sending you there?" she asks, worry lacing her voice.

"The FBI wants me to consult on a case that I was working on before they took it over."

"Both you and your sister gone at the same time? I'm not sure I'm comfortable with this."

"You'll be fine Mum. You and Dad can get some good quality time together."

"Oh rubbish, your dad works as much as you do and when he isn't working, he's making enough kai to feed an entire village. What am I going to do with that much food?"

I laugh. "I'm not moving away forever. I'll be back in no time."

"Yeah, how long will you be gone?"

"Maybe two weeks according to Captain, but I'm not sure."

She continues to fret and tells me all about the colleges Miriama has toured so far before Dad takes the phone and tells me about a new recipe he wants to try this Sunday.

"You'll have to let me know how it turns out," I say and listen as Mum tells him I am going to New York and won't be there for whānau dinner.

"Be safe on your trip son, maybe you can find yourself a girlfriend while you're there."

"Not likely," I chuckle, but warmth rushes through me as I think of seeing Violet.

I hang up with my parents and remind myself that my thoughts drift to Violet because I want to make sure that all three Clark sisters are safe and Sebastian is caught and behind bars.

Right?

Then why am I starting my drive to New York tonight? I ask myself.

I don't want to try to find a flight and have to wait to start traveling. I am antsy to get moving now, so I throw my suitcase into the trunk of my Charger and put New York City into Maps on my phone. I'll figure out where exactly in New York I am going when I get closer.

Right now, I just need to drive.

Chapter 15

Violet

The hot water and steam from the shower feel miraculous on my sore muscles. Each little bead of water is like a mini massage, washing the tension from my shoulders, back and legs, easing the pain from my strained muscles. I wish we had a giant tub for me to soak in like the jetted tub in Mom and Dad's master suite at home.

No, not home anymore, I remind myself. *Although the house still hasn't sold, apparently having a double homicide in the home makes it harder to sell. Weird,* I think sarcastically.

Turning off the shower, I step out onto the fluffy rug and wrap a towel around myself. Wiping the steam from the mirror, I reach to dry my dripping hair, stopping the towel midway when I hear something in the hallway.

I freeze. All my senses go on high alert and I listen for any other sounds. Nobody suspicious would be able to get past the officers watching the entrances to our apartment building, right?

There it is again. Footsteps echo down the hall. Someone is definitely in the apartment.

I quietly wrap the towel tighter around me as I open the door and peek out into the hallway. I don't see anyone. Genevieve and Konnie aren't supposed to be home yet, and Steve normally waits for Genevieve before coming home.

I poke my head out the door. "Genevieve? Konnie? Steve?" I call out into the apartment. No one answers, but I can still hear shuffling feet coming from the direction of Genevieve and Konnie's bedroom.

The ghost stories Konnie told us about our apartment being haunted flood my mind. Is it the cat lady wandering the halls or maybe the serial killer contin-

85

uously looking for his next victim? Despite the hot steam filling the bathroom from my shower, goose bumps prickle my arms and race up my neck.

What if it isn't a ghost at all? What if it's Sebastian, here to finish whatever demented vendetta he is trying to accomplish? I think I might be happier with a haunted apartment than the real-life monster that wants to torment us.

Grabbing a baseball bat out of the closet—from Konnie's softball days in Moncks Corner—I tiptoe as quietly as possible toward the noises. Hoping for a ghost but ready to beat the crap out of whoever is in our apartment, I jump around the corner and swing the bat hard, stopping my swing just in time when I realize it's Konnie, not an intruder.

I just about took my little sister out with a baseball bat.

Konnie screams.

I scream.

"What in the heck are you doing?" Konnie asks in an irritated voice as she pulls the headphones off her head.

"I didn't know anyone was here and I heard noises."

"And you thought it was a good idea to attack whoever it was with a baseball bat? In a towel?"

"Well, I wasn't going to stop and get dressed and wait for someone to murder me."

Konnie rolls her eyes. "Chill out, Violet. I'm going to have one of my friends over tonight. K?"

I'm getting tired of Konnie's constant eye rolling and I clam up thinking about having someone new come over to the apartment. "I don't think it's a good idea to have anyone new come over. I don't know who we can trust, especially after the break in."

Konnie's once friendly brown eyes turn lethal. "You can't keep us all locked up forever."

"I'm not planning on it, but until we know we're safe, we need to be careful."

Konnie erupts, "No one is ever truly safe! Stop trying to act like Mom. You aren't my mother, so stop trying to be."

Konnie stomps back into her room and slams the door hard enough to make the walls rattle, and a picture falls onto the floor with a loud crash. I pick up the photo; it's thankfully still intact. The smiling faces of my family before we were torn apart seem to mock me. I hang the frame back on the wall.

Trying to hold back tears, I wonder if I'm being too paranoid. *Am I holding on too tight?* A knock at the door drags my attention to the front of the apartment. Looking through the peephole, I see the neighbor who dropped off the flowers. The knots in my stomach tighten, but I open the door. Realizing too late that I'm still in my towel as the older gentleman looks at me uncomfortably, his eyes darting around, not sure where to look.

"Hi, sorry. Can I help you?" I ask with a nervous smile.

"Just dropping off some of your mail that somehow made it into my mailbox," he says, averting his eyes and handing me the pile of mail with his gloved hand.

It's weird that he's always wearing leather gloves. My grandpa used to wear driving gloves, but he always left them in the car. Maybe he just wears them until he gets home instead of leaving them in his car?

"Did you talk to the police the day our apartment got broken into?" I ask, knowing that we need more information from him.

"No, I must have missed them."

That's weird. I watched him get into the elevator right before the police walked into the building.

"Do you happen to remember which company delivered the flowers to you by mistake?"

"I don't. I'm sorry. I wasn't paying much attention to who was delivering them. I was focused on figuring out which apartment they were supposed to be delivered to."

"That's okay." I let out a disappointed sigh. "I still haven't caught your name."

We both jump and turn to look down the hall as one of our neighbors drops a package while trying to unlock their door.

"Have a great day," he says when our eyes meet again and turns swiftly down the hall.

"Thank you for the mail," I call after him, frustrated that I still don't have any answers. He seems to make a quick getaway every time I ask for his name, but I can't really blame the guy today. I did answer the door in nothing but a towel.

I try to watch which apartment he goes into, but instead of entering one of the doors in the hallway he gets in the elevator. Closing the door more forcefully than I mean to it slams shut rattling the walls.

Jeez. Not sure how Konnie could think I'm trying to act like Mom. Mom would've been mortified if she saw any of us opening the door wrapped in a towel. I pull on some yoga pants and one of Dad's old sweaters that I saved, pull my still damp hair up into a messy bun and start making myself some tea. Why can't I seem to get anything right anymore? Everything used to come so easily—dance, boys, friendships, being the fun big sister, it used to all seem to flow without any effort. Tears prick the back of my eyes.

Not wanting to start crying once again, I look through the pile of mail the neighbor brought over, shuffling through the bills when another knock comes at the door.

He must have missed some mail that he needed to drop off; at least I have clothes on now. I think before looking through the peephole again.

It isn't the neighbor; it takes my brain a minute to realize the good-looking man on the other side of the door is Detective McAllister. I haven't seen him for months, not since we had our last meeting about my parents in South Carolina. Seeing him here, standing on the other side of the door in all his tall, dark, and handsome glory takes my breath away.

The pesky tears that had been prickling the back of my eyes reach the surface and start trailing down my cheeks as I yank open the door, throw my arms around Detective McAllister, and start sobbing. When he doesn't say anything, I loosen my grip to lean back and look up at him. His dark brown eyes are even kinder than I remember and the shocked look on his face would be hilarious if I wasn't already blubbering like a basket case in our apartment hallway.

I tighten my arms back around his neck and bury my face in his muscular shoulder to hide my embarrassment. He hesitantly wraps his arms around me and warmth spreads like wildfire as my body reacts to his touch.

"Did something else happen?" he asks.

Trying to get control of myself for a minute, I step back and wipe my face. Thank goodness I just took a shower and don't have any makeup on. *Wait, I don't have any makeup on and I'm in my dad's old, ratty sweatshirt.* I can feel my face getting hot. *At least I'm not still wrapped in the towel.*

I remind myself that this is our detective—*was* our detective—I don't need to have makeup on in front of him. I don't need to be hugging him either. *But is he still just our former detective to me?*

"No, nothing else has happened." I continue to dry my face, but the tears just keep coming. "I'm just suspicious of anyone and everyone, and Konnie is mad that I don't want her to invite new friends over to the apartment."

Detective McAllister reaches out and wipes a tear softly from my cheek. My heart stops and my breath catches in my throat. The longing to have someone look at me the way Steve looks at Genevieve crashes back into me. I look up into his kind, dark eyes as he slowly continues to brush his thumb across my tear-stained cheek before dropping his hand back to his side. He looks as startled as I'm after he realizes what he just did.

My heart starts beating double time.

He clears his throat. "Um, well, has Agent Sullivan given you any safety guidelines? You all should probably be extra careful right now, but Konnie having friends over to the apartment is probably safer than wandering around New York City with friends that you haven't even met yet."

"Good point." I'm not sure why I didn't think of that.

"Have you heard anything about the break in?" he asks.

"Nothing yet. They took fingerprints and took the book with them, but I haven't heard if they found anything or not."

He nods. "I was just stopping by to let you, all of you, know that I'm going to be in town for a while, so if anything happens or you're worried about anything, just give me a call."

He looks uncomfortable fidgeting with something in his pocket before making a quick exit down the hall toward the elevators. I back slowly into the apartment and close and latch the door behind me. Relief and mortification flood through me simultaneously. I practically threw myself at Detective McAllister. Yes, I've started to consider him more of a friend than just the detective trying to catch Sebastian, but I have no idea if he feels the same way. At the same time, I'm so relieved to have someone I trust close by.

I feel safer just knowing he is in the city.

Longing for the days when I was carefree, a little bit wild, and hanging out with Genevieve and Livi with nothing to worry about, at least not anything important, I sit down to drink my now lukewarm tea.

Regardless of how ridiculous I just made myself look, having Detective McAllister in town is the first thing that calms me since we were thrown into this never-ending downward spiral.

Chapter 16

Matiu

What was I thinking yesterday? I am still baffled by the fact that I went straight to Violet's—*no. The Clark girls'*—apartment when I got into town. I started driving after work and drove a few hours before stopping for the night somewhere between Charleston and New York. After getting a few hours of sleep, I entered the Clark girls' address into my phone and drove the final eight and a half hours to New York City.

I keep telling myself that I just wanted to check on the girls, but it is more than that. Yes, I want to help the girls and make sure they are all safe, but I also feel drawn to Violet. There is an unexplainable tug to be near her, to hear her voice. When I found out that I was going to New York, it wasn't the case that made me pack up and leave so quickly. It was the thought of seeing her.

Is it completely unethical that I am starting to have feelings for Violet? Crap. I can just imagine what Detective Armstrong will say about this if he ever finds out.

No matter how hard I try to tell myself I was checking on all three sisters and it was purely a professional visit, when Violet opened the door and wrapped herself around me, I felt things I have never felt before. It almost felt like I had finally made it home, which doesn't make sense. How can I feel like that when I had just knocked on an apartment door I had never been to before? The emotion in Violet's eyes when they locked onto mine seemed to promise something more. Yes, she was sobbing and looked like a mess—a hot mess, but a mess all the same—but I finally felt like I was where I needed to be.

And when I wiped the tear off her cheek …

Ugh! I am such an idiot.

These feelings need to be buried deep. I can't have another slip up like that. I need to focus and help Agent Sullivan solve this case and get back to Charleston.

But I don't want to go back to Charleston.

The stern-looking woman at the front desk of the FBI office checks me in after I make it through the security screening and sends me up to the fourth floor. When the elevator doors open, I take in the busy room, desks, offices and lots of well-dressed men and women. I look down at my suit. *I might need an upgrade if I am going to be here for a while.*

Agent Sullivan is making his way to me from the other side of the large room. I head toward him.

"Detective McAllister, thank you for coming," he says with a warm smile, his tan skin creasing as he grins at me.

"Glad to be here."

He leads me to an office. His petite, dark-haired partner I met in Charleston is inside.

He gestures toward one of the empty chairs. "Have a seat. You met Agent Delgado in Charleston."

I glance at Agent Delgado and nod. She gives me a tight smile. Hoping I can make a better impression than I did in Charleston I smile back. I sit down in the chair next to her, trying once again to clear my head. Both of them seem like genuine, caring people, even if Agent Delgado has an attitude. I am glad they are the agents assigned to the Lykaios case.

Agent Sullivan sits and takes a drink of something steaming in a mug before starting. "Have you come across any new leads on the Lykaios case?"

"New leads? I thought the FBI had taken over the case and I wasn't supposed to be looking for anything."

Agent Delgado raises a perfectly shaped eyebrow and gives me a knowing smile. "You seemed pretty adamant the case gets solved when we were in Charleston. We aren't completely incompetent, despite what you might think. We can tell when there is a detective who isn't going to give up."

She looks like she is teasing me, but I can't really tell if she is, or if I am going to get myself into trouble. "I don't think you're incompetent at all."

"So, you're saying you haven't thought about the case at all, haven't looked into any inklings you've had?" She smirks.

My palms sweat; I'm not sure where she is going with this, exactly. "Um, maybe a bit."

This makes her laugh. "I told you Sullivan, this is a case he won't let go of."

"Don't torture the man, Delgado. We thought this case might be one that was sticking with you. You don't have any jurisdiction here, but we figured having your eyes on the case with us for a bit wouldn't hurt," Agent Sullivan says.

The breath I had been holding releases. "Good to know."

Nikau's dinosaur finds its way into my hand again and I fidget with it, rubbing my fingers over its smooth sides.

"What evidence do you have from the break in?" I ask.

"We found some DNA evidence and took fingerprints, but all of them came back as either one of the girls or the boyfriend."

"What about the book?"

Agent Sullivan leans back in his chair. "Forensics was able to confirm that it was a bullet hole, likely a 9mm bullet."

"And the blood?" I ask.

"Pig blood," Agent Delgado answers.

"Was there any camera footage from the break in or the flowers being delivered?" I wonder.

Agent Sullivan leans forward and rests his elbows on the table. "Unfortunately, their apartment building is older and in need of updating. They have cameras in the elevator and the lobby, but not in any of the hallways. To make things even more inconvenient the recordings are only kept as far back as one week. So, any footage of whoever brought the flowers is long gone."

Agent Delgado pulls a photo from one of the files in her briefcase and places it in front of me on the table. "We did get this photo of Violet talking to the supposed neighbor in the lobby."

Scrutinizing the semi-blurry photo in front of me, I can't make out any facial features. His face is partially turned away from the camera and pixelated. The apartment complex could really use an upgrade on their cameras.

"NYPD officers knocked on every door and talked to the apartment managers. No one matching the description Violet gave us lives in the building," Agent Delgado says before taking a drink out of a water bottle on the table.

Could this be Sebastian? There is no way he would be talking to Violet himself, right?

"We need to make sure the girls are protected. Maybe we should move them to a safer location."

Agent Sullivan and Agent Delgado share a look that I can't quite interpret. "We will if we need to, but right now we are hoping to find this man posing as a neighbor if he thinks that nothing has changed. We have officers watching the building entrances around the clock," Agent Sullivan says.

"Don't you think officers should be at least in their hallway if we don't have any cameras? Or should we put our own cameras up?" I ask.

"Right now, we don't want to scare him off; we can't change too much and expect him to show back up."

"So, you're using the girls as bait?" I hiss angrily.

Agent Sullivan at least looks uncomfortable when he answers. "Hopefully we can figure out who this man is quickly and we won't have to for long."

"Have you gotten any closer to finding Sebastian?" I ask.

"We found a death record for a Sebastian Lykaios in Russia who has similar facial features to Mark Lykaios. Whoever *that* Sebastian was, he was killed in a car accident in January 1991," Agent Delgado says and places a picture of, who I assume, is the deceased Sebastian in front of me. This Sebastian does share an uncanny resemblance to Mark.

Agent Sullivan continues where Agent Delgado left off. "We haven't been able to find any current records of a Sebastian Lykaios in the United States. However, we did find records of Mark's mother Irina coming to the States in 2001."

"Are there any other family members that we know of?" I ask, trying to put the pieces together.

"Yes, Irina had two children after immigrating to the states. Mark was her oldest, and she has a sixteen-year-old daughter as well. We went and spoke with both of them. They claim that they didn't see Mark or Sebastian often and the last time they heard from either of them was in January. When we asked why there is no record of Sebastian in the States, she shut down pretty quickly." Agent Sullivan stops to rub his temples like he is getting a headache. "When you were doing your research, did you come across any aliases that Sebastian might have gone by?"

"No, I didn't. Do you think he is using an alias now?"

"I think that Sebastian Lykaios is most likely an alias."

That would make sense why there aren't any records of him, at least none that we have found yet.

I try to pick anything out of the information we have that might lead us to something new as Agent Sullivan continues with his information. "We've been monitoring her and her daughter closely to see if Sebastian makes contact, but so far, we haven't seen or heard anything. From what we can tell, Irina is a single stay-at-home mom with a steady income. We're assuming that Sebastian and his illegal dealing is the source of her income. The hope is that she'll try to reach out at some point now that all the accounts she said Sebastian had access to have been frozen."

"All that we know of at least," I point out.

He nods. "Correct."

Picking up the picture of the deceased Sebastian, I look at it more closely. The resemblance to Mark is unnerving. *What is with the Lykaios family?* It's almost as if they were copied and pasted, creating different aged clones of one another. This Sebastian has slightly darker blonde hair and a kindness in his eyes that the other two Lykaios men don't have though.

Same name.

Similar features—blonde hair, dark eyes, muscular build.

What are we missing? I think before asking, "Did you say that he died in January 1991?"

Detective Delgado turns her gaze back to me. "Yes."

"What day in January?"

She looks at the papers in front of her before answering. "January 29th, why?"

"So, he died during Desert Storm, seems like too much of a coincidence. A Sebastian with the same name and an obvious family resemblance died during the same short time frame where something big happened with the Navy—something that scared straitlaced Tony Clark enough to take classified documents off base when threatened with blackmail."

Both agents' eyes are on me.

I look at the picture for another minute, hoping for something to click into place. My intuition tugging at something in the back of my mind, but I still can't quite put the pieces together.

"So, who is Sebastian, really? And how is he connected to this Sebastian who died in Russia? Are both men connected to Andrei Lykaios who served with Tony?" I ask.

"That's what we need to figure out, as you can imagine NCIS hasn't been very cooperative. I'm already thinking it was a good call to ask you to come assist," Agent Sullivan says.

Agent Delgado doesn't seem so sure when all she says is, "We'll see."

Agent Sullivan ignores her skepticism. "We have reached out to the Russian FBI Legat, our FBI agents stationed in Moscow Russia, trying to get more information. But it isn't going very quickly."

He hands me the stack of files that they have. "All the information we just briefed you on is in this stack. The first thing you can do to help is comb back through it. See if something stands out to you that didn't to us."

Agent Sullivan and Agent Delgado leave the room and I spend the rest of the day going through the documents and searching for anything that might have been missed. By the time Agent Delgado comes and tells me it's time to quit for the day my head is throbbing and my eyes feel like they are full of sand. She helps me clean up the files and put them away before we head toward the elevators.

"I'm curious, why did Violet Clark call you when their apartment got tossed and not 911?" she asks as the elevator doors close and trap us in the small space.

"I guess she's used to contacting me with her questions."

She looks at me for a minute. "Maybe … I'll see you tomorrow, McAllister." She gives me a genuine smile that actually reaches her brown eyes this time, eyes that remind me of Violet's chocolate-colored ones, as she walks away and out the front door of the building.

I got a hotel close enough to the FBI office that it is just a quick subway ride back; I could even walk the distance if I want to. As I walk to the subway station, I call Detective Armstrong.

"Looks like I might be here for a while," I say after he answers. "Everything good there?"

"Despite what you may think, kid, I can handle my job without you for the time being."

I laugh. "Definitely not what I meant. I have no doubt you'll do fine without me."

"So, are you saying you need me to come there to help you do your job?" he teases.

"Nope. I had an excellent teacher."

This makes him chuckle. "Don't be a suck up, McAllister. I'll see you when you get back."

Smiling, I disconnect the call glad that the tension between us seems to have eased and we are back to our familiar patterns, at least for now. I am glad that I am in New York City and I get to help with the case, even if I can't do anything officially here. With an added bonus of being near Violet if anything else happens.

No, not just Violet. *All* three Clark girls, I try to remind myself.

Chapter 17

Violet

'm flying through the air, but I don't feel as graceful as I used to. I land harder than anticipated and stumble out of my leap, grunting in exasperation. How am I going backward? Some things that I excelled at before seem difficult now.

"I think you should take a break, Vi," Jocelyn says.

"I can't take a break. I'm so behind and I swear I'm getting worse, not better."

Jocelyn points at the floor near the mirrors where our bags are sitting. "Sit," she says sternly, "you won't do anyone any favors if you completely wear yourself out."

I scoff. That's all that has ever been drilled into me. Keep trying; keep practicing until you get it. None of my instructors back home told me I could start to go backward in my abilities while rehearsing every day.

Plopping onto the floor grudgingly, I look like anything but a graceful ballerina. I extend and rotate my sore feet and reach for my water bottle. Taking a drink, I notice a flash of red in my bag. I'm sure I didn't pack my red umbrella today; the bright, sunny fall day outside didn't call for rain. Reaching in, I grab for the item that caught my attention and pull out a dark red envelope with my name scrawled across the front.

I look around the studio, but only see Jocelyn.

Opening the envelope, I pull out a red index card with the same scrawling handwriting as the note with the flowers.

I see you.

My heart is racing so fast I feel like I'm still jumping and leaping, falling straight into an abyss. Something drops out from behind the card and I can't catch my breath as I pick it up.

It's a picture of me at the small convenience store just around the corner from our apartment. I'm in line to check out holding a gallon of milk and a small snack size bag of pistachios. This was taken only a few days ago. My blood runs cold and I shiver. I think I might be sick. My stomach feels like it's full of rocks.

Jumping up, I look around the studio again. Still only Jocelyn.

Rushing to the door, I peek my head out into the hallway, looking both ways. I don't see anyone suspicious. Pulling my head back in through the door, I latch it shut.

"Hey, Jocelyn, did you see anyone come into the studio while we were practicing?" I ask.

She steps out of position and walks gracefully toward me. "No, how come?"

Panic courses through me.

I have to get home and make sure my sisters are okay.

"Is everything okay? You look like you've seen a ghost. I didn't know your olive tone could go that pasty white," she teases, but stops when she realizes I'm genuinely terrified. "What's wrong?"

"I got a weird note in my bag. I don't know who put it there."

"A note? Let me see." Jocelyn reaches for the card.

"No!" I practically shout. "Sorry, it's just … I probably shouldn't have even touched it. They're probably going to want to dust it for fingerprints."

"Dust it for fingerprints? What in the world are you talking about?"

"I can't explain right now. I'm sorry Jocelyn. Thank you for helping me practice," I say as I quickly pack my things into my bag and rush out the door, leaving without an explanation. A glance back into the studio shows Jocelyn with a puzzled expression on her face, packing up her bag. I shouldn't be leaving early. I need all the practice I can get, and Jocelyn took the time out of her busy schedule to help me try to catch up.

I'm such a crappy friend right now.

I pull out my phone, sending a text to Detective McAllister as I rush away from Juilliard into the evening dusk and make it to the subway just in time to squeeze in before the doors close.

> Found a creepy note in my bag at school.

> Bring it to the FBI office.

> I'll send you the address.

> I can't. I have to go home and check on my sisters.

> Okay. I'll meet you there.

> Don't touch anything if you can help it.

Too late, I think frantically, trying to call both of my sisters and then Steve. No one answers. *What is the point of everyone having cell phones if nobody answers them?*

Rushing out of the subway exit, the cold air stings my cheeks as I run the rest of the way to my apartment. When my feet start to protest, I realize I left in such a rush I still have my pointe shoes on and I'm not wearing a coat. Ignoring my screaming feet and freezing limbs, I don't wait for the elevator and run up the stairs to our apartment. Out of breath and limping, I burst through the apartment door, startling Genevieve and Steve.

"Violet, you scared the crap out of me," Genevieve chides with wide eyes, her hand on her chest.

"How come you didn't answer your phone?" I ask.

Genevieve looks confused for a minute. "Sorry, it must still be on silent from school." She turns her attention back to the counter. Steve is bent over, looking at something.

"Is Konnie home?" I ask, still trying to catch my breath.

"Yes, she's in her room, as usual," Genevieve says, taking a good look at me. "Did you run home?"

I ignore her as I see what they're looking at on the counter.

Two red envelopes.

Two red index cards.

And two pictures.

All scattered across the counter. The panic rushes back.

"You guys got them, too?" I whisper, creeping closer to the counter.

Both cards have the same scrawling handwriting on them.

I see you.

One picture is of Steve walking through Central Park and the other is a picture of Genevieve sitting on the subway reading a book. Whoever it was had been following us for a while to get pictures of Genevieve and Steve separately. They're hardly ever apart.

"Where did you get those?" I say breathlessly.

Genevieve looks at me, her green eyes filling with fear. "We found them in our backpacks at school."

"Did you see who left them?"

"No, we didn't see anyone."

Silently, I reach into my bag and pull out my envelope, setting it on the counter. Genevieve reaches to open it.

"Don't touch it. Detective McAllister is on his way."

"Wait what? Detective McAllister is in New York?" she asks, puzzled.

Oh right. We were all so busy this morning I forgot to tell Genevieve about him stopping by last night. I'm too panicked to explain anything right now and call for Konnie.

Konnie finally emerges from her room with that permanent sour expression on her face. "What?"

"Did you find a letter in or by your backpack today?"

"No."

"Bring me your backpack."

Konnie rolls her eyes. Again. But grudgingly goes and grabs it, bringing it into the kitchen. Amid protests from Konnie, I start digging through her bag, searching for the red envelope that I'm hoping not to find, but know I will.

Even though I was expecting it, my breath hitches when I see a flash of red. Pulling out the envelope with the same handwriting on the front, I set it on the counter.

"What is that?" Konnie asks and reaches for it.

I know I was told not to touch it, but I have to know. I rip the envelope open and dump out the index card and the picture, trying to touch them as little as possible.

Same creepy message.

And a picture of Konnie sitting with some other teens outside of a café. She has a slight smile on her face, which is an improvement from the scowl she always seems to wear at home.

I may not be able to prove it, but I know this is Sebastian.

I don't know what he wants from us.

I don't know why he is still haunting us.
But I do know we aren't safe.

Chapter 18

Matiu

M y knuckles have barely touched the door when Violet flings it open. She once again wraps her arms around me in a hug and my uncontrollable heart takes flight again.

"I'm so glad you're here," she whispers.

Apparently, we are huggers now, so I return the hug and notice that Violet is trembling. Her obvious fear has me wrapping my arms a little more tightly around her. She fits perfectly in my arms, but I can't be thinking thoughts like that about Violet.

I lean back. "You want to show me this creepy note you texted about?"

Her face flushes a bit as she drops her arms. I already miss the feeling of them being wrapped around me. *Stop! Focus!* I silently shout at myself.

"Right, sorry. Again."

"No need to apologize." I try to give her a convincing smile.

"I wasn't the only one who got the cryptic cards."

She leads me into their kitchen where Steve, Genevieve, and Konnie are all gathered around the counter. They all look up as we walk into the room, and surprise spreads across their faces when they see me.

The cards and pictures laid out on the counter are disturbing. It is apparent that whoever is sending them has been following all four of them for a while. They know their routines, where they go to school and where they shop.

Even if this isn't Sebastian, it is still someone we need to worry about.

"Do you have some gloves and some Ziploc bags I can use?" I had thought about supplies on the way over, but I didn't have any in my car and didn't want to delay getting here by stopping and grabbing some.

Violet quickly grabs some gloves from under the sink and a box of Ziploc bags from a drawer and hands them to me.

"Don't take this the wrong way. I'm glad you're here, but why are you in New York, Detective McAllister?" Genevieve asks.

Sliding my fingers into the gloves, I carefully pick up the contents on the counter and start placing them in individual bags while answering, "I'm assisting the FBI in trying to track down Sebastian."

"Have you found him yet?" Konnie asks, folding her arms defensively.

"No, not yet, but we're making some progress."

"This is Sebastian, isn't it?" Violet asks in a timid voice, biting her lower lip. The motion draws my attention to her lips, makes me wonder what they would feel like against mine.

Stop. Focus, Matiu. What is wrong with me?

"That's who I'm leaning toward. We don't have any definite proof that he's doing this. But after the book was left on your counter, if it isn't Sebastian, it's someone connected to Mark at the very least."

I am convinced that Sebastian is behind this, but I filter other possible suspects to cover all my bases. Mark's mom, his sister, they could have been communicating with Sebastian and Mark more than they admitted. Maybe even a girlfriend or friend we don't know about. Whoever it is had to have known that Mark gave Genevieve that specific book for Christmas, so it was someone that he talked to regularly.

All the envelopes and cards are now safely in bags. The notes are all written in the same handwriting, and whoever wrote them knows all their names and how to spell them correctly. When I get to the pictures, I slow down and scrutinize them. Trying to keep it professional, I focus on taking them all in with a detective's perspective, but my stomach rolls. Anxiety fills me.

Steve in Central Park, Konnie at a café, Genevieve on the subway, and my chest tightens even more when I see Violet in her dance clothes at the grocery store. She obviously had just stopped to grab something quick on her way home from school.

Someone is following all of them.

Someone is following Violet.

My fear quickly turns to anger and my teeth strain against each other as I clench my jaw.

"You all got these while you were at school?" I ask and they all nod.

"And you didn't see anyone near your backpacks beforehand?"

They all shake their heads.

Something is tickling my brain, but I still can't quite grasp what it is. Anxiety comes back. I don't want to scare them unnecessarily, but they need to be on high alert.

I go ahead and tell them what I am thinking. "If this is Sebastian, not only does he know where each of you go to school, he knows where to find you while you're at school. So, it's safe to assume that he knows your class schedules. On top of that, the pictures are plainly letting you know that he also knows where you frequent when you're not at school. This doesn't sit well with me."

Placing the pictures into bags, I continue. "You all need to make sure you're with someone at all times. Don't go anywhere alone. And it might be a good idea to change up your routine a little bit, make yourselves a little less predictable."

I need to convince Agent Sullivan to stop using them as bait and get them more protection. They aren't safe here, but they can't quit going to school even though it is apparent that school isn't safe either.

"Wouldn't changing our routines kinda make it worse? If one of us doesn't show up, it would make it harder for us to retrace their steps too," Violet points out.

That is pretty sound logic. Both ideas have pros and cons.

"I'll leave it up to you about your routines, but try to avoid going anywhere alone at all costs. I'm going to talk to Agent Sullivan about what else we can do."

They all nod and look at me like I have all the answers.

But I don't.

"Each of you have my number, right? Let me know if you're ever nervous or see anyone suspicious. I don't have any jurisdiction here, but I'm here if you guys need anything."

They look so hopeful, like I am going to solve all their problems.

What if I can't?

I am starting to realize what Detective Armstrong was warning me about. Because I have definitely crossed over a line, I am way too close to this. I don't just want to find Sebastian and make sure they are all safe …

I *need* to.

Picking up the bags with the red cards off the counter, I ask, "I need to take these to the FBI agents I am working with. Are you all okay with that?"

"Yes please, why would we want to keep the creepy notes and pictures? We aren't all crazy like Genevieve, keeping creepy mementos from the people who torture us," Konnie says.

Violet wasn't kidding. This is not the same sweet girl who we found in the woods. Konnie has changed—which is totally understandable with what she went through, but it still surprises me.

"Konnie! Knock it off." Anger laces Violet's voice and she narrows her eyes at Konnie, who stomps down the hall and slams a door.

"Sorry about that." Violet looks embarrassed, a blush creeping onto her cheeks. "She's a little bit unpredictable right now, minus the slamming of the doors. That part is a daily occurrence."

She walks with me to the front door. Part of me wants to stay. I don't want to go back to my hotel room alone, I don't want to leave Violet here without protection. But Agent Sullivan made it clear that they want to make Sebastian feel safe enough to continue with his sick game. Having a detective staying in the apartment with the girls would throw that off, and I don't want to give them a reason to send me home after day one.

I need to be in New York right now, not in Charleston.

I pause at the apartment door after opening it and take a step into the hallway, turning to look at Violet. Those warm brown eyes meet mine. I can see the worry in them.

"I'm going to sleep in my car downstairs."

Violet bites her lip. "No, it's fine, really. They have a cop downstairs already. And Steve is here."

Everything in me is screaming to stay. I am so torn between what I should do, what I want to do and wondering what Violet wants me to do.

"I'm only a phone call away," I say softly.

"Thank you. Thank you for everything, Detective McAllister."

Before I can stop myself, I reach my hand up and brush a stray lock of Violet's hair off her face, tucking it behind her ear. She leans into my hand slightly, and touching her, even in this small way, stirs something to life inside of me.

"Matiu," I respond, surprising myself. "My first name is Matiu. You don't need to call me Detective McAllister anymore."

She smiles, her eyes lingering on mine for a moment more before I pull myself away and walk toward the elevator. The sound of Violet clicking the door shut and locking it behind her echoes down the hall.

I'm not sure what I am doing anymore; my emotions are all over the place. But I know one thing for certain.

I will put an end to this madness and protect Violet and her sisters.

Deep in my gut, I know Sebastian is behind this.

I just have to prove it.

Chapter 19

Violet

"You aren't going to have enough energy for rehearsal if you don't eat your lunch, Vi." Jocelyn gives me a worried look.

A brisk breeze rustles the colorful fall leaves in the trees overhead. Last year, sitting at the tables in Hearst Plaza with Jocelyn every day for lunch seemed so grown up and exciting. Now it feels forced, like I'm trying to live this fabulous Juilliard-student-in-New-York-City life. When deep down I know that I don't fit in here. I thought I did, but I don't feel like I do anymore, especially since I don't feel safe anymore. I wish I could lock my sisters and I in our apartment and stay there until Sebastian is found.

More clouds roll in above us, threatening rain, and the temperature seems to drop a few more degrees. The constant soundtrack of traffic in the background creates white noise, and the smells of various foods waft toward us, all smelling a lot more appetizing than the salad in front of me.

I poke a fork around my salad. "I don't have much of an appetite."

"I've noticed. You doing okay?"

I raise my eyebrows at her. I haven't told her about everything that has been happening recently. I know she has questions about the red card that freaked me out at rehearsal, but she hasn't pushed and I haven't volunteered the information. I just want something in my life to feel the same, feel normal, but even while I'm pretending to be a young and carefree college student, I feel exactly like the fraud I am. I may still be young, but I'm definitely not carefree and I live most of my days in fear, suspicious of everyone around me. With only a few people that I trust, Jocelyn being one of them, I really should let her in. I've lost so many people I care about; I shouldn't be pushing away the ones that are still here.

She laughs. "Okay, okay! I know you've had a rough year. You seem to be getting the choreography for the New Dances performance down though."

"Ms. Yvette still has me in the back."

"You'll get back up front. You've got this!"

I smile. "Thanks for always being my own personal cheerleader."

Jocelyn reaches over and gives my hand a squeeze. "You're doing an amazing job for the situation you've been placed in. You're catching up quick in rehearsal and you're rocking it, making sure your sisters have everything they need."

"It's not just trying to keep up with school and taking care of my sisters anymore. There's more going on."

"Like what? Does this have something to do with the card you got the other day? I could tell it really freaked you out."

"Yeah, someone has been following my sisters and me, leaving us creepy notes, sending flowers, and our apartment got broken into."

"What! When did this start?"

"Last month," I say and set down my fork, giving up on the salad.

"How come you haven't said anything? Never mind, don't answer that. Your whole comment about dusting for fingerprints makes a lot more sense now. I take it the cops are involved?"

"Yeah, the FBI and Detective McAllister is in town."

"Wait, the FBI? And isn't Detective McAllister the detective from your parents' case? Are they thinking this is related?"

I nod and pick my fork back up, I'm not sure why, my stomach is so tight with knots that I feel nauseous just thinking about eating anything. "Maybe I need to quit. I don't think I can take care of my sisters, keep them safe, and still go to school."

"You know that if you finish school you'll be in a better position to help your sisters."

"How? I'm not even sure I'm good enough to get hired by a big dance company, which has always been my end goal."

Jocelyn grabs my hand and squeezes it. "You're an amazing dancer, it's just been hard to focus lately, but you're catching up. Hang in there."

"It's not just dance though. Yes, I'm catching up with the New Dances choreography, but I'm behind in all my other classes. I really think I might fail some, everything that is going on outside of school is what needs my focus right now."

"Instead of quitting, have you thought about talking to the school and explaining what's going on?"

I scoff. "They aren't going to hold a spot for a student that can't keep up. It's a privilege just to get into Juilliard, you know as well as I do they have one of the lowest acceptance rates. If I take a break, it would be super unlikely for me to get back in."

She sighs. "Don't give up, Vi. Things are tough and super scary, but regardless of how you feel right now, I think you're the strongest person I've ever met."

Pesky tears prick the back of my eyes again. I didn't used to cry so easily. "Thank you for always being so supportive. Sorry for always being such a hot mess."

Jocelyn laughs; the melodic sound makes me smile. "Don't worry about it. You make life interesting. I don't even need to watch Netflix. Just grab some popcorn and see what's on the Violet show today." Bringing up an inside joke from our first year at Juilliard to lighten the mood.

"Thanks a lot," I say sarcastically as she pulls me into a hug.

"You know I'm kidding." She gives me a mischievous look. "Kinda."

Giving her shoulder a playful shove, I notice someone wearing black jeans and a black hoodie taking a picture of us.

They might be who has been following us, are they working for Sebastian? The need for answers and the urge to protect my sisters takes over. I don't give myself time to talk myself out of my next move as I jump up, grabbing my bag.

"Hey!" I yell and they take off running.

Without thinking, I race after them down 65th Street toward Broadway, ignoring Jocelyn's panicked protests. Dry leaves crunch under my tennis shoes as I run trying to catch up. They rush into the throng of people on the sidewalk along Broadway and, despite trying to follow closely behind, I quickly lose sight of them in the hustle and bustle of bodies. Scanning the street, I can't see the black hoodie anywhere.

Breathing hard and trying to catch my breath, I stop running and pull my cell phone out of my pocket. The heavy clouds that have been threatening rain all day start drizzling cold drops on my head. Digging around in my bag, I feel the handle of my umbrella and pull it out, opening it just in time as the rain starts to lash down from the sky. Large unrelenting drops pound the top of my umbrella, the red standing out against the bleak sky, yet fitting right in with the yellows, oranges, and reds of the falling leaves. I look back at the cell phone in my hand.

For a second, I remember Agent Sullivan's words when our apartment got broken into. Agent Sullivan is in charge of our case now. I should call him not Detective McAllister—Matiu.

After only a moment of hesitation, I call Matiu.

Chapter 20

Matiu

"Is there any way we can get the Clark girls and Steve protective details? Now that we know they're being followed?" I ask Agent Sullivan.

I brought the bags full of the eerie red index cards and the pictures straight to him after I left the girls apartment last night, but we had no luck getting any evidence off them.

"We don't have the resources to have someone follow all four of them wherever they go. Yes, they did get the threatening notes at school, but surrounded by so many people in their classes they should be relatively safe. It's unlikely that Sebastian will make a move with that many witnesses. Plus, we're still hoping that we can find the man claiming to be their neighbor. Like we discussed before if they're constantly with law enforcement that would be unlikely."

"What about when they're commuting to and from school?"

He gives me an apologetic look. "We already have the apartment building under surveillance around the clock, I'm not sure if I can get more approved right now, but I'll see what I can do."

He turns and walks away, and I sit back down and look at the mess I have been trying to decipher. Papers, printouts, and pictures are scattered in front of me on the table that I am using as my temporary desk while in New York. The small FBI conference room we have been working in has windows looking out onto the busy streets. The gloomy sky outside has raindrops pelting against the window, pulling my attention from my work. I have been trying to fit the pieces together for hours now. Nothing is clicking, we are missing something important and my gut is telling me it is here, right in front of me.

I still can't connect the deliveries to Sebastian, either. With only the girls and Steve's DNA and fingerprints on the envelopes, cards, and pictures that were delivered to them at school, we are at another dead end.

And how does any of the information we have about Sebastian connect to the Clark family? It would be helpful if NCIS would share any information with us about Andrei Lykaios. Someone with the same last name as Mark and Sebastian serving with Tony is no coincidence. Agent Sullivan requested documents from the Navy, but we are still waiting. We found some sealed documents attached to Andrei's name, but we are waiting yet again because they are from when he was a minor. Having to jump through so many hoops is frustrating. And nothing is making sense.

Yet.

I *will* figure this out.

My phone vibrates, breaking my concentration. Warmth fills me when I see Violet's name on the screen, quickly followed by dread. What has happened now?

"Hey Violet, is everything okay?"

All I can hear on the other line is heavy breathing for a second before Violet responds. "Someone was just taking pictures of my friend Jocelyn and me. I chased them for a minute but lost them in the crowd on Broadway."

"Did you just say that you chased them?" Irritation and anxiety fill me simultaneously. "Why would you do that?" I snap.

"Because I don't want Sebastian to have any more photos of my sisters or me. If I caught them, they could've led us to Sebastian."

Hurt laces her voice and I realize in my fear I must have sounded much harsher than I meant to. The fact that Violet would attempt to chase after whoever was taking pictures of her by herself has me on edge.

"You aren't supposed to go anywhere alone. I can't believe you just rushed after them without knowing anything about what you were running into." I can't keep the anger from leaking into my voice. How are we supposed to keep her safe if she does things like this? "Why did you do something so stupid? They could have hurt you!"

"No offense, Detective McAllister," she punctuates my name. The way she says it after I asked her to call me Matiu last night and the anger in her voice lets me know she is fully aware of how offensive whatever she is going to say next will actually be. "You've had months to figure this out and have gotten nowhere. Do you really think the person taking pictures was just going to patiently wait for you to get there?"

Ouch. "Well, no …"

"Not that it matters, anyway. I lost them too," she interrupts.

"I'm trying, Violet."

"Well, try harder, detective," she snaps before disconnecting the call.

Sighing, I run my fingers through my hair again. *Well, that went well,* I think. At least the relationship is right back to professional. No worries about Violet thinking she wants anything from me besides finding Sebastian. *Then why do I feel so terrible?* I didn't mean to hurt her feelings, but the terror that swept through me when she told me she went after whoever was taking pictures took over.

And despite what I keep telling myself, I want more than a professional relationship with Violet Clark.

Focusing on Violet will not get me any closer to finding Sebastian, though.

Pulling my attention back to the mess in front of me, I hope something will stand out and send me in the right direction. What is Sebastian's endgame with stalking the girls and creeping them out? They don't have anything that he would want. No access to weapons or weapon designs. But does Sebastian know that? He can't assume that they would have any military documents after NCIS combed through their house.

How do I get ahead of Sebastian when he seems to be several steps ahead of us at every single turn?

Determined, I scan the information in front of me. Picking up the Russian death certificate, I stare at the name. Two men with the same name that share physical traits. Sebastian isn't old enough to be this Sebastian's father. Cousin? Brother, maybe?

The ding of a new email notification comes from my laptop. Glancing at the screen, I see it is from our contact in Russia. Opening it quickly, I read through the information several times.

Detective McAllister,

The deceased Sebastian Lykaios on the death certificate had an older brother and a younger sister.

The brother, Andrei Lykaios, was two years older and immigrated to the USA with his father when he was young. Sebastian and his younger sister, Irina, stayed in Russia with their mother.

As far as I can tell, Andrei never came back to Russia. Their mother died just a couple of years after Sebastian and I couldn't find any current records on Irina.

I will keep looking and let you know if I find anything.

So, the dead Sebastian Lykaios is Andrei Lykaios's brother. What are the odds that another man would choose Sebastian's name as an alias? Clicking off the email, I immediately run an immigration records search for Andrei Lykaios. I find the information easily, and I scan and read as fast as I can. Andrei and his father Anton came to the USA with a green card through Anton's employer when Andrei was only five. Attached to the green card paperwork I find Andrei's birth certificate and divorce documents for his parents. Five years later, Anton and Andrei were granted citizenship.

Continuing to dig, I find a death certificate for Anton. Quickly doing the math, Anton died when Andrei was seventeen. We know from our initial meeting with NCIS that he was listed as MIA in February 1991—shortly after his brother died in Russia and also right in the middle of Desert Storm. Following the paper trail for Andrei after his father's death I hit a dead end. We need those sealed records.

Holding my breath, I check to see if we have access to his minor records yet and I can hardly contain my excitement when I see that we have been granted access. Clicking through them I speed through the information. He had been living in a foster home until he turned eighteen and joined the Navy as soon as he was able. And he enlisted at the same time another eighteen-year-old living in the same foster home did.

My heart races as I finally make a connection to the Clark girls. Andrei enlisted in the Navy with his foster brother Tony Clark. And he was with him and went missing during whatever happened during Desert Storm. So, who resurrected Andrei's dead brother? And why?

A shudder runs up and down my spine.

Apparently, not all ghosts can rest.

Chapter 21

Violet

"**A**dequately done, Miss Clark." Ms. Yvette gives me a curt nod. I'm not back on the front row yet, but at least I'm making progress. Ms. Yvette isn't yelling at me or talking about me standing in the back as a tree today.

Grabbing my water bottle from my bag, I take a long, satisfying drink. Dancers file out of the studio past me.

"I'm going to run to the restroom real quick and then we can start practicing," Jocelyn says as she drops her bag next to mine.

Sitting down next to our bags, I pull my cell phone out and notice a text I missed during rehearsal from Matiu. Guilt floods me for how I reacted at lunch. Konnie's attitude must be contagious.

> Came across some new information. I can stop by tonight on my way home if you all want an update.

I do want an update, and I want to say sorry for being a brat earlier. But if I'm being completely honest, I just want to see him and I don't want it to be with my sisters. I send a reply quickly before I lose my nerve.

> Don't want to worry my sisters. Want to meet for dinner?

> Yes

The reply comes back right away and has me smiling like a giddy teenager. I can't deny how handsome Matiu is, and how excited I feel whenever I see him, or get a text from him. Dinner alone with him might be the highlight of my week, even if it's just eating food while he is going over details of the case. I'm not sure what the information he's found is, but I feel safe and comfortable with him. I can tell him how I'm actually feeling instead of putting on a strong face in front of my sisters to keep us all from falling apart.

My stomach grumbles and I reach into my bag to grab a protein bar to hold me over through practice until dinner. Digging around, my fingers brush across something cold and hard. Confused, I pull it out and quickly drop it back inside.

A bullet.

Why is there a bullet in my bag?

Panicking, I pull it open wide and peer in. Multiple bullets are scattered among my things. The shiny, copper-colored brass jingles as I tilt the bag looking for more. Each bullet has a red tip. Red has always been my favorite color, but it is quickly losing its appeal between the flowers, the cards, and now the red-tipped bullets.

I have no idea if I can get in trouble for having bullets at school, but I really don't want to find out. Quickly zipping it closed, I head outside, sending a text to Jocelyn, letting her know that something came up and I won't be able to practice tonight. My classes are over, so I'm okay to leave school, but I feel bad for ditching out on Jocelyn. Again.

The metallic sound of the bullets moving around in my bag reminds me why I'm not staying to practice. Pulling my phone out, I dial Matiu. He answers after the first ring.

"I found something in my dance bag again," I say instead of a greeting, hoping he can forget about the way I acted earlier. I still owe him an apology.

"Another card?"

"No, not a card this time. I'd rather just show you instead of explaining over the phone."

"Okay. I'm on my way. I'll pick you up from school and we can go to dinner, if you're still up for it."

The uncertainty in his voice tugs my lips into a smile. "Sounds good."

Disconnecting the call, I anxiously wait for Matiu. Not sure if my nervousness is from the bullets, or the thought of having dinner alone with him.

Chapter 22

Matiu

'm not looking forward to seeing whatever new surprise has been left in Violet's bag. I'm not going to lie; I wish she would have given me a little bit of a heads up. Her not wanting to say anything over the phone has me even more on edge.

My phone rings, making me jump. *When did I get so skittish?* I glimpse Detective Armstrong's name before answering with a distracted hello.

"It's time for you to come back to Charleston, McAllister."

No. I'm not ready to go back to Charleston. I am finally making progress with the case. "I just came across some information that I really want to keep pursuing here with the FBI."

"Sorry, kid, no can do. You have to be in court on Monday for the Rolfe case."

"Is there any way you can handle the case without me?"

"This isn't a request. If you're not there, a lot of the prosecution's arguments won't have merit."

Ugh. Worst timing ever. "Okay." I am unable to keep the irritation out of my voice.

"I'll see you in court at 8 a.m. Monday morning. You better start driving tomorrow. Give yourself a little bit of time to relax before work on Monday."

"See you Monday," I say, tossing my phone onto the passenger seat in frustration.

I finally catch a break in the Lykaios case and I have to go home. Agent Sullivan and Agent Delgado are skilled agents, and I know the case is in excellent hands, but I really wanted to be a part of bringing down Sebastian's empire.

121

And then there is Violet.

No matter how many times I tell myself to stay away, she pulls me right back in. I want to be everywhere she is. I want her to call and talk to me about things other than what new terror she has come across that day. I want to know what makes her smile, what makes her laugh, what makes her excited.

Violet is standing on the sidewalk waiting for me as I pull up. She jumps in the car and before I can even ask, she unzips her duffle and opens it wide for me to see inside.

The whole bottom of the bag is littered with bullets. The red tips of the full synthetic jacket bullets are a stark contrast against everything else, like sinister confetti all over the inside of her bag. It doesn't escape my notice that the bullets in her bag seem to be 9mm bullets—the same caliber handgun that Mark was shot with. I would have to measure them to be certain and the Syntech red bullets are obviously not standard issue for the police department, but making sure there is an abundance of red in every message sent seems to be a priority.

She laughs nervously. "You want to know something funny?" I nod and she continues. "Red has always been my favorite color, but now I dread seeing it."

The color red can insinuate so many things: anger, love, danger, sacrifice. Blood. I don't think telling Violet any of this will help the situation at all. She already looks terrified.

And I have to tell her I am leaving.

But I don't want to tell her quite yet.

A wave of nausea rolls through me. Sebastian is obviously ramping up his sick game and I have to leave. I seriously contemplate just not going back, but I can't do that to the team back home who has put so much work into the Rolfe case. They need me there to testify. This is just really horrible timing.

"Is there some place you want to go for dinner?" I ask.

Violet gives me directions to a sushi bar that she loves, and I drive the short distance that takes twice as long with New York City traffic as it would in Charleston. Parking the car, I reach into the glove box and grab a glove and a bag—supplies I grabbed after being empty-handed for the red cards.

Carefully, I pull eighteen bullets out and zip them into the bag. Violet searches to make sure we found them all, but I realize Mark was eighteen when he died. So far everything that has been left has had something to do with Mark's death: the book with the bullet hole and blood, now eighteen red tipped bullets—even the flowers could be connected to his death, the color red for blood and the fact that flowers are the common gift sent when someone dies. I lock the bag of bullets inside my glove box and we walk into the restaurant.

The hostess sits us at a table and we both start looking over the menu. Violet's deep brown eyes keep glancing at me over the menu until she finally asks, "What information did you find?"

"I finally made a connection between Sebastian and your dad. Kind of." Now that I am thinking about it, I haven't directly connected Sebastian to Tony. I just connected the deceased Sebastian's brother to Tony. It's more than we have had this entire time, so I am going to call it a giant win.

"Kind of?" she asks.

"Well, Mark's mom had two brothers, one of them, Andrei, served with your dad. They also had a brother named Sebastian, but he died, so we aren't sure how our current Sebastian is connected to the siblings."

Violet looks skeptical. "So, the brother of Mark's mom served with my dad? How does that help us find Sebastian?"

Now I feel stupid. "Well, um, I'm still trying to figure that out."

To my horror, Violet starts to giggle. Her giggles turn into uncontrollable laughter, and she is wiping her eyes as tears pour down her face. "I'm sorry. I have no idea why I am laughing so hard," she says in between fits of laughter.

"I have to do some more digging, but it's the first concrete lead we've had in a while."

She reigns in her laughter at my serious tone. "I'm sure you'll figure it out. I'm really sorry for what I said earlier today. I didn't mean it."

"You have every right to be frustrated with how long we've been trying to find Sebastian. I'm frustrated too."

Those big, beautiful chocolate eyes search mine. "How do you think someone keeps putting things in our bags at school without us noticing anything?"

"I'm not sure. All four of you need to make sure you're always staying alert. Don't leave your bags unattended if possible. I asked Agent Sullivan if we can get you more protection, especially during your commutes. He is going to see what he can do."

The laughter is completely gone from her eyes now. "Can we talk about something, anything else? I just need a break. I don't want to think about my parents or Sebastian or Mark for just a little bit." She looks at me for a minute. "What about you?"

"What about me?"

"Do you have any siblings? Do you get along with your parents? Were you born in Charleston? Just tell me something about yourself."

"Well, no, I wasn't born in Charleston. I was born in Hamilton, New Zealand. My parents moved to the United States when I was a baby for my dad's job. He still works for the same company."

"That's so cool. I've wanted to visit New Zealand ever since I watched The Lord of the Rings and found out it was filmed there. It looks so beautiful."

"It is. I went to visit my grandparents and family there pretty regularly growing up, but I haven't been back for a few years. I miss it."

"Are you close with your family?" She looks genuinely interested in my answers to her questions, and it makes me smile.

"Very. After we moved to the states, my parents had two more children. My younger brother and then my little sister. My parents are amazingly supportive of everything I've ever wanted to do. My only complaint is that sometimes they can be a little too intrusive into my life, but I think that has a lot to do with the trauma we all went through when my brother went missing."

The smile that had been on Violet's face vanished. "Your brother went missing?"

Yeah, and it is my fault for leaving him alone, I think to myself, but I don't want to say that out loud. Without realizing it, I reach into my pocket and find Nikau's dinosaur. "We were out riding our bikes one summer day and I made it home, but he never did. He was never found. His kidnapping is what drove me to become a detective."

"That's awful." Compassion fills her eyes. "You seem young for a detective," she points out.

"Well, I'm the youngest detective in my department. I pretty much had a one-track mind and worked hard to get to where I am as fast as I did."

"If you don't mind me asking, how old are you?"

"Twenty-four," I say, and Violet looks surprised.

"How old were you when your brother went missing?"

"Nine, and I have never stopped looking for him or his kidnapper."

Violet reaches over and squeezes my hand. It sends jolts of electricity through my body. "I'm so sorry, Matiu. I can't even imagine not knowing what happened to my parents. Not knowing how to handle life without them is hard enough." She pauses and bites her lower lip. "I've noticed you always reach for something in your pocket. Do you mind if I ask what it is?"

I didn't realize I reached for Nikau's dinosaur often enough for others to notice. Pulling my keys out of my pocket, I hold them up for Violet to see—the once blue dinosaur dangling front and center.

"It was Nikau's favorite dinosaur toy. I gave it to him on his sixth birthday and made it into a keychain when I was a teen. I guess I reach for it whenever I get nervous." I smile, looking at the worn toy. "I didn't realize I did it as much as I apparently do."

I have a smile on my face, but when I look at Violet, her face has turned serious. A slight furrow between her brows as her lips turn down in a slight frown.

"Do we ever stop missing those we lose?" she asks quietly.

The warmth of Violet's hand in mine gives me a peace I haven't felt for such a long, long time. "No, you'll always miss them, but the missing changes." I give Violet's hand a squeeze. "The pain doesn't always feel so sharp. It dulls with time, but there are still moments that I miss my brother desperately."

Violet nods. "I still want to pick up the phone and call my parents daily, and then the pain comes back in full force when I realize I can't. At least I have my sisters with me."

Our server brings our food to the table and Violet's eyes light up at the sight of the delicious-looking sushi rolls. My hand feels cold and I immediately miss the contact when Violet pulls her hand from mine to eat. The conversation flows freely and easily as we eat our sushi and continues well after our plates are cleared. When we start to get irritated looks from the servers for staying at our table too long, we finally get up and gather our things. I insist on paying for dinner and we walk out toward where I parked my car.

The rain has stopped, but the warm days of September and October are long gone and it is apparent winter is coming. There is a violinist playing on the street despite the cooler weather and we stop to listen. Violet wraps her coat around her to guard against the chill. I'm not sure exactly how Violet is feeling, but I know I don't want this night to end.

The violinist's melodic tunes turn somber and Violet leans into me. I reach for her hand on instinct, but think better of it and start to pull my hand back. Violet surprises me by catching my hand before it makes its way back to my pocket and laces her fingers through mine. Every nerve in my body seems to be on high alert as she holds my hand. *Since when did holding hands create such potent feelings in me?* I wonder.

When the song ends, I am relieved when Violet tugs me toward Central Park instead of toward the car. We don't walk into Central Park, but Violet stops at a bench overlooking the beauty that is still trying to hold on to some of its color. Some trees still have colorful leaves, while some are already bare. Evergreen trees and shrubs are scattered among the vegetation, giving pops of green to the park that is surrounded by the majestic skyscrapers. The view of Central Park is beautiful. Looking up as far as you can see, it feels like the buildings surrounding the park never stop. I never really thought about why we call them skyscrapers, but looking at these giants, it truly seems as if they are scraping the sky, taller than I can even imagine. The movies don't do New York City justice.

Bringing my gaze back to Violet, I lose my breath for a heartbeat. She is stunning. The streetlights give her olive skin a soft glimmer, her cheeks are rosy from the cold air and those soul-searching eyes watch as the people pass by, coming and going through the park.

I hate to break the peaceful look on her face, but I need to tell her I have to go home. I reach my free hand into my pocket and give Nikau's dinosaur a squeeze to steady my nerves. "I have to go back to Charleston tomorrow."

When she looks at me, the pain in her eyes almost has me ready to quit my job and move to New York. "Tomorrow?" she whispers.

"I found out right before I picked you up. I don't want to go back yet, but I have to."

She looks away, her eyes searching the park. "I'm afraid. I'm constantly afraid now. For me, for my sisters, for Steve. Having you here is one of the few things that has made me feel safe."

A stab of guilt hits me. I want to be here with her too. "Agent Sullivan is a really great guy. He'll be there whenever you need him. I don't have any doubt that he'll be there for you and your sisters if you need help."

She searches my face—I'm not sure what for—before she turns her gaze back to the park. All the emotion on her face, pain, hurt, fear makes my chest ache.

"I'm only a phone call away, Violet, and if you really need me, I'll drive straight back to New York City. I promise."

"You'd really do that for me?" she asks quietly.

"I'm beginning to realize that there isn't a whole lot that I wouldn't do for you."

Violet looks at me with those haunting eyes and I can't help myself. I lean down and brush my lips across hers. Breathing in her intoxicating smell of vanilla and lavender, my kiss is slow and hesitant, but she responds with the same hunger and urgency that I have been feeling and trying to ignore these past few weeks.

The rest of the world disappears.

There is only Violet.

Chapter 23

Violet

My whole body is on fire.

In a good way.

When Matiu's lips touch mine, something happens to me that I've never experienced. It's like I've been starving all my life and was finally given food.

I want more.

I *need* more.

The kiss ends way too soon and we walk, hands laced together, to the car. The drive back to my apartment is quiet. I'm not sure what Matiu is thinking, but all I can think about is how much I want him to stay. That one kiss has me rethinking everything I thought I knew about love. I thought I loved some of my boyfriends in high school. They always came and went and yes, I was sad about it, but this … this is something entirely different. I try to pinpoint the exact moment my feelings started to change, but I can't. I had always thought he was attractive, but he felt unreachable. Like a superhero that everyone admired, wanted, but nobody could actually have.

He pulls up to our apartment building and parks his car, opening the door for me before grabbing my hand again and walking me up to my apartment door. We stop at the door hovering, not wanting to end the night, but knowing he has to go.

Looking into those dark eyes, I think I see some of the same emotions warring within myself, but I'm too afraid to ask, so I don't say anything. I just look and he looks back until he leans toward me again and I don't hesitate to meet him in the middle.

This kiss is just as intense as the first one.

It's almost like there are too many emotions trying to reach the surface at once. Both of us desperate to get more. I reach up and wrap my arms around his neck and he pulls me closer as the kiss breaks and he rests his forehead on mine.

I know this is goodbye and I'm not ready for it. Tears fill my eyes and slowly trail down my cheeks.

"Remember …" he has to stop to clear his throat, "remember I'm only a phone call away, we'll talk soon."

I can't respond, so I just nod my head against his and he pulls me close into a hug. I inhale deeply, trying to imprint his scent into my memory. Hints of cedarwood and citrusy bergamot mingle together to form the perfect blend of fruity and woody spice. I used to think the girls in high school who would have their boyfriends spray their cologne on something—a sweatshirt or a stuffed animal so that it smelled like them—were silly. But now that my parents are gone, I realize how certain scents can bring back vivid memories and now I'm one of those silly girls wishing I could spray some of Matiu's cologne on something to bring back memories of this night whenever I need them. He gives me one last squeeze, his muscular arms pulling me tighter against his body before breaking away and walking back down the hall. I watch him disappear into the elevator with one small, final wave as the elevator doors close before I open my apartment door and go inside.

Genevieve looks up from the homework she's doing at the table when I walk in. A worried expression replaces her smile when she sees my tear-stained cheeks. "Violet! What happened? Are you okay?"

"I'm fine," I say as I swipe at my wet cheeks.

"You don't look fine."

"Matiu is going back to Charleston."

Genevieve's eyebrows shoot up. "Matiu?"

Color floods my face and now Genevieve's worried expression has turned to a smirk. "Okay spill."

"I may have feelings for Matiu."

"Okay, you're going to have to back waaaaaay way up for a minute. When did Detective McAllister become Matiu?"

I giggle. "I don't know."

"Well, do you think he has feelings back?"

"He kissed me, so I think so? Maybe? I hope so." Confusion rushes through me. The emotions I'm feeling are so intense it makes me worry that his aren't the same.

Laughter bubbles back up when I see Genevieve's shocked face. "Did you just say he kissed you?"

"Yes?" I say in a questioning tone. "Is that a bad thing?"

"No. Detective McAllister is definitely hot; I'm just not sure how I completely missed this. Wait, how old is he?"

I roll my eyes. There's the rule-following Genevieve I've always known. "Twenty-four. And don't feel too bad. It kinda snuck up on me, too."

Steve peeks his head out of the bedroom. "Did I just hear Genevieve say Detective McAllister is hot?"

We both burst into fits of giggles, and he leaves his room and walks to the table.

"Do I have something I need to be worried about here? I mean, I know he is all tall, dark, and muscly, but I didn't think I had to contend with the detective on our case," he jokes.

"Nope, you don't need to worry about a thing. Ever." She winks at Steve. "Violet and Detective McAllister were just making out in the hallway," Genevieve teases.

"We were not making out," I say, feeling my face get hot again.

"It apparently wasn't a very good make-out session because she came in crying."

I pick up Genevieve's pad of sticky notes and throw them at her. "Shut up Gen. I wasn't crying because of the kiss—that was awesome. I was crying because he's going back to Charleston."

"Wait, hold up. So, you were kissing him in the hallway?" Steve asks. "When did you and Detective McAllister become a thing big enough to make you cry when he leaves?"

"Don't worry babe, I was just as surprised," Genevieve says.

"Both of you are insufferable," I say as I push back from the table and stand up. "I'm going to take a shower."

I leave them both laughing at the table and walk to the bathroom. Taking a nice long shower, I feel much more relaxed. As I'm towel drying my hair, my phone dings and I can't control the giant grin that takes over my face.

I already miss you.

Warmth spreads through my entire body.

Same.

Stay safe, Violet.

My life may be a dumpster fire right now and I'm terrified of everything that is going on, but I can't help but feel elated.

Finally, something to be excited about, something that feels good and happy and right.

Chapter 24

Matiu

The persistent knocking at my door draws me unwillingly from my sleep. My apartment normally brings me comfort, but not this morning. Being in my apartment means I am home in Charleston, not in New York City with Violet. Walking away from her Friday night might have been the hardest thing I have ever had to do—which is saying a lot because I have had to deal with some tough crap in my line of work. Frustration fills me again. I should be in New York in case something else happens, not here in Charleston. The city that I love so much now feels like a prison.

The knocking at the door continues, aggravating me even more. It is 6 a.m., well before I am supposed to be in court, so I know it has to be one of my family members. Looking through my peephole, I see Mum and Miriama.

As soon as I crack the door open Mum bursts through, wrapping her arms around me and giving me a good squeeze. "It's so nice to have you back, my son." She leans back, looking up at me, and pats me on the cheek. "I missed you."

"I wasn't gone that long, Mum."

"Too long for me," she says and pushes past me into my apartment.

Miriama gives me a hug and follows Mum in, who is now looking through my refrigerator.

"Matiu, why is there no food in here?" she scolds.

"Because I got home yesterday and haven't gone to the store yet. Why are you here so early?" I snap. Immediately feeling guilty for snapping.

Mum just raises her eyebrows and walks into the living room, plopping down on the couch, waiting for me to follow. Miriama and I both find a spot to sit down.

"Sorry Mum, I'm just tired. It's nice to be home. I missed you guys, too."

"I have no doubt you missed us, Matiu, but I know you too well. I can tell you don't want to be here. What's going on? Should I be worried?"

"No, nothing to worry about. I'm fine. I just have a case that's frustrating me."

Mum scoots over to my side of the couch and places a hand on my shoulder. "You'll figure it out. You're brilliant, you're just missing some pieces to the puzzle."

Miriama rolls her eyes at the brilliant comment, and I chuckle. "Thanks, Mum."

"Is this case all that is bothering you?" Miriama asks.

I must wait for a moment too long because both of them are now laser focused on me. Trying to decipher anything I do or say.

Mum scrutinizes me for what seems like hours before she says, "Is there a girl back in New York?"

How in the heck did she jump to that conclusion so quickly? "What? No!" Startled, I respond with a knee-jerk reaction, making it obvious I am lying.

The two women who have always been in my life exchange knowing looks before Miriama leans forward in her seat. "Alright, we need details. Who is she? How did you meet her? What does …"

"Okay, that's enough," I interrupt. "I have to get ready for work. Is there a specific reason you two stopped by, or were you just wanting to wake me up and start making up stories?"

They both laugh. The sound brings a smile to my face, even though I am trying to look serious. I'm not ready to talk about Violet yet. I don't even know what is really happening between the two of us.

"We're going out to brekkie and then to the markets and your place was on the way so we thought we'd drop in. Wanted to see if you'd join us," Mum says.

"Breakfast sounds great, but I have to be in court at eight and wanted to stop by the precinct before."

Mum scrutinizes me one more time. "Remember, you may be the big shot detective, but you got your investigation skills from me." She points a finger at me. "I'll figure out who this mystery girl is. One way or another. I know how to use the Facebook."

"Okay Mum." I laugh and shoo both of them out my door. "Have a great breakfast and fun at the market."

They both give me quick hugs on their way out, and I shut the door behind them. The apartment that I have always loved feels empty without their voices filling it. It has never felt empty before and I can't help thinking that the only change in my life is Violet. What are they going to think about her? Will they think less of me if they know I have feelings for someone from one of my cases? Or … Someone who was from one of my cases, I correct myself.

I am not even sure how I feel about it myself. But there is one thing that I know for sure: Violet is the last thing I think about before I fall asleep and the first thing I think about when I wake up.

On top of the intense feelings I am beginning to feel for her, I also feel like Sebastian is a ticking time bomb that I need to figure out before someone gets hurt. Or worse.

I check the time. It is early enough that if I get ready quickly, I can do a bit of digging at work before I go to court. Hopefully, since I am still technically consulting with the FBI, Detective Armstrong won't give me any grief for looking into Sebastian when I should be working on our current cases here.

— • —

After being in the FBI offices in New York, coming back to my precinct feels like coming home. I have never really realized how much I love working at this station in particular. I love Charleston, I enjoy working with all of my colleagues at the CPD, and being close to my family. The only thing missing here is Violet.

"Good to have you back, McAllister," Detective Armstrong says as I pass his desk and sit at mine. "How was your trip?"

"Good. I don't feel like I was finished with what I needed to do there, though."

"I'm sure the case is in excellent hands."

I nod and turn on my computer. In New York I had been looking through the past, trying to find out who Sebastian could be. But now that I am back home, I'm curious how many times the masked man—who I need to prove is Sebastian—has been spotted here. After a bit of digging, I find multiple pictures and references to someone named Sebastian proving that he has made frequent and regular trips to our city.

What is in Charleston that keeps drawing him here?

How are Andrei and Sebastian connected?

And where does Tony fit into all of this?

Chapter 25
Violet

L eaving school early is not a good idea. I know this, but I do it anyway. It's Konnie's birthday, and I just want to make sure it is special. This is her first birthday after our parents' deaths, so I need to make an effort. Genevieve told me she wanted a quiet birthday at home so hers came and went peacefully in October. As the baby of the family and with her birthday so close to Thanksgiving and the start of the holidays, Konnie has always loved lots of attention from us on her birthday. She has never been one for big extravagant parties, but she usually wants to do something fun, insists that we all sing her happy birthday multiple times, and always wants her favorite: Mom's Italian berry mascarpone cake that she made her every year.

I'm not sure how this year is going to go, since she seems to want to avoid Genevieve and me at all costs. And I don't even want to think about Thanksgiving next week; I don't know how to cook a turkey or make any of our favorite dishes. But I want to make sure Konnie gets all her favorite things on her birthday, even if she might accuse me of trying to replace Mom again. I'm worried about how everything will go tonight, but I can't let her birthday pass by without her favorite traditions.

I wished her happy birthday on our way to school today without a response, but I still want to decorate the apartment before she gets home. I stopped at the grocery store to get everything for her favorite dinner—Chicken Cordon Blue—and all the ingredients for the cake. I hope I can make it like Mom did. Maybe we can finally bring a smile back to Konnie's face.

I'm dreading the holidays coming up. Mom always made such a big deal of birthdays and all the other holidays that I'm not sure what I should be doing.

Should I try to recreate what Mom always did? Should I do something new and just keep some of the traditions?

I'm not sure, but I'll worry about that later. Right now—I have an apartment to decorate. I briskly walk the short distance from the small grocery store to our apartment building.

A girl on a mission.

I'm unstoppable, until I get to the front door of the apartment complex.

My hands are full of groceries and decorations from the store, and I have no idea how I'm going to open the doors. Wrapping my left arm and hand around as many of the brown paper bags as possible, I try to open the dang door.

"Here, let me help you with all those bags."

Peeking around the giant load in my arms, I see the neighbor who delivered the flowers. He still has that same big smile on his face that doesn't quite reach his eyes.

A shiver of fear runs through me. I know the FBI wasn't able to talk to him the day our apartment was broken into and he has been so secretive every time I've asked for his name. This time, I don't want him to rush away without learning his name so I plaster on a big smile, hoping he can't see through how fake it is. "Thank you so much! I wasn't sure how I was going to get through the door."

"No problem at all." He gives me another smile as he opens the door with his gloved hand and grabs some bags.

Peeking over my shoulder and across the street I try to find whatever officer is on watch right now. Maybe I can somehow indicate that this is the neighbor they've been wanting to talk to. But I can't see them right away and he's standing there holding the door so I have no choice but to walk through with him following behind me.

We load ourselves into the elevator and head upstairs to my apartment. The elevator ride feels long and filled with uncomfortable silence.

"I still don't know your name." I try to break the uneasiness; at least he can't run away as soon as I ask while we're in the elevator.

"You can call me Andy. And yours?"

"Violet."

More tense silence follows.

"Looks like you're getting ready for a party or something."

"Yeah, nothing big, just dinner, cake, and some decorations for my sister's birthday."

"Sounds great. I'm sure she'll love it."

Thankfully, I'm saved from responding by the elevator opening on my floor. We walk down the hall and I juggle the remaining bags again to pull out my house key and open the door. He follows me into the apartment and we set the groceries on the counter before I turn to look at him.

"Thank you so much!" I smile as we walk back to the door.

"Anytime," he answers.

This close I realize that something about those dark eyes seems familiar, but I can't quite place what.

"Have we met before?" I ask. "I mean ... have we met before we were neighbors?"

He chuckles softly. "I don't think so. I think I'd remember a pretty girl like you."

I feel my cheeks get hot. "Well, thank you again!"

"Like I said before, that's what neighbors are for, right?"

I nod, say goodbye, and shut the door behind him. Something isn't sitting well with me. My stomach churns. Peeking through the peephole, I watch him walk back down the hallway to the elevator. I pull out my phone to text Matiu.

> That same neighbor helped me with my groceries.
> I tried to look for the officer but couldn't see one.

> He said his name is Andy.

His response comes back right away.

> I'll try and contact them now.

> If he is currently in the building they need to get in there quick.

Andy. It doesn't ring any bells and I can't shake how familiar he looks. But I don't have time to obsess about the neighbor right now. I have an apartment to decorate, dinner to prep, and a cake to get in the oven. Genevieve and Steve are supposed to pick Konnie up from school today and stall getting home as long as possible so I can try to have everything done. I need to clear my mind and leave this in Matiu's capable hands.

I pull the chicken out and try to decipher the recipe. It's obvious the recipe has been used countless times; it's stained with various food splotches and has places missing a few letters where it must have gotten drops of some sort of liquid on it. I follow it to the best of my ability, and while it doesn't look exactly like Mom's, it looks better than I thought it would. Feeling proud of myself, I pop the chicken into the refrigerator and start mixing the cake.

Konnie loves Mom's Italian berry mascarpone cake. The batter isn't too hard, but getting it all put together after the cake layers are baked sounds complicated. Placing the cake layers into the oven, I hang streamers and blow up balloons.

When the timer for the cake goes off, I pull it out of the oven, let it cool, and try to recreate Mom's masterpiece. Let's just say I get an A for effort because it looks more like a Pinterest fail. It smells fantastic, though. Standing back, I look at the cake and the decorations and smile to myself. It looks great, even if the cake is leaning a bit to the right. I can't wait for Konnie to see it.

Almost like I willed them into existence, I hear the front door open and Konnie walks in, followed closely by Steve and Genevieve who both have smiles on their faces.

"Surprise!" we all chorus.

We watch in silence as Konnie takes in the room. Her eyes dart from one colorful balloon bouquet to the other, the cheerful streamers, and then land on the cake. Instead of a smile, her face turns stormy. Then she narrows her eyes at me for a second before she stomps to her room and slams the door.

I look at Genevieve. "What should we do?"

"I have no idea, but we better go talk to Konnie."

I sigh and follow Genevieve down the hall while Steve makes a beeline to his room. I kind of wish I could follow him. Opening the door, Genevieve walks into their room. Konnie is laying on her bed with her back toward us. The ever-present headphones covering her ears.

Genevieve and I walk over to her bed and sit down. She ignores us, so Genevieve reaches over and takes the headphones off. "What's going on Konnie?" she asks softly.

We both flinch when Konnie whips around, glaring at both of us, fire in her eyes. "You're a terrible guardian. I wish I could go live somewhere else!" she shrieks at me.

I've come to expect Konnie's anger, I wasn't sure how she would react, but this still hurts. Does she really mean that she would rather not be with us, her only remaining family? "I just wanted you to have all of your favorite things on your birthday."

"You'll never be good enough and you're just wasting your time trying to take on Mom's role in my life. Just leave me alone." Konnie's words sting and I can feel the seemingly constant tears forming.

I don't have a chance to say anything before Genevieve responds angrily. "Konnie, knock it off. We *all* lost Mom and Dad and we're doing the best we can. Turning on each other won't help anything."

Konnie turns those fiery eyes on Genevieve. "You have no idea what it was like for me. I was there. I was there when the men came into the house and Mom told me to run. I heard the gunshots that took them from us. I should have stayed and helped Mom and Dad."

My heart breaks again. Sitting back down on the bed, I reach for Konnie and pull her into a tight hug. "If you would've stayed, there wouldn't have been anything that you could've done and we probably would've lost you, too."

Konnie pushes me away angrily. "You both have no idea what I went through!" she yells.

And Genevieve explodes in anger, jumping up from the bed with her fists clenched. It's so unlike her it takes both of us by surprise and even Konnie's jaw drops open. "Stop acting like you're the only one who had a traumatizing experience, Konnie! Do you think getting chased and tied up by someone you thought was one of your best friends was easy? Do you think stepping over the dead bodies of the people I was just on a ghost tour with was easy? That watching Mark get shot right in front of me was easy?"

Tears are streaming down Genevieve's cheeks now. "Do you think that identifying Mom and Dad's bodies was easy? I can guarantee you it wasn't. I've spent months trying to cope with everything that happened that night."

Konnie is crying now too and I'm not sure which sister I should try to comfort. I take a step toward Genevieve, but she stops me. "How about knowing that it's your fault all this pain was brought into our lives? A person who was my only friend for months, someone who I thought genuinely cared about me, betrayed us. And the worst part is I can't even yell at him. I can't ask him if any of it was real or if it was all an elaborate show because he's dead, too."

Genevieve looks broken, like the shell of the girl she was all those months ago, the sparkle and excitement for life gone from her eyes. Even her posture is more hunched, like she is curling into herself. "You aren't the only one going through a tough time, Konnie," she says in a haunted whisper full of pain and regret.

"Mark inserted himself into your life. None of this is your fault, Gen," I say.

Silent tears continue to rush down her face, but she says nothing, leaving the room she disappears down the hallway toward Steve's room. Wishing I had Matiu here to comfort me, I turn to give Konnie whatever comfort she'll accept.

"I'm not sure what you want from me. Tell me so I can do better," I plead to Konnie.

But instead of answering she snatches her headphones off the bed and puts them back on with a glare in my direction, I try not to burst into tears of my own as I leave the room and shut the door behind me.

Walking back into the kitchen, I see the cake sitting on the counter. Glimpses of past birthdays full of laughter and family flash through my mind. Mom would always go all out on birthdays. We would always wake up to a decorated house, balloons, streamers, banners, the works. She would make our favorite foods for each meal and always bake a beautiful cake. Some of us, like Genevieve and Konnie, would always pick the same flavor every year. Genevieve's favorite was chocolate raspberry and Konnie always wanted the Italian berry mascarpone cake. I would change it up each year, though. Sometimes I would tell Mom to surprise me and every year I would think I found my new favorite flavor, until my next birthday when she would outdo herself again.

My last birthday at home was my eighteenth birthday. Mom went way overboard. Everyone we knew was invited. The dress attire was formal, and I think we went to at least eight different dress shops before she found one she deemed worthy of my birthday dress. It was beautiful. A slim fitting, mermaid silhouette dress in a rich, dark burgundy color. It had long sleeves, but they were made of a sheer light fabric, so it almost felt like they weren't even there.

I remember feeling silly because I felt like a princess as I walked around the store's fitting room, the long dress brushing the floor with each step. But the biggest surprise was when Mom pulled the dress out on my birthday. She had taken it to a seamstress who had added delicate dark purple violets to the bottom of the dress. The pattern of the flowers that Mom named me after was thick at the bottom and tapered off as they climbed up the fabric, leaving the bodice the original burgundy. I had never seen a more breathtaking dress. As Mom helped me zip up the back, I admired it in the full-length mirror in her room.

"I figured it should also represent your name, along with your favorite color," she said, and smiled at me in the mirror.

"I love it, Mom, thank you so much."

"Love it enough to enjoy your 'over-the-top party?'" She said the last part making air quotes with her hands.

"You have to admit, Mom, the party looks more like a wedding than a birthday."

Placing her hands on my shoulders, she gave me a little squeeze, tears forming in her eyes. "My baby girl is turning eighteen and it might be the last big birthday party I get to throw you. You'll be too busy at college to come home for a party this big for a while."

Little did I know that would be my last birthday party that Mom would ever be at, let alone throw for me.

The beautiful dress hurts too much to look at so it's in a box in our storage unit. When we moved from South Carolina we needed to empty the house so it could sell. We donated what we didn't want, but there were too many of our treasured family possessions. We couldn't fit them all into our small New York apartment. Paying the extra for a storage unit isn't the best option, but it is better than the alternative of losing everything we can't fit into our living space. One day when we all have our own homes and families, we'll want those keepsakes.

Pulled from the memory, I'm brought back to the present, my attempt to make a mom-worthy cake sitting in front of me. Picking up the cake, I walk over to the garbage can and dump it in.

Looking down at the bright, happy, pink cake that is now broken, smushed, and coating the bottom of the garbage can, the tears finally come.

Chapter 26

Matiu

The last few weeks have been full of me trying to juggle finding Sebastian, working my current cases, and giving Violet and my family enough time and attention. While digging through all the CPD reports, I made a map marked with all the places Sebastian was either mentioned in a report or one of the pictures of him wearing his mask was taken.

Finding Sebastian dominates my mind.

The neighbor that Violet keeps running into has me on edge as well. After I got her text on Konnie's birthday, I called Agent Sullivan right away. He called the officer outside of the girl's apartment building and the officer searched the area, but there was no sign of the fake neighbor. I'm not sure how he is getting in and out of the building without the officers seeing him.

Apparently, this time his back was toward the officer while he was holding the door open for Violet. Because Violet seemed to know the man and she didn't look concerned the officer didn't think anything of it. Right after the break in, the apartment management had said there wasn't anyone fitting Violet's description of the neighbor living there, but Agent Sullivan double checked and asked about anyone with the name Andy living in the building. The manager said there is no one by the name of Andy registered in any of the apartments.

Is this guy connected to Sebastian? Or is he visiting or living with someone else in the building without management's knowledge?

Violet says he has always been super kind every time she has talked to him. Her description of him and his burns reminds me of my thoughts that Sebastian might be covering burns up with his masks. Both men are also always wearing gloves. *Could the neighbor be Sebastian?* Would he really risk going to the apartment with an officer watching the building? It also doesn't make sense that he would be so adamant about keeping his face covered, but not cover it when he was talking to Violet. There is no way that the neighbor could be Sebastian, right? I am seeing ghosts where there are none.

Nothing makes sense.

There are other cases that Detective Armstrong expects me to be working on though and if I want to keep my job, I better try to focus on some of them. My current case looks like a drug deal gone wrong on Rutledge Ave last week, but of course nobody is talking, afraid that they will get themselves in trouble.

An email comes through with forensic evidence results from the Rutledge Ave case and I grudgingly close all the tabs on my computer and get all the papers related to the Lykaios case put away. Sliding all the papers into a neat pile, I pause when I notice Rutledge Ave on one of the pages.

I pull out my map marked with possible Sebastian occurrences. Rutledge Ave is a long street but when I look closer, I notice that my current drug-deal-gone-wrong case and one of the spots Sebastian frequented are on the same block.

Following a hunch, I look up homicide cases near those spots on my computer and it lights up like a Christmas tree. So many cases frequent these specific areas, many of them looking like drug deals that have turned violent.

This can't be a coincidence.

I request more files from the archives and start digging into the ones I have already. Sebastian is suspected of multiple crimes, including drug and weapons dealing and he was regularly seen in these areas, but never within the time frames that any of these crimes were committed.

It seems like Sebastian may not be who is actually killing these people, but he sure leaves a trail of bodies in his wake.

My phone dings with a text. Hoping it is from Violet, I pull my phone out of my pocket quickly but see a text from Mum.

> Let me guess. The one that's stolen your heart is a fancy FBI agent.

More guilt floods through me. I have never kept anything from my family like this before. Mum has turned it into a game and I get several texts a day trying to guess who the mystery girl is. The fact that she hasn't even guessed that it is someone from a case I was working on makes me even more nervous to tell them.

Nope

Don't you worry. I'll figure it out.

Laughing, I can picture Mum going through every scenario that she can think of until she figures out who Violet is.

When are you going to come say hello to your whānau?

Major holidays don't count as regular visits.

I don't think I have ever gone this long between visits and I miss my family. Thanksgiving went as it normally does—lots of delicious food, family time, and football. However, I was constantly thinking about how Violet and her sisters were handling their first Thanksgiving without their parents.

Work has been busy. I'll visit soon!

Good.

Bring this mystery girl of yours with you.

I roll my eyes. She will never let this drop.

I need to stop by my parent's house soon just to say hi, like I used to, but the last few months have been intense. Trying to keep up with my regular workload and still trying to find information about Sebastian.

And now Violet.

Violet is like a bright light in the darkness. I feel like I didn't even know I was living in the dark until she showed up and gave me what I was missing.

She excites me, looking forward to where this will go, but she also terrifies me. I have never had feelings this strong, this quick for anyone. There has never been anyone that would draw my focus away from my work. Violet is a big distraction. A pleasant distraction, but a distraction all the same. If I am thinking about her, there is no thinking about anything else.

Before I left New York City, I dropped the bullets she found in her bag off to Agent Sullivan and he scrutinized me for a moment before saying thanks and going about his day. Then with Mum realizing I was keeping something from her right away and immediately deciding it was a girl … I must not have as good of a poker face as I thought I did.

We have talked every night since I got back to Charleston. The past few nights, Violet has seemed more stressed than usual, which is baffling because with everything going on, she is always stressed right now. I replay our conversation last night back in my head, looking for any indication of what could be adding to her stress.

"How was school today?" I asked.

Her laugh had a bitter edge to it. "Well, I didn't get kicked out of my group for the New Dances event, so I guess it was okay."

"Are you still in the back?" I asked, wincing after. I probably shouldn't have brought that up.

"Yep, pretty sure that's my new spot for the foreseeable future."

"Give yourself a little grace, Violet. You're juggling a lot right now."

Her long sigh filtered through the phone. "I don't have time to give myself grace. Everything is happening now. I don't have the luxury of waiting until later to figure it out."

As she told me what happened during Konnie's surprise party, I got angry for her. Konnie is not making anything easy for anyone. Reminding myself that Konnie just turned seventeen, she is still just a kid—a kid who has been dealt a pretty crappy hand this last year. I don't even think she realizes she is pushing her sisters away. I think she is so wrapped up in her own pain and anger that she doesn't have the ability to see what she is doing to the only family she has left.

Regardless of her age or her intentions I don't want to make the same mistake and push my family away by avoiding them and the questions I don't want to answer. I am not ready to tell them about Violet, and Mum seems to have made it her life's mission to find out who the mystery girl is.

"Time to head home, McAllister," Armstrong says from his desk. "Any fun plans tonight?"

"Nope, just headed home for a night in."

He nods. "Sounds good. See you tomorrow."

I shut my computer down and pack up my things, shoving the file I have made on Sebastian into my laptop bag.

When I get back to my apartment, my eyes scan the living room, taking in the bare walls and what I thought used to look like a cool bachelor pad. Now it just looks empty to me. I pull everything back out of my laptop bag and go through all that I have for what seems like the millionth time. There is something to all these unsolved cases and the places Sebastian frequents, but I am interrupted by a phone call from Violet.

"Hey. How was your day?" she asks after I answer.

Hearing her voice is the best part of every day. I worry about how this relationship is going to work. I was her detective. She lives in New York and I live in Charleston. There are so many forces against us.

"It was pretty good. How about you?"

"Well, Konnie didn't yell at any of us today, so I guess that's a bonus." I can hear the smile in her voice.

"Yes, definitely a bonus."

"I miss you." Her words hit me right in the gut. I didn't even know that I could miss a person as much as I miss Violet. We have known each other for a while now, but this intense need to be near her is new. Although now that I look back, I can see that it has been slowly building for a while.

"I miss you too." Saying it out loud has my pulse racing. "How are you holding up?"

I listen to her trying to sound positive, but I can tell she is really struggling with school and especially with Konnie. A nineteen-year-old shouldn't have to carry all of this on her shoulders, and she definitely shouldn't have to deal with this impending danger constantly hanging over all of their heads. None of them are safe while Sebastian is still free.

Life isn't fair, I remind myself.

Little brothers shouldn't go missing, parents shouldn't be murdered, bad guys shouldn't be roaming around free.

But they do. And they are. And it is my job to fix some of that.

I have been so worried about what my family will think about Violet, wondering if my feelings for her are unethical and trying to find Sebastian. I'm now realizing it doesn't matter how this relationship will go or how it will end. I am already too far in.

Regardless of how our relationship moves forward, if it ends and Violet is torn away from me, it is going to hurt.

December

Chapter 27
Violet

The bright lights are blinding. Seeing into the audience is near impossible, but it doesn't matter because the rest of the world disappears as I step into the tombé pas de bourée that will take me across the stage in the combination. I glide across the floor and spring into the grand jete before taking my place in the next formation toward the back.

We've rehearsed so much that my nervousness from backstage dissipates as soon as I'm on stage and muscle memory takes over. The music and the movements suck me so deep into their world that I almost forget that I never got my front row spot back. It's just my troupe and the music. My body takes over as I continually count beats to make sure I'm where I'm supposed to be at all times.

As the routine ends, the roar of applause from the audience startles me, pulling me back to the real world from my own little universe—a universe that makes sense and brings me joy. I want to live in that universe; the real world is too depressing for me right now.

Taking my place with the other dancers, we form a line and curtsy. Despite the bright lights, I can see Genevieve beaming up at me from the front row, always one of my biggest fans. A stab of pain hits me as I realize my parents and Konnie should be in that front row with Genevieve. The pain doesn't stay for long as the applause grows deafening when Ms. Yvette steps out and takes her place among us.

Genevieve is on her feet now, applauding wildly. It's so unlike her to draw attention to herself. She must have noticed that I was missing our parents. I watch as she mimics how Mom used to applaud, with so much animation and exaggeration that I can't stop the smile that spreads across my face.

The curtains descend and the heat from the lights disappears. I follow the rest of the girls off the stage.

"That was amazing!" Jocelyn says as she twirls her way down the hallway. Laughing, I follow her into the dressing rooms and change back into my jeans, sweatshirt, and tennis shoes. "Are you going to come out with us tonight?" she asks.

"Not tonight. Genevieve is here. I think we're just going to head home."

"Awwww. Come on! We *have* to celebrate. New Dances is over! No more Ms. Yvette."

I laugh. "That *is* something to celebrate, but I don't want Genevieve going home alone. Let's get together during Winter Recess though!"

Rehearsals for New Dances had taken over all of our lives, so I'm relieved the performance was the first weekend in December—maybe I'll have some extra time these last two weeks of the semester to catch up on homework. My grades aren't good.

"Fine," Jocelyn pouts, but quickly gets animated again as the group gets ready to leave.

Zipping up my bag, I make my way to the lobby, where I find Genevieve waiting for me.

"That was amazing, Violet." She squeals as soon as we find each other.

"Thank you. I wish I got my spot back in the front though."

"I don't care what spot you're dancing in, you always look like an angel on stage."

I look at her with my eyebrows raised and we both burst into laughter as we exit the building and step out onto the street.

I've been living in New York City for over a year now and the streets never cease to amaze me. In a city this big you'd think that the stench would be horrible, but it isn't. It isn't necessarily pleasant, but the unique smell of exhaust, wood smoke, various foods and the almost constant scent of weed mingle together, giving the New York City streets their own distinct aroma.

It's a pleasant night. The bitter cold that accompanied this first week of December has warmed some since this morning, and melted the dusting of snow that coated the streets.

"Do you want to walk home instead of taking the subway?" Genevieve asks.

"Sounds good to me. Let's walk part of the way through Central Park since it isn't dark yet."

She nods. "I'd love to be walking through Cypress Gardens right about now."

"Me too." I know Genevieve misses all the places she frequented in South Carolina.

Genevieve's phone buzzes with a FaceTime call from Livi and she answers.

"How was the performance?" she asks as soon as Genevieve picks up. "You were supposed to FaceTime me, Genevieve!"

"I know! I'm sorry. They didn't allow any recording or anything."

Livi huffs. "Fine. What are you guys doing now?"

"Walking home through Central Park. What about you?" Genevieve asks.

"Did you know Central Park is actually super haunted? I mean, there have been so many murders and stuff it can't not be, right? Did you know the first murder in Central Park was in 1870, the year the park was completed? Some guy was stabbed. What sucks is that the person who stabbed him thought it was someone else," Livi says excitedly.

Genevieve glances over at me, her face paling a little bit, and I poke my head into the view of the camera so Livi can see me. "Don't scare Genevieve. Konnie already has her paranoid that our apartment is haunted. We have enough real-life scary crap to be worried about. You two don't need to be adding ghosts to the list."

"What! Your apartment is haunted? Now I'm even more excited to come visit you guys!" When she sees the worried look on Genevieve's face, she changes tactics. "Not all the ghosts are scary, Gen. What scary crap are you guys dealing with?"

Oh right. I haven't told Livi about anything that has been going on. Apparently, Genevieve hasn't either.

"Liv, it might be a good idea to postpone your trip. It's been kinda crazy here," I say before Genevieve interrupts me.

"Ghosts are always scary Livi," Genevieve says, bringing the subject back to ghosts. For her to voluntarily talk about anything creepy means she must really not want to talk about the flowers, the cards, the pictures … the book.

"No, seriously! The Van Der Voort sisters aren't scary. Janet and Rosetta's dad was like super strict and never let them go anywhere, but they lived right next to Central Park so the one place they were allowed to go was ice skating in the park. After they both died in 1880, people started seeing their ghosts ice skating."

"Still creepy," Genevieve says.

Livi rolls her eyes. "The Dakota is right by the park too! It's supposed to be super haunted. And John Lennon was shot in its archway."

"Okay, change the subject Livi," I intervene before Genevieve gets too creeped out. We were supposed to have an enjoyable walk through the park, not one where Genevieve is checking over her shoulder the whole time.

A chilling breeze ruffles Genevieve's hair and I wrap my coat around me tighter.

"You guys should go check out the Suicide Cave; its real name is Ramble Cave. It's bricked over now, but it used to be where all the teenagers would go to be naughty. Between that and after a bunch of suicides, they bricked it over, but it is supposed to be super haunted."

"Umm, yeah, I think I'll pass on trying to find that cave," Genevieve mumbles.

The sound of shuffling feet behind us makes me tense up. I glance over my shoulder, but there are a lot of people walking in the park. A couple bundled up in their warm coats wander past us as they walk their dog. A man wearing a red scarf wrapped around his neck and face, moves to the side of the path when their dog tries to greet him excitedly. *Get it together, Violet,* I chastise myself. Genevieve shivers next to me. I'm not sure if it's the chill in the breeze or the ghost stories Livi is telling, but I'm glad when Livi says she has to go and disconnects the call.

"How come you cut me off when I started telling Livi to postpone her trip?" I ask. "With all the weird stuff happening, don't you think it might be a good idea for her to wait to visit?"

Genevieve lets a heavy sigh out before responding. "Yeah, it probably would be a good idea. But Vi, I'm struggling. I miss Livi, I miss home, and having Livi here the week between Christmas and New Years is something that I've been looking forward to all year. I really don't want her to cancel her trip. I need this."

"Okay, but don't you think we should at least warn Darla and let them decide?"

Darla, Livi's mom, was one of Mom's closest friends and I know she'd want to know what has been happening anyway, even if Livi wasn't coming to visit.

"How about we warn Livi and let her make the decision?"

I raise my eyebrows. "You know Livi won't tell Darla and come anyway."

"Exactly."

Laughing, I shake my head and link my arm with Genevieve's. We walk in silence, the sounds of traffic floating into the park sound more distant than they actually are. Walking in Central Park almost feels like you are in a terrarium—immersed in nature, yet surrounded by the gigantic buildings on every side. The buildings in New York City feel unreal when you are standing at the bottom. As you look up into the sky, they just keep going. They are majestic in their own way, but the park has a tranquility to it, even with the throngs of people that make their way through the slice of nature each day. We should have spent more time here when the weather was nice.

Taking in the surrounding beauty, I notice that the same man with the red scarf is still behind us. Goosebumps that weren't already there from the cold prickle my flesh and I tighten my hold on Genevieve's arm.

"Are you okay?" she asks.

Peeking over my shoulder again to glance at the man, I whisper, "I think that man might be following us."

Genevieve whips her head around, looking for the man in question. "Why do you think he's following us?"

"He's just been behind us for a while."

"We're on a walking path, Violet. He may just be walking in the same direction. We're probably just creeped out from Livi's ghost stories."

Good point. "Okay, well, let's make some turns and find out. I don't really want him to follow us home."

Genevieve and I wander the pathways, taking random turns and glancing behind us every once in a while. The last couple of turns have taken us into a more isolated part of the park and my heart races when I look behind us and the man is still following. The pink and orange rays of sunlight are quickly lowering below the horizon and dusk is turning into dark.

I don't want to be in Central Park in the dark with this man. And now we're the only people around.

Glancing around us, I try to remember where the closest exit to the park is and tug on Genevieve's arm as I run toward it. She follows without me having to say anything. The bare trees and brown grass rush past us as we sprint toward the closest exit. But in our haste to try and lose the man in our twisting path, we've wandered much farther from any of the exits than I'm comfortable with.

I've never wanted to be surrounded by the crowds of the New York City streets more than I do at this moment.

Heavy footfalls sound behind us as the man picks up his speed. My heart picks up its frantic rhythm. Looking around, I panic as I realize I don't know where we are. The exit I thought we were running to is nowhere in sight and nothing looks familiar.

My tired limbs from my performance find new strength as adrenaline kicks in and I tug at Genevieve to run faster. We dash along the path, trying to get as far ahead of the man as possible, but we're both slowing down, gasping for air as we run. My dance bag feels like I'm carrying a bag full of bricks and I lose steam. A bridge looms off a side path and I pull Genevieve off of our current path, through the trees and grass toward the bridge.

We run through the brush surrounding the bridge and duck underneath. The damp earthy smell under the bridge assaults my senses as we crouch and try to make ourselves as small as possible, sitting on my dance bag to keep some of the cold at bay.

The pounding of the man's boots sound like thunder to my ears as we hold our breath, silently praying that he won't find us.

Minutes feel like hours and time seems to slow down and nearly stop as the man walks back and forth looking for us. The crunching sounds of footsteps walking through the dry leaves and sticks near the bridge has both of us trembling. It's so dark now that we can't see him, which thankfully means he can't see us. The lamplights of the park have turned on, but our area is unlit, which proves that we've wandered much farther off the main walkways than we should have.

He rustles through the brush for a while and it even sounds like he begins to venture under the bridge before we can't hear him anymore. We let out the breath we've been holding and gulp huge breaths of air into our lungs, but I still don't have any idea which direction he went or where he is. For all we know, he could be waiting silently for us to show ourselves.

"Is it safe to leave?" Genevieve whispers.

I have no idea. I'm too afraid to attempt it. Pulling my phone out of my pocket, it lights up and the bright light in the dark reminds me of the blinding lights of the stage. Ironic that not long ago I was feeling so peaceful for the first time in so long, and now I'm once again filled with terror.

Frantically I turn the brightness of my screen and the volume of my phone all the way down and FaceTime Matiu.

It rings and rings, but he doesn't answer.

"Try again, Vi," Genevieve hisses.

Pleading silently for him to answer this time, I press the button and call again.

Chapter 28

Matiu

Violet is trying to FaceTime me again. The first call made me think she had forgotten about the late meeting I was having tonight, but a second call right after has me worried. I excuse myself from the meeting, earning disapproving looks from everyone in the room. Armstrong glares and follows my path to the door with his eyes and Captain raises his eyebrows and folds his arms across his chest, making his irritation very apparent on my way out of the room.

Accepting the FaceTime as soon as I get into the hallway, I hold my breath and my hands tremble as worst-case scenarios flash through my mind. Violet and Genevieve's terrified faces finally fill the screen. The blue glow from Violet's phone screen seems to be their only source of light. Both girls have wide, panicked eyes and Genevieve has tears rolling down her face. It is dark enough on their end that I can't see much past their faces, and even those aren't completely clear.

"What's wrong, Violet? Where are you?" I ask.

I strain to hear Violet's soft whisper. "I can't hear you, Matiu. I turned the volume all the way down, but we need help. We're hiding somewhere in Central Park by a bridge. A man was chasing us."

What! Instant panic fills me as my worries are confirmed and I realize Violet is in danger.

And I am hundreds of miles away from her.

Trying to calm my racing heart, I try to focus on how I can help her. Once again, Violet is calling me when she should have called 911.

Rushing to my computer, I tap the keyboard to wake it up, drumming my fingers impatiently on the desk while I wait for the screen to load. When the lock screen finally pops up, I type in my password and hit the enter button with more force than I mean to. I do a quick search for bridges in Central Park and my stomach drops.

Forty-two.

There are forty-two arches and bridges in Central Park.

I am sure that Violet FaceTimed me so that I can see the surrounding area, but it is so dark on the other end I can't make out anything other than some unidentifiable vegetation that they are crouching in. I send her a text trying to get some more information.

> Do you know what bridge you're under?

I am not very familiar with Central Park, so I might not even recognize a significant landmark if I saw one.

> We aren't sure

> We started walking Bridle Path after we walked down 65th Street from The Peter Jay Sharp Theatre at Lincoln Center.

> We left the path when we were trying to see if the guy was following us.

> After that, we started running and we aren't familiar with this part of the park.

Running my hand through my hair in frustration, I reach for the phone on my desk and dial Agent Sullivan. I have never been so grateful for workaholics when he answers on the second ring, well after business hours.

"Sullivan speaking."

"Hey Sullivan, this is Detective McAllister."

"Hey McAllister. Everything all right? You sound stressed."

"Violet and Genevieve got themselves into some trouble and need help."

"What sort of trouble?"

"Someone was chasing them through Central Park. They're currently hiding under a bridge."

"Do you know what area of Central Park they're in?"

"She said they entered at 65th Street and started walking on Bridle Path but ended up leaving the path when they were trying to see if the man was following them. I'm on a FaceTime call with her right now, but can't see much because of how dark it is."

Sullivan is silent for a moment and I can hear typing on his end. "Can you ask her some questions for me?"

"Of course."

"What was the last street entrance she remembers passing before leaving Bridle Path?"

I text Violet and wait for a response.

"She says that they left Bridle Path when it started curving around the lake and got on another path, but she isn't sure what the name is."

"Okay, ask her what the bridge they're under is made of and whether there is water or a path going underneath it."

My foot taps nervously underneath my desk as I watch those three little dots indicating Violet is typing a response. When her response finally comes through, I release a breath I didn't realize I was holding.

"She says the bridge is made of stone and there is a small creek and a narrow footpath that goes underneath the bridge. I also don't see much light on the FaceTime call, if that helps narrow it down at all."

"I actually think I might know where they are. I'll head to The Glen Span Arch and Bridge and start there."

I sigh in relief. "Thank you."

"No problem, McAllister. I'll head over there and call 911 on the way. We'll talk again after I find the girls and get them home safe. I have a few questions for you." His tone sounds accusatory.

I thank him and hang up the phone. Uneasiness rolls through my stomach. I'm not sure what questions he has, but I am willing to answer any of them as long as he gets to the girls before someone else does.

Sending a text to Violet, I let her know he is on the way and to watch for him. I slam my fist down on my desk, hard. Pain shoots up my arm. I should be in New York helping. Armstrong could have handled this case without me; I shouldn't be here in Charleston. Seeing Violet on the FaceTime call gives me some comfort. I know both girls are okay.

For now.

Violet's head whips to the right, panic taking over her features again. Her brows furrow in concentration, like she is trying to listen to something I can't hear.

"Violet! What's going on?" I shout before remembering that she can't hear me. I pick up my empty Dr. Pepper can from lunch and launch it across the room in frustration.

When beams of light flash across the girls' faces, my body tenses until I can hear the call of "FBI" coming through the FaceTime call. Violet jumps up and must drop her phone in the process. I can hear her yell "over here" before she picks the phone back up and I can see her face again.

I watch as the tension leaves her features, smoothing out the creases of her worry that were evident between her eyebrows and the tightness in her jaw.

"The FBI is here, Matiu," Violet says and looks straight at me for the first time during the call. "Thank you."

"Can you hear me now?"

"Yeah, I just turned the volume back up."

"Are you injured?"

"No, we're shaken up, but neither of us is hurt."

I hear Agent Sullivan's voice in the background and Violet looks away, listening for a minute before she comes back to the call.

"Agent Sullivan has some questions for us. I have to go. I'll call you later."

I don't have time to reply before Violet disconnects the call.

Relief floods through me, but I still feel antsy. I have got to figure out how to get back to New York until I know Violet and her sisters are safe. I help people for a living and feeling completely helpless as I watched Violet and Genevieve hiding in fear is not something I ever want to do again.

Taking a deep breath, I walk back into the meeting. I am not sure how long I was gone. It felt like hours. I quietly take my place next to Armstrong, straighten my pen and notebook, and attempt to listen to what is being said.

"Glad you decided to join us again, McAllister," Captain says.

"I'm sorry, there was an emergency I had to take care of."

Armstrong glances at me with concern lacing his eyes. "Everything okay?" he whispers.

"I think so," I whisper back.

Nothing feels okay.

I try to listen to the information being presented in the meeting, but my thoughts keep going back to Violet. I want to hear her voice. Did they find who was chasing them? She has to be terrified. My knee bounces nonstop, and I can't seem to stop fidgeting with my pen, tapping it on the desk. My restlessness must be getting on Armstrong's nerves because he reaches over and grabs the pen out of my hand.

My phone vibrates and I pull it out of my pocket. I sigh in relief and relax back into my chair, my knee stopping its continuous bouncing when I see the text from Violet.

> **We're both home safe.**

That could have ended so much differently. A smile spreads across my face as I get notifications that Violet, Genevieve, and Konnie have all started sharing their locations with me.

Hopefully, there isn't a next time, but if there is, I will be able to send Agent Sullivan straight to them.

A sharp sting from Armstrong kicking my leg under the table snaps my head back up from my phone. The entire room is looking at me and it is obvious I missed something I should have responded to. I look at Armstrong for help, but he just exhales a disappointed sigh.

"Get it together, McAllister," Armstrong says as he shakes his head.

Mumbling an apology, I put down my phone and try to focus.

Chapter 29

Violet

The icy wind bites at my cheeks as we walk to Konnie's school from the subway stop. Wrapping my coat tighter around my shoulders and trying to bury my face down into my coat to escape the wind, I glance over at Konnie.

"Why do I have to share my location with Detective McAllister?" Konnie asks, giving me a death glare. "And why did you think it was okay to share it with him last night without asking me?"

I can't stop the sigh that escapes my lips. "I already told you, Konnie. If he could've seen our location on Saturday, it would've been a lot easier for them to find us."

Steve and Genevieve were both totally okay when I said our locations always needed to be on and sharing with each other. If Genevieve thought it was weird to share her location with Matiu, she didn't say anything, but Konnie is clearly not thrilled with the idea.

"I'm not sharing my location with a cop. Especially one that I don't even know."

"You do know Matiu."

"No, *you* know Matiu." She rolls her eyes and says Matiu's name in a snotty voice.

"Just leave your location on and sharing with all of us please, Konnie. I really can't handle your attitude today."

"Yeah, well then, maybe you shouldn't."

What is that even supposed to mean? I massage my temples to relieve the headache that is forming. "I'll be here to meet you when school gets out."

With yet another eye roll, she turns and walks toward her high school and I watch until she disappears inside with the rest of the teenagers. I turn and start walking toward Juilliard.

I'm afraid.

I'm afraid for my sisters to go to school.

I'm afraid to walk the short distance to my school.

Fear seems to rule my life now. Sebastian knows where we go to school. He knows our class schedules. The notes and pictures we received prove that. He could be inside the school waiting for Konnie right now. I watch her walk into the school and my chest hurts and my fingers tingle as panic rears its ugly head. The need to keep my sisters safe overwhelms me. How can I keep them safe when I can't see the threat?

The urge to go home floods through me.

Not home to our apartment.

Home to Moncks Corner.

Moncks Corner, where I know every street, and went to school with the same kids from elementary school until we graduated. Where Twirling Dreams Dance Studio is, the dance studio I grew up dancing in—the same studio that threw a party for me and cheered me on when I got accepted into Juilliard. Miss Evelyn, who taught all of us with kindness and patience, overjoyed when we would grow, versus Ms. Yvette, who thrives on our fear and failure. Moncks Corner, where I always felt safe and loved.

Until I didn't.

You don't have a home in Moncks Corner anymore, I remind myself. Our parents are gone. Our grandparents are gone.

All of them are gone. I can't go shopping with Mom, or listen to Dad's corny jokes, or watch Grandma make a fresh batch of cookies. Our support system dissolved one member at a time until there was no one left.

But that's not true. We have a community of people who have loved and cared for us our entire lives, I remind myself. We have Darla and Livi. We have Matiu.

Moving home is sounding like a brilliant plan until I remember why the house hasn't sold.

Could we really live in a house where our parents were murdered?

A shiver runs through me at the thought, but then memories of my family at our house flood me. Our nightly family dinners where we could vent or laugh or cry in a safe space. The weekly movie nights with popcorn and candy and Dad's running commentary about the movie the whole time. Playing games before Thanksgiving dinner. Wearing our new ugly Christmas sweaters we all picked out for each other every Christmas Eve. Our house was always full of love and laughter.

Can one horrible night overshadow all the love we felt there?

Thoughts of going home consume my mind. *Would we be able to get past the tragedy?* Genevieve needs to go to school to reach her dreams of being an architect, but that doesn't have to be in New York. Juilliard is exactly where I need to be if I want to be a professional ballerina. But my dreams of being on stage performing every weekend don't seem as bright as they used to be. I still love dancing, and when I'm performing the rest of the world disappears, but it also feels a little bit like a chore now.

It would probably be frowned upon to pull Konnie out of school, and I'm sure Konnie would throw a fit, but maybe I should look into online schools just in case. Maybe the best thing I can do for my sisters is take them back home to Moncks Corner.

Noticing the time, I rush the last of my walk to class and slide into my desk just in time for Dance History to start.

"Are you ready for the test today?" Jocelyn leans toward me to ask.

"Oh crap! I totally forgot about it."

Jocelyn frowns in worry as I pull my phone out of my bag and text Genevieve.

> I forgot I have a test today. Can you guys pick Konnie up?

Sure.

Who is going to walk home with you tho?

Oh right.

> Should we all meet for dinner after?

Sounds good. Have a good day at school, sis!

I'm not sure how much more of this I can handle. I was already struggling to keep up with life before we knew we were still in danger. Now I feel like I'm drowning in fear and uncertainty, but the need to keep my sisters happy and safe pushes me forward.

As if the universe wants to add a cherry on top of my emotional upheaval, a graded assignment gets placed on my desk. The bright red D- glares up at me.

Red is definitely not my favorite color anymore.

I groan and lay my head on my desk. Why can't I catch a break?

Chapter 30

Matiu

Papers and pictures from the Lykaios case litter my desk at home, and I have way too many tabs open on my computer. Armstrong saw me working on the case a few days ago and told me I would be written up if he caught me looking into it at work again.

I can hear his gruff voice still. "What you do with your time when you're with the feds is up to them, but while you're here on my time you'll be working on the cases I tell you to. Understand?"

My eyes grow heavy. Now that I can't look into Sebastian at the precinct anymore, it has to wait until I get home. Working all day and then coming home to dig into Sebastian until the early morning hours is taking its toll. I should get some sleep. I have to get up for work in just a few short hours, but I can't stop.

Staring at the mess of information, I wait for an aha moment, but it doesn't come. The pictures of the Sebastian listed on the Russian death certificate taunt me. *Could this be the current Sebastian? Did he somehow fake his own death?*

From what I can tell, Andrei, the other brother, was never located and there aren't many pictures of him.

How is Sebastian connected to these two brothers?

We know that Mark called him his uncle, but who is he really?

So far, the only thing tying the brothers to Sebastian is Irina. Sebastian has to be connected through Irina. But how?

There are no records of any other siblings; all the extended family is accounted for. Maybe he isn't related to the brothers. Maybe Irina is the missing link. Could Sebastian actually be Mark's father, assuming Irina's dead brother's identity? That would make more sense why she sent Mark to live with him and explain how similar Mark and Sebastian's eyes are.

Sending an email off to Agent Sullivan suggesting to look into Irina's history, I switch gears and go back to looking at all the dates that coincide with Sebastian being in town and suspected weapons deals.

I stop breathing.

My whole body fills with heat as July 21, 2009—the date that changed my life forever catches my eye.

The day Nikau went missing.

I click on the file and read the words like they are oxygen and I have run out of air. Sebastian has slipped away so many times when he should have been caught. He is one slippery snake of a man. This particular weapons deal, there was a team ready and waiting. They knew the time and the place, but apparently the location changed last minute, and when the team arrived, no one was there. It is unknown if the deal happened somewhere else or if it didn't happen at all.

A file of surveillance pictures associated with the missed weapons deal is scattered in with all the other information. I open it and click on the file labeled July 21, 2009. Pictures fill my screen, several of Sebastian wearing one of his masks catch my attention—pictures taken just a few blocks from where I raced away from him on my bike.

A dash of color catches my eye in one of the photos and I stop scrolling to zoom in. Dread fills every fiber in my body as I realize what I am seeing.

Propped up against one of the walls behind Sebastian is Nikau's bike. The bike that we never found.

The bike that went missing with my innocent little brother.

Why is his bike there? I scour the image for any sign of Nikau, but he isn't there, only his bike leaving behind a whisper that he had been.

Sometimes Nikau would take detours down alleyways if there were big puddles to race his bike through, always trying to make a bigger wave of water spray each time he rushed through them. The thunderstorm the night before had left massive puddles of water. He had wanted to go down several alleys on our way to get ice cream, but I was too eager to get to the store. What if without me there to keep him from stopping, he rode down one of the alleyways with enticing puddles and stumbled upon Sebastian? What if he saw something he wasn't supposed to? From what I have come across so far, Sebastian would let no one, adult or child, who had witnessed something they shouldn't have leave with that information.

Especially if they had seen his face.

What did Nikau see?

Fumbling for my phone, I call Armstrong.

"I think Sebastian is linked to Nikau's disappearance," I practically yell into the phone as soon as he answers.

"What are you talking about?" Armstrong's groggy voice comes through from the other end and I realize it is way too late to be calling him.

"I found a picture of Sebastian with Nikau's bicycle in the background during one of his suspected weapons deals."

Thinking Detective Armstrong would be as excited as I am to find a clue to the case that has haunted us for years, I am surprised when his tone turns icy. "Leave the past in the past, McAllister. Why are you still poking around in the Lykaios case at all?"

Solving cold case files is part of our job. What is this 'leave the past in the past crap'?

"I thought you'd be glad to have any kind of lead in Nikau's case. How did you miss this during the initial investigation?"

"Nikau is gone, kid. Move on. And the Lykaios case is out of our hands now. Let the feds do their jobs and you stick to doing yours. I already warned you what would happen if you kept digging into Sebastian," Armstrong says curtly and hangs up the phone.

Anger curls its ugly fingers through my body. I could listen and do what Armstrong told me to. I know Sullivan and Delgado are excellent agents. I have no doubt they will catch Sebastian.

Eventually.

But eventually is not soon enough and there is no way I am going to let them take Sebastian down without me. No matter how many times Armstrong threatens me; I will be the one who puts this monster behind bars. For Violet. For Nikau.

New determination fills me.

Sebastian is behind Tony and Charlotte's murders and he continues to torment the Clark girls now, making Violet live in fear every day. I can't prove it yet, but my gut tells me I am not wrong.

And now, with a sick twist of fate, I have evidence that Sebastian may be connected to Nikau's disappearance.

Sebastian will not tear apart another family like he did ripping Nikau from my family or making Violet and her sisters orphans.

I will find him.

And I will make him pay for what he has done.

Chapter 31

Violet

Matiu's angry voice on the other end of the line echoes through the kitchen. I take him off speaker phone, but he is loud enough that I'm turning down the volume again as Genevieve and Steve give me questioning looks. Walking into my small room, I shut the door behind me and sit down on my bed.

"He told me to leave the past alone. We haven't had any sort of lead on Nikau's disappearance and as soon as I get one, he tells me to leave it alone! I just don't understand."

The anger in his voice can't mask the pain underneath. "Maybe he just doesn't want you to get your hopes up. It's a case that I'm sure has been weighing on him, too," I say.

"Yeah maybe. Violet, I really think Sebastian is behind Nikau's kidnapping."

Matiu told me his brother's kidnapping was what made him want to be a detective during our dinner before he went back to Charleston, but he never told me the entire story. The sadness lacing his voice makes me wonder if he needs to talk about it.

"Do you want to tell me what happened?"

"I left him," he whispers. The pain in his voice makes me ache for him.

Matiu pauses long enough that I wonder if the call disconnected. Looking at my phone to make sure, I wait until he is ready to continue.

I listen to him recount the day in vivid detail. So much so that I can taste the ice cream. I can feel the sticky heat of summer, clothes damp with sweat sticking to my skin. I can see a young Matiu riding away from his little brother, and it brings tears to my eyes.

"Oh Matiu, you were so young. You can't blame yourself for his disappearance."

"But I *do* blame myself. Nikau never came home and the last thing I did was laugh at him when he asked me to wait."

Blinking back tears, my heart aches for Matiu. What a heavy burden to carry on his shoulders for so long. I'm no stranger to regret. Every day I wish I would've taken Genevieve's worries more seriously. Dad probably would've been in prison, but at least he would be alive. And Mom …

Matiu's voice pulls me from my own regrets. "That is when Detective Armstrong came into our lives. He's always been able to do no wrong in my eyes. I watched him search for Nikau and then he took me under his wing and I got to watch him solve so many cases, bring so many families the closure they needed." His voice catches and he clears his throat. "I wanted to help him solve the mysteries that came across his desk and I guess I have always assumed that we would eventually give my own family closure by solving Nikau's case together. I don't understand why he doesn't want to follow the lead as much as I do."

"I'm so sorry Matiu." I scramble for something to say that might ease his pain, but I don't know how to help. Listening to the silence on the other line, I bite at my bottom lip and pick at a stray thread on my comforter, trying to come up with the right thing to comfort him. Maybe what he needs most is to just get it out. Tell someone about the guilt he has been carrying. Maybe all he needs from me is for me to truly hear him. Let him feel the pain he keeps buried.

Matiu breaks the silence. "We prayed for so long that Nikau would be found, that he would come home and we could be a complete family again."

As horrible as the situation my sisters and I are in, I think it is probably easier knowing what happened to our parents instead of always wondering and never knowing.

"I don't think I can ever forgive myself for leaving him behind that day," he whispers.

"It's a horrible situation, Matiu, but you can't blame yourself for something you had no control over."

He laughs bitterly. "I didn't have control over whoever took him, but I shouldn't have left him."

"If you had stayed, whoever took Nikau might have taken both of you and your family would've lost two sons."

"If they were going to take someone, I wish they'd taken me." And there it is. What lies beneath all Matiu's guilt. My breath catches. I wish that Matiu's family didn't have to go through that horrible experience, but I will forever be grateful that Matiu is still here.

As soon as I think it, I feel the shame creep in. One child getting kidnapped over another doesn't make the situation any less horrible. I wish this world wasn't full of heartache and people hurting other people.

But it is.

As much as we want to, we can't control what other people do. There are monsters in this world and it is the good people like Matiu who are willing to fight those monsters that gives me hope.

Matiu sighs heavily. I can picture him running his hand through his hair. Something I've noticed that he does when he isn't sure what to do next. "If I was there, maybe Nikau could have gotten away."

I don't know what to say to help Matiu. I don't think there is anything I can say. "Do you really think Sebastian is behind Nikau's kidnapping?"

"My gut is telling me that my poor little brother was in the wrong place at the wrong time and saw something he shouldn't have. And yes, I definitely think Sebastian is connected."

"I hate him." The venom in my voice surprises me.

"Me too Violet." His voice fills with determination. "I'm going to find him."

"I know you will."

I wish I could give him a hug, actually be there for him instead of miles away. An overwhelming need to see Matiu consumes me and I touch the Face-Time button on the screen to switch to a video call. He answers and judging by the messy look of his hair I can tell I was right—he's been running his fingers through it. His hair is the longest I've ever seen it. It makes him look younger, more laid back, less intimidating. I just stare at him for a minute without saying anything, and he stares right back. His muscular frame and usual military style haircut make him look intimidating, but anyone who has ever looked into these eyes would be able to tell that intimidating or not, Matiu is kind. He is kind and compassionate and genuinely wants the best for people. His dark eyes look pained, but I watch as he switches over to worrying about me. Taking an assessment of how he thinks I'm doing, even amidst his own turmoil.

The anger leaves my voice. "I miss you."

"I miss you too." I can't stop the small smile that spreads on my face as I watch him drag his fingers back through his hair again. "But I'm not sure how to handle our relationship, Violet."

My smile vanishes. "What do you mean?" *Are we in an actual relationship?* I've been trying to figure that out myself. Besides worrying about my sisters' safety, Matiu dominates my thoughts. I'm not quite ready to tell him that though.

He sighs. "I don't know what we are, but I know that wherever you are is where I want to be."

My heart skips a beat before speeding up. I feel the same way, but I can tell that wasn't the end of his train of thought. "So then, what's the problem?"

"I'm the detective on your case, and it's probably unethical for me to be in a relationship with you."

"Are you worried I have Stockholm Syndrome?" I laugh.

He chuckles. "No Violet, I didn't kidnap you. I'm not worried about Stockholm Syndrome. That would be more like White Knight Syndrome."

"Don't let your head get too big; maybe you have the Nightingale Effect."

"So, you've looked it up. See, I'm not the only one worried here."

Crap. Totally walked myself right into that one. Yes, I may have Googled if it was a common occurrence. White Knight Syndrome can be found in two different scenarios, someone who feels like they have to rescue broken people or where someone falls in love with their rescuer. Technically that could apply to both of us, but the Nightingale Effect is when a caretaker thinks they have feelings for the person they're trying to help or take care of. But from everything I read, when it does happen, it's usually short-lived. This doesn't feel like fleeting emotions to me, but I'm still not sure how Matiu actually feels.

My fingers tremble as nerves take over, and I look away from the phone. "This doesn't feel fake to me, Matiu."

I've been so nervous to say anything about my feelings, but I don't want to brush them away and add more to my long list of regrets if I say nothing.

Biting my lip, I make eye contact and once again wish I could reach out and touch him. Feel his warmth, remind myself that this is real whether it should be or not. Remembering the jolt of electricity that seemed to course through my whole body when our fingers touched, lacing together the night before he left, I know that regardless of how he feels, this is extremely real for me.

"I'm not sure exactly where your feelings are, but you aren't our detective anymore, and although that might be how we met, that doesn't have to be what keeps us connected," I say, trying to sound confident.

"It doesn't feel fake to me either, but we live hundreds of miles apart and even though I'm not your detective anymore, I'm still sometimes consulting on the case."

"So, stop consulting. Let Agents Sullivan and Delgado handle it," I snap in frustration.

Anger flashes in his eyes. "How can you ask me to do that especially now that I know he might have something to do with Nikau's kidnapping? I will never stop searching for Sebastian and I can't believe you would want me to."

Do I want that? I don't know exactly what I want, but I know I want to see where this relationship will take us. The question is, if it does come to choosing between a relationship with me and being able to stay on the case, which one would he choose?

I'm not sure I want to know the answer, but I do know that I can't ask him to stop searching for answers about Nikau.

"I do feel safer knowing you're trying to find Sebastian. We don't have to put labels on anything right now. I just wish you were here."

He's quiet for a minute before responding. "I wish I was there, too."

A roller coaster of emotions floods through me—excitement, fear, longing, and maybe even love. Love seems like too big of a word right now, but I know I feel every emotion I have more strongly toward Matiu than I've felt for anyone else. Just hearing his voice can bring a smile to my face, but does he want to be here for me or for the case?

After we say goodbye and disconnect the call, I can't stop thinking about what to do. Should I be worried that these feelings aren't real? They feel very real to me. My whole body craves being next to Matiu, like a physical ache now that he's not here.

Genevieve knocks quietly on the door before poking her head in. "I'm sorry Vi, I came to talk to you and overheard the last bit of your conversation."

I groan and pat the bed next to me. Genevieve sits down and wraps her arm around me. "Are you doing okay? Everything good with you and Detective McAllister?"

"Ugh, don't call him that." I put my hands over my face and fall backward onto my bed. "I've never had feelings this strongly for someone before. But he brings up some valid points."

"Like what?"

"Like what if the feelings aren't real? What if I just see him as my knight in shining armor?"

Genevieve lies back on the bed next to me and turns her head to look at me, waiting until I turn to look at her as well. Her dark green eyes seem so serious tonight.

She plucks at a stray piece of hair that has fallen onto my face and tucks it gently behind my ear. "Your feelings seem real to me, Vi, and yes, maybe you see him as your knight in shining armor, but maybe you see him like that because he is your knight in shining armor."

She lets that thought sit for a minute before she says. "I think it's okay for him to take that role in your life *and* for you to have feelings for him."

She gives my hand a squeeze before she gets up and leaves my room, quietly shutting the door behind her.

Tears trail down my cheeks, dropping onto my comforter. Regardless of how I feel, if Matiu decides that this isn't something he is okay with, I might end up with my heart breaking more than it already has.

Chapter 32

Matiu

Detective Armstrong might have told me to leave the past in the past, and now Violet might want me to remove myself from the Lykaios case, but I can't. Armstrong has been keeping a close eye on me at work, regularly reminding me that if I mess up, it will tarnish his record as well because he vouched for me and he is training me.

But he can't stop me from looking when I am at home.

My apartment with the bare walls now has one section of wall completely covered in case file photos from Nikau's case, another with photos from the current Lykaios case plastering its empty space and a map of Charleston in the middle—a push pin for every suspected Sebastian sighting from 2009 until now littering the map.

Files and note cards with notes jotted down on them during my late nights cover the couch, and now there's no room to sit. It doesn't really matter though since I am usually up pacing around the room anyway. A half-eaten pizza still sits in its box on the coffee table. I really hope Mum and Miriama don't stop by unannounced anytime soon. This would worry them.

After I made the connection between Sebastian and Nikau, I pulled all the files and security footage from Nikau's case. I have been digging through all the original information of the case every night after work. Sticking pictures on the wall or placing pins on the map. Looking for anything that could have been missed. It seems like a pretty tight investigation, minus the whole Nikau's bike leaning up against the wall behind Sebastian thing. It looks like Armstrong investigated every lead thoroughly, but hit dead ends on each one. *So how did that slip past him unnoticed?*

Something doesn't feel right.

I know I should be trying to find out where Sebastian is now, but I am currently going back through all the security footage saved from the day Nikau was taken. The quality of the video now is so much better. It is a miracle that they could catch anyone with the camera footage used back then.

There is a video caught on a security camera where a man with dark hair forcefully takes my little brother and his bike. He turns down an alleyway and they disappear. I have watched the footage over and over again since I got it, trying to find a better-quality image of Nikau's kidnapper. A familiar rock settles in my stomach even though I have watched the video countless times. His dark hair proves that Sebastian wasn't the actual person who took Nikau, but I have to identify the man if I am going to have any chance of linking Sebastian to the kidnapping.

The facial features of the monster who took Nikau are so pixelated it could be anyone and there isn't any footage of where he took Nikau after he pulls him into the alley. The man who took him, however, had interesting fashion choices with what looks like a snakeskin patterned shirt and orange pants. Yuck. That outfit definitely wouldn't have blended into a crowd.

I run my hand through my hair and then down my face. I need some caffeine.

I walk to the fridge and grab a Dr. Pepper, chugging half of it down on my way back to the laptop. I push some papers and files aside to sit down on the couch, pulling my laptop from the coffee table onto my lap and taking another swig of the cold soda.

Watching the footage again isn't going to do me any good, so I scroll back through the higher quality pictures that were taken during surveillance. Someone got a lot of good photos while they were getting ready to bust the weapons deal that was supposed to be happening that day including the picture with Nikau's bike in the background, maybe there is something else in there.

My breath hitches as one of the men in the pictures catches my attention.

Not wanting to get my hopes up quite yet, I zoom in on the photo. Holding my breath, I pull the grainy video footage of the man who took Nikau back up and take a screenshot.

Pulling up both the screenshot and the image from the weapons deal surveillance on my screen, I stare at the two images in shock.

Even with the poor quality, it is obvious that the man in the video footage is wearing the exact same horrible tacky outfit as the man in the crystal-clear surveillance photo.

I scroll faster through the pictures, watching for those awful orange pants to see if there is one where I can see Nikau's kidnapper's face.

Until one catches my attention.

I can hardly believe what I am seeing. My hand shakes and my heart races as I zoom in on the image.

I finally have a face to the man that took my brother, and he is standing right next to a masked Sebastian.

Sebastian's face is partially covered as usual, but the face of the man in the hideous outfit is uncovered and crystal clear. I don't recognize him, dark hair that falls down onto his forehead, green eyes that remind me of a snake—fitting right in with his choice of wardrobe. The acne-scarred face has a smirk on it showing a chipped front tooth. He looks like he found whatever Sebastian just told him amusing.

I stare long and hard at the face of the man who tore my family apart, burning the image into my mind. I don't know who this man is, but now I have a face to look for.

And I just found proof that Sebastian is connected to Nikau's kidnapper.

I grab my keys off the coffee table next to me and hold Nikau's dinosaur in my hand. Searching for Nikau has always been one of my driving forces and ever since Violet came into my life searching for Sebastian has become one as well. Now the two paths have converged leading me toward keeping my vow to Violet and my vow to find out what happened to my little brother. Both paths lead to Sebastian.

There is nowhere he can hide that I won't find him.

If it takes me until the day I die to catch him, so be it.

Chapter 33

Violet

The blood red index cards Konnie and I received today sit on the counter and leer up at me.

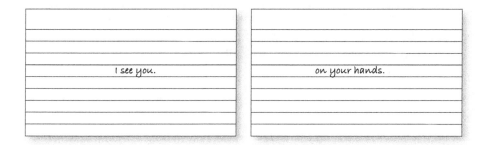

I see you.

on your hands.

Written in bold, black ink.

These don't make any sense. Steve and Genevieve are on their way home with their cards, maybe when we put them all together it will. All four of us got the sinister red index cards at school today.

Again.

The tiny fingers of fear claw their way through my body and I shudder, rubbing at the raised flesh on my arms.

This time, the notes were found when all of us were in different classes at our various locations—the high school, the City College of New York, and Juilliard. Different classes, different buildings even, than where the previous disturbing red cards were slipped into our bags. It's like Sebastian is trying to prove he knows where we are at all times.

That he is watching us wherever we go.

No place is safe, no *one* is safe.

We have nowhere to hide.

Message received loud and clear. *But why?*

Why is he watching us? Why does he care what a bunch of emotionally beaten and broken teens are doing and where they are going? And what exactly is his end game here? Is he just trying to scare us? Or is this a warning of more to come?

My eyes are fixed on the cards, like if I stare long enough they will reveal all their secrets.

But of course, they don't.

How can we hide from someone who vanishes like they never existed every time law enforcement thinks they have found another lead?

Ghosts from my past mingle with the ghosts of my present, making my grip on reality feel like it is slipping away. Just out of reach—my fingertips barely brushing the answer before it disappears all together.

Dread settles heavy in my stomach. The need to look over my shoulder is now constant, as my paranoia that Sebastian is watching us has once again been proven a legitimate concern.

Why can't we just live in peace? Haven't we been through enough already?

I inhale a shaky breath and pick up my phone to call Matiu. Regardless of the unknown status of our relationship I really need his comfort right now.

He answers after the first ring, but his hello is filled with barely controlled rage and I can tell something has happened. "What's wrong?" I ask.

"I found actual proof Sebastian is connected to Nikau's kidnapping, but when I told Armstrong about it, he wrote me up for disobeying orders."

"What? Really?"

"Yes. I don't understand why he doesn't want to finally close Nikau's case," Matiu rants. "I didn't even get a chance to send the information to Agent Sullivan. I should have right away, but now Armstrong has revoked all access to any files in the network unless it's on my computer at work. And I had to turn in all physical files; I'm not allowed to take any home."

Suspicion blossoms in my subconscious. Why wouldn't he want Matiu looking into his brother's case? Maybe he just doesn't want Matiu to get sucked into a case he feels is unsolvable?

"That does seem weird. I kinda get why he doesn't want you looking into Sebastian anymore, but anything to do with Nikau is still his case, right?"

"Yep. I finally put a face to Nikau's kidnapper and I get in trouble for it." He lets out a harsh laugh. "Go figure, right?"

We're both silent for a few seconds before Matiu speaks again, his voice still angry but losing a little bit of its edge. "Sorry, I'm in such a bad mood. How are you? Were you calling for a specific reason?"

This is definitely not the put-together detective I'm used to talking to, and it sure isn't the sweet man whose voice I crave. This is a side of Matiu I haven't seen before. He sounds angry and broken and I can't give him anymore stress right now. There's no way I can tell him we got more notes today. I'll call Agent Sullivan and let him know instead.

They aren't anything new.

Same sinister red cards, same creepy message.

This can wait to tell Matiu.

I try to force the uneasiness out of my voice and sound supportive. "Nope, just wanted to see how your day was going. I'm so sorry it hasn't been a good one."

I wish I could help Matiu. I long for the chance to hold him tight and let him know he isn't alone. I'm here and I want to help.

But I'm not sure if he would even want that. I'm afraid to bring up our last conversation. I don't want him to tell me that he doesn't want to pursue our relationship.

That he doesn't want me.

So, I don't bring it up and neither does he. We end the call with tense good-byes weighing heavy with words unspoken by both of us.

The red cards on the counter catch my attention again and I can't help but wonder if it's too late. Too late for a relationship with Matiu, too late for a normal life—it's definitely too late to bring my parents back.

The rain pelting angrily against the living room window draws my eyes away from the cards. I watch from the kitchen as the storm brewing outside ramps up its vengeance. The rain turns to sleet and the noise, as it batters the window above the couch, covers up all the other noises in the apartment. The Christmas tree's lights reflect in the window, the sparkling colors reminding me that this Christmas, only a few days away, will be a tough one for all of us. The tree next to the couch is the only indication in the apartment that we've come into the holiday season.

The storm's intensity continues to grow, and the apartment is drenched in darkness as the power goes out. Grabbing my phone, I switch on its flashlight, catching the vivid red cards on the counter in the beam of light.

Konnie comes out of her room guiding herself with her cell phone's light.

"The power is out," I say as she comes and stands next to me.

"No, really? Thank you, Captain Obvious."

I don't even justify her snarky comment with a response. Both of us study the cards that seem to glow an even brighter red with only the light from our phones.

The silence of the apartment is shattered as the apartment door crashes open with a bang, shaking the walls and knocking my umbrella over onto the ground. Screams rip from our throats as the umbrella rolls into the kitchen where we're standing, its red color bright in the dim light.

Genevieve makes it through the door first with Steve following close behind. "Sorry guys. I didn't mean to scare you."

Breathing a sigh of relief, I pick up my umbrella and lean it back up in its spot next to the door. I hate the color red. It may have once been my favorite color, but next week I'm donating anything I own that is red to Goodwill.

"Let me see your cards," I say. "Do they say anything different than the last time?"

"Yeah, they don't make sense though."

Genevieve places her card on the counter with ours.

This won't end until yours is on mine.

We didn't get pictures this time, just the cards. My gut twists. I'm not sure I want to know what this new message is.

"What does yours say Steve?" I ask.

He pulls his card out of his backpack and adds it to the counter with the others.

You all have blood

"See they don't make sense," Genevieve says looking over my shoulder at the cards on the counter.

"Some of these don't have punctuation. I'm pretty sure we have to put them together for it to make sense."

Moving the cards around until they make a sentence my hand hovers above the counter when I realize what it says. I can't breathe, icy fear shivers through my body.

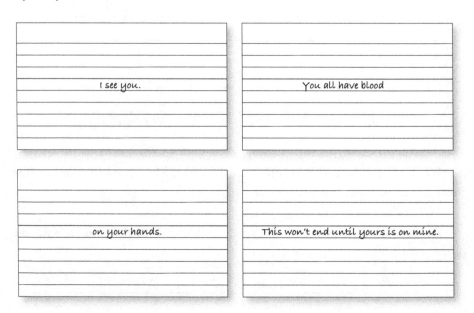

I hear Genevieve's sharp inhale as she reads the message. I don't wait for anyone to say anything, ripping a gallon Ziploc bag from the pantry and sliding the cards into it I head for the door. Grabbing my coat, I slide it on before opening the door into the dark hallway outside our apartment.

"Where are you going?" Genevieve calls after me.

"I'm taking these cards to Agent Sullivan and getting us some protection. You three stay here and lock the door. Don't answer it for anyone."

Ignoring Genevieve's protests, I listen for the lock behind me and head toward the stairs. Emergency lights give a faint glow where the exit is, but I use my phone's light to navigate my way down the stairwell.

Bursting out of the apartment building into the storm I bury my face down into my coat, trying to avoid the sleet hammering down from the sky. Picking up my pace I jog to the nearest subway station where a subway employee tells me that the subway isn't running due to the power outage, but suggests a different station that runs off of a different power grid. It's only a few blocks away.

I rush toward the station, jumping at every shadow and noise. I don't slow down or give myself time to catch my breath until I'm sitting down in the subway car, racing toward the closest stop to the FBI offices. Hoping and praying that they still have power and Agent Sullivan hasn't left yet. I should have called first.

As the train screeches to a halt and I squeeze out of the claustrophobic metal tube with the crowd of people, I push through the arms and body odor until I reach the sidewalk up above. As soon as I'm free from the confinement of bodies, I sprint toward the building Agent Sullivan works in, thankful when I see lights shining brightly through all the windows.

Brushing the wet blobs of sleet off my coat I walk toward the front desk and tell the lady behind it that I need to speak to Agent Sullivan. She gives me an irritated look before calling Agent Sullivan and telling him I'm in the lobby.

I wait impatiently pacing back and forth until he finally appears. "Miss Clark. What can I help you with?"

Shoving the Ziploc bag carrying the disturbing message into his hands I say. "We got these today. We need protection; the cop outside our building isn't enough."

He peeks at the contents of the bag before gesturing for me to follow him. We take the elevator up to the third floor and he leads me into his office. Sitting down in one of the chairs across from his desk my knee bounces uncontrollably as he studies the cards in the bag.

"Do you see what it says?" I ask. "He's pretty much telling us that he's out for blood. We aren't safe."

"I agree. Let me show this to my supervisor, I'll be right back."

Agent Sullivan stands and walks out of his office. Unable to sit still I stand and peek out the door, watching him go into an office a couple of doors down the hallway. I have to know what they're saying so I quietly step out of the room and tiptoe toward the door he disappeared through. I slowly inch down the hall until I'm close enough to hear what is being said, holding my breath to keep from making any noise.

"Sir, these girls aren't safe, we need to move them. Put a detail on each of them at the very least."

"Sullivan that would be four agents and officers around the clock, we already have one officer monitoring the apartment building. You have no concrete proof that these notes are even from the same man. A man you have yet to successfully identify. People get threatening notes all the time, we can't send protective details every time that happens. I'm not approving this; you'll have to wait it out or bring me more evidence."

I scurry back as Sullivan leaves the office in a rush of anger before spotting me in the hall. I follow his angry steps back into his office.

He sits down in his chair hard before speaking. "I'm sorry. Maybe I can get installing one of our cameras in your hallway approved."

I glare across the desk at him. "How am I supposed to keep my sisters safe if you can't even do it?"

He stares back at me for a moment, his gaze filled with guilt. I stand up and stalk out of his office before he responds.

I rush out of the building heading back toward the operating subway station, anger and frustration surge through my body, making my temperature rise. The ice-cold sleet that is still coming down almost feels good as it hits my hot face. When I reach the station and descend the steps, I'm confronted with a large crowd of people waiting. Due to some of the other stations being closed from the power outage this one is now backed up and it's apparent that I'm going to have to wait a while. I take my place in line and needing something to do, I pull out my phone and click on Matiu's contact, but remembering how angry and upset he was earlier I change my mind and call Livi. She answers on the second ring.

"Hey Vi, I've been needing to ask you what all I should pack. Am I going to need anything dressier?"

I know Genevieve will be upset with what I'm about to do. She needs to see her best friend, but I can't add trying to keep Livi safe to my already never-ending to do list.

"I'm so sorry Livi, but you're going to have to postpone your trip."

"What? Why?"

"It's not safe. We just got messages threatening our lives today. You can't come here right now."

"I already have tickets. I'm supposed to fly in next week."

"I know and I'm sorry, but I'm serious Livi. Don't come here right now."

After more protests and some choice language, an angry Livi hangs up the phone, but I know I made the right decision. Now is not the time for Livi to come visit us.

This goes deeper than we know; whatever is going on is so much bigger than Matiu, bigger than my sisters and I.

How far is Sebastian willing to go for revenge? I vow to keep my sisters safe, if it is the last thing I do.

Maybe no one can help any of us now.

Chapter 34

Matiu

My desk rattles and several pens roll onto the floor as I slam my fist down onto its surface. Several other detectives look my way before turning back to their own work. I'm not sure what cases have them here this early, but a couple of them look like they might have been here all night.

Sebastian and Violet are all I think about now.

Christmas yesterday with my family was almost torture. Instead of being present with them, I was itching to get back to work. The need to find Sebastian is consuming me and I caught worried glances between my parents multiple times before I made up an excuse that I was getting a migraine and needed to go home and go to sleep, leaving the Christmas festivities early. They would have more fun without me there dragging down the mood anyway. I spent the rest of the afternoon going over all the information I have and then going over it again. Only pausing to wish Violet a Merry Christmas over the phone.

I know I am really pushing my luck digging deeper into Sebastian at work, but with my privileges revoked to sign into the precinct's system on any other computers besides the desktop here, I am risking it.

So here I am at work three hours early, trying to find something.

Anything.

Before Armstrong, my once-mentor-turned-tyrant, gets into work. He will stop my research before I find anything.

No matter how hard I dig, I can't find anything about Sebastian's true identity. The Russian FBI Legat hasn't been able to find anything on his sister Irina either, but to be honest, I'm not sure how hard they are looking.

I have to be missing something.

Pulling up some photos of the masked Sebastian, I glare at them. Something tugs at the edges of my mind, but I can't quite grasp what it is. His eyes are so familiar, yet unfamiliar at the same time. We may not be able to see his entire face in any images, but those cold eyes stare back at me.

Dark eyes that match Mark's but colder, harsher, unrepentant, evil.

Okay, this is going nowhere. Maybe if I start back at square one, I will see something I missed. Pulling up the initial information we got from Genevieve and the blackmail texts we pulled off Tony's phone, I search for anything that can lead me in the right direction.

When nothing there catches my eye, I pull out the manila envelope with the threatening pictures that the blackmailers sent to Tony. Flipping through the pictures of Genevieve and Steve walking in Charleston, Konnie in the yard, and Charlotte at her desk, I pause when I get to the picture of Violet dancing at Juilliard. She looks so happy and peaceful. That version of Violet had no idea what the next few months held for her.

I hope she can get that spark of joy back.

But I have to find Sebastian before that can become a reality.

I flip to the next picture of Tony with his naval squad, scanning the men grouped with Tony. This picture was obviously taken before Andrei was listed as MIA and before whatever happened during Desert Storm took the light out of all these men. They all have smiles on their faces, their eyes still happy and full of youthful innocence.

Except one.

I stop when I get to Andrei's face. He is older than his enlistment photo, but it is obvious it is him. His resemblance to Mark is even more apparent in this picture. But the look in his eyes doesn't match the other men.

His cold eyes look full of anger, contradicting the smile on his face. I take a picture of the photo and email it to myself. Pulling it up on my computer, I crop Andrei out of the picture and run it through facial recognition against all the partials we have of Sebastian.

It is a potential match.

I know I couldn't hope for more with the limited images we have of Sebastian, but this is enough to get me excited. Grabbing my phone, I call Agent Sullivan.

I start talking as soon as he answers. "I think Sebastian might be Andrei. Can you generate an image aging the photo of Andrei that was sent to Tony? Oh, and add a scar under his right eye?"

"Yeah, we can do that."

"Add some burns to his face, too. Like what someone might look like after having bad enough burns on their face to require skin grafting."

"We'll start on that and let you know what we come up with."

"Thank you. Oh, and Sullivan?"

"Yeah?"

"Can you keep this conversation between us?"

"Yes. Do I even want to know why you're asking me not to say anything?"

"Probably not."

"All right. Stay out of trouble, McAllister," Agent Sullivan says before disconnecting the call.

If only he knew how unlikely that would be.

Armstrong will show up to work soon. I have got to get everything put away. I send the information I just found to Agent Sullivan and shortly after, he sends me the image they were able to generate.

I feel like I am finally seeing Sebastian's full face for the first time since this whole thing started.

Those dark, evil eyes seem like they are taunting me.

Sebastian *is* Andrei, and he was blackmailing Tony with classified information because he already knew it. He was there with Tony during whatever incident the Navy wants to keep hidden.

And nobody knew he was still alive.

Chapter 35

Violet

We have too much to do. With school and everything else, we've let the apartment get dirtier than we usually would. It is well past due for a deep clean. Genevieve was not happy with me when she found out I told Livi to postpone her visit, keeping her busy on the day she was supposed to arrive is probably a good idea. She needs the distraction.

The apartment is so small; we have a storage unit for most of Mom's decorations and family heirlooms that we wanted to keep, things we don't want to lose, but can't fit into our small space. So, a few days before Christmas we pulled out the tree, but not much else. We let both the holiday and my birthday, a few days before, pass uneventfully, exchanging small gifts with each other Christmas morning. I had a short phone call with Matiu who seemed distant and distracted the whole time, which made me worry for the rest of the day that our relationship—or not relationship, whatever it is—is ending.

Not wanting to add more worry onto Genevieve, I've been texting Jocelyn non-stop about Matiu. I haven't told her he is our former detective; just that he is a police officer back in Charleston. Sometimes I wonder what I'm doing.

But then I remember the spark I felt when our lips touched, how just holding his hand made me feel like everything would be okay, the heat that trailed after his fingers when he tucked a strand of my hair behind my ear, breathing in his cedarwood scent.

"Where do you want me to put the tree skirt?" Genevieve asks, jarring me out of my thoughts and back into reality.

"Just set it next to the storage bag, I'll shove it back in there with the tree after we get all the branches in."

She folds up the knitted red tree skirt and sets it next to the bag, the flash of the dreaded color as she walks past me sets my nerves back on edge. We carefully take the ornaments off the tree and wrap them in tissue paper before placing them into boxes, where they'll sit until next Christmas.

When we're done, Genevieve moves on to picking up items tossed all over the living room and takes them back to their various places—Konnie's backpack that needs to be hung up by the front door, some of my dance clothes that should have been washed days ago, and a water bottle that Steve had left on the coffee table. I take the branches off the Christmas tree and try to get them to fit back into the storage bag. After all the branches are safely stored for next year, I send Steve to the storage unit with all of the Christmas decorations. As he shuts the door behind him, Konnie comes out of the bathroom where she had been cleaning and starts vacuuming the hallway and living room.

Not too much time passes before Genevieve finishes putting the sofa pillows in place and steps back to look at our hard work. The living room looks immaculate. Lighting a candle, Genevieve sets it on the counter, filling the room with a sweet vanilla scent.

"I think you might have Mom's talent of making a room feel inviting," I point out.

"Thanks, it always makes me feel like they're still with us when I can see little aspects of Mom or Dad in you and Konnie."

"Me too."

My phone rings, distracting me from the conversation and the counter I was wiping.

A smile spreads across my face when I see who is calling. "Hey, Matiu."

"The man you girls didn't know in the Desert Storm photo with your dad, the guy I told you was named Andrei—he *is* Sebastian."

Okay, not the conversation I thought we were going to have. "What? Sebastian served with Dad?"

"Yes." He lets out a harsh laugh, "He even sent your dad a picture of himself while he was blackmailing him. What an arrogant snake.

"That's how he knew the information to blackmail Dad with."

"Correct. I'm going to text you a rendered photo of what we think he looks like now from all the information we have."

Matiu sounds so formal. Uneasiness fills me. I'm not sure if it's because he's sending me a picture of Sebastian, or because I'm worried he's decided our relationship isn't worth pursuing.

Maybe both.

My phone dings as the text comes through and I put him on speakerphone to look at the image. My stomach drops and a gasp escapes my lips.

Blonde hair that I know is now sprinkled with gray, cold blue eyes, a scar underneath one eye, and the uneven skin that looks like it's healed from a burn.

I know him.

I've seen him regularly for months.

"Violet? You okay? Have you seen him around?"

"Yes."

"What? When? Where?" Matiu sounds frantic.

"The picture you just sent me looks almost exactly like the neighbor I keep running into."

"Are you kidding me? I should've looked into him harder. I'm going to call Agent Sullivan."

Good luck with getting any more help from the FBI, I think bitterly. Agent Sullivan's supervisor made it pretty clear that we weren't high on his priority list. Disconnecting the call, I show Genevieve the picture, feeling numb with shock. I've been talking and feeling neighborly with the man who had my parents killed. Even when I started to get uneasy around him, I never once thought that he could be Sebastian. The numbness mingles with disgust and anger. *What kind of sick person would try to befriend us and torment us at the same time?*

Genevieve snatches the picture out of my hands and studies it, her brow furrowing. "It definitely looks like the guy in our apartment building. I don't know how I didn't see it before. The scarring must have thrown me off. He really does look so much like Mark." Her voice sounds sad, and it makes me wonder if it's Mark who haunts her nightmares.

Needing something to do, I check to make sure the deadbolt on the apartment door is locked and then walk through the apartment making sure all our windows are as well. I make a mental note to get a heavy-duty padlock for the window in Steve's room that leads to a fire escape. Knowing that Sebastian has been in our apartment building has my skin crawling.

As I run through all our conversations in my head, I realize that I never saw Sebastian going into or coming out of an apartment. I always saw him in the lobby or the elevator, or he was knocking on our door. He doesn't live here; he has just been lurking, tormenting us all.

I walk back out to the living room, where Genevieve is still staring at the picture on my phone. A knock on the apartment door has us both looking toward it.

"Did Steve forget his apartment key?" I ask.

"I don't think so; he's driving his Jeep so he should have all of his keys."

The now familiar sensation of fear and dread snake through my body as I walk to the front door and peek through the peephole. Genevieve comes to stand behind me.

"Who is it?" she whispers. "Is it him?"

I'm not sure if the *him* she is referring to is Steve or Sebastian, but a torrent of new emotions wash through me. Relief, confusion and even a small glimpse of happiness and I turn the door knob.

Livi bursts through the front door. "I missed you both so much!" she squeals, her pink-tipped ebony hair bouncing as she jumps up and down before wrapping an arm around both Genevieve and me.

"What are you doing here?" I manage to get out between Livi squeals.

"We missed you too," Genevieve mumbles against Livi's shoulder.

I give another squeeze before pulling back and making eye contact with Livi. "It's really good to see you Liv, but you have to go home."

"Umm, no. I just got here," Livi responds, irritation evident in her voice.

Steve walks down the hall from the elevators and interrupts our reunion. "Hey. I thought your visit got postponed?"

"Vi told me to postpone, but I ignored her," Livi says and gives Steve a bright smile and a hug.

"I can't say that I'm surprised." Steve says and looks up at Genevieve and me.

At this point all the panic I've been feeling for the last few months finally reaches its breaking point. "Steve, I need you to take Livi back to the airport. She CANNOT be here right now. *We* shouldn't be here right now."

Genevieve and I share a worried glance that Steve catches, sending us both a questioning look. "Okay, what did I miss?" he asks.

I clear my throat. "The neighbor that brought us the flowers and we keep bumping into is Sebastian."

"What! Sebastian has been living in our apartment building this whole time?" Steve asks incredulously and Genevieve nods worry pinching her face.

"I don't think he actually lives here, but he does have a habit of showing up," I say.

Livi's gaze darts between the three of us. "Wow, you guys really do attract all the crazies."

Genevieve reaches for Steve's hand and pulls the picture back up on my phone and shows him. Steve swears under his breath and pulls Genevieve closer so that he can wrap his arm around her. His eyes aren't focused on anything and he looks deep in thought, but he still places a kiss on the top of Genevieve's head and she leans into him.

"Well, you two are obviously still grossly obsessed with each other," Livi says and then pretends to gag, which brings a timid smile to Genevieve's face. Turning to me, she says, "I just got here. I'm not leaving, so don't even bother trying to convince me."

"We should all leave," Genevieve says softly.

"I agree Gen, but where are we going to go? You know how hard it was to find an apartment that we could afford that wasn't a studio. We're already burning through the life insurance money fast; we can't afford to stay in a hotel long term. The FBI won't do anything else. I don't know what to do or how to keep us all safe."

"Maybe you guys should come back to Moncks Corner. You have a house there," Livi points out.

"Sebastian knows where our house in Moncks Corner is too. I think it's safe to say he would probably find us no matter where we go. Are we all just going to drop out of school? He knows our class schedule, for crying out loud. Even if we could find a new apartment and move, he could still find us at school and follow us home."

Panicked thoughts race through my head, trying to solve a puzzle that seems to have all mismatched pieces. No matter what idea I come up with I realize there is no escape. We won't be safe in this disturbing game until Sebastian is no longer a player.

"I'm scared," Genevieve says.

I let out a shaky breath. "Me too. Livi I really would feel better if you went home."

Livi narrows her eyes at me. "Vi, you guys have been getting these creepy messages for months now. Honestly, what are the chances that he decides to go completely diabolical during the five days I'm here?"

"You usually attract trouble, so I wouldn't be surprised," Steve pipes in.

Despite all our nerves, or maybe because our nerves are already so frayed, a giggle erupts from my throat, turning into uncontrollable laughter. Genevieve, Steve, and Livi all join in and soon we are wiping tears from our eyes. Genevieve, Livi, and I jumble into a three-person group hug as our laughter turns into tears and Genevieve and I quickly turn into blubbering messes.

Despite my fear and worry, a small spot of happiness at seeing Livi and having this piece of home finds its way into my warring emotions. The noise we're making pulls Konnie out of her self-induced seclusion, and she peeks her head around the corner before rolling her eyes, returning to her room and shutting the door behind her.

"What's Konnie's problem?" Livi asks.

"Everything," Genevieve and I answer in unison.

"Konnie hasn't been handling all the changes in our lives well," I say.

"We've all been trying our best," Genevieve says and gives my hand a squeeze.

"You're all in therapy, right? Even my mom made me go to therapy after everything. My therapist is actually pretty cool. And hot. He is pretty hot, too."

Genevieve's eyes widen. "You think your therapist is hot?"

"I feel sorry for that guy," Steve says.

Livi smacks his arm and switches the subject. "Okay, I have so much I want to do while I'm here. I want to see The Statue of Liberty, The Empire State Building, Central Park, Ellis Island, and eat so much yummy food."

Despite the stress I laugh, this is Livi to a T. "Pace yourself Livi, you're only here for a few days. Not to mention that we shouldn't be running all over the city with Sebastian on the loose."

Livi looks at me like I don't have two brain cells to rub together. "Umm, I think sitting in your apartment where you're secluded and have no witnesses is a lot more dangerous that being in gigantic crowds of people, with lots of witnesses and more of a chance for someone to step in and help if something does go wrong."

"Livi has a valid point there," Steve says. "Especially with school out for winter break, going to all the big touristy spots might be safer."

My uneasiness doesn't go away, but I can see the logic behind what they're saying. If the FBI isn't going to help us and we don't have enough money to take ourselves someplace else, immersing ourselves in the mass of tourists might be our safest place.

"So where should I put my stuff?" Livi asks. "Also, can I take a shower? I feel gross from traveling."

Livi, as usual, looks completely put together, perfect makeup with a black sweater and a cute skirt over warm leggings, cute black boots covering her feet. She doesn't look like she has been traveling all day. We wheel her suitcase into the living room and I get her a clean towel and show her where the bathroom is.

"Where is Livi going to sleep?" Konnie grumbles, coming out of her room as soon as Livi closes the bathroom door.

"In your room, she's going to take Genevieve's bed," I respond.

I'm still contemplating shoving Livi back out into the hallway after she is done with her shower and locking the door until she comes to her senses and goes home.

"Why do I have to share a room with Livi? She hates me."

"Livi does not hate you," I say. Genevieve raises her eyebrows and Konnie gives me a look like I've lost my mind. "Okay, you guys might not get along the greatest, but she doesn't hate you, Konnie. Where else are we supposed to put her?"

Konnie huffs. "On the couch."

"How about you can sleep on the couch and Genevieve and Livi can have the room?"

"Like Genevieve would sleep in there anyway. I don't even know why all her crap is in my room, she's never in there."

I notice her word choice calling it her room, not their room. Life is too stressful already; I don't need Konnie arguing over whether she shares a room with Genevieve right now. We have someone threatening our lives and Konnie is still stuck on petty things like if Genevieve's stuff should be in their room. She's lucky all four of us aren't sharing a room in a studio apartment. Konnie's attitude isn't just annoying anymore, it is almost unbearable. Trying to bite my tongue and ignore her immaturity I grab a set of clean sheets out of the linen closet in the hallway and push past her to change the sheets on Genevieve's bed.

"Why did she have to come during winter break when I have to be home while she's here?" Konnie whines.

"Konnie, can you just be pleasant for a few days? I could really use a break from your constant negativity."

"Sorry I'm such a burden to your perfect life!" Konnie seethes and surprise, surprise stomps over to her bed pulling her headphones over her ears and turning the music up loud enough that I can hear it from across the room.

Perfect life? That's hilarious. I sigh and look at Genevieve who is tidying up her nightstand. "Do you think she's going to be like this permanently? I miss the old Konnie."

"Me too. I don't know. She's obviously processing everything differently than we are, but I don't understand why she wants to push us away."

"Me either."

Tears prickle the back of my eyes, but I refuse to let them come. I finish making the bed and Genevieve and I make our way to the living room where Steve is sitting on the couch scrolling through his phone.

"Gen, what are we going to do?"

"I don't know. Try to stay alive," she whispers.

Her comment leaves rocks in my stomach as Livi comes out of the bathroom, looking refreshed, her hair damp and her makeup washed off. She wraps us both in another hug. "I've missed you both so much. Oh, and I was thinking we should totally go on a ghost tour for old times' sake."

The room hushes into an apprehensive silence, tension slamming back into the room. We both pull away from Livi in astonishment. Even Steve looks at Livi in surprise.

"Have you lost your mind?" Genevieve asks with wide eyes. "I never want to go on a ghost tour again."

"Come on, Gen. Think about how many tours we went on. Out of all those tours, only one of those was traumatizing," Livi says. "I still think we should go on the ghost tour. I found one that is in a museum and it sounds super cool, also it's pretty popular so, you know, more people, more safety."

"I'll go with you," Konnie says, startling screams out of all of us. Despite Livi's carefree demeanor, we're obviously all on edge.

"Holy crap Konnie, you scared the heck out of me," Livi says as she turns to look at Konnie.

"I'll go too," I say.

Livi looks at Genevieve expectantly, but Genevieve shakes her head. "I don't think so."

"Come on Gen, you need to face your fears if you're ever going to get over them." Livi pleads, her bluntness is one thing I have *not* missed.

Genevieve looks at Steve and they seem to have a conversation with their eyes. She sighs and reluctantly says, "Fine, I'll go as long as Steve's there with me."

My ears ring with Livi's excited squeals echoing through our apartment.

I send a text to Matiu, letting him know that Livi came to visit even though I told her not to and a response never comes, even hours later.

These next few days might be more than we bargained for. I hope it's only Livi's plans we have to deal with and not Sebastian's.

Chapter 36

Matiu

I have to get back to New York.

At this point I am thinking about driving up there whether I can get the time off work approved or not, but it would be better if I can get there with my captain's approval. Only an hour into the workday and it seems like the day will never end. Morning light shines brightly through the windows prompting one of the detectives to lower the blinds.

I dial Agent Sullivan and wait impatiently for him to answer, fidgeting with Nikau's dinosaur on my keychain while I listen to each agonizing ring on the other end of the line.

As soon as he answers, I jump right into my question without so much as a hello. "Now that we have so much new information, would it be possible for you to request my assistance to help comb through it all?"

"That's probably something I could do," he answers slowly.

I let out a breath. "Thank you."

"But before I agree to anything, how about you tell me what's going on between you and the Clark girls? Particularly, the oldest Clark girl."

I should have known Sullivan would pick up on this. I have seen how good of an investigator he is. My stomach drops, filling with heavy anxiety. "Yes, it's Violet."

"Well, are you in a relationship with her? She called you 'Matiu.' I heard it at the park. So, you're obviously on a first name basis."

"I honestly don't know what's going on."

He doesn't sound like he is done questioning me about Violet yet, but he changes the subject anyway. "Can you keep your emotions out of the case?

200

Especially since you also said that you found evidence that Sebastian is connected to your brother's kidnapping. I never got that evidence from you, by the way."

"Yeah, Armstrong blocked me from accessing files from home. I can tell you which files to request though. And yes, I won't have any jurisdiction there. I'll just be helping sort the information so there wouldn't really be any conflicts of interest, right?"

"I guess, I'm not even going to ask why Armstrong blocked you from accessing files. As long as you keep it professional while you're here, you have a lot of personal connections with this one. I could really use your instincts though."

"Understood."

I disconnect the call and try not to fidget. I don't know how long it will take for Agent Sullivan to request my help, or if Captain will even approve it or not, but I want to be on my way to New York City already.

Not only to see Violet and help catch Sebastian, but to get away from Armstrong. Writing me up for finding evidence he couldn't find himself pisses me off. I'm not sure how I will feel about him after this initial anger passes, but the man, the mentor that I put on a pedestal my entire life, has dropped down quite a few pegs.

As if I willed him into existence by thinking about him, Detective Armstrong walks over and leans against my desk.

Arms folded, he asks, "How long are you going to hold a grudge against me for writing you up?"

I try to compose my face into some semblance of calm, but my anger can't be completely covered. "I'm not as mad about getting written up as I am about the fact that you don't want to follow the new information about Nikau." I toss the pen I was holding angrily onto the desk. "I thought you'd be excited about the new lead and instead you're trying to make it disappear."

"There are just some things that are better left alone. Leave them in the past, McAllister."

I glare at him and before my brain can catch up to my actions, I am already around my desk and pulling Detective Armstrong toward me, my fist clenching his shirt. "The disappearance of a child is not one of those things."

Why does he want Nikau's case to be left alone? Something isn't adding up.

Several other detectives are now up on their feet, ready to intervene if they need to, but I still don't release him.

"I found evidence that Sebastian might be linked to Nikau's kidnapping and you just want to ignore it? We've identified him as someone posing as the Clark girls' neighbor. He doesn't have long before we catch up to him."

"Oh yeah, how did you identify him?" he asks through gritted teeth.

"That's none of your business, it's not your case anymore. Remember?"

"McAllister, cool it. Captain is on his way over," I hear someone warn me.

I shove Detective Armstrong back, letting go of his shirt, and he lands roughly in his chair, a scowl on his face.

Thankfully, before he can say anything, we are interrupted by the captain and I don't have to continue the conversation. "McAllister, the FBI has requested you assist them again with some new information on the Lykaios case. They want you there as soon as possible. Where are you at in your cases here?"

"Nothing that Armstrong can't handle without me," I say, glancing over at Detective Armstrong. The color has drained from his face and he looks like he might be sick.

"I think we should keep McAllister here," Armstrong objects.

"Are you saying that you can't handle your cases without him?" Captain asks.

"No, I just don't think that sending him back to New York is the best choice."

"Why not?" Captain asks. I look at Armstrong too, waiting for his pitiful excuse.

"He was already there helping. What more can he do? Why don't they handle their own investigation?"

"Armstrong, unless you have a valid reason to keep McAllister here, I'm sending him to New York. Do you have a valid reason?"

Armstrong loses even more of his color. He almost looks ghostly now. "No."

"Okay, McAllister, pack up and go. You have a full day of traveling ahead of you."

"Thank you, sir," I say as Captain retreats to his office.

I grab my laptop and phone, shoving them into my bag. Most of my things pertaining to Sebastian are at the apartment now. This should be all I need from the precinct. I grab my keys and notice Detective Armstrong's eyes following Nikau's dinosaur as it dangles from my fingers. I shut down my computer, clean up my desk and leave without even saying goodbye.

— • —

Flights to New York are a mess today—weather has canceled a bunch of flights and everything is backed up and overbooked. I am not waiting for the weather to clear, so it looks like I will be driving again. I may get away with leaving without saying goodbye to Armstrong, but that will not fly with my family. So, after I am all packed up and ready to go, I drive to my parents' house.

When I get there, Mum and Miriama are in the living room watching one of their girly shows that Dad and I make fun of.

"What are you doing here, Matiu?" Mum asks. "Aren't you supposed to be at work?"

"Yeah, I am working. I'm going to New York again, just stopping by to say goodbye before I leave."

"Why are they sending you to New York again?" Miriama asks.

"To consult on the same case I was there helping with before."

"Your dad will be sad he missed you. I'm worried about you, son. This case seems like it might be dangerous."

"Mum, all my cases have the potential to be dangerous."

She grabs my hand and squeezes it. "I know. But this one feels different."

She has no idea. I haven't told them anything about the new information I found on Nikau.

"I'll be fine, Mum."

"Be careful, please. And make sure you call me every day," Mum chides.

I give both Miriama and Mum hugs before heading out the door. A hint of vanilla lingering on one of them brings Violet back to the front of my mind.

"I'll be careful. Tell Dad bye for me."

"I will." Mum gives me a mischievous smile. "Bring your mystery girl home with you this time."

I just laugh and shake my head as I walk out the door. Climbing into my car, I start the long drive to New York City.

Nervous energy makes me jittery, and I turn on the radio to distract myself. I am not sure what I am more nervous about: being able to spend more time with Violet and making this long-distance relationship, or whatever it is we have, even harder, or that I might actually close two cases.

I have been so lost in my own world I have been bad about responding to Violet's texts and calls, leaving my phone on silent most of the time. There will be days I miss a call and don't notice until the early morning hours and don't want to wake her up by calling back. Same with texts. By the time I check my phone, sometimes I will have several unanswered text messages from Violet before I respond. For all I know, when I get to New York, Violet might want nothing to do with me. Especially after the conversation about where our relationship is going. My gut twists again.

I just need to focus on these two cases. I am good at what I do; the pieces are falling into place and I am almost at the finish line. I can feel it.

I just need to put them together quickly and keep Violet safe at the same time.

And possibly come face to face with the monster I have been searching for all my life.

Chapter 37

Violet

Livi never runs out of energy. And her zest for life attitude is clashing horribly with mine and Genevieve's constant state of worry. I've seen more tourist spots in and around New York City in the past couple of days than I have since I moved here over a year ago. Some of them I had already seen, like the Empire State Building and the Statue of Liberty, but there were a lot of hidden gems that Livi found that were really interesting, like the Hard Hat Tour of Ellis Island. Livi is making the most of her time here and I'm glad she's having fun even if I can't fully enjoy her visit. Being surrounded by so many people has been both nerve wracking not knowing if Sebastian is hidden in the crowd watching us, but also reassuring that it would be hard to do anything to us without being noticed by so many people.

I'm exhausted.

It's New Year's Eve, but if the ghost tour's doors didn't open at 9:20 p.m., I would probably already be in bed. The tour might actually keep me up until midnight tonight. Livi, of course, wants to be in Times Square when the ball drops, so we plan to stop by there on our way home from the tour. Surrounded by thousands of people is most likely safer than bringing in the new year at home with our small little group. If the tour ends on time, we should be able to get to Times Square in time to see the ball drop.

Trying to stifle a yawn, Jocelyn and I follow Steve, Genevieve, Konnie, and Livi off the subway, climbing the stairs to the bustling city streets above. Cold air stings my face as we start the walk from the subway station to the ghost tour.

I haven't been able to spend as much time with Jocelyn since my sisters moved to New York and I miss my friend. We were pretty much attached at the hip my first year at Juilliard. Not only did we have all our classes together, but we were roommates before I needed to find a place big enough to fit my sisters and Steve. I asked Jocelyn if she wanted to room with us, but she declined. I think she knew we needed to heal together. I'm glad she decided to come with us tonight.

We both trail after the group. I pull the collar of my coat up around my face to combat the cold. According to my phone, we have about a seven-minute walk to the Merchant's House Museum, where Livi has scheduled the tour.

Livi is at the front of the pack babbling about everything as usual. I notice Genevieve has a tight grip on Steve's hand. Between everything we have going on and how nervous she is about the tour; I'm surprised she still came.

My mind wanders to Sebastian. None of us have seen him since we figured out who he was. It makes me even more paranoid. *How would he know we figured it out?* It's too much of a coincidence that he disappears as soon as we know he's Sebastian. *Did he bug our apartment? Can he hear our conversations?* I file my questions away for the next time I talk to Matiu.

Speaking of Matiu … we haven't talked as much as we normally do after our conversation about our relationship. The last phone call we had was when he called about Sebastian's identity. We've sent texts, but he waits so long to respond or sometimes doesn't respond at all, like my last text about Livi coming to visit. I worry he's trying to pull away.

It hurts, and it doesn't make it any easier when he's constantly on my mind. Having Livi here keeping us super busy has been an excellent distraction from both Matiu and the constant fear Sebastian will show up at our apartment and make good on his promise to get our blood on his hands.

My phone dings and I pull it out of my pocket. The text from Matiu has me excited and nervous at the same time. Every time I get a text, I fear it is going to be the one where he tells me we can't have a relationship.

> Left Charleston midmorning. On my way to NYC.

206

I squeal and almost drop my phone, but don't reply as I watch those three little dots appear and disappear multiple times before the next text comes through.

Can I see you tonight?

Or do you want to wait until tomorrow?

I don't know how late I'll be.

Tonight! I'm going to see Matiu tonight! My sleep deprived brain wakes up like it has just been given a high dose of caffeine.

Definitely tonight!

Livi wants to go to Times Square for the ball drop so we'll be up late anyway.

Can't wait to see you.

That has to be a good sign, right? He said, 'can't wait to see you.' Not, 'we need to talk,' or something else equally nerve-wracking.

"Whoever you just got a text from seems to have put you in a good mood," Jocelyn teases.

"Matiu is coming back to New York tonight!"

"Wow, talk about last-minute warning."

"I don't even care. I'm just excited I get to see him."

She gives me a skeptical look. "Is this the same Matiu that you have been worrying is going to break up with you? Or not break up with you. I guess you guys would have to officially be in a relationship for him to break it off."

"Yes, same Matiu. It's complicated, okay?" I grumble.

She laughs. "I would say so."

Pulling my phone out to reread the texts, I notice a new email notification. Pressing on the notification, I see it's an email from the Dean's office at Juilliard.

Ms. Clark,

Your presence is requested at the Dean's Office at 8:00 a.m.,
January 2nd.

I stop reading. This can't be good. Spring semester doesn't start until the 16th of January. I didn't even realize that faculty would be at the school during break. Putting my phone back in my pocket with shaking hands, I try to calm myself down—which is kind of hard between the email, Matiu's texts, and Sebastian's whereabouts unaccounted for.

Of course, Jocelyn notices. "Hey, I was just kidding. I'm sure you guys will figure it out."

"It's not that. I just saw an email from the Dean's office. I'm supposed to be at a meeting on January 2nd. This can't be good, right?"

Jocelyn tries to hide her shock. "I don't know. Maybe they're going to give you an extension or something with everything you've had going on this last year."

"Yeah, maybe."

My stomach does somersaults. I know there's no use worrying over something I can't control, but I feel like a ticking time bomb of nerves. I look toward my sisters and see that apparently I'm not the only one having trouble with my nerves tonight. Genevieve has her arms wrapped so tightly around herself she might lose blood flow. It's her tell-tale sign of anxiety. I watch as Steve puts his arms around Genevieve's shoulders and whispers something in her ear. Whatever he said seems to make Genevieve relax a little bit.

Hope blooms in my heart. Maybe Matiu does want a relationship; maybe I'll have the same comfort Genevieve gets from Steve in the near future.

Or maybe I won't.

My mind seems to be at war with itself and I don't realize that we're at the Merchant's House Museum until we're following Livi up the steps of the tall red brick house. Its green shutters on the windows stand out against the brick and it towers above us. With an empty lot on one side and some construction scaffolding on the other, it looks to be in its own little world. Even surrounded by the tall modern buildings, the beautiful old house looks untouched by time.

We walk into the narrow hallway. I gaze around in wonder as I look at the house that makes it seem as if we've traveled back in time. Getting glimpses into a couple of the rooms on our way to meet the tour guide, I notice a dining room table set as though it is ready for dinner to be served; the kitchen looks like someone is in the middle of meal preparations. It's as though the family who once lived here might just be out for a bit and will be home any minute for the evening meal. Jocelyn lets out a soft "whoa" next to me as she takes in our surroundings.

Livi checks us in and we only have a brief wait before a tall, slender man, who must be our tour guide, greets us, and moves us from the hall into the family room.

"Thank you all for coming tonight." The man smiles at the group before continuing. "I'm going to start the tour off with some information about this beautiful house before we delve into the scarier parts. The house was built in 1832 by a man named Joseph Brewster. The architecture of the house was very popular at that time and these 'row houses' were common. The houses were built from pattern books by men of other various livelihoods. For instance, Joseph Brewster's day job was making hats."

The guide pauses and lets us look around the family room for a minute before continuing. I take in the beautifully crafted red couch. A table and chairs with intricate woodwork that we don't see often in the modern styles. An enormous fireplace sits on the wall opposite the couch.

The guide's informative voice echoes through the room. "This particular house is unique because out of the hundreds of row houses built in the area occupied by the wealthiest of Manhattan society at the time, it is the only one still standing. The Tredwell family moved into the house in 1835 and many believe they never left."

The skin on the back of my neck prickles and I pull my coat tighter around me as I shiver and the guide continues. "Seabury Tredwell was a hardware merchant and made his living by importing various hardware items, pretty much anything made of metal, such as nails, doorknobs, and even cast-iron skillets. His family lived here, and the house remained largely untouched due to his youngest daughter Gertrude never marrying and living here her entire 93 years of life, leaving the house unchanged."

The tour guide leads us up the creaking narrow stairs to the second level, talking the whole way up. "A minimum of eight people died in this house during the almost 100 years the family lived here. Gertrude, who died in 1933, was the last of the Tredwell family. She was the youngest of eight children and was born in this very house. As Gertrude outlived her entire family, there were no shortages of deaths and funerals in the house."

We follow him through one of the parlors furnished with beautiful red couches and chairs, long elaborate curtains, also in a dark shade of red, frame the windows. The house already feels alive with past spirits, but with all the pops of red sprinkled throughout the house, I'm even more on edge. I once would've loved all the red accents, but after the past couple of months I associate the color red with dread.

He stops the group at a dark brown piano that is in remarkably good shape for how old it is. No paint seems to be peeling and despite its age, the keys are still pristinely white and black instead of yellowing and chipped, their color fading.

I can't take my eyes off the beautiful instrument, and I long to reach out and tap one of the keys as our guide gives us more information. "Since the museum opened in 1936, there have been paranormal phenomena happening in the house. Workers that were getting the house up to code reported seeing members of the Tredwell family as well as doors opening and slamming, voices calling out, and floorboards creaking. But it didn't stop there. Many have recounted seeing a young woman wearing a brown dress that most believe to be Gertrude, carrying a cup of tea. And this piano, which has long since stopped playing, has been heard playing a haunting melody."

The air around me seems to drop a few degrees. I shiver and look around. Livi's at the front of the group eating up everything the tour guide is saying; Konnie standing next to her looks just as interested, the usual scowl missing from her face. Turning to find Jocelyn standing with Genevieve and Steve, I notice Genevieve's pale face.

"You doing okay, Gen?" I ask quietly.

"I really don't want to be here. I don't like getting scared and all these rooms just make me feel trapped."

I can't even imagine what Steve, Genevieve, and Livi went through during that ill-fated tour in Charleston, but I can tell that Genevieve is trying hard to hold it together. Maybe we shouldn't have pushed her to come. Steve and Livi were both on the tour and they both seem fine. Trauma is so weird. The same trauma can manifest so differently in each individual.

We follow the tour guide up to the next level. The steep stairs have me reaching for the hand railing to make sure I don't tumble back down them. The bedrooms on this floor seem a normal size for today's standard, with dark wooden flooring and lavish four-poster beds in each room. Pristine marble fireplaces take up a large section of wall in both rooms.

"These were the bedrooms of Mr. and Mrs. Tredwell. There have been self-guided tourists who have had encounters with different apparitions that were so vivid that the tourist talking to them thought it was an employee playing a part. Sometimes they will talk with them about the family and other times they are angry and tell the people touring the house to leave. Several times, the tourists have been able to positively identify the ghost they were talking to when looking at a family photo of the Tredwell family." When the tour guide finishes, I'm almost convinced that we'll see Mr. Tredwell standing in his room as we follow the guide to another set of stairs.

The narrow steps up to the fourth-floor groan and creak as we climb up. We shuffle behind our guide, who almost seems bored as he talks. "This level is where the children's bedrooms are located; these rooms are now used as employee offices. Employees of the museum have seen what looks like swirling mist and sightings of Gertrude, her brother Samuel, and her father Seabury throughout the house. One notable story is when neighbors saw who they believed to be Gertrude run out of the house to scold noisy children playing near the house. Another is when three men were giving themselves a self-guided tour and were blocked from continuing by an elderly man who told them they needed to leave."

We walk past the closed doors and climb single file up the last set of stairs. The stairs seem to become more and more narrow the higher we climb, and the temperature drops dramatically. Goosebumps pepper my skin and I shiver, pulling my coat even tighter around my shoulders. I'm not sure if the temperature change is from the old house with inadequate heating in December, or the ghosts that they say live here.

Either way, I'm ready to leave.

"These four rooms were the rooms of the family's Irish servants. In 2011, paranormal investigators claim to have made contact with two chatty servant girls. The same investigators were able to capture several instances where the ghosts of the house answered questions. Despite whether each particular tour has an encounter with one of the Tredwell family or their servants, it is thought that this house is one of the most haunted houses, not only in the country but in the world." When the guide is done talking, our group makes our way slowly back down each set of stairs and into the gardens located at the back of the house.

Genevieve hurries down the stairs and out into the winter chill. The cold weather with a brisk breeze almost feels warmer than when we were in the house. I follow her into the landscaped garden, tall red brick walls on each side and a small fountain near the back. She stops and sits down on one of the stone benches, taking in calming gulps of fresh air. Steve comes and takes a seat next to her, rubbing his hand in small circles on her back. Livi and Konnie are finally getting along as they walk through the dormant garden, pointing out things of interest.

"Well, that was cool, but creepy," Jocelyn says as she stands next to me, looking at the intricate fountain void of its water due to the cold winter months.

"Right. It was eerily beautiful. I really wouldn't have been surprised if a ghost had walked right past us during the tour." I say before looking back toward the house as Livi and Konnie join us.

I see movement in one of the shadowed corners of the garden and freeze. Squinting into the darkness, I can make out the shape of a man watching us wander through the landscaping. Blonde hair reflecting what little light can reach into the shadows. I reach for Livi and point toward the house. All the color drains from her face. Livi finally showing signs of fear makes my stomach twist. Her wide eyes fill with terror instead of her normal playfulness or defiance, making everything creepier. My eyes have been on Livi and when I look back toward the house, the man is gone, even though Livi is still staring into the dark corner. Jocelyn notices our gazes locked on the spot and gives me a questioning look.

"There was a man standing there. I know I saw him," I whisper, my hand tightening on Jocelyn's arm.

"Who did you think you saw? Was it Mr. Tredwell?" she asks.

Without taking her eyes off the shadows of the dark corner Livi answers, "It was Sebastian. He looks so much like Mark." Her voice shaky, something I've never witnessed. Livi's confidence never seems to waiver.

Genevieve and Steve join us and Jocelyn tries to put our worries at ease. "You guys are probably just both spooked from the tour. I doubt it was Sebastian, but maybe it was one of the ghosts!"

Genevieve shivers. "Sebastian or one of the Tredwell ghosts. I'm not sure which one would be scarier."

"Sebastian," Steve and I both say in unison.

I glance back into the empty corner of the garden as we make our way into the house and out the front door. If it was Sebastian lurking in the corner, this was the first time he's shown himself since we identified him. I send a text to Matiu.

> We might have just seen Sebastian outside our ghost tour.
> We aren't completely sure though.

He texts back quickly.

> Make sure your location stays on.

> Don't go anywhere you won't have good service.

I copy the text I sent to Matiu and send it to Agent Sullivan as well. My skin prickles the entire trip to Times Square.

Despite being with my group and surrounded by so many people in Times Square, my skin crawls. Amidst the chatter of thousands of people, the bright lights, and flashing screens all around us, I feel as though someone is watching me. But no matter how many times I look around, I never see anyone looking in our direction. The uneasy feeling stays with me and I wrap my coat around myself tighter to ward off the chill of the night air. My heart races and my goose bumps multiply by the second as the crowd around us grows. Too many faces surround me. Scanning the people around me, my mind sees Sebastian everywhere, sending me into a panic—until I focus on the faces and realize it isn't him. But he could easily be hiding in the massive group. I hope we're right and the number of people around us gives us the protection the FBI won't provide.

More people press into us as the crowd grows, I feel claustrophobic as we're squished together, the smell of alcohol is strong amid the smiling faces happy to bring in the new year. I once again scan the faces of the people around me until my eyes meet the brown eyes I've been longing to see for so long.

Matiu's tall, muscular frame is the most beautiful thing I think I've ever seen. His hair has grown a little bit longer since the last time I saw him. A little bit of a wave that I've never seen making itself known in those dark locks, now that his hair isn't cut so short. But aside from feeling how attracted I'm to him as he makes his way toward us, I take in his presence. And with all his good looks and charm, I see strength, I see protection. Our eyes stay locked on each other, and I see determination and love staring back at me.

Forgetting my worries about what will happen between us, I push through Genevieve and Livi, who seem to be deep in conversation and squeeze through the bodies of Times Square visitors to get to Matiu. When I reach him, I jump up and wrap my arms and legs around him. His arms circle around me and I finally feel at peace. I don't care what Matiu thinks is ethical or unethical, or whether he thinks I have White Knight Syndrome or whatever else. I never want to be anywhere Matiu isn't.

Ever again.

When he goes to pull back to look at me, I hold on even tighter and he laughs. The low melodic tones are like music to my ears. Matiu walks the short distance back to my group with me still clinging to him like an octopus out of water.

The shocked look on Livi's face is comical as she says, "I'm apparently miss-ing out on some juicy information." Even though she's back to joking, her tone is more subdued than usual and she still seems troubled underneath her carefree façade.

Genevieve giggles and I finally unwrap myself from Matiu and stand next to him, clenching his hand with mine. My sisters and friends count down with excitement and we watch the ball drop. Genevieve has relaxed and a smile spreads across her face before Steve claims her lips with his for a New Year's Eve kiss. Livi, Jocelyn, and Konnie all laugh and yell out Happy New Year with the rest of the crowd, and when I meet Matiu's eyes everything and everyone around us disappears as our lips crash together.

I give all of my fear, frustration, and longing to Matiu through our kiss and he takes it, returning my emotions with his own full of desperation.

"Good gravy Violet, and to think you had the audacity to give me grief about thinking my therapist is hot," Livi teases and I reluctantly pull my lips away from Matiu's.

As the crowd disperses, we start our trek home and drop Jocelyn off at her apartment first before getting back to ours. I finally feel safer than I have in months with Matiu beside me. When everyone files past us into the apartment, Matiu smiles at me and he doesn't look like someone who is going to break my heart.

At least not tonight.

January

Chapter 38

Matiu

The group goes into the apartment and the door closes behind them leaving it open just a crack. When I met Livi last year after the incident at the Old City Jail, she was quiet and had just gone through a traumatizing experience. During my conversations with Violet these past few months she told me stories of how her life used to be when Genevieve, Livi, and her were an inseparable trio. I had trouble picturing Livi as the vibrant, wild girl described to me, but after watching her at Times Square and listening to her chatter non-stop on the walk back to the apartment I can see it now. I tug on Violet's hand wanting to have her to myself for a second before we follow the group through the door.

She pauses and looks up at me with those beautiful eyes full of emotion. I pull her toward me and wrap my arms around her. Needing her closer. Her arms wrap around my neck and she pulls me even tighter, crushing her body against mine.

And it is the first time my mind has felt at ease in weeks.

All thoughts of Sebastian and Nikau have finally taken a back seat, allowing some semblance of peace to fill me.

I nuzzle my face into the soft spot between her neck and shoulder, breathing her in. Her calming scent of vanilla and lavender fills me.

"Should we go into the apartment?" she asks, and I groan.

"We probably should, but I need a minute with just you. I can see the Livi you talked about now; she is so different from the girl I met during the investigation."

"She's actually a little bit subdued right now, she's normally even more animated. And fair warning, the girl has no filter." Violet laughs, the sound bringing a smile to my own face. But her smile quickly falters, the laughter coming to a halt. She pulls back so she can see my face. "I was worried you had decided against moving forward with any sort of relationship. You've been distant the last few weeks."

"I'm sorry. I've had a lot on my mind. I didn't mean to make you feel like I was pulling away," I say and brush my thumb across her soft cheek.

Cradling her neck in my hand, I lean down and place a soft kiss on her mouth.

"Holy crap! They're kissing again. It wasn't just a New Year's Eve kiss in Times Square," I hear Livi squeal from the other side of the apartment door and Violet stifles a laugh.

"Stop spying on them through the peephole Livi, that's weird," Genevieve's voice floats through the cracked open door.

"That's not weird. What's weird is that I look like this and I'm still single and both of my best friends have somehow landed smoking hot boyfriends," Livi whines.

Violet giggles. "I don't think they know we can hear them."

"I didn't know Livi thought I was smoking hot," I tease.

This has Violet rolling her eyes at me. "Anyone that sees you would think you're smoking hot Matiu and you know it."

"Well, I do now."

She pushes me playfully. "Don't let it go to your head."

Violet pulls away from me and opens the door. I want to pull her right back, missing the warmth of her body next to mine, but follow her into the apartment instead and she deadbolts the door behind us.

Livi is trying to act like she isn't paying any attention to us as she watches Genevieve making mugs of what looks like hot chocolate in the kitchen. Steve is sprawled out on the couch flipping through movies on Netflix and Konnie must be in her room. I can't see her anywhere.

I have seen this countless times during my career as a police officer and a detective. When people are in turmoil and their lives have been turned upside down, sometimes they will shut down and go numb. But more often than not they will try to create small moments of normalcy, where they feel in control of their situation, where they can pretend that their lives might one day be okay again. And for some reason most people turn to a hot drink when they feel the need for solace. Coffee, tea, hot chocolate, any warm drink seems to be present when humans are trying to comfort themselves.

"Mmm, a cup of Mom's hot chocolate sounds amazing right now," Violet says, lacing her fingers through mine and pulling me into the kitchen behind her.

Livi watches us walk into the room, and her eyes lock onto our intertwined hands. "Okay, I can't take it anymore. When in the heck did this happen? And why didn't anyone tell me about it?"

"It's fairly recent, and I didn't tell you about it because it wasn't my business to tell you, so quit giving me dirty looks," Genevieve says, giving Livi a pointed look.

Livi turns her gaze to Violet and raises her eyebrows, waiting for an answer. "I've had a lot going on if you haven't noticed," Violet says.

Livi rolls her eyes. This girl might have the most dramatic eye roll I have ever seen. She has definitely perfected it. "Well, obviously you guys are as obsessed with each other as these two." She gestures from Genevieve in the kitchen to Steve on the couch.

Violet laughs and glances at me nervously as Genevieve hands us all mugs of rich hot chocolate. I take a sip and my eyes widen at the delicious flavor.

"Be careful. Once you have a cup of Mom's hot chocolate, you'll never be able to drink the regular stuff again," Violet warns me.

"Too late. Regular hot chocolate has already been ruined. This is delicious," I say before taking another drink.

Steve gets up and makes his way to the kitchen. "I know I said we could watch a movie, but I'm exhausted and it's almost two o'clock in the morning. I think I'm going to go to bed."

Genevieve yawns. "I think I'd fall asleep within the first five minutes of a movie anyway. I'm ready to get some sleep, too."

"You're both party poopers," Livi whines, but Genevieve pulls her down the hall with her, leaving Violet and me in the kitchen alone.

It doesn't last long as a grumpy Konnie comes into the kitchen and sighs loudly when she sees us. "Vi, I'm so tired, and I just want to go to bed. If you two are going to be staying up, can I just sleep in your room with you tonight so I can lie down right now?"

"Sure Konnie, go to bed. I'll try to not disturb you when I come in," Violet answers and we both watch Konnie shuffle back down the hall toward where I am assuming Violet's room is.

Realizing I have been in their apartment, but I have never seen the whole thing I scan the area. Steve disappeared to the left where his room must be, and Konnie, Genevieve, and Livi all went down the hallway to the right. The kitchen has a counter with bar stools that borders the living room and another entrance that leads to the front door and a small hallway that also connects to the living room.

Violet bites her lower lip and nervously looks up at me before walking into the living room with her hot chocolate and sitting down on the couch. I follow her and sit beside her, placing my mug on a coaster on the coffee table in front of me.

"Sorry about that. Konnie and Livi don't get along. They shared a room the first night but it didn't go over very well so Konnie opted for sleeping on the couch instead of having to share a room with her while she's here."

"I can imagine Livi can get overwhelming sometimes. Were you serious when you said that this is a subdued version of her?"

"Yeah, she's been off ever since the ghost tour we went on earlier tonight."

"I've been meaning to ask you what would possess all of you to go on another ghost tour after everything that happened during the one Steve, Genevieve, and Livi went on?"

Violet chuckles. "Livi is what possessed us. She's always pushing us to do things and she's very convincing."

Violet yawns. I'm not ready to leave yet, but she looks exhausted. Her eyelids seem heavy and she has dark circles under her eyes.

"Sorry I know it's late," I say. "I can go get a hotel and we can catch up tomorrow."

"I don't want you to go," she whispers. "This is the first time I've felt safe in a long time."

I smile and drape my arm over her shoulders. "Good, because I probably wouldn't have gotten a hotel anyway, I would have sat in the hallway all night making sure Sebastian didn't show up, especially since you think you saw him tonight."

"You really are my knight in shining armor," she says with a small, sad smile tugging at her lips. "I have to know though Matiu. What's going on between us? Because I'm getting some mixed signals. When we're together, I feel like you want to be with me, but when we're apart, you always seem so torn."

I go to run my hand through my hair, but Violet catches it and pulls it back down to my lap, tilting her head up so she is still cuddled up to me but can see my face.

"I do want to be with you, Violet, but there are still things that worry me."

"Like what?" she asks.

"Things we've already covered, like the fact that I was the detective on your case, that I'm worried that your feelings for me aren't real, that this is just some form of White Knight Syndrome …"

She stops me with a finger to my lips before I can continue with my list. "Matiu, I've never felt anything more real in my entire life. These past few weeks, when I thought you were pulling away, I've never been more terrified. Not only because of everything going on with Sebastian, but because I was terrified I was going to lose *you.*"

A tear escapes her eye and winds its way down her cheek. I wipe it away and we sit in silence as I war with my emotions. I want to be with Violet; I know that. I'm not sure why I keep telling myself that it would be unethical. I haven't been her official detective for months now. I think what it comes down to is that the powerful emotions I feel toward Violet scare me. I don't want someone else that I love taken away from me, but I can't live my life walking on eggshells because of something that *could* happen.

I play with the ends of her hair, tucking a stray piece back behind her ear before responding. "I'm not going anywhere, Violet. At this point, I'm not sure I could let you go even if you told me to."

"That will never happen," she says right before her lips crash into mine.

We kiss like we are short on oxygen and the other one holds all the air in the room. All the feelings and emotions that both of us have been holding back come to the surface at once. I am on fire and feel cold at the same time. My fingers weave into her hair and I deepen the kiss, which Violet matches in return.

"Jeez, we leave you two alone for a second and you're all over each other." Livi's voice breaks the spell we were under and we pull apart. Violet's face flushes in embarrassment.

Livi takes a drink of water, eyebrows raising. "Don't worry, just getting a drink. I'll be out of your hair in just a minute and you two can get back to whatever you were planning on doing."

Violet groans. "Go to bed, Livi." And tosses a throw pillow at her.

Livi dodges the pillow, laughing, and walks back down the hallway. I hear the click of the door as she closes it.

Violet brings her hands up to her cheeks to cover the blush that has spread across her face. "Well, now that we've clarified that neither of us is going anywhere, what exactly does that mean for us?"

I kiss the tip of her nose. "It means that I am yours and you are mine. And nobody is going to take you away from me."

She smiles. "I can live with that."

Snuggling up tight next to me, I hold her in my arms glad that at least for tonight, I can give Violet the comfort and a small bit of normalcy that she craves. I listen as her breathing pattern changes into the slow, calm breaths of sleep. My eyelids feel heavy and I feel calm myself, peaceful for the first time in so long. With Violet in my arms, my world finally feels whole again. Leaning my head onto the top of hers, I close my eyes and drift off to sleep next to her on the couch.

— • —

Bright sunlight streaming through the window wakes me. This is the first night in a while that I have gotten multiple hours of uninterrupted sleep, even if it was sitting on a couch. I'm not sure what time it is, but I feel more refreshed than I have in months and waking up with Violet nestled up next to me just makes everything seem brighter.

My arm has fallen asleep, so I try to shift just enough to return blood flow without waking her up, but the movement has those beautiful eyes fluttering open anyway.

"Good morning," I say smiling down at her.

She stretches an arm up and rolls her neck. "Good morning. What time is it?"

"I'm not sure I just woke up."

She slides away from me reaching for her phone on the coffee table. "Wow! It's after ten o'clock. I can't remember the last time I've slept this late. I haven't been sleeping well for a while."

"I haven't either."

Knowing that Violet was protected took a huge load off my shoulders last night. "Would you be okay if I stayed here while I'm in New York? I'll try and stay out of everyone's way and I'm totally fine with sleeping on the couch."

"I think we would all sleep easier knowing you were here," Violet says as she walks toward the kitchen.

I follow her into the kitchen and help her cut up some fruit, fry some bacon, and scramble some eggs for everyone else. One by one they all emerge from their rooms rubbing sleep from their eyes, the smell of freshly fried bacon beckoning them.

Everyone is exhausted and it's a holiday so none of us have school or work. We spend the day watching movies on Netflix, playing board games, and just spending time with each other. Even Konnie is semi pleasant, keeping her anger confined to the occasional eye roll instead of her snide comments.

I could get used to this.

But underneath this peace and calm I am feeling today, spending time with these people I am coming to love, especially Violet, uneasiness still settles in my core.

Chances are this is just the calm before the storm.

— • —

My brain is foggy and I can't seem to focus or pay attention to anything. I stayed up way too late talking to Violet again last night.

It's only the second day of the new year and every part of me feels heavy— my arms, my legs, my eyelids. Between the drive to New York and the two late nights after, I am exhausted.

But the need to be near Violet apparently outweighs my need for sleep. At least that is how I felt last night. I was definitely regretting the lack of sleep when the alarm on my phone went off early this morning.

Slowly walking into the FBI building, I check in and make my way up to Agent Sullivan's office. I close my eyes and lean the back of my head against the wall of the elevator. The ding of the elevator as it stops gives me a bit of a heads up before the doors open. My eyes are gritty, they feel like sandpaper. I just want to go back to the apartment and take a nap, which isn't a good sign since I haven't even started the workday yet.

This is going to be a long day.

I knock softly on Agent Sullivan's office door and he tells me to come in. When he sees it is me, he stands up and shakes my hand.

"Hey McAllister. Good to have you back," he says.

"It's good to be back. Thanks for having me."

"I'm on my way to meet with Viktor Gusev. He is currently incarcerated for weapons dealing here in New York, but he was positively identified in the pictures we got from the CPD files you had me request." He pushes his chair under his desk and grabs his coat. "Good call on having me take a closer look at those files. We still need to have a chat about why getting those files was so urgent, but if he was both here in New York and in Charleston with Sebastian I am hoping he was privy to a lot of Sebastian's operations before he got arrested."

This news wakes me up pretty quick. This is huge, finally getting to talk to someone who worked closely with Sebastian. When we took Clyde Fletcher into custody after the night at the Old City Jail, he claimed to never have even talked to Sebastian himself. Everything was relayed through Mark. I am doubtful that we will get much out of this Viktor, but it doesn't stop the hope from swelling within me.

Agent Sullivan pauses next to me on his way out of his office. "He's been in prison for almost ten years now, so his information is probably outdated, but I figure it's worth checking into. Want to tag along?"

"Yeah, that sounds great."

Following Agent Sullivan back to the elevator we descend to the lobby and make our way to his car and start our drive to the prison.

"Viktor is serving twenty-five years in Sing Sing right now for multiple charges being served consecutively. Apparently, he's willing to talk if we can get what's left of his serve time to be concurrent," he says while weaving through New York traffic.

"Can you do that?"

"It can happen. It won't be easy, though. It would have to be some really good information for me to even try. I'm not sure I want him out in the world any sooner than he needs to be, anyway."

The roughly thirty-mile drive goes by in a blur. After Agent Sullivan parks and we get checked into the prison, we wait in uncomfortable plastic chairs for Viktor to be brought to us. The cold, hard chairs add to my impatience.

We can hear them coming for a long way as doors open and bang closed multiple times until finally the door into our room opens. When the correctional officer walks in with Viktor, my stomach churns. Acid threatens to rise up my throat and I feel lightheaded until Viktor smirks at us cockily with his acne-scarred face and his dark hair falling into his eyes. Whatever emotions I was feeling before turn to red fiery anger.

No, anger isn't a strong enough word.

Rage.

I am filled with rage as I recognize Viktor from the photos and surveillance videos I have watched countless times.

I seethe as the man who took Nikau sits down across the table from us.

"You good?" Agent Sullivan asks as he notices my barely controlled rage.

No! No, I am not good. I want to reach across the table and rip him out of his chair. Demand that he tells me what happened to Nikau before knocking out his teeth with my fist.

But I can't do that, we need information from him. Information that might lead us to finally catching Sebastian. So instead of reaching across the table and strangling the man, I nod and let Agent Sullivan do the talking.

This is his interview, this is his interview, this is his interview, I repeat in my head. I have never wanted to kill a man, but that instinct burns bright and hot right now. I clench my fists.

"We hear that you have some information you think might be helpful to us," Agent Sullivan starts the interview.

"Did you get my sentence reduced?" Viktor asks that ugly smirk back on his face.

"That depends on how helpful the information is and if it leads to detaining Sebastian. If it's good information that actually leads to us finding him, then yes, I'm confident that I can get your sentence reduced ... some."

Viktor's reedy eyes narrow on Agent Sullivan. "Well, that doesn't sound too promising."

"I'm not making any promises until I know what type of information you claim to have," Sullivan says.

"Sebastian has several safe houses and some warehouses around the city that aren't attached to his name. He used them all pretty regularly when I was working for him."

"And you know the addresses of these houses and warehouses?"

"I know several of the addresses. I could take you to all of them."

"Nice try, we're not taking you on a field trip. Give us the addresses that you know."

Agent Sullivan writes down the addresses that Viktor lists before looking back up at him. "Just curious, why are you willing to part with this information? You aren't worried about backlash from Sebastian?"

"I've been in here for almost ten years now and he hasn't tried to get me out. No help with lawyers, nothing. It's time for me to help myself."

"Sounds like you may have pissed Sebastian off. How do you know your information is accurate?"

Viktor fidgets. "I don't know if it's still accurate or not. Like I said, I've been in here for a while."

"So, these five addresses are the only information you have for us? Nothing else."

"Like I said, there are a few other safe houses, but I don't have their addresses memorized. I'd have to take you to them myself."

"Can you draw me a map? Like *I* said, I'm not taking you on a field trip and I'm not too sure you have any information that is still relevant anyway."

I can't hold my tongue any longer. "You may not have any new information, but what about some old information?"

Those uncaring eyes switch from Agent Sullivan to me. "Like, what type of old information?"

"July 21, 2009. There was a big weapons deal that was supposed to be happening in Charleston, South Carolina, but something spooked Sebastian and he changed his plans last minute. On the day of the supposed deal, you were seen on surveillance taking a little boy. His name was Nikau. I want to know what happened to him."

"You know, I actually remember that day." That ugly smirk shows back up on his face. "I don't know what happened to the kid, though. I took him because he saw something he shouldn't have and I brought him to Sebastian. That was the last time I saw him. I wouldn't hold your breath though, because people who know too much about Sebastian tend to disappear."

"And you have no idea where he'd put the boy?"

Viktor laughs. "Nope. That wasn't my specialty. You should be asking that detective in Charleston for more information."

Dread fills me. The feeling is thick inside my chest. I force a calm, slow breath. There are over a dozen detectives in CPD, fewer that were also detectives fifteen years ago. The faces of each one flash across my mind, settling on the familiar father figure that I have looked up to for most of my life. Armstrong and his insistence I leave Nikau's case in the past and his orders to stop my search for Sebastian comes to mind. But then memories of all Miriama's and my birthday parties he attended, all the family dinners he joined us for, the study sessions with him that fast tracked me to becoming a detective follow the thought. Armstrong can't be dirty, he follows every rule, there is no way he would do that.

A cruel smile spreads across Viktor's face, but he doesn't respond. Before I even realize what I am doing, I am out of my seat and leaning over the table, the collar of Viktor's jumpsuit clenched in my fist.

"What detective in Charleston?" I ask.

Viktor's harsh laugh echoes around in the empty room. All logical thought leaves my head and I yank Viktor across the table, pulling back my other fist, ready to make contact with that ugly smirk of his.

But I don't have time for my fist to connect with his face before Agent Sullivan grabs the back of my shirt and pulls me out of the room. Viktor's cruel laugh follows us into the hall.

"What in the heck was that, McAllister? If you want to be a part of this investigation in any way, you need to pull yourself together!"

Breathing heavily, I nod; embarrassed that I can actually feel tears building up, trying to reach the surface. He leaves me out in the hall while he goes back in to finish the interview with Viktor.

When he comes back out of the meeting room, he walks past me and I follow. He leads me out of the prison, back to his car and after we both close our doors the air is filled with thick tension hanging like fog around us.

"I'm sorry Agent Sullivan, it won't happen again."

"It better not," he says sternly, but the look of compassion he gives me contradicts his stern words and I am mortified when tears actually start to fall down my face.

"I'm sorry," I say again as I swipe at the hot tears rolling down my cheeks. "I wasn't expecting to come face to face with the man who took my little brother today."

"I'm going to need a little bit more of an explanation," he says and then sits quietly, waiting for me to continue.

The story of the day Nikau was taken, how Armstrong took me under his wing and helped me become a detective comes pouring out. Then I continue to when I found the picture of Nikau's bike behind Sebastian and saw the first image of his kidnapper—who I now have met face to face—he wrote me up and restricted my access to the files.

"That's why you sent me the cryptic message to request those files."

I nod and wipe my wet face again.

"When we get back to the office, I need you to show me these photos you're talking about. Kidnapping also lands firmly in FBI jurisdiction and if it's also linked to my current case, I think it's time Nikau's cold case becomes an open FBI investigation."

"Thank you. The guilt I've felt since Nikau disappeared has been eating away at me for the last fifteen years. It's been long enough that I have given up hope of finding him alive, but I do need to find out what happened to him. I just want to find Sebastian and get closure on both of these cases. Did you get the name from Viktor?"

Agent Sullivan sighs and leans his head back against his head rest. "No. He claimed that Sebastian never told him the name of the dirty detective and that he never saw him, he just knew of him. And after questioning him more about the other safe houses he admitted that there weren't any more. The five addresses he gave us are the only safe houses he knows about. He's grasping at straws to try and get out of prison early."

"Is it bad that I'm kind of glad that we didn't get much information from Viktor? I want him to rot in that cell for the rest of his life."

Agent Sullivan smiles. "No, I don't think that's bad. The world is definitely a better place with people like Viktor Gusev behind bars."

I dry my face and apologize again.

Agent Sullivan starts the car and says, "Look McAllister, you're bright and you have good instincts and I want your help on this case, but you have got to play by the book."

I nod.

Agent Sullivan sighs, "And just call me Alec, for crying out loud. With all the calls from you as the Clark girls' personal 911 and all the information we've shared, I think we're on a first name basis."

A slow smile creeps onto my face. "Alright Alec, where are we headed next?"

He calls Agent Delgado and references the addresses Viktor gave us with the addresses tied to Irina Lykaios that were already checked during the initial search for Sebastian. Out of the five addresses Viktor gave us, there is only one that hasn't been looked into.

After disconnecting the call with Agent Delgado, Alec says, "I guess we're headed to Chelsea to check out the only new address we got from the visit."

But when we pull up to the address, an empty lot stares back at us. The strong emotions I was feeling earlier turn into a numb hollowness that crawls through me.

Another dead end.

Alec parks the car and we get out and walk to the nearest business, an art gallery, pushing the door open he walks in. I follow him and the bell above the door rings a second time as it closes behind us.

A professionally dressed woman wearing a black pantsuit strolls toward us. "Hello. What can I help you fine gentlemen with today?"

Alec flashes his badge. "I'm Agent Sullivan with the FBI; do you happen to know what used to be in the empty lot to the west of your building?"

"It was an old warehouse. It got demolished about six years ago."

Alec thanks her before heading back out the door. I follow and once we are back in the car I clench my fists in frustration.

"So, our visit to Viktor was no help at all."

Alec nods. "That seems to be how most of the leads in this case turn out. We really need Sebastian to mess up."

He puts the car in gear and starts driving back to the office. We stop for lunch on the way back and eat our fast food in the car. "Was your commute to the office okay this morning?"

I panic, trying to run all the possible scenarios through my mind about how this next part of the conversation could go. I am afraid of what will happen if he knows I am staying with Violet. Alec glances over at me and raises his eyebrows.

I clear my throat. "I took the subway, where I'm staying isn't too far from the office."

"That's good. Where are you staying this time?"

I search for a way around the direct question, but can't find any. "I'm actually staying with the Clark girls."

Alec looks at me with those raised eyebrows again, but doesn't say anything.

"I feel like they need more protection and they aren't getting any. I might as well be the one keeping an eye on them at their apartment," I try to reason.

"I've requested a protective detail multiple times. I'm not sure this is a good idea with your relationship with Violet, but I'm glad they have some protection since I haven't been able to get them more yet. Especially after the last notes they got."

Wait? What notes? "Which notes are you talking about?" I ask.

He gives me a quizzical look, his eyebrows coming together. "The ones where he talked about getting their blood on his hands."

Why wouldn't Violet tell me about them? I thought she was running everything past me. It stings more than I thought it would knowing that she gave Alec information that she didn't share with me. We finish the rest of the drive in silence, and when he parks the car he shakes his head as we take the elevator back up to the office.

I settle back into the same temporary desk in the conference room as last time and search Viktor Gusev in the database. Maybe Viktor can still lead us to Sebastian in some way. At this point I will take any clue I can find, even if it seems inconsequential.

I don't know what Sebastian's next plans are, but I can feel the time running out.

Chapter 39

Violet

My empty stomach is in knots and even though I was too nervous to eat breakfast or lunch today, my stomach feels as if it is going to rid itself of any contents that might still be in there. Pushing the heavy door open, I walk into the administrative building. My footsteps echo as I walk down the empty hall, each one rubbing at my frayed nerves as I get closer and closer to my fate. I'm not sure what this meeting is about, but I have a feeling it isn't going to be a good one. I didn't tell anyone at home about my meeting today, only Jocelyn knows about it. I took Konnie to school and then came to Juilliard, wandering the campus, lost in my own thoughts and worries about what the Dean will tell me.

Stopping at the desk of the Dean's secretary, I wait nervously for her to finish her phone call and acknowledge me. The secretary looks prim and perfect, not a single one of her blonde hairs out of place. She speaks to whoever is on the phone with an overly friendly and accommodating voice that sounds too cheerful to be authentic. Looking down at my jeans and cream-colored sweater, I subconsciously try to make myself more presentable—brushing out any wrinkles and then reaching up to smooth back my hair and hope that the messy bun I wrangled my dark locks into doesn't look too messy. *Why didn't I dress nicer?*

The room is immaculately decorated, everything neat and tidy, making me feel even more out of place. Someone is taking down the Christmas tree in the corner and I watch as they carefully remove the glittering glass ballet slipper ornaments from the tree and wrap them before placing them into a box. I normally would think the decorations were beautiful and take notes for when I'm decorating my own home, but today it feels stifling and judgmental. I won't ever have my act together enough to have such a beautifully decorated house.

Thoughts of the last time I was in this office put me even more on edge. Wiping my sweaty palms on my jeans, I try to calm my racing heartbeat. It was mid semester when I got the horrifying knock on my apartment door letting me know my parents had been murdered, Genevieve had been held at gunpoint, and Konnie was missing. To top it off, they were having an officer watch my apartment because they had evidence that I was being followed and until they found Konnie and knew we were all safe, the NYPD insisted. After closing the door in shock, emotions battered me. Heartbreak, anger, disbelief, and terror all washed over me at once, and I collapsed against the apartment door and sobbed. Jocelyn wrapped me in a hug and let me cry. So much was running through my mind at the time that I hadn't even realized she was standing right behind me the whole time the officer was speaking to me.

That next morning, Jocelyn walked to the Dean's office with me. Following Jocelyn through the hall, I didn't even register my surroundings during that trip. Thankfully, Konnie had been found in the woods behind our house. She was injured, but despite knowing both my sisters were okay, an overwhelming numbness had taken over me. The Dean looked imposing behind her large desk when Jocelyn and I took seats across from her. Although she had a no-nonsense vibe and a serious expression, she didn't feel cold or uncaring. As I told her the news I had received about my family, her eyes filled with compassion. Jocelyn and I left the office that day with an excused leave for me to go back to Moncks Corner to be with my sisters and bury our parents and an extension to catch up on all my current coursework during the summer months.

"Can I help you?" the secretary asks in an overly cheerful voice after finishing her phone call.

"I'm here for a meeting with the Dean."

"Okay, hun." She gives me a warm smile that seems practiced. "What's your name?"

"Violet Clark," I say in an unsteady voice.

That fake smile never leaves her face. "Go ahead and have a seat and she'll be with you in just a moment."

I nod and sit down in one of the overstuffed chairs. I can't sit still, shifting my position every few seconds and bouncing my leg with anxious energy.

Fidgeting with the umbrella in my hands, I give my fingers something to do. Despite the forecast of rain and possibly snow today, I almost didn't grab it. Now I'm glad I have it as I unsnap and snap the strap that cinches it together when not in use. My cell phone dings and I pull it out of my pocket, welcoming the distraction.

> Sebastian was the last person to see Nikau alive.

> And I think there's a dirty cop in my precinct who may know what happened to him.

Sebastian didn't just tear my family apart; he ripped Matiu's family apart well before we were even on his radar.

What a monster.

Before I can respond to Matiu, the Dean's office door creaks open. She nods at me and asks me to come in and sit down. I follow her into the office, flinching when the door thuds closed behind me.

Taking a seat in a chair, I sink down into the soft padding. I'm sure that it is supposed to be cozy and comforting, but it feels claustrophobic. The surrounding walls seem to shrink and I feel like a trapped animal, the urge to get out of this office is overwhelming.

The Dean gives me a tight smile, watching me squirm in the chair that feels like it is trying to swallow me up. "Hello Violet, how are you doing?" she asks in a curt voice.

"I'm okay."

"I know that this has been a horrible year for you."

"Definitely hasn't been the greatest year, that's for sure," I say timidly.

"I hate to do this over the holiday break, but we need to chat about your grades." Any hint of compassion in her voice disappearing, she pulls up something on her computer and scrolls through it before continuing. "You failed all of your academic classes last semester and you had Ds in most of your dance classes. It looks like you had one C in Ballet."

I swallow hard, making eye contact with her hard, judgmental gaze. "I know, I'm so sorry. I'll do better."

"The semester before that was the same. With the limited spots at Juilliard reserved for those who are dedicated to succeeding here, we can't have students who aren't willing to put in the work required. Due to your circumstances, I've been lenient; giving you far longer than any other student would have gotten to catch up." She steeples her hands in front of her, leaning back into her chair like a judge about to read my sentence to me. "I'm sorry, but it has come to the point where you are going to have to find another school to continue your education."

What? Heat rushes through me followed by numb tingling in my extremities. My lungs seem to have forgotten how to work properly, screaming that there isn't enough oxygen in the stifling room. My sweater that is usually one of my favorites and a go-to for comfort feels restraining and itchy against my skin. There's no way I heard her right. *Did I just get kicked out of Juilliard?* Juilliard has been my dream since as far back as I can remember. I sit in silent shock, trying and failing to fill my lungs with much needed air, staring blankly at the Dean without uttering a word.

When I don't respond, she continues without a hint of the previous compassion in her eyes. "Termination will be effective immediately. I'm truly sorry and wish you the best."

With the obvious dismissal, I force myself to my feet as numbness washes over me and my vision tunnels. Somehow, I make it out of the office and leave the building, a blast of cold air hitting me in the face. The dark clouds above threaten rain and I tighten my grip on my umbrella as I walk the seven blocks to Konnie's school on autopilot. The bright red of the umbrella against the dreary gray of the city is the only thing I pay attention to as it swings back and forth as I walk.

Normally I would take the subway and I startle when a car horn blasts next to me. I quicken my pace to get out of the crosswalk, the car racing past me and I realize where I am. Konnie's school looms in front of me. The shrill school bell rings and it isn't long before Konnie walks toward me with her ever present scowl. She puts on her headphones and starts walking toward the subway station without a backward glance, oblivious to my emotional distress.

The damp smell of the subway mingles with the smell of too many bodies in one space assaulting my nose. I take a seat next to Konnie and stare at the doors as they close us inside. The jolt of the subway as it starts moving and speeds up jars me enough that my numbness begins to wear off and the dam of emotions inside of me cracks. The realization of my dreams vanishing from my grasp makes my stomach clench painfully, anger at myself for not being able to succeed makes my hands start to tremble, and the overwhelming sadness of everything that has happened this past year snatches the breath out of my lungs. Tears are now threatening to fall and I tuck my umbrella tighter under my arm, willing myself to hold it together for just a few minutes longer.

The muffled beat of Konnie's music mixes with the sounds of the other commuters rustling. The flip of a page of a book, someone is tapping a pen on one of the hand railings, a baby starts to wail a few seats over. All the noises, the smells, the blinding lights, become too much. Closing my eyes, I try to block out some of the visual stimulation, but with my eyes closed, my ears overcompensate and the overwhelming noise of the subway car becomes almost deafening. Newspaper pages rustling, someone humming along with whatever music they're listening to, a toddler wanting more snacks.

I know we need to stay on the subway. This isn't our stop, but I have to get out of this subway car, packed with people like a tin can full of sardines. When the train screeches to a halt and the doors open, I spring up from my seat, desperate to get to fresh air. Rushing out of the doors, Konnie stands, grabbing her backpack and sprints after me in surprise. The gloomy sky is barely visible as I start jogging. I need to be outside; I'm too hot but starting to shake as if I'm cold. I know I'll feel better if I can feel the breeze on my face; I just need to get out of this station.

I don't see Sebastian following us off the subway train until it's too late.

Icy fear snakes its way through my veins as he grabs my arm. His voice hard and emotionless when he says, "Don't make a scene or you'll both be dead."

He steers us up the stairs and out into the open air. Large snowflakes are floating down from the clouds and accumulate on the sidewalks as we exit the subway station. I finally get to feel the breeze on my face that I had been craving, but it doesn't offer any relief now. Konnie's wide, terrified eyes meet mine as he takes both of our cell phones, turns them off, and drops them into a garbage can. So much for anyone being able to track our locations. Ripping Konnie's backpack off her shoulders, he tosses it into the garbage can next.

His cold eyes assess us both. "Get rid of your headphones and anything else in your pockets."

He watches Konnie as she drops the items and her headphones into the trash can. I look around desperately for anyone who might be willing to help us. If we had gotten off one stop sooner, we would still be in a heavily populated area, but between the bad weather and the rundown buildings surrounding us, the street is uncharacteristically empty.

Sebastian's attention turns to me. "You too."

As he turns and pats down Konnie, making sure she isn't trying to hide anything, I walk toward the garbage can, patting my own pockets, double checking that there isn't anything that I can use to help us.

There isn't.

With Sebastian's concentration on Konnie, I stand in front of the garbage can and scan the isolated street again. This time making eye contact with a homeless woman, huddled in an alleyway darkened by the shadows of one of the tall buildings. Bundled up, she blends in with the wall.

Pleading in silent communication with my eyes, I drop my umbrella behind the garbage can instead of dropping it inside. The weathered woman's eyes follow the umbrella to the ground, the bright red a stark contrast against the fresh snow.

With one last glance toward the shadowed alley, I turn back toward Konnie and Sebastian. Biting back tears, I meet Sebastian's eyes as he checks my pockets.

The snow comes down thicker, hiding our footsteps as we walk down the street. Looking up into the flakes, I will them to stop falling. The flurry erases any evidence of where Sebastian is taking us, his threatening presence looming behind us as we walk.

I reach for Konnie's hand and squeeze it tight. One last attempt at trying to console my little sister, because despite the hope and courage I'm trying to give to Konnie, I know this is not going to end well for us.

Chapter 40

Matiu

Walking briskly toward the subway I try not to worry about Violet. It has been hours, and she still hasn't responded to my text. I am acutely aware of how whiny that sounds even though I am only thinking about it in my head, but it is weird. She usually texts me back pretty quick and something is pestering me about it. Something feels off. I don't want to text again and seem needy, but I thought she would want to know more about my interview with Viktor.

Dread settles like a weight on my chest. Maybe she is getting sick of me hanging around. Maybe she doesn't want me sleeping on her couch. Or maybe now that we are in a better place she is realizing that she really doesn't want to be with me. *Am I asking too much of her?* I have never thought of myself as clingy before, but maybe I am and I am freaking her out.

I really need to talk to someone about Nikau, but the only person I want to talk to is Violet. I don't want to dredge up the past with my family again if we still don't get any answers. It would be like rubbing salt into a wound for no reason, but the fact that I now know that he was handed straight to Sebastian has my head reeling. *What did Sebastian do with Nikau?*

I probably don't want to know.

But at the same time, I need to know what happened to my little brother after I left him alone on the street. Another wave of guilt floods me as I find a seat on the subway, but before I can go too deep down the guilt rabbit hole, my phone rings and I fumble, reaching for it, hoping it is Violet.

Genevieve's name lights up the screen. Maybe Violet's phone is dead or something. That would explain why she never responded to my text. I answer with a quick hello.

"Hey Detective McAllister, I mean Matiu," Genevieve corrects herself. It has been weird for both her and Steve to see me as anything other than the detective that was there on one of the worst nights of their lives. "Are Violet and Konnie with you?"

An uneasy feeling snakes its way through my body, settling in my stomach. "No, were they supposed to be with me?"

"No, not that I know of." She pauses before continuing like she doesn't know what to say. "I was hoping they were with you and Violet just forgot to tell me about her plans or something. Neither of them came home after Konnie got out of school and both of their phones are going straight to voicemail."

With trembling fingers, I put Genevieve on speaker phone and pull up Find my Friends, clicking on Violet's name. I watch as that little rotating circle goes round and round until "no location found" pops up. I try Konnie next and get the same result.

Frantically, I click on Violet's name again, hoping that it was a mistake the first time. Or maybe they didn't have good service and now they do. But the words on the screen seem to burn themselves into my mind.

No location found.

"Are you still there?" I hear Genevieve ask. She sounds far away; everything seems to get farther away, like someone is zooming out on a picture. Except this isn't a picture, this is real.

The real world comes crashing back into me. Everything seems too bright, too loud. I take her off speaker phone and hold my cell back up to my ear with a trembling hand.

"When was the last time you heard from either of them?" I manage to ask.

"When Violet left to take Konnie to school this morning. Now that I'm thinking about it, I should have gone with her. Her school hasn't started back up yet, so she would have had to come home alone after dropping Konnie off."

"Well, if she didn't come to pick Konnie up from school, Konnie would have called you, right?"

"I would think so, but I should have gone with her. Why didn't I think about that? She seemed super nervous this morning before she left, but when I asked her if she was okay, she said everything was fine."

"Okay, stay at the apartment. I'll be there soon."

Genevieve agrees. I disconnect the call and immediately call Agent Sullivan.

"Hey Matiu, did you find something new?"

"Violet and Konnie didn't come home when they were supposed to today, and their location isn't showing up on my phone."

"Okay, are you sure that they didn't just make a stop on the way home?"

Frustration bubbles up and despite me trying to keep calm, my voice sounds harsh. "No, I'm not sure, but after everything the girls have gone through, there is no way Violet would ever let Genevieve worry like this. I know something's wrong. I can feel it."

"You need to calm down. I know I'm asking a lot, but I need you to be the detective right now and not the worried boyfriend."

"I know that," I snap. "But they were supposed to be home hours ago, Alec."

"Since the girls have been threatened multiple times we have reasonable suspicion, I'll call into the office and open an urgent missing persons case. Have you started looking for them anywhere yet?"

My fists clench in frustration. "No. Not yet."

"What subway stop do the girls get on and off of when they're going to school?"

I give Alec all the information I know about the girls' routes to and from school as I rush out of the subway station and start sprinting toward the apartment building, weaving through all the commuters heading home after work.

"Bring Genevieve and Steve to the office. I'll get some units to help search and request the footage of the subway stations," Alec says before hanging up the phone.

Steve answers the apartment door when I rap my knuckles against it. He opens the door wide for me to walk in. Genevieve is pacing back and forth across the living room. Livi is sitting on the couch watching Genevieve pace with a worried look on her face.

When I walk into the room, she stops her pacing and rushes toward me. "Have you heard anything?"

"No. You both need to come with me. Livi, you too."

Genevieve nods and quickly scrawls a note for Violet to call her if she gets home, leaving it on the counter before following me out the door. We quickly make our way through the snow to my car and Livi and Genevieve climb into the back seat. The air around us feels suffocating, electrified, heavy with tension as the doors shut and we are all trapped together in the small space. Steve and I share a worried look before I put the car in gear and drive toward the FBI office. The expressions on Genevieve and Livi's faces in the rearview mirror bring back memories of the first night I met them—terrified, covered in blood.

They aren't covered in blood this time and I hope and pray Violet and Konnie won't be when we find them either.

But all the sinister red messages flash through my mind—Sebastian has been warning us he was out for blood for months. We knew something was coming, but we still weren't fast enough to outwit him in the end.

I hit the steering wheel with my fist, making both girls in the backseat jump. Apologizing, I grip the steering wheel tight enough to cut off the circulation to my fingertips and focus on the slick roads.

We need to find the girls before it is too late.

It might already be too late, but I can't let my mind go there. Right now, I need to think like a detective, not someone who is terrified that his girlfriend and her little sister are missing.

My girlfriend. The label doesn't feel quite right. Violet feels like more than a girlfriend to me. Girlfriends come and go, but Violet feels like forever.

Does Violet feel the same way?

I still don't know, but I desperately want the chance to find out.

I send out a silent plea. *Hold on Violet. I'm searching for you.*

Chapter 41

Violet

A sour taste fills my mouth, and my head is pounding. Slowly, I crack my eyelids open. Blurry images greet me and I blink multiple times to focus on what I'm looking at.

Where am I?

A slow and steady dripping comes from somewhere in the room. My shoulder aches and I shift my position to give it some relief from the cold concrete I'm laying on. I can't shift too much, though; my hands are tied behind my back. The abrasive rope stings my skin as I try to adjust my weight off my shoulder. The gag in my mouth tastes metallic and rancid; it takes everything in me not to heave up the last thing I ate—although I can't remember what that was.

Sifting through the fog in my mind I try to recall the last thing I can remember. The disappointment is crushing as memories of meeting with the Dean flood back in.

Getting kicked out of Juilliard.

Following Konnie onto the subway.

Sebastian.

Adrenaline surges through my body as I bolt to an upright position. Dragging my feet in front of me, I groan. They're tied together too and I'm secured to something cold and metal coming out of the wall. A pipe maybe?

Propping myself up into a sitting position I lean against the cold metal and my head spins. Waves of nausea threaten the contents of my stomach again. Trying hard to quell the queasiness, I swallow the saliva that has pooled in my mouth. I don't want to find out what happens if you throw up with a gag in your mouth.

The nausea takes a back seat in my worries when I remember Sebastian has Konnie too. Heart racing and my vision still blurry, I frantically search the room around me. Pulling at my restrained wrists, the already raw skin breaks and becomes slick with blood. As my vision finally starts to clear, I can see her lying on the floor, tied up just like me, a few feet to my right.

Relief fills me and then terror follows closely behind.

Where are we?

Is Konnie okay?

Where is Sebastian? Searching the surrounding area, I don't see any signs of him.

"Kaa-eee," I call out quietly. It doesn't sound anything remotely like her name with the gag in my mouth. I don't want to alert Sebastian that we're awake, wherever he is, but I need to know she is okay.

Konnie doesn't move. Squinting my eyes, I watch her still form for movement.

Nothing.

Is she hurt?

Or worse?

I can't tell if she is breathing and I hold my breath and watch to see if her chest is moving up and down. I tug against the ropes binding my wrists again, I need to get free, but the twisted fibers don't stretch. Instead, they dig deeper into my already raw and bleeding skin.

Calling out to her again, louder this time, a sigh of relief rushes through my gagged lips as she starts to stir. Her eyelids flicker open and her eyes widen in fear. She looks just as disoriented as I was, and she fights against her tied wrists, pulling hard on the metal pipe she's tethered to. Terrified screams muffled by the gag in her mouth fill the musty, cold room.

In an attempt to calm Konnie down, I mumble for her to stop yelling, but she can't understand my muffled words and I have no idea what she's saying. Shaking my head I try to tell her to be quiet with a shh, but it comes out more like a loud, fast breath. Ugh, these stupid gags are so frustrating. And gross. I don't even want to know what's on mine.

Both of our coats are gone and I realize that Konnie isn't wearing her glasses either, so she probably can't even see me shaking my head. I give up and slump against the unforgiving metal behind me. After a few minutes, Konnie, shivering from the cold, finally stops screaming and tries to say something that might be my name.

The temperatures outside have been rapidly dropping the past few days and whatever room we're in isn't heated. Sitting on the concrete floor tied to metal pipes, we're going to freeze.

I have no idea if we'll be okay.

Or how to get untied.

This might be our last moments alive on this Earth.

But there is no way I'm going out without a fight.

I will not live in fear any longer. The monster I've been running from has finally caught up to me. I may not be Mom, or able to do anything like the woman we all loved, but I'll do everything in my power to protect my little sister.

Even if I die trying.

My eyes scan the room for my phone, but then I remember Sebastian dropping it into the garbage can by the subway station. The room seems to be empty aside from us and the pipes we're tied to. The persistent dripping noise is coming from a corner too dark to see into. Each plop of liquid echoes through the darkness.

Wriggling my wrists again, they have more movement now that my skin is slippery from the oozing sores the rope has left behind. I yank hard against the ropes, sucking in a breath and bite back a scream as the rough, abrasive strands slash into my skin. Not just a raw sore anymore as my skin gives way to the rigid restraints, hot blood trickles down to my fingertips. Switching my attention to my feet, I flex my ankles. These ropes aren't quite as tight as those around my wrists. Wriggling my feet back and forth, I work on getting them free.

If I can get the ropes off, I can also untie Konnie. Maybe we can find a way out before Sebastian comes back. And if we can't, maybe I can attack him when he comes through the door and at least give Konnie the chance to run. Another sound mingles with the dripping water, a distant thud. Pausing my attempt to free myself, I sit motionless, listening for what might be coming. My heart freezes and the cold cuts into my limbs.

Is Sebastian coming back?

Chapter 42

Matiu

"Any news?" I ask as I burst through Alec's office door with Steve, Genevieve and Livi following behind me.

"We have officers canvassing the areas around Konnie's school and the usual subway stations they use. I've requested subway surveillance footage as well."

Genevieve wraps her arms tightly around herself. "Did you find out if Konnie was at school today?" she asks.

"Yes, Konnie was present at school. Do you know if Violet was planning on going anywhere else today?"

"Not that I know of."

"What about Jocelyn? Have you talked to her?" I ask.

Genevieve shakes her head and pulls out her phone, scrolling through her contacts and clicking on Jocelyn's name.

"Put it on speaker," Alec says and we all wait for her to answer. The deafening ticking of the clock grates on my nerves as we wait. Jocelyn finally answers; I thought the call was going to go to voicemail.

"Have you heard from Violet today?" Genevieve asks.

"No. And I've been worried. I tried calling her to see how her meeting went, but she didn't answer and hasn't called me back."

Genevieve's brows scrunch in confusion. "What meeting?"

"She got an email from the Dean's office about a meeting this afternoon."

Why would Violet be at the school during break?

"But Juilliard isn't even in session," I say.

"I know that's why she was so worried. Is that Matiu? What's going on? Is Violet okay?" Jocelyn's voice turns frantic.

"We don't know," Genevieve responds, her voice shaky.

Alec leans toward the phone. "If you hear from Violet or think of any information that might help us find her please let us know."

Jocelyn agrees and Genevieve ends the call. Alec tells us to sit down and does a search for the Dean's information and we listen to his end of the conversation as he speaks with someone on the phone.

I can't just sit here and wait.

Shoving my chair back with a shrill screech, I stand up. "I'm going to go look for them."

Alec motions for me to sit back down and finishes his call before turning toward us. "You going to go search the whole of New York City by yourself?" he asks with an irritated look on his face.

"If that is what I have to do, then yes," I bark back in anger.

Alec sighs and rubs a hand over his eyes before the ding of a text has him looking at his phone. "Sit down Matiu, you're not going anywhere until we have an idea of where to start looking." He turns his attention back to Genevieve. "The Dean's secretary said that Violet was at her meeting this afternoon, and officers talking to Konnie's classmates have verified that they saw Konnie walking toward the subway station with Violet after school."

"That means they were fine this afternoon," Livi points out.

"Yes, this is helpful because it narrows down the hours that they could have gone missing. We don't have to search footage of this morning" Alec says before looking back at me. "I need you to go through the footage when we get it and see where they got off the subway, or if they even got on it to begin with. We have witnesses saying they saw them walking toward the station, but we don't actually know if they got on a train."

"Do we know what the meeting with the Dean was about?" Genevieve asks.

Alec shakes his head. "The secretary didn't know, but I'll keep trying to get a hold of the Dean."

Steve pulls Genevieve tighter into his side before asking, "What do you want us to do?"

"We need the three of you to stay here where we know you're safe. You can help by calling anyone that might have seen Violet or Konnie, or anyone that they might have gone to see," Alec says.

"What time is your flight?" Steve asks looking at Livi.

Livi's eyebrows reach toward her hairline. "Who cares, there's no way I'm leaving right now. I can't just fly home not knowing if Violet and Konnie are okay."

Genevieve reaches over and grabs Livi's hand and the two best friends hold tightly to each other.

Agent Delgado walks into the room. "We got the footage from the subway station cameras. It should be in your inbox," she says before taking a seat in the chair next to me.

Alec pulls up the email and stands up. "Matiu go through the footage and see what you can find while I make some more phone calls. Delgado, can you take these three to a conference room and get them settled."

Delgado nods and Genevieve, Steve, and Livi follow her out the door.

"Let me know if you find anything," Alec says before putting his phone back up to his ear and walking out into the hall.

I skip all the morning footage and jump to the video taken this afternoon around the time Konnie's school ends. It doesn't take me long to spot Violet and Konnie amid the crowd; they walk through the station and onto the subway. Konnie has her headphones on and looks grumpy, but that isn't anything new. Violet looks distracted, clutching her umbrella tightly. She might look a bit distressed, but she doesn't seem frightened and no one else seems to be with them. I watch them disappear into the subway car before clicking onto the footage of the other station that was sent.

The train I just watched them get onto arrives. Holding my breath, I watch all the passengers pouring out of the open doors.

Violet and Konnie aren't present in the throng of commuters.

Racing out of the office I almost run into Delgado and Alec who is still talking on the phone in the hallway. "I saw them get on the subway, but they didn't get off at their usual stop." I run my hand through my hair. "How long will it take us to get footage from all the other stations where that train stopped?"

"I'll request it now," Delgado says before pulling out her phone.

The same fear, the same helplessness, the same need to do something comes rushing back. It is like I am reliving Nikau disappearing all over again. But this time I am not ten years old. This time I am an adult. I am a detective for crying out loud; I know I can find Violet if I put my mind to it.

Violet and Konnie will not share the same fate as Nikau.

Whatever that dark fate was.

I will see Violet again and when I do, I won't hide my feelings anymore.

Life is too short to not show those we love just how much we truly love them.

Pacing down the hall I go to the conference room to check and see if Genevieve, Steve, or Livi have heard anything. They are quietly huddled together. Livi grasps a mug in her hands and Genevieve's eyes meet mine as soon as I walk into the room.

"I found footage of them getting on the subway, but not getting off. We're waiting for video from other stations to see where they exited the train."

Snow has started falling again. I watch the delicate flakes float down to the ground outside the conference room window. It looks so peaceful, but I am feeling anything but peace.

Glancing over at Genevieve, Steve, and Livi, I see the same fear and helplessness reflecting in their own eyes.

I should be doing something.

Taking one last look at the snow accumulating outside, I push myself off the wall I have been leaning against. "I'm going to go help search," I say to the three teens that I feel responsible for. No, not responsible, that's not the right word. They feel like family, like my world wouldn't be quite right if any one of them was missing from it.

Genevieve stands up and surprises me when she wraps her arms around me in a tight hug. "Find my sisters, please," she pleads quietly. "She loves you, so find her and then hold on tight. Please don't break her heart; we've all had enough heartbreak in our lives."

Genevieve pulls back her eyes brimming with unshed tears. I can't find the words I want to say, so I nod and am relieved at Alec's impeccable timing as he walks into the conference room.

"Matiu, I need you to go back to the apartment for some of Violet and Konnie's clothing for the K9 unit to locate the girls."

Relieved to finally be able to go do something, Genevieve hands me her apartment keys and I don't wait to be told twice before I leave the conference room and make my way back down to my car.

Driving faster than I should, I weave in and out of traffic to get there as quickly as possible, even though I don't think it is saving any time. I squeeze out of my lane and through the next to park on the street in front of the girls' apartment building.

I sprint to the doors narrowly avoiding a fall as I slip, the snow making the sidewalk slick. Barreling through the lobby and into the elevator I push the button to their floor multiple times before the doors close and it starts ascending at a snail's pace. The doors aren't even open all the way when I push myself through and race down the hallway to their apartment door.

The door is cracked when I get there and I can smell a hint of smoke. Pulling my gun from its holster and pushing the door all the way open with my foot I call out, "Police, make yourself known!"

I don't hear any movement, but smoke wafts out the open door, curling along the floor. On high alert, I check my surroundings and make my way into the apartment. The air is heavy and acrid, the visible gray vapor getting thicker as I near Violet's room. Reaching for her doorknob I jerk my hand back from the heat emanating off the metal knob.

I know from my training that if a doorknob is that hot I shouldn't open it, but if a fire is confined to only Violet's room maybe I can put it out. I still need a piece of clothing so the K9 units can help find her—if the smoke hasn't erased her smell from the fabric already.

Using the sleeve of my coat I go against my better judgment and open the door. A blast of intense heat forces me to the ground, singeing my eyebrows and stealing the breath from my lungs. The uncontrollable flames roar out of Violet's room, catching the walls of the hallway on fire in an instant. The fiery inferno surrounds me, blocking my exit.

Chapter 43
Violet

The thuds continue to get closer morphing into heavy footsteps. The steady rhythm brings to mind the executioner drum roll that I've seen in movies—each step one moment closer to what may possibly be the end of our stories.

The door handle rattles.

He came back too soon.

I haven't been able to free myself or Konnie.

I haven't been able to do *anything*.

I glance over at my little sister, who had also been trying to get her wrists free. The door opens on creaky hinges and we both freeze, trying to hide any evidence of our attempts to escape. Deep down I know that the person coming through the door will be Sebastian, but fear still makes a home in the pit of my stomach when I see his scarred face.

The same face that I thought was a kind neighbor—although no kindness shows on his face now. His face is contorted in anger and he looks at Konnie and then me in disgust.

He walks into the room, pacing back and forth between us, mumbling under his breath. The drum roll continuing with every footfall.

He stops suddenly, startling me, and glares in my direction. "Why did you have to ruin everything?"

What? How did I ruin everything? If anyone is to blame for ruining anything, it would be him. For taking away our parents, for forcing me to become a caretaker instead of a just turned twenty-year-old that still needs to be taken care of herself.

When I don't answer, he rips the gag out of my mouth with so much force it makes me cry out, the fabric pulling against my teeth and lips painfully. He doesn't seem to notice though as he gets close, forcing me to look at him. "I said, why did you have to ruin everything?"

His voice is cold and unfeeling and the angry void of his eyes sends more waves of panic coursing through me. "I … I don't understand what I ruined."

Sebastian laughs bitterly. "Everything was going according to plan. Years and years of planning, waiting, watching for my moment and in one night your family derailed everything. Your sister and her boyfriend by getting Mark killed and your stupid father, always trying to be the hero, getting himself killed. I was so close to getting what I needed."

The blueprints. I try to remember everything Genevieve told me about the plans Sebastian was blackmailing Dad for. A weapon big and scary enough that very few people had access to the information. Dad being one of the few.

"What did you want the weapon blueprints for?" I ask.

"There are people who need to pay for their crimes." He starts his restless movement again, each step echoing through the bare room. "I used to think that people in general were good. Until some of those good people massacred an entire cruise ship full of innocent women and children."

Ironic since he himself now terrorizes innocent women and children I think, but know better than to say it out loud.

Those soulless eyes meet mine again. "The world had already hardened me by the death of my father and foster care. Not many people are willing to take in an angry teenage boy, but your father always told me to look for the good things in life, not to focus on the bad. He was in foster care with me and was happy, so I tried. I tried to find the good in the world, but it just wasn't there."

He pauses, staring into the darkness behind me, his eyes focused on something I can't see, reliving whatever haunts him. "The screams of the burning people who survived the initial explosion that night was the worst sound I had ever heard. But when it became obvious the ship wasn't carrying weapons or cargo, that it was transporting civilians, we still did nothing. I tried to put down life rafts and start pulling people out of the water, but orders were to cover up the mistake and disappear as quickly as possible."

Sebastian clenches his fists, his jaw tight. "We were going to leave them all there to drown. Do nothing, leave them to die. Your father telling me that we needed to be the good in the world when it wasn't there, played on repeat through my mind. I couldn't ignore the screams of the children, the wails of their mothers asking for help, so I jumped overboard. I needed to try and save some of them, any of them."

The room fills with tense silence as he is lost in his memories, and then he focuses back on me. "Did you know that if there's enough oil in the water, things can still burn, the fire dancing along the top of the water like it doesn't exist?"

I shake my head. Is this what he was blackmailing Dad with? I don't know if I want to hear any more of this story, but the longer I keep him talking, the more time it gives me to figure out how to get away from him.

Grabbing my jaw roughly, he turns my head to look at him. Sharp pain radiates through my cheeks. "Look at my face when I'm talking to you." He lets go of my face and I focus on him out of fear as he continues his rant. "I wasn't able to save a single one of those people and what did I get for it? Severe burns and a ship full of what I thought were *good* people leaving me for dead. Nobody even bothered looking for me. They covered it up. That's what I need the weapon for, the people who made the decision to do nothing, to cover everything up, to leave me behind need to pay. They don't deserve to go on with their unaffected lives while I'm forced to live in the shadows."

I don't know how to respond, but it doesn't matter because now that he is telling his story, he doesn't seem to want to stop.

"Against all odds, I survived and made my way back to Russia, only to find that my brother and mother both died while I was gone. I hadn't seen them since I was a child. By some miracle, I found my little sister. It had been so long since the last time I was in Russia everything had changed. My Russian was rusty. I hadn't spoken Russian for years. I knew I couldn't make a life for my sister and myself there. We needed to come back to the states, but there was no way I could immigrate under my name after being labeled MIA by the military."

I try to recall all the information that Matiu told me they found. Sebastian was actually his brother's name, not his. He came to the USA with his father as a child after his parents got divorced. His dad died, sending him into the foster care system as a teen. The man in front of me was my dad's foster brother, Andrei, at one point. They joined the military together. I'm trying to put all the pieces together, but I still can't figure out how Sebastian turned from someone who seemed to want to do the right thing into a villain.

He continues with a sneer. "After years of doing jobs for vile people, I finally got the connections I needed to smuggle myself back into America. My sister used all the proper channels so that we could have legitimate avenues for our needs, but I vowed to never let anyone tell me what to do, or tell me that there was any semblance of good in the world ever again. There are no good people Violet, all humans are selfish creatures that will always put their needs above those of others."

"But there is good in the world, just because there's bad too doesn't mean the good isn't there," I say, shaking my head. "And making the world a worse place won't help anyone."

He whips his body around fixing a glare on me, moving so fast that it takes me a second to register the sting of his slap across my cheek. The pain mixes with my anger and fear.

"The world is already a horrible place. Taking what I want doesn't even matter."

I know I should stop. I shouldn't push it any further, but all of my anger and frustration from the past several months comes bubbling to the surface. "It does matter! It matters that you took our parents from us, it matters that you took Matiu's little brother from him, and it matters that you took Mark from this world too!"

"I did not take Mark. Genevieve did that," he growls.

"No, the only reason Mark was around Genevieve at all is because you sent him there. Genevieve didn't ask Mark to befriend her, Genevieve didn't ask Mark to betray her, and Genevieve definitely didn't ask to be held at gunpoint and watch someone she considered a friend get gunned down in front of her. That wasn't Genevieve. That was *you*."

The fire in Sebastian's eyes seems to reflect that horrible fire so long ago he had been talking about. I look into his dark, empty gaze and say, "The world may be broken and there are so many horrible things that happen, but there are good things that happen too. It's a choice that *you* have to make. Are you going to make the world a better place, or are you going to make it worse?"

Sebastian stills and I think he might be listening. His posture seems to soften for a moment before he stiffens again, his back rigid. "You sound just like your father. Good never prevails in this world, and if you think otherwise you're naïve just like he was." He doesn't sound as angry anymore, just broken and tired.

"What are you going to do with us?" I ask.

"As soon as I get Genevieve and Steve here, you'll find out," he says, his lips tugging into an evil smirk. "But thanks to your cop boyfriend, I have to figure out how to get them out of the FBI office first."

Relief washes through me and I can't help but repeat what he just said. "Genevieve is with Matiu?"

"Isn't that what I just said?" Sebastian snaps.

He seems to be done talking, but if Matiu has Genevieve and Steve, he knows we're missing. I need to stall long enough for him to find us. Trying to figure out how to get Sebastian talking again, I think about Nikau and before I can think better of it, I ask, "What happened to Matiu's brother?"

"Who?" Sebastian's brows pull together in confusion.

"Years ago, Matiu's brother disappeared in Charleston. He was only a child at the time, but the last time he was seen by anyone was when he was brought to you."

"I actually remember the Charleston kid. I rarely run into having to deal with children. It wasn't personal. He saw something he shouldn't have and I couldn't have him talking to anyone."

"He was a child. How threatening could he have really been to you? Would he have even understood what he saw?"

"He wandered into a secluded alley and watched wide eyed as one of my men killed someone who didn't do their job. So yeah, I'm pretty sure he understood what he saw."

Poor Nikau must have been terrified. Even now, tied up to a frigid pipe and terrified about my own future, my heart hurts for him.

"What did you do to him?" I ask in a whisper.

"I got rid of him, just like I'm going to get rid of you three. I should've gotten rid of you long ago and disappeared again, but I wanted the four of you to know what it feels like to lose everything. And I mean *everything*, just like you all did by ruining my chances for my plan to continue and by taking my nephew from me. I wanted you to fear what was coming next, always watching over your shoulder, waiting for your ghosts to finally catch up to you."

This guy is delusional. How did we take everything from him? *He* took our parents from us.

"You still have your sister and niece."

His harsh laugh stops me from continuing. "My sister hates me. She's more than happy to take the money I give her and live an extravagant lifestyle, but she wants nothing to do with me."

"Well, maybe she wouldn't hate you if you didn't take her son away from her and then get him killed."

Pain floods my head, and I can taste the coppery tang of blood in my mouth. It takes me a moment to process that Sebastian hit me. My vision blurry again, I spit out the blood. I must have bitten my tongue. When my head stops spinning my gaze meets Konnie's wide eyes filled with fear, silent tears leaking down her cheeks. My poor little sister has been through so much, and now this.

I don't know what's going to happen.

I don't know how we're going to get out of this situation.

But maybe if I can get him talking again, if I haven't already made him too angry, maybe, just maybe, I can stall long enough for Matiu to arrive.

If he can find us in time.

Chapter 44

Matiu

Groaning timbers creak around me, some form of liquid hisses loudly as the intense heat continues to make a path through the apartment. The fire rages out of control, consuming everything it touches.

Dragging myself across the floor, trying to keep low below the smoke, I cover my face with my shirt and make my way to the apartment door. Pulling myself to my feet when I get to the entry, I grab a handful of the jackets and coats hanging by the front door, hoping that any of them belong to Violet and Konnie.

This building is even worse than we thought for safety standards. Violet's apartment is completely consumed in flames and no alarms are going off. The only sound is the roaring fire behind me. Spotting a fire alarm in the hallway I yank it down before pushing through the door to the stairs, taking them two at a time, racing to the bottom. Grabbing my cell phone, I call Alec and he answers as I finally make it outside to fresh air.

"The apartment is on fire. Send the fire department quick," I manage to get out, my lungs burning with every breath I take.

Alec doesn't ask questions, giving orders to get emergency personnel to the building. Throwing the armful of clothing onto the passenger seat I jump into my car and speed back toward the office. The glow of the fire against the darkening sky becomes visible in my rearview mirror as flames break free through one of the windows, climbing up the building with their devastating tendrils.

"Did you see what started the fire?" Alec asks his voice too loud as my phone connects to the speakers in my car.

"No. Whatever it was came from Violet's room, but that's all I know."

"Are you injured?" he asks as a violent fit of coughing takes hold of me, making it hard to focus on the icy road.

"I don't think so. I didn't really check though." I can still feel the jittery rush of adrenaline surging through me. "I seem to be in one piece."

"We need to get you checked out. It sounds like you at least had a good dose of smoke inhalation."

"I'll get checked out when we find Violet and Konnie," I say before disconnecting the call.

— • —

After making it back to the office, Genevieve identified one of the jackets I grabbed as Konnie's. Delgado left with it to get it to the K9 units, but the acrid smell of smoke coming off it is likely to cover any of Konnie's scent. Thankfully, the rest of the subway station footage came in while I was at the apartment.

The conference room is quiet despite Steve, Genevieve, and Konnie being in the room with me. The three of them are texting and sometimes calling anyone else they can think of that might have seen Konnie and Violet. The dinner that someone brought for all of us sits untouched on the table.

Alec and I split up the videos of each station between us. Clicking on the next file in my group I watch the last of the sun's rays completely disappear below the horizon as it loads. It is officially dark now and we still don't know where to look. The door bangs open and Alec comes in with a grim look on his face.

"What's wrong? Did they find them?" I ask.

He shakes his head. "No, no sign of the girls yet, but I just got word that the entire apartment building is now engulfed in flames. From what I understand, the fire department was able to evacuate everyone safely, but they haven't been able to get the fire under control yet."

The distress in the room is almost tangible. The tears Genevieve was holding back now make slow trails down her cheeks before she hurtles her phone at the conference room wall. The shattered pieces fall to the ground like tinkling glass in the silence, her uncharacteristic demonstration of anger shocking us all. Steve hesitantly reaches for her, their fingers linking together before she melts into him. Livi, for once, is at a loss for words and stares silently at her two friends.

Alec leaves the room to go back to searching his files of video. The same uncontrollable urge to find Violet that has been burning inside of me since we found out she was missing now turns into an unquenchable inferno. Where is she? Turning my attention back to my laptop I continue to scour the footage we have.

Until I see Violet.

Leaning closer to the monitor, the tingling of fear starts to feel more like panic as I watch her rush out of the subway doors, a wide-eyed Konnie following close behind. They seem to be alone still.

And then I see *him*.

He exits the train just before the doors close and follows behind Konnie and Violet. His coat is pulled up around the bottom of his face, but those cold dark eyes are the eyes of the man in all of the pictures I have been staring at for months. My worst fears are confirmed.

Sebastian has Violet and Konnie.

He walks up and roughly grabs Violet's arm, leaning forward to say something into her ear before ushering the girls up the stairs. When they reach the top of the stairs, before they leave the view of the camera, Violet turns to look behind her. Her eyes are full of fear, terror written across her beautiful features, but there is also a determined set to her jaw as she frantically searches the station for some form of help.

I have watched in awe for months at how strong the three Clark girls are. I know that despite her fear, Violet will do anything to protect her sisters.

It fills me with hope that she will be determined enough to survive until we find them. Followed by dread that she will do something to protect Konnie and get herself killed before I get there.

Fueled by fear and the need to find Violet, I grasp Nikau's dinosaur in my pocket. It doesn't comfort me this time and I stand up, my chair making a horrible screeching noise as it slides across the floor.

"Alec! I found them!" I shout pointing to the screen on my laptop.

He rushes over and squints at the station footage. "A couple units have already started canvassing that station. They've been moving down the subway line one station at a time."

Alec gets back on the phone sending all the units to the correct place, but I can't wait here any longer.

There is no more time. I need to find both of them.

Now.

Before it is too late.

The elevator won't be fast enough for me tonight, so I push through the stairwell door and sprint down the stairs, taking two or three at a time until I burst out into the snow filled air. The cold burns my lungs as I race to my car. I don't have a snow scraper, so I pull my coat sleeve over my hand and wipe at the snow on my windows.

Starting the car, I speed as fast as I can through New York City traffic to the subway station where Violet and Konnie were last seen. I don't even bother parking my car in an actual parking spot as I slide on the icy road before screeching to a stop near the subway exit. Checking my weapon, I make sure it is loaded and that the safety is on before pushing my door open and stepping out into the cold.

Police officers and agents are swarming the area. Nodding at a couple of the agents that I recognize, I look for anything that looks out of the ordinary. Where would Sebastian take the girls? It would have to be somewhere relatively close. An officer to my right pulls Konnie's backpack and then two cell phones out of the trash. I recognize the ballerina with the red tutu on the case of Violet's phone.

Someone had to have seen something.

In an alley not too far from the subway station, a group of homeless men and women huddle together against the cold. One of them is holding a red umbrella, blocking the snow from falling on her. Logically, I realize that there are many red umbrellas in the world, but I know that this one is Violet's.

Making my way toward them, one agent stops me. "We already talked to the group. They said they didn't see anything."

"I just have a couple of questions for them," I say.

"Good luck," he says with a frown before turning his focus back to the officers, looking for more clues around the garbage can.

Back home in Charleston, anyone living on the streets is always leery of officers. It has taken me many hours of genuine compassion and concern to have the reputation of someone they can trust.

And I need to get this woman to trust me in a matter of seconds.

I walk up to the frail old woman holding Violet's umbrella. "Where did you get that umbrella?" I ask, trying to sound as unthreatening as possible.

"I found it," she answers in an irritated tone.

"Where did you find it?"

She answers with silence and a defiant look in her eyes.

I squat down so that I am eye level with her. "There are two girls that I care about deeply that are in extreme danger. I need to find them before something happens to them. And that," I nod toward the umbrella in her hand, "is one of the girls' umbrellas."

Two of the homeless men look at each other warily, but it is the old woman that speaks up. "We didn't see anything."

I sigh in frustration finding Nikau's dinosaur with my fingers. What can I possibly say to make her trust me?

"Violet, the girl who owns that umbrella, is my girlfriend." I pause and make eye contact, hoping that she can see how much I mean what I am saying. "The only thing I care about right now is making sure she is okay."

I watch as a K9 unit pulls up, and the officer walks over to the garbage can with the dog. Even if the smoke covered any trace on the jacket I grabbed, Konnie's backpack will have her scent all over it.

I wish they would move faster.

"I never saw the girls or the man you're talking about," the woman says.

I didn't tell her they were with a man.

She did see them.

The first inklings of hope sprout in my chest. Observing her weathered face, I take her hand in mine before responding. "I never told you there was a man with them."

A flash of shock skirts across her face as she realizes she messed up. Giving her hand a squeeze I say, "I just want them to be safe. I need to find them. I promise they won't be in any danger from me."

Her eyes, surrounded by wrinkles, look like they have lived more than one lifetime. There is wisdom in them and I wonder for a brief moment how she ended up here.

"I believe you," she says quietly, pulling her hand from mine and pointing down the street. "The man took them down the street a couple of blocks before they disappeared into the old, shut down community center."

"Thank you," I say and take off running down the street in the direction that her frail finger is indicating.

Logic tries to win. I should call Alec. I should tell the agents and officers searching near the exit what I have found. I should find out more about this building I am running toward before I attempt to enter it.

But I am spurred on by the overwhelming need to find them.

Find them like I never found Nikau.

So I run.

I run through the snow-covered ice on the sidewalk.

I run like something is chasing me.

Maybe I am running from my past, or maybe I am running toward my future.

There is one thing I am certain of though.

I am running toward Violet.

I will always run toward Violet when she needs me.

Chapter 45

Violet

Sebastian is unhinged.

Whatever he's trying to do doesn't seem to be going well and despite my worry for Konnie and myself, I'm glad that Genevieve is safe from whatever horrible things he plans to do to us.

It makes me love Matiu even more.

I wish I hadn't been too afraid of my own feelings, or so worried that Matiu was pulling away. We wasted so much time.

Sebastian paces back and forth, muttering to himself. His sanity seems to unravel as we watch him walk between us. In all honesty, I'm not sure he has ever been completely sane, not with all the horrible things he has done, but his mental state seems to be deteriorating at a rapid pace.

Konnie and I are both shivering violently now. The sound of our teeth chattering fills the room.

"Can you give us back our coats?" I ask.

Turning toward me his pacing stops and his lips pull into a creepy smile. "You won't be around long enough to need your coats."

Numbness settles in as I realize that Konnie and I aren't making it out of this alive. Not only did he tell me some of his secrets, but he just insinuated we won't be surviving whatever he has planned. *If he's going to kill us anyway, what is he waiting for?*

Desperate to find any way out of this situation, I try to pull any semblance of human emotion out of Sebastian.

"You seem to have loved your family deeply. Do you really think that this is what your mom, your dad, or your brother would want you to be doing? Do you think they would be proud of you for hurting innocent people?"

He scoffs, giving me an irritated look.

"It's not too late to let us go. You can disappear and we won't say anything," I try again.

He responds by putting the rank gag back into my mouth. Konnie's eyes still hold the fear they did before, but now as I look at her, tears glisten her haunted eyes and I see so many of my own emotions reflecting back at me.

Fear, pain, remorse, anger.

Hopelessness.

His phone rings and he answers. I can't understand anything that's being said. He must be talking in Russian to whoever is on the other line. His Russian accent is getting thicker as his stress level rises. He must have lost most of his accent when he moved to the US as a child, because until now it hasn't been noticeable.

In a fit of rage Sebastian disconnects the call and hurls his phone across the room. It shatters when it hits the wall above Konnie making her whimper and curl into herself. Sebastian ignores us, cocking his head to the side. He goes silent and listens like he can hear something on the other side of the door.

Maybe it's not something, maybe it's someone.

I yell as loud as I can with the gag in my mouth. Everything I can do to make noise. I kick my feet against the concrete and bang my back against the pipe I'm tied to. My spine screams in pain, but I want to make as much noise as possible.

Closer to the door than I'm, Konnie's eyes go wide as she hears whatever Sebastian is hearing. She joins me in my attempt to make noise.

Sebastian whips around, facing me, pulling a gun out of his jacket, he points it at my chest. "Stop."

The gun he holds in his hands silences our attempts.

Alarm jolts through me as I look down the barrel pointed straight at me. If he pulls that trigger who will take care of Konnie? Would either of my sisters be able to recover from another loss? I would never see Matiu again.

"Violet? Konnie?" Matiu's deep voice on the other side of the door has never sounded as beautiful as it does right now.

Yelling once again through my gag, Matiu pounds against the door until it bursts open and I get to see his face for a moment. That handsome face that I wasn't sure I would ever see again. Hope fills me for a few short seconds before the air is shattered by two deafening bangs.

Fire rips through my abdomen and I hear Matiu yell something.

My vision blurs. I try to focus on Matiu, but my brain fills with fog and everything goes black.

Chapter 46

Matiu

My relief at seeing Violet and Konnie alive dissipates quickly as the air splits with the loud sounds of gunshots. Two shots, his gun pointed at Violet. Fear courses through me with an electric jolt. Sebastian is still holding the gun, rotating to the right toward Konnie. With his concentration on the girls, I don't give myself time to think, and rush toward him, tackling him to the ground.

My ears ring as another gunshot explodes through the room, but the gun clatters across the floor out of Sebastian's reach. Pain surges through my jaw as his fist makes contact with my face, resulting in a split lip. Tasting blood, the force of his punch throws me back and I lose my grip on him. For an older guy, he is surprisingly strong.

Taking advantage of slipping away from me, Sebastian scrambles toward the gun lying on the ground, just out of reach. I lunge for him, throwing all my weight into his frame, knocking him off balance, and we both tumble back to the ground. I try to hold him down while I reach to secure his arms, realizing too late that I have nothing to restrain him with.

I should have told Alec where I was going.

Sebastian wrenches one of his arms free, knocking me to the side. He manages to swing and lands a hard punch to the side of my head.

Darkness surrounds the edges of my vision from the impact. Willing myself to stay conscious I focus on Violet's still form lying on the ground and stand back up. As my vision clears, I dodge another punch before elbowing him with all the force I have. The crunch of his nose as my elbow connects with his face has him shouting out in pain.

But instead of backing off he kicks me. The powerful impact of his foot against the back of my knee has me hitting the ground again, both of my knees shooting pain through my body as they connect with the concrete floor.

I underestimated him.

I was cocky, so sure of my own size and strength, I didn't even worry about being able to subdue Sebastian.

Blood pours out of Sebastian's nose, running down his face.

One of my eyes is swelling, making it hard to see clearly.

I'm going to lose this fight to a man twice my age.

Rallying all the strength I can muster; I reach up and yank his head down toward the ground as hard as I possibly can. He slips out of my grip at the last second and my hand collides with the concrete, sending white hot pain shooting up my arm.

He smiles wickedly at me, blood coating his teeth.

I raise my arms to protect my head, waiting for the next blow to come.

Instead, I hear a dog barking and the sweet sound of footsteps pounding toward us.

Sebastian is ripped off me by officers and his arms are secured behind his back with handcuffs.

Scrambling to my feet, I swipe a hand across my bloody lip, instructing one of the officers to call for an ambulance and I rush toward Violet.

Please let her be alive, I plead silently.

Searching the room for Konnie, I see she is awake and alert. "Someone check Konnie for any injuries," I shout.

Kneeling next to Violet, I feel for a pulse. It is there, but it is faint.

She is slumped over, a dark stain covering her torso. Untying her as quickly as I can, I carefully lower her to the ground and lift her shirt.

Blood pools out of two gunshot wounds to her abdomen. Ripping my jacket off, I apply pressure.

"Stay with me Violet," I whisper.

I visually check over the rest of her body. Her chest moves up and down with each unconscious breath.

An officer helps untie Konnie and pulls the gag from her mouth. A heart-wrenching sob escapes her lips. "Violet! Is Violet okay?" she cries.

Konnie crawls over next to me. With tears running down her face, she grabs one of Violet's hands. Her other hand holds pressure on her own arm where the bullet must have grazed when I tackled Sebastian, blood seeping through the fabric.

"I'm sorry, Vi," Konnie sobs. "I'm sorry I've been so horrible. Please don't leave me too."

Knots form in my stomach. These poor sisters have been through so much.

Everything seems to move in slow motion. Someone takes a sobbing Konnie and helps her out of the room. She needs to get checked out, and she doesn't need to see her sister like this.

I know the officers called for ambulances and additional support. I heard them, but it feels like we are running out of time.

Giving myself something to concentrate on, I count each rise and fall of Violet's chest. Pleading and praying for help to get here soon, as each breath comes slower and slower.

I have wasted so much time trying to figure out if my feelings for Violet are acceptable or not. I should have told her how I felt months ago.

How I still feel.

Color is draining from Violet's face, and tears stream down my cheeks.

"Fight, Violet!" I plead. I can't lose her now.

Both of my hands are sticky with her blood, my jacket soaked through.

The room fills with even more people as emergency personnel arrive. I didn't notice them take Sebastian out of the room, but he is gone and I relinquish my hold on Violet to the EMT who starts to work on her. She calls out information to her partner that I know my brain should understand, but I can't seem to keep up. They load Violet onto a stretcher and rush her outside.

Following behind we pass a handcuffed Sebastian who gives me a sinister smile and sneers. "All good things must come to an end, Detective."

Without thinking I launch my fist at his face. The crack as my knuckles meet his cheekbone reverberates through the air. Sebastian falls back onto the hood of the police car he was standing next to and slides to the ground, officers scramble to pick him back up and pull me away.

"Not today," I say, pulling my arm from the officer holding me back and take one last look at Sebastian. His nasty smirk is gone and a new cut on his cheek has blood winding a path down his face.

Violet and Konnie are both loaded into ambulances and I climb into the ambulance with Violet. Two EMTs work hard to keep her with us on the way to the hospital.

Reaching for her face, I brush my thumb across her pale cheek, leaving a streak of blood behind. Leaning forward, I rest my head on the stretcher next to hers.

"I love you Violet, please don't leave me," I whisper through my tears, reaching down to grab her hand.

I am never letting go again.

Chapter 47

Violet

I t hurts to breathe.

Fiery pain shoots through my abdomen with every breath I take.

Wincing, I open my eyes and try to move.

Nope.

Moving is a bad idea.

One hand has an IV in it and the other is wrapped in Matiu's. He has a tight grip on my fingers even though he has fallen asleep, his head lying on my bed. Looking around what is obviously a hospital room, I see Genevieve asleep in a chair by the window.

"Gen," I try to say, but my throat is so dry that what comes out sounds more like a croak. Croak or not, it is enough to wake Matiu, who breathes out a sigh of relief when he sees me looking back at him. He looks exhausted with dark circles under his eyes and his shoulders sag with the burden of the emotions he has been carrying for months and maybe something more. Is Konnie gone? I don't know if I can survive losing another family member.

"Violet," he whispers.

The way he says my name carries a weight I've never heard before. It's laced with a million things he's not saying, and a thousand more I wish he would say.

"How are you feeling?" he asks me quietly.

"Not good," I say in a raspy voice that tickles my throat and makes me cough. The cough rips through me, spreading the fiery pain to areas that I didn't notice before.

Matiu reaches for a bottle of water, opens it, and holds it up to my lips. Taking a small sip, the coughing recedes and I realize just how thirsty I am.

"Don't drink too much too fast," Matiu cautions.

The small amount of water does wonders for my dry throat, and I'm finally able to talk. "Where's Konnie?" Fear raises its ugly head again and I'm afraid to hear his answer.

Matiu waits for my searching eyes to meet his. "Konnie's okay. She has a minor wound, but they checked her out and she was discharged. Steve and Livi are with her."

"But she's okay?" I ask, to reassure myself.

"She's okay Violet, you're both going to be okay."

Our conversation wakes Genevieve, and she rushes over to my hospital bed. Tears of relief spilling from her dark green eyes. She holds my gaze, silently speaking the quiet things that only a sister would understand.

"I thought you were gone," Genevieve says through her tears. "I can't lose you Vi, I need my big sister here with me."

"I'm not going anywhere," I say as my own tears wet my face.

Our family is already so much smaller than it used to be. I can't even fathom the pain one of us would feel if we lost a sister.

I reach for her hand, grasping it in mine to reassure her before turning my attention back to Matiu. "What happened?" I ask.

"Sebastian shot you twice. Both wounds were in your abdomen and relatively close to each other. Thankfully, the bullets didn't hit anything that the doctors couldn't fix." Worry spreads across Matiu's face as he continues. "You're going to have a long recovery ahead of you. We need to see if you can take a leave of absence from school."

Squeezing my eyes closed, I groan. "I won't have to worry about that."

"What does that mean?" Genevieve asks.

"It means I'm no longer a student at Juilliard. I flunked out."

Shock fills Genevieve's face. "That's what the appointment with the Dean was about? Why didn't you tell me?"

"I was going to when I got home, but Sebastian had other plans." I find Matiu's eyes. "Where's Sebastian?"

"He's in custody. With what he did to you and Konnie, we have him on kidnapping and attempted murder. Between those charges and everything else in the case Alec is building against him, he should be going away for a very long time."

Does that mean we're finally safe? We don't have to look over our shoulders anymore? My hope mingles with grief as I remember everything Sebastian told me about Nikau.

"Matiu." He must hear the change in my tone because his eyebrows crease together in worry. "Sebastian told me what happened to Nikau."

It tears at my heart to be the one to tell Matiu his innocent little brother is gone. "I don't know what he did with his body, but he told me that Nikau witnessed a murder and he couldn't let him live."

My own eyes fill as I watch tears trace long winding trails down Matiu's cheeks. I try to lift my arm to wipe them away, but wince in pain.

Matiu reaches up to swipe away a stray tear from his face. "Thank you," he whispers. "I knew he was gone, but it's still painful to have it confirmed."

"I'm so sorry, Matiu," I say and lace my fingers through his.

"Don't worry about any of that right now, Violet, just worry about getting better. Is there anything you want or need right now?" Matiu asks.

"Actually, next time you go back to the apartment, can you bring my pillow back with you?" I ask Genevieve. "This one isn't very comfortable."

Matiu and Genevieve share a look before Genevieve responds. "I won't be able to do that. Our apartment is gone."

"What do you mean it's gone?" I ask in confusion.

"Sebastian set the apartment building on fire. It was a complete loss," Matiu says in a soft voice.

Shock and anger rush through me, and then tears of grief roll down my cheeks. "He told me he wanted us to lose everything like he did; apparently, he meant *everything*. A lot of my keepsakes from Mom and Dad were in the apartment," I whisper.

Genevieve carefully grabs the hand that Matiu isn't holding again. Cautious of my IV, she gives my hand a small squeeze. "I know. We're all going to be okay, we still have everything in the storage unit. We'll figure this out. Right now, all you need to worry about is healing."

Looking from Genevieve back to Matiu, I close my eyes and drift back into the welcome arms of sleep.

February

Chapter 48

Matiu

Last month went by in a blur.

Between spending my evenings at the hospital with Violet and my days at the FBI office with Alec, time seems to be moving in fast forward. To make sure Sebastian never sets foot outside of prison walls again, the FBI has been working tirelessly to get as much hard evidence against him as possible. With Violet and Konnie both as eyewitnesses to Sebastian confessing about his knowledge of Nikau, more charges are piling up against him.

Thankfully, Alec pulled some strings to keep me here to help compile evidence for the prosecutor. We need a solid, airtight case by the time Sebastian goes to trial. So I get to help close up Sebastian's case and I still get to be in New York City with Violet while she is healing.

Once again, I'm surrounded by files and photos of Sebastian's misdeeds. "Alec?"

He looks up from his own pile of notes and files. "Yeah?"

"Something Viktor said when we were interviewing him at the prison is bugging me."

"You mean you were actually listening to what he was saying when you tried to strangle him with his own jumpsuit?"

I roll my eyes. "Ha ha, so funny. But seriously. He said, 'you should be asking that detective in Charleston for more information.' I've been growing more and more suspicious throughout this entire investigation. There are too many times that there was a team ready to move against Sebastian with solid information and whatever deal they were trying to bust just happened to get changed at the very last minute."

"I've noticed that too. Someone in Charleston PD is definitely on Sebastian's payroll."

"Yeah, there aren't many in the department that have been around that long. But how do we find out for sure who the dirty cop is?" I ask.

"I don't know. Let's go ask Sebastian."

"Do you really think he'll tell us?" I ask skeptically.

"It's worth a try."

The thought of seeing Sebastian again brings back the fiery heat of hatred. He almost took Violet from me—he did take Nikau from me. But Alec is right. Why wouldn't we go straight to the source and see if we can get anything out of him? I nod.

Alec calls to give a heads up that we are coming, and the drive to the MDC Brooklyn, where Sebastian is being held, doesn't take long. We wait in a small room until a cuffed Sebastian is brought to us. His tan prison garb washes out his face and his scarred skin has a sickly yellow tint to it. He looks smaller in here, but he still smirks at us like nothing will keep him in here for long.

He wishes.

I let Alec take the lead. "We need some information from you about your corrupt detective in Charleston."

He doesn't even look at Alec, maintaining eye contact with me. "What detective in Charleston? I don't know what you're talking about." That evil smirk shows back up. "How's your face McAllister?"

I know he is just trying to push my buttons and get a reaction out of me. It took a while for my face to heal up, but no permanent damage.

"How's yours?" I ask in return.

Those cold, dark eyes flash with anger. "How's Violet?"

Clenching both my fists under the table, I try to keep my cool. My fingers find Nikau's dinosaur and I squeeze it as Sebastian and I have a staring contest sitting across the table from each other. No remorse shows in his frigid gaze.

Alec interrupts our silent showdown. "You don't get to ask the questions here, Sebastian. Tell us which detective you have in your pocket."

Sebastian tears his eyes from mine and looks at Alec. "Why would I give you any information?"

"Because you're already going away for life, but if you cooperate, I might pull some strings as to which facility you end up in."

Sebastian scoffs. "I'll be walking out of here in no time."

"Okay, good luck with that. Have fun wherever you end up." Alec stands, but Sebastian turns his gaze back to me and a sinister smile spreads across his face.

"I'll tell you the name of the detective in Charleston, but not because I think I'll need your help to pull any strings for me."

Alec sits back down. "Oh yeah, you're just going to tell us out of the kindness of your heart?" he asks sarcastically.

Sebastian's grin grows and the sadistic gleam in his eyes flashes in glee. He doesn't break eye contact with me which sends my heart racing. I'm not going to like where this is going.

"Detective Darryl Armstrong."

The words feel like a physical blow to my gut. Sebastian's eyes light up with unrestrained vengeance and I know he isn't done torturing me.

"And while you're chatting with your good pal Darryl, why don't you ask him what he did with Nikau's body?"

I struggle to get air into my lungs as my mind tries and fails to process the information Sebastian just dropped on me.

Darryl Armstrong?

My mentor, my friend. He has been a friend to my family since Nikau disappeared. He has sat at our dinner table, eaten our birthday cakes. He is one of the reasons I am where I am today.

He can't be a dirty cop.

He can't be the one who disposed of Nikau's little body.

How could he look my devastated mother in the eye and tell her he was doing everything in his power to find my baby brother when he knew where he was the entire time?

But he did everything he could to keep me away from Nikau's case and off Sebastian's trail.

I thought Sebastian was the worst monster I had crossed paths with.

I was wrong.

A wave of nausea crashes into me and rolls through my body as bile attempts to climb up my throat.

Sebastian watches with a diabolical smile plastered on his face as I take in the devastating news. Then he starts to laugh.

A horrible, grating sound that has my skin crawling.

Alec motions for the guards. "Take him away. We're done here."

The guards take Sebastian by the arm and walk him back out the door toward his cell, his haunting laugh echoing through the halls. The sound cutting new, fresh wounds until a door we can't see shuts behind him and the noise is blissfully cut off.

Numb denial fills me as I silently follow Alec back to the car. We both get in and buckle our seatbelts, and he starts the car before saying anything.

"We can't let him know we're onto him. We're going to have to find everything we can to prove that Armstrong is dirty, and then you're going to have to go back to Charleston, Matiu."

Ask him what he did with Nikau's body.

Sebastian's words run back through my mind.

I'll do more than ask him where my little brother's body is. I vow to make sure he never takes another step without shackles around his ankles for the rest of his life.

I will take Armstrong down with Sebastian even if I have to take myself down with them to make it stick.

And I will find Nikau and finally … finally put my little brother to rest.

Chapter 49
Violet

The incessant beeping of the oxygen sensor grates on my nerves. I don't know why I still have to wear one of these, and it seems like more often than not it's just getting in the way. It's always going off for one reason or another—I'm laying on my arm weird or the sensor has moved and isn't reading my oxygen anymore, or a million other reasons it thinks I'm not breathing. I'm so ready to get out of here. I would've been released weeks ago if a secondary infection hadn't taken over, requiring more surgeries on top of the multiple I already needed to repair all the damage. One of the many things that can go wrong with gunshot wounds to the torso. I just want to go home.

But I don't have a home, I remind myself.

Spring semester just started for Steve, Genevieve, and Konnie, and they're busy with school, homework and life. The only person I haven't seen yet is Konnie. Every time I ask Genevieve why Konnie hasn't come to visit there is always an excuse. She continues to distance herself from all of us, and it hurts. They're staying in a hotel until we figure out where we're going to live. Which means I spend most of my days alone in my hospital room, binge watching shows on Netflix and scrolling through social media. Until Matiu gets done with helping Alec each day or until Genevieve, Steve, or Jocelyn take mercy on me and come to visit after school.

But this afternoon is different.

Matiu walks into the room in a daze and makes his way to the window. He stares at the street below, but doesn't fully focus on anything and I immediately know something has happened.

"Matiu, what's wrong?" I ask, worry creeping into my voice.

I've seen him go through so many different emotions during this entire ordeal, but this empty shell of my boyfriend isn't something I've seen before, and I don't know what to do.

Careful not to twist or unplug anything, I pull all my wires and tubes with me as I gently place my feet on the ground and slowly walk to Matiu. When I reach him and place my hand on his back, fingers brushing his firm muscles, he turns to face me, and the dam he had built to hold back whatever emotions he has been keeping hidden collapses.

The man I love crumbles in front of me and sobs, grabbing onto me like I'm the only thing that can keep him afloat in his sea of torment.

Wrapping my arms around him, I hold him until his tears stop. Worst-case scenarios rush through my head. I'm anxious to know what has happened. But I don't want to rush whatever he is feeling.

"I'm sorry, Violet, you shouldn't be standing this long yet," he says when he finally speaks.

"Matiu, what happened? You're scaring me."

"Detective Armstrong covered up all of Sebastian's crimes in Charleston. And according to Sebastian, Armstrong is the one who actually disposed of Nikau's body."

Shock radiates through me. Matiu has always talked about Detective Armstrong with such respect. I know he's always looked up to him, I can't even imagine what he's feeling right now. Not knowing what to say I wrap my arms around his neck and pull him close, ignoring the twinges of pain in my abdomen. He circles me in his arms in return and crushes me into his body, burying his face between my neck and shoulder.

"You really should sit back down," he says, words muffled against my shoulder.

"Only if you come sit down with me."

We make our way back to my hospital bed and he helps me climb in and get situated, but when he steps back to go sit in the chair by my bed, I catch his hand. Scooting over on the bed, I pat the empty spot next to me and Matiu climbs up carefully. Laying my head on his broad chest, I drape my arm across his body and listen to the rhythm of his heartbeat, the sound of each breath entering and exiting his lungs. He runs his fingers through my hair absent-mindedly and plays with the ends.

"You know I love you, right?" I whisper into the quiet of the room.

With my head still on his chest I can't see his face, but I feel him catch his breath before letting my words break through his grief.

"I think I loved you the moment you walked into the precinct to pick up your parents' belongings, Violet Clark." He lets out a long, slow exhale. "I tried to tell myself that the emotions I was feeling were because I needed to solve your case, but you have been haunting my dreams ever since."

"If that's the case, what in the heck took you so long, Matiu McAllister?" I tease.

The rumble of his chuckle vibrates through his chest, and he tightens his arms around me. Despite his chuckle, his voice is somber when he says, "I'm going to have to go back to Charleston."

I knew this would come eventually, but I'm still not ready for it. The thought of being away from Matiu for an extended amount of time makes my chest ache.

"I know," I say, taking a deep breath.

"I don't want to."

"I know." I say again.

"On a brighter note, my mum has been pestering me about when she'll finally get to meet you."

I laugh. While I was in surgery and he needed comforting, it was his family that he called telling them the entire story over the phone. And after my infection set in keeping me in the hospital, Matiu wanted to give my cell phone number to his mom and sister, and asked if I was okay with it. I've been talking to both of them regularly for almost a month now. They are already starting to feel like family to me.

I still haven't been able to speak to them in person, but Matiu's mom is an amazing lady and I can't wait to meet her myself.

"I'm excited to meet her, too."

Another stretch of comfortable silence fills the room before Matiu speaks again. "What did I ever do without you?"

"Probably worked way too much," I joke.

He laughs. "You're not wrong there." Kissing the top of my head, he leans his head back and closes his eyes.

I fall asleep listening to the sound of Matiu's beating heart and feel true peace for the first time since my parents died.

It doesn't matter that I won't be going back to Juilliard, or that I don't know what I'm going to do next.

As long as Matiu is by my side, I know everything will be okay.

Chapter 50

Matiu

know I needed to come back home, I need to be here, see it with my own eyes. But I am not sure if I can handle today without breaking. Following Alec and two Charleston-based FBI agents into the Charleston Police Department, I try to ready myself to see Armstrong again.

To think that he spent all those years invited to all our family functions, pretending to do everything he could to find Nikau. When, in reality, he discarded my little brother like he was nothing more than a piece of trash that had gotten in the way. It makes me sick to my stomach every time I think about it.

Armstrong sees us coming and a look of resignation washes over his features. He knows why we are here. He stands up and peacefully puts his hands behind his back as the agents arrest him, reading him his rights, but his eyes don't leave mine.

On their way out, Armstrong pauses in front of me. "I knew you'd figure it out eventually. You've always been too observant."

My body stiffens and my fists clench. Reaching for Nikau's dinosaur, I look at him but don't respond. His gaze follows and lands on the keys in my hand. He knows what the dinosaur key chain is—he has watched me carry it around for years.

He doesn't deserve a single thing from me.

"For what it's worth, I'm sorry" Armstrong says with a pained expression.

After all the lies, I'm not sure if the regret I am seeing is for his actions or because he got caught.

Looking into the eyes of my mentor, the betrayal feels like a physical blow and almost knocks me to my knees, but somehow, I stay standing and don't break eye contact.

"Where is he?" The only words I am willing to speak to the man in front of me.

Armstrong looks away and I watch them walk him out of the precinct in cuffs, headed to the FBI offices for interrogation. I trust Alec to ask the questions. I can't handle being in the same room with Armstrong for another second. The amount of time I spent idolizing him will haunt me for the rest of my life.

Walking out of the building, I cross the street and make my way to the Brittlebank Park fishing pier and look out at the Ashley River. I let the rhythmic sounds of the lapping water calm my nerves. I don't know how long I stand staring out into the water, it must be hours before Alec comes and stands beside me.

"Armstrong admitted to dumping bodies for Sebastian and covering up various crimes. He didn't confess to killing anyone, but he told us where he disposed of the evidence. The FBI is coordinating a massive search off the coast of Charleston."

"Will they even be able to recover anything?" I ask.

"Well, according to Armstrong, they placed the bodies in weighted barrels, so it's possible, but after fifteen years under the water, who knows if they'll find anything."

Alec places a comforting hand on my shoulder and we watch the sun sink below the horizon, sending spectacular shades of orange and red across the sky.

— • —

It took over a week, but they were able to recover several bodies, and positively identify the remains, including Nikau's.

Watching as Nikau's small casket is lowered into the ground, I squeeze the little dinosaur so hard it breaks skin. My plan was to put it into the casket with Nikau, but when the time came, I just couldn't. I need a private moment to say goodbye to my baby brother, away from the eyes of everyone mourning him.

I wrap one arm around Miriama and one around Mum, who clings to Dad. Even though we all knew he was gone, I think we all held out hope for the possibility that maybe one day he would be found.

At least the wondering is over.

Watching my family's wounds—the wounds we have long tried to heal—get ripped open has been torture, but we can finally have a proper funeral for Nikau and lay his little body to rest. The sound of the dirt hitting the top of the casket has me wincing with every shovel full.

When the service is over and my family walks to the car that will take us to his celebration of life, I stay behind. Taking slow, hesitant steps, I walk over to the freshly placed dirt and drop to my knees.

"I'm so sorry, Nikau. I'm sorry that I wasn't there for you. I'm sorry that I left you behind."

The tears are coming fast now and I can hardly make out the patch of dirt in front of me. Pulling the dinosaur that has been my constant companion since I was ten years old out of my pocket, I grasp it in my hand. Not ready to let go, but knowing I need to. Digging a small hole in the soil with my hand, I place Nikau's faded blue Long Neck into the soft earth, pressing it firmly down before filling the hole back up with dirt and covering the dinosaur with it.

Still kneeling with my hand on top of the ground above Nikau's casket, I feel someone place their own hand on my shoulder. Trying to wipe the tears from my face, I look up into Dad's also tear-stained face. "Your little brother loved you so much. He wanted to be just like you and I know in my heart that he wouldn't harbor any resentment toward you. It's time to forgive yourself, Matiu. It's what Nikau would want, it's what we all want."

A fresh wave of tears stream down my cheeks as Dad pulls me up and wraps me in his arms. Sobbing, we both let out years of grief and guilt before we walk to the car to join Mum and Miriama.

In the silence of the car ride from the cemetery to the house, Mum reaches for my hand. "We're all grieving today as a whānau, but we've been grieving for years. Son, tomorrow you need to go back to New York."

Looking up in surprise, I meet Mum's eyes with my own. "You want me to go back to New York?"

With a sad smile, she gives my hand a pat. "The woman you love is recovering in the hospital. As much as this breaks your mother's heart, and as much as I want you here with me, it's Violet who needs you the most right now."

Gratitude and love for Mum fill me. "Are you sure?"

"Yes, my son, I'm sure. I can't wait to meet the girl who broke through that tough exterior of yours."

With a smile, I wonder why I was ever so worried about telling my family about Violet. Not a single one of them thought anything was wrong with me having feelings for her, even if I was a previous detective on her case.

"Thank you, Mum, I'll leave tomorrow morning. I don't know what I'm going to tell my captain though."

"Worry about one thing at a time, Matiu. Things have a way of working out. You have time off saved up. Use that for now before you make any decisions."

I nod and watch the beauty of downtown Charleston pass as we drive back home, already itching to start the drive back to Violet.

— • —

I park in the hospital parking garage and walk to the elevators. Juggling my phone and the flowers I brought for Violet, I push the button that will take me to the hospital's rehabilitation wing and wait for the doors to open. I haven't seen her for several weeks. I needed to be there when they arrested Detective Armstrong and I needed to see Nikau properly buried.

The elevator doors open and I walk down the brightly lit hall that smells of cleaning chemicals and an underlying tone of something unpleasant. Hospitals are really a weird zone—a place where life is brought into the world, but also a place where death waits around every corner. The rooms can be filled with utter joy for some and despair and heartbreak for others.

Shaking off the melancholy, I plaster a smile on my face before walking into Violet's room. She looks irritated, or maybe it is boredom that is evident on her face, but as soon as she sees me walk into the room with the large bouquet of flowers, her face lights up.

"Hello beautiful, how are you feeling?" I ask.

"Much better now that you're here, but I'm ready to get out of this place."

I laugh. "We need to make sure you're healed up enough and your infection is cleared before you leave."

"I know. I just want to go home."

I watch her face fall as she once again realizes that there is no home to go to. "I know, I'm so sorry Violet. You'll get out of here soon enough and you'll get settled into a new apartment."

She nods and looks out her window. Her beautiful features set in concentration. I don't know where her mind has taken her, but it is obvious whatever she is thinking about is weighing on her.

I walk over and set the bright, happy flowers on the table and sit in the seat next to her bed. She reaches for my hand.

"Thank you for the flowers. They're beautiful."

Giving her hand a squeeze, I look over at the flowers full of so many different shades of colors—orange, purple, blue, yellow, pink.

But no red.

"You're welcome. I didn't want to come empty-handed after being gone for so long."

"I know it was only a few weeks, but it felt like forever." She looks at me with those chocolate-colored eyes. "I missed you. I don't like being so far away from you."

"Me either," I say with a sigh. "We'll figure it out."

She just nods again and turns her attention back out the window.

"Violet? You sure you're doing okay?" I ask. I'm sure she just has a lot on her mind, but she isn't usually so despondent.

Her lips form a sad smile. "I'm not sure I'm okay right now. But I know I will be." Pulling her gaze from the window, she focuses back on me. "How was the funeral? I'm sorry I couldn't be there with you."

"Don't be sorry, you needed to be here healing. It was hard, but good. We finally were able to put him to rest. And now that we know, even though it's not what we hoped for, at least we don't have to wonder anymore."

Reaching for my hand again, she laces her fingers through mine. "Fear of the unknown has stopped me from doing a lot of things in my life, and I will not let fear stop me from doing the things I want to do ever again."

Before I can respond, she tugs at my hand to pull me closer and I close the gap between us, our lips colliding. She leans into me even more and I scoot closer to the bed, wrapping my arms around her, careful not to bump any healing areas, but she doesn't seem to notice.

It is like she is letting out all her emotions in our kiss. Her fear, her despair, her longing and my remorse, pain, and need for her meet her warring emotions, mixing, mingling until her emotions are mine and mine are hers. We both tremble under the weight of it all.

Her hand reaches up and trails through my hair, which is growing out. I haven't had time for a haircut lately. She pulls me closer one last time before we break for air.

"Matiu." She whispers my name.

"Yeah?"

"Please don't leave me."

I don't know if she means right now, or in the future, but if there is one thing that I know for certain, it is that Violet is a part of me. Leaving her would be like telling my lungs they need to learn how to breathe underwater.

Impossible and never going to happen.

I don't know how we are going to make our situation work, but I am going to do everything in my power to figure it out.

"I couldn't leave you, even if I tried," I say into her hair, breathing in her sweet vanilla lavender scent before planting a kiss on her forehead and holding her until she drifts into sleep.

Chapter 51

Violet

As long as I do well during my physical therapy today and all my blood tests come back clear of infection, I'll finally be discharged. I've moved from the ICU, to a regular room, and to the rehabilitation center attached to the hospital during my stay. I'm still not sure where exactly we're going to go, but just getting out of here seems like a good place to start.

A knock at the door has me looking up to find Matiu. I'll never get sick of looking at him—tall, dark, and handsome—giddy doesn't even come close to explaining what I feel every time I see him.

"You ready to get out of here? Have they told you that you can leave yet?"

"Not yet, still waiting on some tests, and I think the doctor wants to do one last checkup. I really want to go home, Matiu." At the look of pity that crosses his face, I rush on to explain. "Not home to my apartment. I want to go home, home. I want to go back to Moncks Corner."

His eyes go wide with shock. "You want to go back to Moncks Corner?"

"Yeah. I've been thinking about it a lot. I've had a lot of time to think in here." A small chuckle escapes me before I turn serious again. "The house still hasn't sold. Most likely because there was a double homicide in the front living room."

His pity now looks like worry. I'm sure he's probably worried that I'm losing it, dark humor and all. "I thought you didn't want to be in the house after what happened."

"I didn't. But I grew up in that house, Matiu. It holds so many memories of my parents, of my family when it was whole. Why should one night take away all the wonderful memories we have there?"

To my frustration, tears well up in my eyes and I angrily swipe them away. "We can remodel the whole area where everything happened so that it isn't a reminder if we need to. But I want to go home."

"Okay. I'll take you home and do my best to help you with anything that I can. I can't deny that I'll be excited to have you close. New York is a long commute."

We're interrupted by Genevieve and the doctor walking into the room. He tells me my blood work came back clear and checks my healing wounds, having me do various movements before declaring me free to go with a follow up appointment in two weeks and regular physical therapy.

"You ready to go?" Genevieve asks as she grabs an armful of some things that will be leaving the hospital with me.

A nurse wheels me down to the exit in a wheelchair, with Genevieve and Matiu following behind. They put the items they're carrying into the trunk, and Matiu helps me out of the chair and into the car.

"I want to stop by the apartment before we go to the hotel," I say.

"I'm not sure that's a good idea, Vi," Genevieve responds nervously.

Looking at my determined face in the rearview mirror, she realizes I won't be backing down. She drives toward where our apartment once stood, parking next to the charred earth and eerie looking remains of the building. Pulling on the door handle, I climb out of the car and walk toward the rubble. The acrid smell assaults my senses, stinging my nostrils and leaving a sour taste in my mouth. My legs are still a little wobbly from weeks of sitting in a hospital bed, but Matiu takes my arm and steadies me as I wander toward the debris. I don't realize I'm crying until Matiu softly wipes away some of my tears.

Starting over twice in such a short amount of time is overwhelming.

And so unfair.

But if life has taught me anything in these twenty years I've been alive, it's that life isn't fair. It is not fair at all, but it is beautiful.

Beauty lies in the hug from a friend on a bad day, a kiss from the person who holds your heart, the chance to start over when the world pushes you down.

Life is hard, but the hard is always laced with beauty if you take the time to really try to look for it.

Genevieve walks up next to me and wraps her arm around me, resting her head on my shoulder. We sit in silence, staring at the ashes of what we once hoped to be our fresh start.

I carefully climb over the caution tape and I'm grateful that neither Genevieve nor Matiu try to stop me. Making my way slowly through the rough terrain of destroyed lives, I search for anything familiar.

So many people lost their homes because of one man's vengeance against my sisters and me. Despite my need to find anything familiar in the rubble, nothing stands out and minutes pass as I search before I decide it's time to go. It's time to stop digging through the past and move ahead with our future.

I reach for Matiu's hand, who has followed closely this whole time, but still lets me do what I needed to do on my own. I tug him back toward the car where Genevieve waits and after one last backward glance at the destruction; I turn back around.

Determined not to let this break me.

— • —

After resting at the hotel for a little bit, Matiu asks if I want to get some fresh air. I nod and we walk for a short way, hands laced together until we get to a quiet bench in Central Park and sit down.

The sounds of the busy city can still be heard, but they're muffled by the snow and bare trees. Even though the chill is subsiding and today is a warm day for February, I wrap my coat around me tighter. The snowy landscape is beautiful in its own way and I breathe in the cold crisp air before leaning my head on Matiu's shoulder. I'm surprised that he feels rigid and when I look at him, I realize after taking in his stiff posture and clenched jaw that he's super tense.

"Is everything okay?" I ask as I run everything that has happened between us through my head, searching for something that could have upset him.

Maybe when I asked him not to leave me I scared him. Maybe he made sure I got released from the hospital and now he's going to break up with me. Dread fills me and my heart starts to race.

"Violet I …" he stops to clear the emotion from his voice. "I thought I was going to lose you."

"But I'm still here."

"I know, but there were moments I thought you weren't going to be. And I realized I don't want to spend any more time apart."

I breathe a sigh of relief. Thank goodness this isn't a breakup. "Well, good thing we're moving back to South Carolina as soon as spring semester ends."

"No, that isn't good enough."

My mouth drops in shock as I watch Matiu get up and kneel in front of me. There's no way what I think might be happening could actually be happening.

"I never want to be anywhere you aren't ever again. You're the first thing I think about when I wake up and the last thing that crosses my mind before I fall asleep, every day that I'm with you makes me want you more than the previous one. I know we're both young, but I know what I want and I hope you feel the same way. I love you Violet Clark, will you marry me?"

I tell myself to close my mouth, but my pause must make him nervous because he adds, "and if you need any more convincing, you shouldn't have to navigate raising a teenage girl alone. That's scary."

I laugh and swipe away tears, happy tears this time. "I don't want to be anywhere you aren't either. Of course I'll marry you!"

Matiu stands up off the frosty ground and pulls me up with him. When his lips meet mine, it's more than a kiss, more than a promise. I know that wherever we end up, Matiu will make it feel like home.

I know we're still going to struggle to get through and overcome these past two years.

But we *will* make it through.

And I choose to seek out and find the good in the world. Because if we look for it hard enough, we will always find it.

Acknowledgments

Last year I couldn't believe *Haunted by You* had become a reality and having a second novel enter the world seems just as mind blowing. Writing *My Haunted Vow* was not easy, the deadlines set to release this sequel seemed impossible at times and I honestly still don't quite know how I managed to get to this point. But I do know that this novel would not be here if I didn't have so many amazing people in my life. I am going to try my best not to leave anyone out. If I do happen to miss someone, I am so so sorry!

To my husband, his faith in me and his willingness to let me reach for my dreams has made this book possible. His hard work to help fund my writing means the world to me. I love you!

To my rambunctious boys that call me 'Mom,' for being my biggest cheerleaders and understanding when Mom has to lock herself in the office and write.

To my parents, all of them, biological, step and through marriage. Thank you for all of your support and encouragement.

To my alpha readers: Susan, JoAnna and Erin. Thank you for reading my roughest of drafts and pushing me in the right direction.

To Susan and JoAnna, thank you for always being there for brainstorming sessions, meltdowns and when I need someone who understands the ups and downs of the writing world. Your friendship and unwavering support mean more to me than I can express. And Susan, thank you for reading and re-reading sections of my manuscript over and over again as I tried to shape this story into what it is today.

To my editor, Erin Huntley, for helping me polish the story and being willing to answer my never-ending questions. Hopefully your job was a little bit easier than last time.

To my proofreaders: Mom, Tara and Emily. Words cannot express how grateful I am that you were willing to adapt to an ever-shrinking timeline as my deadline approached. Thank you for catching those pesky errors that somehow make it through multiple rounds of edits.

To Rylan with Voodoo Art and Design, thank you for taking my vague ideas and creating amazing book covers that not only catch the eye, but incorporate the book into one intriguing image.

To all of my friends and family who were excited to see where this story would go and encouraged me to keep writing. Thank you for the phone calls, texts and everything in between. All of your loving words and support have meant so much to me.

To all the wonderful friends in Ladies Night and Book Group—both which force me to take a break—for being genuinely interested in how my writing is going, and supporting me even though I only pop out of my writing cave for a moment before jumping right back in again.

To Chantel, who's amazing artwork brought my characters to life. Thank you for taking the time and effort to make character art that so fit the image of the characters in my head.

To Shannon and Lindsey with Emerald Frost Design, for creating such amazing book trailers for my books.

To Amber, who answered all of my law enforcement questions and took the time to explain them to me. And to Dave via Susan, for all of your FBI insights.

To all of you who connect with me on social media. Your kind words and support have made me feel seen and heard. Sabrina, Alice, Jen, Alexandra, Wenna, Kiana, Shannon, Dani, Jill and so many more new friends. I am so grateful that our paths crossed on Bookstagram. Your friendships have been a bright spot in my life and I will always read anything you write or tell me is a must read.

To Ashley and Jess, for being amazing coaches and continuing to push me to reach for the stars even after I have graduated from your course. And for all my fellow Author Accelerators that have continued to cheer me on.

To Natalie, for making sure all of my New Zealand dialogue was accurate. You really brought the characters in Matiu's family to life.

To the whole Morgan James team for believing in me as an author and supporting me along the way. Thank you for all of your hard work and dedication to design and create a book we can all be proud of.

To my amazing launch teams, both for *Haunted by You* and *My Haunted Vow*. This series wouldn't be where it is today without your help.

To all of those who graciously donated to fundraisers to help fund the costs of this novel. Carolyn Hardy, Joni Norton, Salina Dingler, George and Kari Archibald, Sherry Archibald, Dori McAllister, Kris Anne, The Shupe Family, Chani Drouin, Sabrina Nilsson, Steven Michael, Katelyn Benning, Mariah Stoker, Dani Elias, Annie McClellan, Cin Pinnock Art Gallery, Alice Rosegold, Barry and Susie Smith, Kara Oberhansley, Nicky Hemsley, Carol Passey, Melissa Peterson, Jennifer Evans, all those who wished to remain anonymous, and to anyone who donated after the manuscript was submitted. If I could add your names I would! I am so extremely grateful for your support and your help making the production of My Haunted Vow possible. And a gigantic thank you to the two amazing ladies, Emily Black and Joni Norton, that were so passionate about making book two happen they decided to run fundraisers to raise the money when I couldn't. Also, Emily, I am so grateful for all your beautiful and delicious cookie donations. Thank you!

To all of my animals who brighten my day with all of their antics and keep me company while I write.

To God, for instilling in me the love of stories, the drive to write, and placing all the people and places in my life to help me along the way.

And once again, thank you to YOU. Thank you for reading this book. Thank you for being a reader and keeping stories alive and thank you for making my dream of becoming a full-time author one step closer to becoming my reality.

About the Author

Louise Davis is a powerful, up-and-coming young adult author with an innate ability to draw readers into her stories using dramatic realism. Her commercial and accessible writing style blends with highly riveting and twisting plotlines to craft truly unique works of literary art. Her debut novel, *Haunted by You*, artistically showcases her wide range of writing skills, weaving in romance, mystery, and suspense all in one thrilling book. Her lifelong love of reading led her to earn a bachelor's degree with a focus on creative writing,

Photo by Kelsey Pease

which paved the way to writing her own books, including her children's book, *Grandpa's Boots*. Through Louise's profound character development and realistic storylines, she enjoys entertaining her readers while delivering valuable life lessons in the process. When Louise is not sharing her love for writing with the world, she enjoys reading, going on adventures, and spending her time with her five boys, husband, and various animals on their peaceful 3-acre ranch-style home in the Idaho Falls, Idaho area.

Connect with Louise online: www.louisedavisbooks.com
Instagram: @louisedavisbooks
Facebook: @Louise Davis

A free ebook edition is available with the purchase of this book.

To claim your free ebook edition:

1. Visit MorganJamesBOGO.com
2. Sign your name CLEARLY in the space
3. Complete the form and submit a photo of the entire copyright page
4. You or your friend can download the ebook to your preferred device

A **FREE** ebook edition is available for you or a friend with the purchase of this print book.

CLEARLY SIGN YOUR NAME ABOVE

Instructions to claim your free ebook edition:
1. Visit MorganJamesBOGO.com
2. Sign your name CLEARLY in the space above
3. Complete the form and submit a photo of this entire page
4. You or your friend can download the ebook to your preferred device

Print & Digital Together Forever.

Snap a photo

Free ebook

Read anywhere

www.ingramcontent.com/pod-product-compliance
Lightning Source LLC
Jackson TN
JSHW020028141224
75386JS00027B/735

* 9 7 8 1 6 3 6 9 8 4 3 1 5 *